Shoreseeker

Book One of The Farshores Saga

Brandon M. Lindsay

Dear Khalil,

Enjoy the book!

Cover art and design by Jeff Brown
www.jeffbrowngraphics.com

Copyright © 2019 Brandon M. Lindsay

All rights reserved.

ISBN: 9781690732013

For my family
My first fans and my biggest supporters

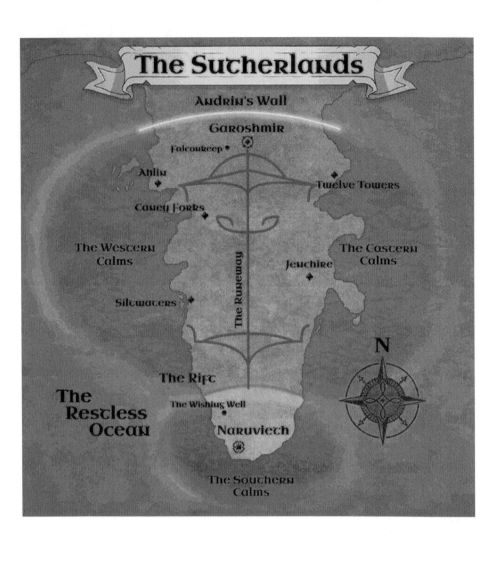

Table of Contents

Prologue: Twelve Towers

S had Belgrith fell to her knees on the stone balcony. She stretched her arms out to both sides with palms facing skyward, shuddering as the rain trickled down her naked flesh. It wasn't long before her glossy brown hair, at least what remained of it, was plastered to her neck and back in rain-saturated clumps.

She waited there. For how long she waited, she could not tell, but she waited until she had Matrollis's attention again.

Lightning flashed, shattering the darkness of the overcast sky.

"Matrollis. If my actions be unworthy of your sufferance, may you strike me dead where I kneel, bare before you."

She stared up at the sky, eyes squinting in the rain as she awaited his displeasure. But none came. No bolts struck her. At times like this, when Shad knew she had transgressed against him, she wondered if Matrollis, or any of the apoth, were even real. She didn't like this feeling of doubt wriggling inside her, though, so she ignored it as best she could. After all, her father had believed in them. She supposed that was reason enough. It would have to be.

After a while, the sky grumbled softly. Apparently Matrollis would not punish her for the sins she was about to commit.

It was all the sanction she needed.

Letting one arm drop to her side, she gestured with her other hand impatiently. Her servant, Erianna, strode forward with a leather bundle tucked under one arm. In her hands, she carried a hammer and pair of pliers. Her hair, normally a wavy, light brown, clung to her scalp, yet even so she didn't look half as much like a drowned rat as most people did in the rain. Most women would have envied Erianna for her beauty, but Shad was the mistress and Erianna was not. As far as Shad was concerned, Erianna had nothing to envy.

Without a flicker of emotion on her face, Erianna knelt a pace away from her naked mistress, set down the hammer and pliers, and unrolled the leather bundle between them. Strapped to the leather were sharp, needle-like objects, some as long as a finger, some shorter. Some were as thick as carpentry nails, while others would be suitable for the most delicate stitchwork. All of them were made of gleaming steel. Of the one hundred and fifty spikes she had begun with, fewer than half remained.

The rest of them pierced Shad's skin.

Shad closed her eyes and ran her fingers along the spikes before her, letting the feel of them guide her choice. As always, one forced itself upon her awareness as her finger touched it, sending an electric thrill up her arm. She didn't know how, but she could always find the right one.

She opened her eyes and drew a sharp breath. It was the thickest spike left. She exhaled slowly. "This is the one today."

With an expression perfectly schooled to show nothing, Erianna drew the spike from its sleeve. "As you will, mistress."

Shad inspected herself. Eighty-two piercings adorned her flesh from head to toe. Piercings on her arms, piercings on her legs, piercings on her stomach and her back and even the tops of her feet. Over twenty of them were in her face and ears, along her eyebrows, in her nose and lips, even three along her forehead. A strip of scalp down the center of her head had been shaved away to make room for more piercings. She had discovered that keeping that shaved was a chore, but her servants were up for the task.

She had even tried piercing one of her eyelids. Luckily the blindness passed only a few days after she realized how much of a mistake that had been, but even now, her left eye was slightly milkier than the emerald green of her right one. It had been the only piercing she'd ever removed.

Shad didn't have many places left to pierce—at least not many that wouldn't irritate her. She did, however, find a spot on the inside of her thigh that wouldn't get in the way of much. She hadn't had a man in quite some time, after all. "Here."

"Is ... is my mistress certain?"

"Your mistress is always certain. Now do it."

Still holding the spike in one hand, Erianna nodded and picked up the hammer. She leaned close.

Shad pinched the bit of flesh and looked away. Not because she couldn't stand the sight of her own blood, but because she didn't want to know when it would—

Metal clanged. Steel bit into flesh.

Blood, diluted with rainwater, streamed out of the new wound in Shad's thigh and over her fingers.

"Now," she said between ragged gasps, "the pliers."

Standing in the wavering candlelight of her high-ceilinged dressing chamber, Shad stared at her reflection in the gilt-framed mirror as Erianna dressed her. The skin around the spike, which had been bent with the pliers to form a crude ring like all the others, was swollen and pink and would doubtless ooze rancid-smelling pus before the week was out. She found, though, that she was getting used to the smell.

Erianna deftly wrapped the strip of satin cloth, green to match Shad's right eye, over her breasts, crossing her back, between her legs, over the shoulders. Shad would be clothed enough to be decent by some standard, but she wanted all of her piercings—especially the new one—to be exposed to the air.

That was, after all, the point.

Someone knocked at the door. At a gesture from Shad, Erianna pinned the wrap in place and hurried to the door. Erianna whispered to the unseen servant and shut the door. "The ambassador has arrived." Erianna immediately resumed clothing her mistress. Shad had heard a faint tremor in her voice.

"Did he bring anything with him?" she asked.

"Yes," said Erianna, fingers deft as she cinched and tied the cloth into a belt. Once the ivory clasp that kept her garment from falling open had been fitted into place at the small of Shad's back, Erianna stood with her head bowed, her task finished. "He brings a gift for you, mistress. A small knife."

A thrill of anticipation ran through Shad. "Good," she said, idly fingering one of the rings on her elbow. "Time to put these to use."

The clicking of her heels on the white marble-tiled floor became muted as Shad stepped onto the carpet in the center of the foyer, toward the sitting room where her guest waited. Shad couldn't help but grin like a fool. How long had it been since anyone south of Andrin's Wall laid eyes on such a ...

Such a what? Man? Creature? She couldn't rightly say what the ambassador was, though of course stories dating back before the construction of Andrin's Wall called them something entirely different.

Monsters.

Shad knew such appellations were utterly meaningless. Monster was merely what you called an outside force that thwarted your plans. She had been called a monster herself at times, and she was none the worse for wear as a result. In fact, she found that the title suited her nicely. *And so I go to*

3

a meeting of monsters.

As two of her servants pushed back the heavy doors to the sitting room, Shad allowed herself to imagine what he would look like. Of course, the stories that had trickled down through the centuries had likely been exaggerated with each telling, and likely begun by people who had never even seen the sheggam. As the stories told it, the sheggam had nearly annihilated mankind and had driven the few thousand that lived to build the Wall and cloister themselves off from the world, so it was somewhat understandable that every description of the sheggam tried its best to tap into some universal fear of wildness and the unknown. This often led to saying that the sheggam had beast-like attributes—fangs, fur, scales, and whatever else a limited imagination could conjure up.

Shad believed none of it. The sheggam clearly were not as gruesome and barbaric as the stories painted them; the mere fact that one was here to speak to her, calling himself an ambassador no less, was testament to this.

But that didn't mean she trusted him. Until now, Shad had only spoken to the ambassador by proxy. That way, if something went wrong, Shad would only lose a servant, and not her own life. But now that Shad was getting what she wanted, she had decided it was time to meet the ambassador face-to-face.

A pair of guards holding spears pushed open the twin doors as Shad approached. She nearly missed a step as she entered, fixated on the hulking form standing in the center of the sitting room.

Shad next noticed what he wore. A fine white cloak trimmed in pale blue silk, adorned with delicate embroidery of deep blue. It was, by most standards, a beautiful thing. She had at times met with governors and councilors from most of the other lands of the Accord, and none would be ashamed to wear such a garment.

Almost immediately, she realized what the cloak was: a disguise. A mask.

Indeed, the cloak covered the ambassador entirely. Not even his boots were visible beneath its hem—if he even wore such things. The cloak disguised him well, revealing little of his true shape, only suggesting. Yet while the cloak hid his shape, it did nothing to disguise his size. He was massive, at least two heads taller than Shad, even hunched down as he was. She had expected him to be more … more like the monsters she was used to. More like herself.

It was odd. With as many lamps as were hanging on the stone walls, she

4

should have been able to see his face clearly from where she now stood. But the hood completely obscured the ambassador's face, shrouding it in unnatural shadow. Not even a glimmer escaped the darkness there. Shad tried to smile to take the edge off her nerves, but only succeeded in stretching her lips into a thin line.

"Ambassador Orthkalu," Shad said, "welcome to Twelve Towers. I'm glad to finally meet you in person. I apologize if you've been waiting long." When he said nothing in reply, her eyes flicked to the small knife lying on the wooden side table. It was a gorgeous piece. Light danced off the jewels in the hilt. She licked her lips, and silently chided herself for such a wanton and careless display. But the truth was that knife awakened something in her, a hunger, like she had never known.

She knew that the knife itself was not the gift, but rather the means to receiving it.

"I see you want it," came Orthkalu's voice. Shad had expected a voice harsher or rougher. Not quite so ... refined. "Go on," he continued. "Pick it up."

The seductiveness of his offer nearly overwhelmed her. Nearly, but not entirely. A lifetime of politics had inured her to such easy trust. "Are you sure there's nothing you want for all that you and your people have given us? Not only for your expertise in building the Runeway, but ..." She gestured faintly to the knife. "This."

The ambassador spread his massive gloved hands wide. "Your friendship is all we ask."

Shad knew that those words, whenever uttered, were lies, no matter who was doing the uttering. No one merely wants friendship, especially not at such a price as what Orthkalu had given her. Not knowing what he truly wanted made her uneasy.

"Well," said Orthkalu, "there is perhaps one thing."

Ah. She smiled and gave the hulking monster a slight bow, more than she had ever given anyone in her life. "You have but to name it." Making a promise wasn't the same as keeping it.

Orthkalu studied her, though whether to determine her sincerity or merely unnerve her, she didn't know. But he was definitely doing the latter. "A trifling thing. Arrange a meeting with the land's rulers."

"You wish to speak to the Council of the Wall." Shad frowned, which was little more than a tightening of the skin around her brow piercings. "Consider it done. What would you like me to say to them on your behalf,

Ambassador?"

"You won't be speaking on my behalf, Governor. You will be there to make my introduction."

Shad paused to consider the request. It was possible, she knew. But she would have to be careful. Merely harboring a sheggam would cause an uproar throughout the Accord. Superstitious mobs would form with the aim of seeing her hang from a tree, her remains burned and buried to keep her soul from reaching Farshores. She would have to keep Orthkalu's identity a secret until she got him in front of the Council, and once they decided to deal with him, he would all but have their sanction. And so would Shad. She would be just as untouchable as they were.

Briefly, she wondered what her father would think of her speaking to a sheggam like this, like an equal. Her gaze drifted back to the knife.

"Go on," Orthkalu said again, gesturing to it. "For all the hospitality you've shown me, and for what you do for both of our peoples."

Shad paused a moment before crossing the floor to the table where the knife lay. All that existed in the moment was the knife. She ran her fingers along its cool silver surface. It was worth a fortune, she knew—but the true value lay in what it would give her.

Power.

She picked up the knife, gripping it firmly, and stepped back from the table, eyes fixed on Orthkalu. "I am ready."

And she was. The sensitive flesh around her piercings tingled with anticipation.

Though she couldn't see his face, she could sense a smile form under that hood as the cloak parted to reveal silk-gloved hands.

With unexpected deftness, Orthkalu plucked at the fingers of his glove, loosening them, before removing the glove. A hand twice the size of her own was revealed, skin pale like that of a corpse. The stories had been right about one thing: heavy black talons tipped each finger. Orthkalu could shred her just as easily as crush her skull with that hand.

Instead, he raised his bare hand, exposing the palm to her.

Before she lost her nerve, Shad slashed at his palm with the knife, then hurriedly set it back on the table.

As far as she could tell, Orthkalu hadn't even flinched as the blade bit into his flesh. Blood trickled from the gash in his palm, spoiling the pristine lace at his wrist. Still she waited.

Then her gift came.

White mist, as thick and heavy as smoke, oozed out of the wound. It wormed through the air towards her like the tentacles of some sea beast. She took another step back, then hardened herself. *No. I wanted this. I want this.*

She spread her arms wide, exposing herself.

The tentacles of mist brushed along her skin, burning it with a subtle and unseen energy. Then the mist found a piercing.

The pain made her collapse to the floor, screaming.

Like wolves on a wounded elk, wisps of smoke attacked her, pouring into her through her piercings. It felt like being flayed alive.

None of that prepared her for the moment it found the piercing on the inside of her thigh, still damp with fresh blood.

She cried her throat raw for Matrollis to save her from the agony, but Matrollis never came. Neither did her father when she cried for him.

There was only the sheggam, his low chuckle barely audible beneath the sounds of her screaming.

Chapter 1: Words in Blood

Tharadis crouched down with his elbow resting on his knee, his eyes taking in the horrific scene before him.

Over a hundred birds lay scattered about on the ground, unmoving except for the stir of feathers in the hot breeze rolling through the narrow, shaded alley. Tharadis recognized many of the birds, from smaller birds such as petrels and crakes to even a massive buzzard, and many more birds he'd never seen before.

All their heads were smashed, beaks twisted at sickening angles or broken off entirely. The plaster wall was painted with blood and gore, flecked with chips of bone and bits of feather. Tharadis knew what had happened. He had seen the cloud of shrieking and cawing birds dance over the rooftops before surging down this alley in a frenzy. He had even heard the birds sweep down the alley to smash into the wall before him now, the sounds of their impacts a quick succession of sickening crunches.

Yes, he knew what had happened. What he didn't know was *why*.

Tharadis realized he was gripping Shoreseeker's hilt when his fingers started to ache, so he let go and gave his hand a brief shake, admonishing himself to relax. A crowd of people were gathered behind him, clambering over each other to catch a glance. They were curious, but not alarmed. It wouldn't do for them to see how disturbed Tharadis was by this. He was the Warden of Naruvieth; he had best act the part.

He took a calming breath and stood, turning to Rellin, his second-in-command. Rellin was old enough to be Tharadis's father and had been second-in-command of the Shoresmen back when Tharadis's brother had been Warden. He had doubtless seen much, but now a worried expression darkened the man's face. His eyes met Tharadis's.

"Send a runner for Larril," Tharadis said. "There's not much for us to deal with here."

Rellin nodded, a glint of relief in his eyes, and turned to the line of six Shoresmen holding back the crowd and relayed the message to one of them. The man nodded and shouldered his way through the crowd.

Rellin turned back to Tharadis. "Should we go then?"

Tharadis could tell the man was eager to leave and let someone else deal with it. Tharadis felt a bit of that, too. He didn't know if this … situation, or whatever it was, had anything to do with Patterning. He had little interest in such arcane matters. But he wouldn't be doing his job as Warden if he didn't at least ask the resident Patterner if there was something he should be worried about. "We'll wait for him. It shouldn't take more than half an hour for him to arrive."

Rellin scratched at the stubble on his chin. Flecks of gray had started showing up in recent months, matching the streaks of gray in the man's otherwise night-black hair. "What about the stranger in the plaza? And the woman in the carriage? You want me to go see them instead?"

"No. I'll go see why they're here once Larril comes." Tharadis turned a corner of his mouth up in a half-smile. "We'll let them sweat a little longer."

Rellin harrumphed. "*I'm* sweating in this heat." With the back of his thick forearm, he wiped his forehead. "Outlanders? You'll be lucky if they're not piles of ash before you get there."

Tharadis forced himself to smile. The back of his linen tunic clung to him as if he had just gone for a swim. Foreigners would be having a tough time indeed.

But the banter felt hollow. The grisly scene behind him was an insatiable itch drawing his attention. Strangers rarely came to Naruvieth. Tharadis didn't like the fact that they had shown up not long before the birds had committed their collective suicide.

It was bad enough that Tharadis was supposed to be preparing to leave for Garoshmir. And what if he'd decided to leave early this morning instead of tomorrow? That had been his original plan, after all, and he hadn't really understood why he had waited an extra day. He'd just had a feeling, like he was forgetting something and if he only waited a little longer, he'd remember what it was.

Tharadis kicked the toe of his leather sandal against the alley's loose paving stones to free a few bits of sand that had worked their way under his toes. Too many coincidences. Truth be told, Tharadis didn't want to wait for Larril to show up. He was afraid the Patterner might actually have something to tell him.

Tharadis turned his attention to a small commotion in the crowd. Cursing and curt shouts were thrown about, and a thin, older man elbowed his way to the front.

Tharadis felt a chill run through him when he saw who it was.

9

"Larril," Rellin whispered. Only a few minutes had passed since he'd given his order. The runner wouldn't have even made it to Larril's house by now. "Let him through."

The Shoresmen stepped aside to let Larril through. He dusted off the lap of his sleeveless red tunic as if he had crawled across the dusty streets to get here. He looked thinner than usual, though Tharadis was always surprised at how thin the man was on the rare occasions they'd actually met. There were shadows under Larril's eyes as if he hadn't slept for days. Larril didn't even glance at Rellin, but he cast a long, searching gaze at Tharadis before he wordlessly stepped forward to examine the wall, completely ignoring the dead birds scattered in the dust.

Tharadis frowned. The wall? What was so special about it? He'd only given it a cursory glance before; his attention had been fixed on the birds.

As Warden, Tharadis was no stranger to the sight of blood. But seeing so much of it sprayed across the wall like this churned his stomach. It was starting to dry, leaving a dark brown crust along the edges. Yet he saw nothing there to draw the Patterner's interest.

Larril, however, squinted as his inspection intensified. "I came as I soon as I found out."

"Found out what?" Tharadis asked.

Larril abruptly turned and shooed Rellin out of the way as if he were a cat that was underfoot. Larril then stepped aside and gestured for Tharadis to stand where the Patterner had just been. "See for yourself."

Tharadis looked to Rellin, who merely shrugged helplessly. Another moment passed before Tharadis moved to the spot indicated.

He turned back to the wall.

The scene hadn't changed at all—the blood was exactly where it had been before. But now, from this angle, Tharadis could almost see a design forming. It looked like … *words*. He blinked and briefly glanced away, but when he returned his gaze to the blood, the words were still there.

"You can read it, can't you?" Larril whispered, stepping close. "What does it say?"

Almost as if his lips moved of their own will, Tharadis spoke. "'*To the land of the dead, one must go. To find what was lost. Blue stands against Green.*'" Tharadis shook his head. The hazy feeling left almost as quickly as it came. He noticed Rellin frowning at him as if Tharadis were more worrying than the blood on the wall.

"Can you read that?" Tharadis asked him.

Rellin's frown deepened. "Read what?"

Tharadis spun to Larril, who was eyeing him like a snake eyes a hawk. "Can you see it?"

Larril shook his head, keeping his voice pitched low so only Tharadis could hear him. "I knew it was there. But I didn't know who it was keyed to." He hesitated. "I had my suspicions, however."

Keyed to? "Larril, what's going on? What is this?"

"It's a prophecy. And it was meant specifically for you."

Tharadis felt his skin prickle. "You're joking."

But there was no hint of a joke in Larril's shadowed eyes. The Patterner shook his head. "I'm afraid this," he said, gesturing at the birds, "will have no explanation that you or I will accept, other than it was a message meant for you."

The message. Tharadis had been so focused on the existence of the prophecy that he hadn't given any thought to its meaning.

To the land of the dead.

What could it possibly mean? A land where people died? That could be anywhere. A graveyard? The site of a battle? There weren't too many of either of those south of Andrin's Wall. No, that made no sense. And what about the rest of it?

Tharadis sighed, scrubbing a hand over his jaw. He wouldn't figure out the meaning standing here in this alley—if he could even *trust* such a prophecy. Why would such a thing be meant for him? Questions piled upon questions with no answer in sight. And even though he could feel Larril's heavy, expectant gaze on him, he couldn't bring himself to ask the Patterner any of those questions.

"Warden, sir," Rellin said. "I'll see that this gets cleaned up if you want to head over to the plaza now."

Tharadis nodded. "Good idea." Rellin was right; he had other matters to attend to—matters that were actually in his capacity to deal with. He would deal with the armed stranger first and deal with the woman in the carriage after. "Are you sure you don't want to be Warden?"

Rellin scratched his stubble again, feigning a look of deep thought, though Tharadis could see the sparkle of a smile touching his eyes. "Tempting," he said with a sideward glance, "though I'd rather keep my sanity."

Tharadis snorted. "At least one of us should." He nodded to the Shoresmen to step aside and let him through. Before he could leave, Larril seized him by the arm.

"Tharadis." The Patterner's eyes were hard. "I know you think this message wasn't meant for you. But I assure you, it wasn't meant for anyone *but* you."

Tharadis didn't want to make any promises. "I'll give it some thought," he said. Larril seemed to understand this was all he would get and let go of his arm. As Tharadis turned to go, he could feel that vague sensation of having forgotten something creep up on him again, and he knew that this prophecy, or whatever it was, wasn't through with him yet.

Chapter 2: The Lone Knight

Dransig sat under the blazing Naruvian sun in the middle of the city's main plaza, but it wasn't merely the heat that made him want to flee this place. From where he was forced to wait at the fountain's edge, he couldn't see much through the throngs of people wending their way through the plaza. That didn't stop his eyes from casting about, searching as many faces as possible. None were faces he recognized, but that only made him more anxious. Sweat ran down his forehead, stinging his eyes and dampening his beard, and again he wondered how in the name of the apoth he ended up in this heat-scourged city.

White plastered buildings of different sizes, roofed with blue tiles, were packed together as far as the eye could see. The plateau upon which Naruvieth sat was not flat, and many clusters of buildings were on small rises with flights of stone stairs connecting them, making the whole of the city feel huddled together. The resulting shade did make the unnatural, scorching heat a bit more bearable. The fountain where Dransig now sat, however, was over a hundred paces from the three- and four-story buildings at the west end of the plaza. He was as far away from shade as possible.

Dransig felt he was being cooked alive in his mail shirt, the quilted gambeson underneath, and the heavy woolen tabard on top. He eyed the belted linen tunics and sandals that the Naruvians wore with growing envy. It was just so *hot* here. He had heard the Patterners' explanations for it before—how the Rift, the magical barrier separating Naruvieth from the rest of the Sutherlands, interfered with this land's natural climate. But crossing the Rift over the Runeway had been like crossing a bridge to another world entirely. The change from the damp, temperate weather of the Accord to the desert-like weather of Naruvieth had been shockingly abrupt.

And it hadn't gotten any better in the half day since he had arrived. Under very different circumstances, Dransig would have been half-tempted to kick off his boots, roll up the hems of his trousers, and dip his feet in the fountain's pool behind him, but he would have to content himself with the spray rising up from it. He couldn't even remove his leather gloves, though his hands were soaked in sweat. Baring any of the skin below his collarbones would raise questions he was not prepared to answer.

Besides, he couldn't afford to relax. Not now.

Naruvieth was barely a mid-sized city compared to the cities of the Accord, yet there was more bustle here, in Naruvieth's plaza, than Dransig had seen in the wealthiest market streets of Garoshmir. Deals were struck with laughter and pats on the shoulder, teams of mules pulled carts loaded with lumber, and packs of shrieking barefoot children chased each other through the throngs of people going about their business. Everyone here moved with purpose, even if that purpose, as in the case of the children, was simply enjoying the moment. They seemed to know what they were about and were pursuing it with fierce determination.

Which only made his situation, being forced to sit here and wait, all the more unbearable.

None of these people was being hunted. He was.

Dransig turned to the nearest of the four soldiers standing guard nearby. "How much longer until I meet this Warden of yours?" He didn't bother to mask his impatience.

The question earned him a long, flat glance but no response. One of the other soldiers had Dransig's weapons: a steel-capped wooden staff and a short arming sword. If these Naruvians had an inkling of the history of the Accord, they would know what these weapons signified. Only Dransig's order of knights carried such weapons, and there were plenty of towns in the Accord—ruled by superstition, of course—that would lock Dransig up merely for carrying them. A few might even execute him for the monster they suspected him to be.

And would they be wrong? he wondered, not for the first time.

Dransig wiped the sweat from his forehead with the back of his gloved hand. The absence of his weapons didn't concern him. Even without them, the four men were no match for him. Dransig was likely older than any of their fathers, his close-cropped hair and trim beard more gray than not, but that would work to his advantage. They would doubtless see an unarmed old man and underestimate him. And they would regret it.

He hoped it didn't come to that. He hoped they let him go. Dransig had lost his pursuers in this city, but it wouldn't take them long to catch up. They didn't need to see him to know roughly where he was.

They could feel his presence, just as he felt theirs.

He had never even wanted to come to this apoth-damned city. He hadn't

14

wanted to cross the Rift, or even go south. His destination had been north, to Garoshmir, yet a number of chance events conspired to force him down here to Naruvieth, as far south as a person could go before being run into the sea.

Dransig snorted. Chance events rarely conspired. No, there was more than just chance at work here. His path here felt guided. This whole situation reeked of Patterning. Though if the result of the World Pattern— what uneducated men sometimes called *fate*—or direct interference from a Patterner, Dransig had no idea.

The heat only exacerbated his anxiety. How much longer could he afford to wait here, while the other Naruvian soldiers fetched their so-called Warden to come meet him? They had said they were treating him as they would any dignitary from the Accord, but he knew that although he was an old man, he was armed and a stranger. They didn't trust him and they weren't going to let him go until their leader got a good look at him.

A large bell in a tower at the corner of the square tolled, marking the hour. Dransig began fidgeting, idly grinding the loose bits of stone under his boot and wondering if he could take all four of them down without hurting them too much, when he noticed a change in the crowd. There was something in the way their gazes shifted, in how they seemed to stumble just the tiniest bit. The strange effect, so subtle that Dransig wondered if he was really seeing it, seemed to ripple through the crowd. Someone even dropped a clay pot, shattering it and spilling wine over her sandaled feet, eliciting curses from a couple of passersby. More than a few heads turned towards the east end of the plaza, towards the source of the mysterious disturbance. Dransig's own attention was drawn that way, so strongly that it seemed against his will.

It didn't take long to find the source of the commotion.

A man, walking toward him. Dransig knew, almost instinctively, that this was the Warden.

He was not old, certainly not by Dransig's standards. He couldn't have been a day over thirty and was likely younger. How could someone so young become the effective ruler of what was, until recently, a sovereign nation?

Like the rest of the Naruvians, he wore a long, cream-colored tunic, but his had sleeves coming to his elbows, hemmed by fine, deep blue embroidery, stylized as crashing waves. Over this he wore a shaped leather cuirass riveted with metal scales.

A narrow strip of pale green leather affixed with a small gold ring in the center circled his head and kept his slightly long, straight, brown hair out of his face. Within the ring was a small ceramic disk which, too, was painted with crashing waves. As far as Dransig could tell, this mark of office was the only such mark he wore. At his right hip hung a sword in a light blue lacquered sheath.

Shoreseeker.

Dransig had heard of the sword, of course—everyone in the Sutherlands had. Rumor had it that Shoreseeker's blade was as blue as the sky and utterly indestructible. Blue was strange enough, but indestructible? Dransig found that hard to believe. There weren't many Crafters alive these days—if there were even any at all. And none of them had created anything even close to indestructible.

Dransig picked up his steel conical helm from where it sat next to him and tucked it under his arm. Slowly, so as not to rile the four guards watching him.

When the Warden and his small retinue of soldiers stopped a few paces ahead, Dransig bowed his head. "A pleasure to make your acquaintance—" What sort of title to use in this situation? "—eh, Lord Warden. My name is Dransig."

"Not Sir Dransig?" asked the Warden in a friendly tone after looking him over.

Dransig raised his head. "No longer, no." Smiling, he met the man's eyes. But then his smile withered. Up close, there was a terrifying keenness to those bright blue eyes, as if they were stripping Dransig's secrets bare. Dransig forced a smile again to cover his discomfort but couldn't find any words to break the silence.

The Warden's words puzzled Dransig, and it took him a moment to figure out why. True knightly orders were a thing of the distant past; none had existed for centuries. At least, save for one—the Knights of the Eye. The realization chilled Dransig. *How much does he know?*

After a long moment, the Warden smiled and extended his hand. "I'm Tharadis, the Warden of Naruvieth," he said in the same casual tone a potter would have used. "Thank you for keeping my men company. They don't get out much, so I have them mingle in the square sometimes. I hope their constant jabbering didn't cause you any grief." The guards hadn't said a word and Tharadis knew it. Dransig decided he liked him somewhat—but that didn't mean he trusted the man any more. Less, since he was so

16

obviously trying to disarm him.

Dransig shook his hand. "A fine grip you've got."

Tharadis released him and patted the cloth-wrapped hilt of his sword. "A swordsman's grip."

"Of course." So. The sword wasn't ornamental, and Tharadis wanted him to know that.

"What brings you here?" Tharadis asked. "We don't get too many visitors from Accord lands."

Now that the Rift had been bridged, the Council of the Wall considered Naruvieth to be a part of Accord lands, but Dransig didn't think it wise to argue politics with the man. "Truth be told, I'm here entirely by accident."

Tharadis cocked an eyebrow at this. "Really? There's only one way across the Rift, and that's the Runeway. There's nothing south of the Rift but Naruvieth and the sea. And there's nothing out at sea save death." A hint of warning came into his voice. "So how exactly does one come here by accident?"

Dransig took a deep breath, considering his options as he exhaled. The Warden seemed to be someone who wouldn't want to be misled. But if he told the truth, Dransig might be detained until the mess could be sorted out—Tharadis was a lawman, after all, and who could say that Dransig wasn't a criminal evading arrest? Dransig had to admit, travel-worn as he was, he did look suspicious. It was no wonder that Tharadis's men kept him under guard until Tharadis could inspect Dransig himself.

Carefully, Dransig cast his senses westward. His pursuers were closing, but how much time did he have? He couldn't be sure. Tharadis had nine men with him, and if he was smart, likely more out of sight. Unless there was an exceptional fighter among their ranks, Dransig could break free of them—but it would be a near thing. And the crowd would work against him, too, perhaps slow him down enough for Tharadis's men to recapture him.

No, fighting his way out was not an option. Much as he would rather not, he would have to trust this man.

"I'm being pursued."

The Warden nodded, as if Dransig had merely confirmed something he suspected.

Tharadis gestured to the patch of dark brown on Dransig's tabard, shaped like a wide-open eye circled with flames. It was darker than the surrounding fabric only because it had once been covered with embroidery. "Does it have something to do with that?"

Dransig nodded slowly.

"How many men?"

"As few as four, as many as ten."

"Which direction?"

"West. I don't know how long. An hour maybe, two at the most."

Tharadis frowned for a moment, then turned to one of his men. "Find them and keep a watch on them. Don't be too obvious, but don't worry about being seen. They'll likely know you're there. And don't engage them unless they try to harm someone. Cycle a man out every quarter hour but send him my way only if they start getting too close or if the situation changes."

"Warden." The man saluted, then trotted west.

Dransig turned to Tharadis, eyes narrowed slightly. "Am I under arrest?"

"Did you commit a crime in my city?"

"No."

"Do you plan to?"

Dransig watched him carefully as he shook his head. "Do you know who the Knights of the Eye are?"

There was no change in Tharadis's posture, but the air between them crackled with tension. "Yes."

"How?" The Knights were well-known but not often spoken of in Accord lands, as if merely uttering their name would summon a lifetime of bad luck. And as Tharadis said, Naruvieth didn't get that many visitors. What few they did get weren't likely to casually mention the Knights of the Eye.

Tharadis turned and gestured for him to follow. "Come. Let me show you."

Dransig jogged a couple steps to catch up. "Where are we going?"

"To my mother's house."

Chapter 3: The Last Night

Much to Dransig's relief, Tharadis's mother's house was on the east side of town, taking him further from his pursuers. By the time they arrived, the sun had fully set, reddening the sky. Lamp lighters began their rounds, and light began to spill from open windows and from between the slats of shutters upon the road. When they finally arrived in the small dirt yard of a nondescript house that could have belonged to anyone, Tharadis gestured to his man to hand Dransig back his weapons.

Dransig buckled on his sword belt and checked the blade in its scabbard. Then he took the staff. "I'm surprised you're giving these back."

"If I thought you were a threat, I wouldn't have."

"Can you be so sure I'm not?" Dransig asked. The man who had given him back his weapons tensed.

Tharadis shrugged. "Perhaps I can."

The front door to the house banged open. A small black-haired girl, no more than eight or nine years old, stood in the doorway with her tiny fists propped on her hips. A string of painted wooden eggs hung from her belt. Even at the top of the steps her eyes weren't level with Tharadis's, but she still managed to glower down at him.

"Uncle Tharadis! Where's dinner? I'm hungry!"

"Sorry, Nina. I've been busy today."

Her face broke into a wild grin as she leapt down the steps and threw her skinny arms around his waist. Though she couldn't have weighed much, Tharadis staggered back a step before wrapping his arms around her in a tight embrace.

Dransig looked away. It had been a long, long time since he had ever held anyone like that.

Tharadis released her. Holding on to her uncle's hand, she took a step back and sized Dransig up with a frown. He noticed the wooden eggs were painted like smiling raccoons. "What's a Knight of the Eye doing here?" she casually asked. She looked up at Tharadis. "Are the sheggam coming over the Wall?"

Grinning, Tharadis mussed her hair. "No, Neensy. No monsters are coming. He just got lost and is trying to get back home."

Dransig felt his hackles raise. Even the *children* here knew what he was?

She turned back to Dransig. "Where's your sigil? Did they throw you out of the order?"

Tharadis lifted Nina's chin up to look at him. "That's not the kind of questions we ask strangers. He's minding his own business. And so should you."

She nodded. Then, grinning, she ran over and seized Dransig's hand without letting go of her uncle's. "Did you know," she said as she dragged both of them towards the house, "that Uncle Tharadis has a copy of *First Night, Last Night*? It was written by a man named—"

"Prothugesh," Dransig finished with a hoarse whisper.

Nina cocked her head. "You know him?"

"Yes," Dransig said, half-dazed. "He founded my order before Andrin's Wall was completed." *And before the Rift came into existence*, he realized. If there was anything close to a holy text for his order, it was *First Night, Last Night*. But when the Knights of the Eye had been heavily persecuted hundreds of years ago, every known copy of the work had been destroyed. *Well*, he thought, *every copy known to those in the Accord*. "May I … see it?"

Before Tharadis could open his mouth to stop her, Nina nodded and dashed inside with a wild grin. Dransig heard the pounding of his heartbeat in his ears as he waited. He felt as if some ritual should be observed before such a holy moment, but when Nina returned, she handed him a book as if she were loaning him a doll.

"It's pretty old," she said, "so be careful with it." Tharadis stood behind her, arms folded and shaking his head with a small smile.

But Dransig didn't care about them. The world faded from his attention; all that existed in that moment was the book in his hands.

The binding was intact, but very, very brittle. So much so that Dransig feared to ruin it by opening it. Much like his own sigil, the title that had been embroidered into the leather was gone, with only the discoloration of the leather and the pockmarks where the thread had been to indicate where it once was.

From what he could tell, it was the genuine article. Which meant that Dransig held his order's holiest relic in his hands. "I'd very much like to read it," he said when he rediscovered the use of his tongue.

"I'm sure you'll agree that there's no time for that now," Tharadis said.

"You can read it on the road. I'm taking it with me. It's one of the few things of value I own, and I may need to barter it." Tharadis shrugged. "As you can tell, I'm not that wealthy."

A hundred questions competed for the use of Dransig's tongue. *"Barter it?"* he finally asked in a horrified tone. Reluctantly, he handed the book to Tharadis.

A woman stepped into the doorway. She had the typical Naruvian coloring—olive skin, thick black hair, but streaked with bits of gray. It was pulled back in a bun, though a few skeins hung loose to frame her face. Dransig guessed she was the owner of the house, and thus Tharadis's mother. She raised an eyebrow at Dransig before turning to Tharadis. "Taking in strays now, are you?"

"Just doing my job. He isn't trouble himself, but trouble's on his tail. So I'm taking him back to the Accord."

Dransig raised his hand. "That's not necessary. If you just let me go, I'll be able to fend for myself."

"I'm the Warden," Tharadis said. "Protector of Naruvieth. Even if you are not a Naruvian yourself, I will make sure you're safe until you are out of Naruvieth. Besides," he added, "I wouldn't want you to *accidentally* stick around." It seemed Tharadis thought since Dransig had come against his will, that he likely wouldn't be able to get himself out.

And perhaps he was right. "I understand your concerns. But you don't need to escort me all the way to Rift. I can take care of myself once we're free of the city."

Tharadis's mother disappeared inside and reappeared only moments later, holding a heavily-laden pack. "So, it seems you're changing your plans again," she said as if Dransig had never spoken.

Tharadis walked up the steps, took the pack, and hugged his mother. "I should only be gone a couple weeks. Once all of this is taken care of, I'll head right back home. I don't want to spend any more time in Garoshmir than I have to."

After sliding the book in, he shouldered the pack and gathered his niece up in his free arm. "Behave, all right? Listen to your grandma. By the way, where's your aunt?"

"She didn't say where she was going," Nina said. "Probably out at the Face."

"I bet you're right," he said, mussing her hair again as he straightened. "Listen to Aunt Esta too, Neensy. Unless she gives you bad advice."

Nina smoothed her hair out with an expression of mock distress.

"Dransig," Tharadis said, turning. "It doesn't look like you've got any supplies besides your weapons. I've got enough to share until we reach the outpost down in the lowlands." Just then a soldier trotted up to Tharadis, saluted, and whispered something in his ear. Tharadis nodded and said, "Take care of it. Slow them down." The soldier saluted again and left, taking two others with him.

Tharadis turned to one of those that remained. "Rellin, I'm leaving you in charge until I get back."

"What about the woman in the carriage?" asked Rellin.

Tharadis sighed. "I won't be able to deal with that now. Larril will just have to take care of it all himself. He has the final word on the matter. Do whatever he says to do about her."

He spared one final smile for his niece before looking back at Dransig. "Let's go."

Chapter 4: The Face of Naruvieth

A warm breeze ruffled the hem of Esta's sleeveless yellow dress and stirred the dark brown curls of her hair. With the trees at her back, she sat with her knees tucked against her chest, arms wrapped around them, sandals tossed aside. A mere two paces beyond her bare feet began the steep incline of the Face, which separated the city of Naruvieth from the lowlands sprawling before her, stretching towards the horizon. The hilly lowlands were mostly covered in drytrees, but here and there pockets of land had been cleared for farming.

Beyond the lowlands was the Rift. For as long as Naruvieth existed, so had the Rift, the magical barrier separating their little tip of peninsula from the rest of the world. Esta had seen the strange orange light of the Rift up close years ago, when she was still a child. She was enraptured—there was a thing of *magic*, close enough, if not safe enough, to go up and touch— and, at the same time, incensed at the unfairness of it. The Rift was all that kept her from being able to go explore the world she had read about in all the stories, the world she desperately wanted to see and experience.

Her favorite story was of the Steeds Who Would Not Yield, horses so large that six people could sit atop one. Some of the stories of the Steeds were simply too fantastical to believe: that light shone through their skin as if their muscles were made of fire, and that they could read minds. But knowing that an element of the fantastical lived in her stories only made her eager to find out more, so that she herself could distinguish fact from fiction and truly know what kind of world she lived in.

Yet, as she got older, she gradually began to accept that the world she loved would stay right where she had found it: in the telling of stories. *That* world was forever beyond her reach; she was stuck with Naruvieth.

All of that changed last year, when she was just eighteen. She remembered where she was when she heard the news: sitting at the wheel in the back of Melnek's pottery shop, face streaked with red clay. In front of her sat her latest "creation," though the small, lumpy jug seemed more of an abomination at the time. She sat there, staring at the pathetic thing in disappointment, when someone had crashed into the shop, screaming the news: *the Rift has been bridged.*

Her yearning to see the world, which had been tamped down to a few mere sparks, roared to flame like never before.

With each passing day, her desire to leave Naruvieth only deepened. Yet with each passing day, leaving seemed more unlikely.

It didn't take long for people to start complaining about the new bridge—called the Runeway by the people who built it. The complaints came in from all quarters, save the merchants, who saw the Runeway for the tremendous opportunity it was. Worse, her brother shut down the construction of the Runeway, saying it was his duty as Warden of Naruvieth to do so, given all the complaints. Since then, there had been a very uneasy truce between Naruvieth and the Accord lands.

All because of her brother.

Worst of all, he was using that very same Runeway to travel to the Accord's capital city to petition them to put an end to the construction of the Runeway permanently. While Esta was forced to stay here.

It was almost as if he were using that stupid sword of his to cut out Esta's heart.

She sighed. That wasn't true; she knew he was just trying to do the best he could for his people. But she couldn't help but suspect that he was secretly trying to get back at her for all the trouble she caused when she was younger, sneaking out of the house and getting lost in the lowlands.

Esta stood and dusted off the back of her dress before lacing up her sandals. As she did, she inspected her hunting gear arrayed next to her, just to make sure it was all accounted for. She knew it was, but checking it was also a good habit that she needed to keep up. She wasn't a kid anymore, getting tangled in brambles and crying until her big brother came and saved her. She could take care of herself.

She stuffed everything in her pack, slung it over her back, and picked up the spear, feeling its heft. It was a good weight, perfect for the boars that ran wild down in the lowlands. She couldn't fire a mug to save her life, but she knew how to make a good, simple spear.

Much as she thought about it, Esta couldn't just leave Naruvieth behind. Though she thought she was more of a burden that not, Melnek still depended on her. And so did her mother and Nina. She had to go to Melnek's shop in the morning.

But the night was hers. To Farshores with anyone who thought otherwise. She began walking towards the main road leading to the switchbacks down the Face when she heard something beyond the tree line.

It sounded like dry, brittle plants crushed underfoot.

Esta spun into a crouch, spear leveled in front of her, heart pounding in her ears.

When she saw who it was, she dropped the tip of her spear and let out her pent-up breath. "Nedrick, what are you doing here?"

"There's only one reason I would come out to the Face," he said, "and that's to find you." His narrow face wore its typical stern expression, an expression Esta saw far more than she liked. It turned to disappointment when he saw what she was holding. "I don't like it when you're out there by yourself at night. It's not safe. If something happened to you, who would you call for help?" He held out his hand for her to take but didn't step closer. "Why don't you just come back to town with me?" His eyes were wide with apprehension.

Esta knew Nedrick hated the Face. It frightened him. Most things did. Including Esta. She sometimes wondered what he saw in her, why he continued to pursue her. She knew he thought of her as his betrothed, even if he wouldn't outright say it. But neither did he deny it when others teased him about it. He just laughed along with them with a helpless shrug, as if attraction made people into fools.

Esta was no fool.

She made no move to take his hand.

"Come on," Nedrick said. He inched closer to her. "Just take my hand. You don't have to go hunting. There are other things you can do, in town. Useful things."

"Hunting is useful enough."

"I'm not denying that." He leaned forward. Slowly, as if reaching towards a venomous creature. "I just care about you. I don't think this is the right thing for you, Esta." He dropped his hand in exasperation. "Look, I know you hate working at Melnek's. He told me that he got upset and yelled at you today."

"That's not why I'm here," Esta said in a tight voice, hoping the tears threatening to spill wouldn't put the lie to her words.

"I'm not saying it is. But I've been talking around town, keeping an eye out. I think I've found something that will be more … suitable for you."

Esta didn't trust her voice enough to ask what it was.

Nedrick seemed to sense that. "Horses."

"Horses?" she asked. They had all died out in Naruvieth over two hundred years ago. They had only been reintroduced this year, since the Rift had been crossed. "Who do you know who could afford them?"

"Hender. His trade's been good recently, and he wants to expand. He has four of them coming in from the Accord, and he's hoping to breed them on his plot just west of town. He's looking to take on new staff, too, people who have a way with animals. I mentioned you right away." Nedrick grinned weakly as he gestured at the spear in Esta's hand. "I may have left out some of the details, though."

Horses. She had seen them, of course, from time to time. The few merchants allowed to come from the Accord all drove teams of horses, and the dignitaries that had visited her brother since the Rift was bridged had come in horse-drawn carriages. Townsfolk, especially the children, always crowded around the beasts, making it difficult to see them, even when they were standing in front of Esta's own house. She had caught glimpses but had yet to touch one.

If she were working with them, she might even be able to *ride* one someday.

Nedrick extended his hand again. "Come on. Let's go home."

She looked over her shoulder. The strange orange light of the Rift was over the horizon, out of sight. Perhaps it would stay that way forever. The Steeds Who Would Not Yield would always remain in the stories; deep down, she had always known that, even if admitting it was sometimes too hard to do. Esta would have to settle for regular steeds.

Wearing a smile she didn't quite feel, she set down her spear and took Nedrick's hand. She realized at that moment that it was softer than hers.

They began walking, Esta following Nedrick's lead. Her thoughts were too jumbled to lead right now. She was actually grateful for him at that moment. He seemed to sense that and squeezed her hand. And despite herself, she felt reassured.

Before they got to the tree line, Nedrick froze so suddenly that Esta bumped into him from behind.

Frowning, she asked, "What is …" The words died on her tongue as she looked ahead.

Two men stood on the path, wearing mail shirts under brown tabards and steel helmets. Heavy, brown cloaks hung down to their ankles. Short swords hung from their hips, and in their hands were long wooden staves, capped with steel.

On each chest was embroidered a wide, white eye wreathed in flame.

26

Chapter 5: One of Your Own

S o," Tharadis asked, "how dangerous are they?"

Dransig was at his side, struggling to keep up with the younger man's pace. They passed the last of the houses. All that lay between them and the forest ahead were pens holding pigs and goats and an empty field. The road leading from the main avenue towards the Face was more of a wide footpath made of hard-packed dirt.

He had stumbled once on the shallow wheel ruts in the dim light of the night sky. Dransig could improve his eyesight easily by drawing on his magic, but there were costs to that he wasn't willing to pay. Unlike with Patterning, drawing upon the shegasti magic could ruin a man, no matter how intelligent he was.

The weight of all his years, which he felt keenly whenever he wasn't drawing on shegasti, would remain on his shoulders for now. He would simply do his best to keep his footing and watch where Tharadis stepped.

Dransig didn't need to ask who *they* were. "As you may already know," he said, still stunned by the fact that Tharadis had a copy of *First Night, Last Night*, "the Knights are forbidden from taking human lives. That doesn't restrict them from *ruining* a man's life. I've watched as a Knight broke a man's knees with his staff for trying to cheat at dice." He caught Tharadis's gaze. "And that's just what I've seen. I've heard much worse."

"And they weren't punished for it?"

"Reprimanded? Yes. But not punished." Dransig shook his head. "If anything happens to your men, it will be because of me. I apologize if they suffer on my account."

"You aren't harming my men."

"No. But they're only in danger because the Knights followed me here. They're desperate to get a hold of me, and I've frustrated them so far. I fear for your men."

The needle-encrusted trees flanking the dusty road were large and gnarled, twisting at odd angles. As the lights from the edges of town faded behind them, only starlight and moonlight shone on the forest ahead.

"Why are they so desperate to get you back?" Tharadis asked, ducking under a branch that had grown low over the road.

"I betrayed them," Dransig said quietly. "And I plan to betray them further."

Tharadis spared him a long glance, but thankfully, he didn't press the point.

Dransig followed close behind, so deep in his thoughts that he only realized what the two points of light up ahead were—not light that he saw with his eyes. Instead it was shegasti magic he sensed. He seized Tharadis's sleeve. "Two, up ahead." He tamped down his draw upon the magic. Hopefully, they were as distracted as he had been and hadn't felt him yet.

Tharadis crouched down beside him. "Up ahead is the Face. That's where we need to go if we want to get off the plateau and down into the lowlands."

Dransig focused on his shegasti sense while trying not to draw too much of it into himself. It was a difficult balancing act, but one that all Knights of the Eye trained for—to see, but not be seen. *Too bad they were trained the same as me,* he thought. Still, he only used a tiny trickle to see beyond what his mundane eyes could.

North. The two didn't flicker, so they likely hadn't sensed him. Good. He cast west, and then south. What he saw there made him drop his guard briefly, letting too much shegasti in. He stifled it immediately, but he knew that they had sensed him. He cursed silently to himself. "There are more behind us."

"How many?"

"Eight. And I'm sure they felt me."

Tharadis paused briefly before nodding. "All right. Let's hurry north." As Dransig took a step, Tharadis grabbed his arm to hold him back. "Are you willing to kill one of your own?"

Dransig bared his teeth in a humorless grin. "The Knights? I don't count them as my own anymore."

Tharadis tightened his grip. "Can you kill them?"

Dransig hesitated. He had been a Knight for many years; breaking the habits and beliefs drilled into him for so long was difficult. Yet he was here because that was exactly what he had done.

He nodded sharply. "If I must."

Tharadis released Dransig's arm. "Then let's go."

Chapter 6: Eyes of a Predator

T ell me." The man who spoke lowered the steel-capped end of his staff. There was no explicit threat in his change of stance, but Esta felt her whole body tense up in response. "Have you seen anyone looking like us come this way?" His voice was low and soft, but again, Esta felt as if it were a challenge.

Her blood rose as the man's eyes fixed on hers. She knew that look; she had seen it many times before. It was the look of someone who expected to get what they wanted, no matter what.

"No," Nedrick said. His eyes briefly flicked to Esta's face with obvious concern. "We haven't seen anyone at all."

"Maybe we have," Esta said. "Maybe we haven't. What we have or haven't seen is no business of yours." Her fist was so tightly clenched at her side her knuckles ached. These two may have been dressed as soldiers, but Esta knew what kind of men they really were. Bullies. Brutes.

"As I said." Nedrick gave her hand an imploring squeeze. "We haven't seen anyone." Nedrick tried to guide her around the two soldiers, and after a moment Esta let herself be led.

But then the soldier who had spoken stepped into their path. "I wasn't talking to you, boy." As he spoke, his dark eyes never left Esta's face. The man's companion, standing slightly behind him, grinned widely, his lips twisted by a scar that snaked across his face.

Nedrick turned to her, his expression pleading. "Esta, just tell him what he wants to hear."

Esta knew it wasn't what he wanted to hear that mattered. It was what he wanted to see.

Fear. Submission. Well, she would show him neither. "Get out of my way," she said.

The scarred man chuckled. Neither of them stepped aside.

"Esta." Nedrick's voice dropped nearly to a whisper, but the soldiers were close enough that they would doubtless hear, too. "Not all of us can hide behind your brother's sword."

"I'm not hiding." Esta glared at Nedrick before returning her gaze to the soldiers. They weren't merely brutes. No, they were something else entirely.

Predators. Esta had dealt with predators before. They would let her pass if they were staring down the length of her spear.

As if he could sense her intentions, the scarred man suddenly stopped smiling. No one had moved, but the air had changed. It was filled with the promise of violence.

"You don't want to do that, girl." The first soldier's voice was almost a growl. Esta didn't think he knew about the spear—it was far too dark to see it—but somehow, he and his companion knew she was planning something.

Her spear was behind her, tucked under the brush. Three steps back, and it would be in her hands. She didn't know how, but these men knew she wouldn't back down without a fight. And now, she suspected, neither would they.

Esta spun and leapt for the spear.

Something rushed past her, stirring her hair. She slammed hard into the ground, and just as her fingers were about to close around its shaft, the spear was yanked out of reach.

Esta looked up. The soldier stood there, holding her spear in both hands with his own staff slung over his back.

Impossible. How had he moved so fast?

With no visible effort, he snapped the shaft in half and tossed both halves over his shoulders. They disappeared beyond the cliff's edge, clattering as they bounced down the Face.

Behind her came a thump and a grunt. Esta turned, clambering to her feet. Nedrick lay face down in the dirt, not moving. The scarred man stood over him, staff in hand. He shrugged, almost apologetically. "He moved."

Loose pebbles and gravel crunched under the first soldier's boots as he stepped around Esta to join his companion. He was watching her with his predator eyes, but Esta refused to give him the satisfaction of meeting his gaze, staring off to the side instead. He stopped not three feet from her and raised his staff. Esta felt the cold steel of its capped end pressing hard against her cheek, forcing her to look at him.

"Now, he said. "You were just about to tell us something."

Chapter 7: Sword and Staff

Staring down the shaft of the soldier's staff, Esta felt her fear finally catch up with her.

She glanced down at Nedrick's limp form again. She couldn't tell if he was breathing. For all she knew, he could be dead, and she would be next if she didn't tell the man what he wanted to know.

She knew she should feel regret for what happened to Nedrick, but all she felt was anger. At these men, for what they did, and at herself, for letting it get as far as it had. But she knew she couldn't let her anger get the better of her. She knew when she was outmatched. The image of her spear broken and discarded flashed in her mind. She didn't doubt the man could do the same to her.

She looked at Nedrick. She hoped he was still alive. Despite his faults, he didn't deserve this.

It was time to end this and get Nedrick out of here. These men would get what they wanted, and it wouldn't cost Esta more than few words and a little dignity. Besides, she had to live in order to make them pay.

But before she could open her mouth, both soldiers turned to look down the path as if they'd heard a sound, even though Esta had heard nothing. Then the men shared a glance.

Behind them, someone rushed out of the trees straight towards the men, a bared sword in his hand. In the darkness, Esta couldn't make out his face. But she caught sight of the blade, unmistakable even in starlight. *Shoreseeker.*

Both soldiers spun in surprise. Esta didn't stop to consider why her brother was here; he'd created a distraction—and she'd be damned if she didn't take it. She shoved the tip of the staff away from her face and grabbed hold of its middle, intending to wrench it out of his hands.

The soldier holding the staff barely seemed to notice as he started to swing it. Esta's eyes widened as she was lifted off her feet and flung aside, as if she weighed nothing. Before she knew what was happening, she crashed to the ground, her lungs screaming for air.

* * *

Tharadis parried the man's first attack, keeping his motions light and close. His opponent, a Knight with a scar running down his chin, was fast—faster than Tharadis had ever seen a man move. On the second strike, that steel-tipped staff whistled past Tharadis's ear, nearly splitting his head open.

It was then that he noticed Esta, looking as if she were trying to wrestle the other man's staff from his grip. The next moment she was flung away like a twig. Before he could make sense of that—how could a man be so strong?—his own opponent cracked Tharadis's shoulder with a thrust. He danced back. Foolish, taking his eyes off his opponent like that. Luckily, it had been his left shoulder. It throbbed with agony, but he could still fight. The scarred man straightened and grinned, spinning his staff as if he hadn't a care in the world.

This man was dangerous, maybe more than Tharadis could handle. But two of them? Tharadis could hear his heart pounding in his ears as he readjusted his grip. *Come on, Dransig! Where are you?* The other man, the one who had thrown Esta, sauntered over, his face a mask of cool anger.

"Interesting sword," the scarred one said, though his eyes never left Tharadis's. "Too bad you'll never hold it again. Not after I break every one of your knuckles."

Both men began to move, slowly trying to get on both sides of him. Tharadis stepped backward, knowing he couldn't let that happen. He was finished if they flanked him. He ached to check if Esta was safe, but he knew he couldn't afford to do that either. Distractions were death. Whatever had happened to her, she would have to wait.

The scarred man suddenly swung his staff in a tight circle, the tip a blur. With no time to pull back, Tharadis tightened his grip and twisted his wrist.

Shoreseeker, its matte blue blade a dull gray in the starlight, cleaved the tip of the staff from its shaft, sending it flying into the trees. The scarred man gaped, but only for a second, for the next moment Shoreseeker's blade was buried in his eye, its tip punching out the back of his skull. He slumped to his knees and finally to his side as Tharadis drew Shoreseeker free.

He turned to the sound of staves clacking. Dransig, seemingly from out of nowhere, had engaged the other man and was already pressing him back. For an old man, Dransig certainly held his own—but there was no need for him to, not with someone to help him. Tharadis sprinted forward and, before the other Knight could react, sliced the tendon above his heel.

The man collapsed, screaming. His scream was cut short as Dransig's staff spun, smashing his throat. Somehow the man survived, thrashing and writhing on the dirt, but Tharadis paid him no mind. He was no longer a threat.

Tharadis sheathed Shoreseeker and ran into the trees, scanning the darkness for the shape of his sister. He couldn't remember where exactly she had been thrown, or how far. But only a few moments passed before he found her lying on her stomach, coughing.

"Esta!" He crouched next to her and scanned her for injuries. No blood or broken bones that he could see; only a couple twigs tangled in her hair and a short rip in her dress. "Are you hurt?"

Behind him, Tharadis heard a loud crunch. He didn't have to turn to know that Dransig had finished the downed man.

Esta flinched at the sound, but when Tharadis didn't, she merely shook her head. "Wind was gone," she said, grimacing with every word. "Now it's back. Where's Nedrick?"

Tharadis shook his head. "I didn't see him."

With some effort, Esta got to her feet, shaking off Tharadis's attempt to help her. "He might be ... hurt. I have to help him." She staggered back to the mouth of the trail and froze when she caught sight of Dransig, crouched next to another form lying not far from where Tharadis had been moments before. He hadn't even noticed it during the fight; had he taken a few more steps to the left, he would have tripped over it.

Tharadis sensed Esta tensing up. He touched her arm. "Don't worry. He won't harm you."

Dransig looked up at Esta, his expression weary, though Tharadis could see it was beyond physical weariness. He gestured to the still form at his feet. "A friend of yours?" He rose and turned to Tharadis. "This man's still breathing. The both of them should be gone when the others come."

Tharadis couldn't agree more. "How long?"

Dransig shrugged. "Minutes. I drew in more than I should have. They'll know exactly where we are."

"More are coming?" Esta asked. She sounded more angry than afraid. She didn't wait for an answer, but merely moved to Nedrick and pulled his limp arm over her shoulders and hoisted him up.

"Hide in the woods for now," Tharadis said. "Maybe until morning. They won't be looking for you."

Esta paused and met his gaze. "What about you?"

"Looks like I'll be going to Garoshmir ahead of schedule."

She hesitated before nodding. "Stay safe."

"You too."

She started dragging Nedrick into the woods.

Tharadis walked back to where he had dropped his pack and shouldered it again, forcing himself not to worry about her. She would be safe as long as she stayed off the road, especially now that their pursuers knew where their quarry was.

When Tharadis came back, Dransig was standing near the ledge and peering over. He turned back, his face grim. "If we head down these switchbacks, they'll have the advantage. I don't want to have the high ground to my back."

Tharadis nodded, rubbing the ache in his shoulder. It didn't seem broken, but the pain nearly made his eyes water. "There's another way down the Face. We might be able to lose them that way, but you'll have to keep your magic tamped down."

Dransig grunted. Then something happened. It was almost as if he aged ten years before Tharadis's eyes. His skin looked paler, his posture more bent. He looked less like a warrior and more like … a regular old man. "There," Dransig said, his voice little more than a hoarse rasp. The corner of his lips curled up slightly. "I feel almost human again."

Tharadis stared a little longer than he should have. "This way."

Chapter 8: The Edge

The Face, as it was called by the Naruvians, was more of a steeply inclined slope than a sheer cliff, but Dransig's stomach still flipped as he followed Tharadis along its curving edge. Only a few feet of ground separated the edge from the trees, forcing them to watch their step, but it was all Dransig could do to keep from peering down to the ground far below. If he were to fall over the edge, he would tumble down the Face rather than smash directly onto the ground. At least with a sheer cliff, it would be over quickly.

Dransig glanced back over his shoulder, though the road where they had fought his former comrades had long been obscured by the drytree forest as they followed the curve of the Face. Likely the eight that pursued them had found the corpses he and Tharadis had left behind. What would they do if they caught up to him? Unlike Dransig, they still held to their oaths, and couldn't kill him. But they could leave him within an inch of death and simply let nature take its course—however long that might take. A more merciful death awaited him at the bottom of the Face. Perhaps it would be best if Dransig just threw himself over the edge and was done with it.

No, it was too soon to die. He still had too much left to do. And he wanted to see his daughter's face one last time.

All he had to do was survive. Yet drawing only a trickle of shegasti power—just enough to keep him alive—it was difficult to keep up with Tharadis, even though the younger man slowed whenever he saw Dransig lag.

"Not much farther," Tharadis said. "The road we were on doesn't come this way. A separate road leads to where we're going. As long as the Knights aren't drawn by your magic, they won't find us." He stopped, turning back. The concern on his face was evident even in starlight. "Are you all right?"

The lie came easily. "I'll be fine." Dransig even managed a smile.

Tharadis didn't look convinced, but neither did he challenge him as he continued forward.

The narrow path widened as the tree line crept back from the ledge, and soon Dransig was able to walk without fearing his knees buckling and sending him over the edge. He glanced up at the two moons, judging by their position that they'd been walking for half an hour.

"Here," Tharadis said.

Dransig stopped as they entered a clearing. Looming in the darkness was a large construction of some sort, leaning up against the edge of the Face. Dransig drew in a bit more shegasti to sharpen his vision. It was a large wooden platform. Sturdy timbers reached up over it, a pair of pulleys hanging from them over the center. Ropes stretched from those pulleys out over the Face all the way into the lowlands, disappearing in the trees down there.

"We're … riding that thing?" Dransig didn't mind heights, but he didn't relish standing on such a heavy platform with nothing but air below him. Those ropes didn't look nearly strong enough to hold it. It wasn't hard to imagine them snapping, sending him to the merciful death he now dreaded.

"No," Tharadis said, tossing his pack onto the platform before striding to the dozens of barrels and crates stacked on the other side. Dransig realized this was likely how much of the trade between the lowland farmers and the city craftsmen was done. "It will take too long, and we'd be easily spotted." Tharadis pulled off the lid to a crate, looked inside, then replaced the lid before doing the same to another.

"What are you looking for?"

"Found it." Tharadis tossed him something long. "Catch."

It was hard to judge where it was in the darkness, so Dransig instinctively drew in more shegasti than he would have liked. He snatched the object, which turned out to be a leather belt, out of the air before dampening his power. But not before silently cursing himself for a reckless fool. He glanced over his shoulder. He didn't know if their pursuers had felt it, but he didn't want to hang around to find out. "I think it best if we leave soon, Warden."

Tharadis paused a moment to glance up at him before returning his attention to a barrel. With Shoreseeker's pommel, he cracked the lid. Liquid lapped over the barrel's edge. "That's the plan. Come here and soak your belt."

Dransig did as he was told, submerging his belt in the water. His stomach turned as he realized what they were about to do. "Who's going first?" he asked, voice quavering.

"I will." Tharadis looked up at him then. "You may need your magic to hang on."

Dransig hesitated before giving a brusque nod. He knew then that he would be holding onto as much shegasti as he safely could. *Safety?* he thought wryly. *I'm worried about that now?*

Tharadis walked to the platform and slung his pack over his head and shoulder. Holding onto one end of the belt, he tossed the other end over the ropes before catching it in his other hand. He tugged down on both ends of the belt, putting most of his weight on them. The ropes barely flexed. He tossed a long glance over his shoulder at Dransig and nodded again.

"See you at the bottom." Then he leapt.

Dransig feared the man would lose his grip immediately, falling to his death, but amazingly he held on as he slid down the rope.

Fear knotting his insides, Dransig crossed to the platform and tossed his belt over the ropes as Tharadis had done. He tugged down on it. The ropes would hold his weight, of course; but would the belt see him safely down before the friction burned through it? He shook his head. It either would or it wouldn't. *And apoth take me if it doesn't.*

Taking in a deep breath, he drew upon his magic.

Three points of light blazed in his awareness, rushing straight toward him. They were less than a minute away.

How had they found him so quickly? It didn't matter. He exhaled, whispered a brief prayer to the apoth, and jumped beyond the platform's edge.

Chapter 9: The Fall

Air rushed all around Dransig, his cloak snapping like a whip behind him. Eyes watering as he shot down the length of the rope, he involuntarily glanced down. Nothing but two hundred feet of empty air lay between the ground and his swinging feet. His knuckles ached from holding the ends of the belt so tightly, even with as much shegasti as he was holding in. But he dared not loosen his grip even the slightest bit.

Up ahead, he saw the patch of darkness where the rope disappeared into the drytrees. Moments later, Tharadis himself disappeared into it.

Dransig realized then he hadn't asked Tharadis when to let go of his belt. What lay at the end of the rope? A wall, for him to smash into? Dransig cursed himself for not asking and Tharadis for not telling him. A dozen horrific scenarios played out in his mind in the space of a heartbeat. Despite that, and despite the fact that he was hurtling through the night air, an odd calm came over him. It was the calm of a man with no choices left to him save death.

But as he approached that patch of darkness, he knew that the calm was a lie. He still had choices to make.

Such as when to let go.

Darkness swallowed him as he heard the crisp rustling of drytree needles all around him. With even starlight obscured, whatever lay at the end of the rope would be hidden from him. Not even his shegasti would help him in darkness this absolute.

Now.

He let go of the belt, drawing in even more shegasti than he had before to prepare for when he hit the ground.

Dransig expected the ground to rush up to meet him at any moment, but as he continued to plummet, he knew he had fatally misjudged how high he was.

His knees cracked when he did finally land. The shegasti power coursing through him was all that kept his legs from shattering. Still, they folded underneath him, and he collapsed to his back on the needle-strewn forest floor. He lay there a moment if only to feel himself breathe. He had lost count of the times he thought he would die this night, and it felt good just to take a breath.

The moment was shorter than Dransig would have liked. He scrambled to his feet and made for wherever Tharadis had ended up. It was a struggle to dampen the shegasti—it was getting harder and harder to reject its sweet, poisoned promises—but he managed to hold in just enough to keep him going. The forest floor sloped upward and he would need the energy just to climb it, yet he knew that if he relied on it much more, it would be over for him.

Starlight poured in through a large gap in the trees ahead, revealing a timber framework much like the one at the top of the Face, though of course the moving platform was absent. Tharadis stood there with his sword drawn—strange, how it didn't seem to shimmer at all—looking up the length of rope, towards the top of the Face. Dransig turned to follow his gaze.

A gap in the branches revealed three forms, small as insects at this distance, sliding down the rope. It seemed that Tharadis wasn't the only one who'd had that idea.

"Stand back," Tharadis said. Dransig turned to see the Warden had raised his sword. Then he swung it, its edge whistling through the air.

It cut through the rope.

Dransig threw himself clear as the taut rope snapped with the sound of a thunderclap. It whipped past him, splintering branches. He pushed himself to his knees and peered back towards the Face. The three small forms were no longer sliding down the rope but falling through the air. Within the space of a heartbeat, they disappeared from view.

"Shegasti or no," Tharadis said, sheathing his sword, "nothing can survive that fall." He crossed to Dransig and offered him a hand. Dransig took it and let himself be pulled to his feet.

He didn't doubt the truth of the Warden's words. Even after all that had happened, Dransig felt their loss like a dagger in the heart. "There are still five more," he said after a moment. "Coming down the switchbacks."

Tharadis nodded. "Then we'd better keep moving."

Chapter 10: Bound to the Moon

The walkway leading up to Larril's cottage on the outskirts of town was a mastery of subtle Patterning. Fist-sized granite stones, rounded smooth by the ocean, made up the walkway. It wended up the small hill upon which the cottage sat, looking like a flat snake that had fallen asleep mid-slither. The hill itself was not natural; it was the result of the Patterning. Each granite stone was positioned exactly as it needed to be to bend this particular Pattern to its needs. The Pattern had caused the earth to shift, to tremor, to *adjust* itself ever so slightly, so slightly that the process wouldn't be noticed as it happened—but the result, the small cottage raised up over the course of months and years to peer out over the roofs of its nearest neighbors, could not be ignored. The walkway itself had even adjusted to the Pattern, adapting to it; it was now more of a stairway leading up to the cottage.

Indeed, the stones were positioned so artfully that there were over a hundred layers of redundancy in the Pattern; even as stones were shifted out of place when visitors walked the path, the Pattern would still be effective until the stones could be placed back in their original positions. An untrained eye would never see this subtle Patterning implicit in this walkway, but Noredren's eyes were far from untrained.

His ghostly form crouched at the bottom of the hill to examine the Pattern. Then he stood, streamers of ephemeral blue smoke drifting off of his translucent body like steam. At least he thought it was blue. The red moon, Aylia, was full in the night sky. The feeble light it provided tainted and distorted everything, making everything it touched looked soaked in blood. Noredren hated that moon, hated it more than almost anything.

He had enough time for hate later. Now that he was here—at least *partially* here—there were more important things than that. He had a job to do, events to set in motion.

As Noredren approached the humble little cottage, the wooden door swung inward. A clean-shaven older man in a red tunic stood in the doorway. He stood, barefoot, staring at Noredren for a long time.

Noredren smiled. "You look like you've seen a ghost."

40

"Ghosts are the spirits of the dead. You're not dead." Larril shook his head and stepped to the side. "I don't suppose shutting the door will keep you out, will it? Come in. I've been … expecting you."

Out of habit, Noredren ducked his head under the top of the low door frame and stepped in. The cottage was as unassuming on the inside as it was on the outside. A single room, if larger than some of the nearest houses, four posts supporting the joists. Gray wooden furniture, much of it rough, a sleeping mat rolled up and tucked in the corner, an unlit fireplace, oil lamps hanging from the poles and a smattering of smoky candles. The only extravagance was a stained wooden shelf bulging with books and scrolls. The window shutters were wide open. Through the window, Noredren could see Aylia's red face shining brightly.

"Yes, I suppose you have." Noredren turned to face Larril. "But do you know what I am? Why I am here?"

"I imagine you are here to tell me something, seeing as there is little else you can do right now. If I knew what it was you were going to tell me, you wouldn't need to be here to tell it to me, would you?"

Noredren nodded his head to concede the point.

"Would you like some tea?" asked Larril. He went to the counter, where a number of dishes were stacked.

"I'm afraid I don't have much time. By the time you get a fire going—"

Larril returned, holding a steaming cup of tea. The half-smile on his face held little humor.

"Impressive," said Noredren, "for a mortal man." When he reached for the cup, Larril let go of it. It passed through Noredren's hand and shattered on the floor, spilling its contents. Noredren had forgotten, briefly, that his form was not material. Judging by the mildly amused expression on Larril's face, the Patterner had not forgotten.

Noredren decided there was something else he hated almost as much as the moon.

"As for your first question," Larril said. "I can't really say that I do know what you are. But there is one thing that I know: now, here, you are *powerless*."

If Noredren's body had been real, the bones in his clenched fist would have creaked. "Now, yes. Here, yes. But not forever, *Patterner Larril*."

Larril's smile widened. "Oh, so you know my name? I'm not surprised, as it's my doorstep that you came to. Now what is it you came all this way to tell me?" He gestured to the mess on the floor and the broom leaning

41

against the wall. "I have very important tasks to attend to."

Noredren forced himself to calmness. His emotions couldn't get the better of him, not if he was to have any success tonight. "There isn't much you don't already know, I imagine," he said. "But perhaps there is one thing you don't know. You've heard the footsteps, yes?"

It was difficult to tell in the poor light, but Larril's face seemed to pale slightly. His answer was quiet, his voice hoarse. "Of course, I have. The whole world trembles with them."

"But few are sensitive enough to feel it, and only you are useful enough to do anything about it."

"I suspected as much." Larril's eyes sharpened. "And?"

"They are but echoes of something far greater, far more powerful than me and my brothers and sisters. Something far more terrible."

Larril stared at Noredren for a long time. He said nothing.

"If you're half the Patterner I suspect you are," said Noredren, "you know I'm telling the truth."

"Yes," said Larril, closing his eyes. "You are." He breathed out deeply and opened his eyes. "But I can't help but feel you are manipulating me."

"Don't disappoint me, Patterner. You know as well as I that all human interactions are exercises in manipulation. I doubt very much that you've allowed me to speak to you out of concern for *my* well-being."

With a grunt that could have been agreement, Larril moved to a small table against the wall. Scraps of paper covered it. Written on them were a number of complex symbols, pieces of a writing system that Larril no doubt developed himself to describe the concepts he dealt with. Larril's eyes flicked across the symbols quickly. Occasionally, he shuffled through them. A few of them looked old enough to crumble under his fingertips; these he handled gingerly. After a short while, he ignored the papers, staring at nothing, deep in thought. Then he stood.

"I hate to admit it, but you're right," Larril said.

"You know what you must do? To set things on the proper path?"

Larril consulted his papers. "A carriage. A blue one, with a bird painted on the door. A woman will ask me … Shores, this can't be right." He scrubbed his face. "He will never forgive me."

Noredren shrugged. "A problem for another day. A day that will come, because of what you do here and now." He began walking toward the open door. Beyond it, the first bit of blue sky broke over the horizon. Noredren could already feel his presence here waning.

Z

"Wait."

Noredren turned, pretending to rest his hand against the door frame, though it could have just as easily passed through the wood. "Yes?"

"What are you, really?" The Patterner's voice was dry, his face deeply troubled. "Are you an apoth?"

"An apoth?" Noredren laughed and continued walking. As he did, he began to fade, as if the substance of his body were licked away by an unseen wind. "You do me an injustice, Patterner, comparing me to a mere god."

Larril watched him go and dragged his chair over to the window and sat in it. He stared out the window at the moon Aylia. Briefly, he thought he saw it flash a bit brighter, as if something glimmering had returned to it, but realized that it had only been his imagination. He also realized that he hadn't asked the man's name, and that it didn't matter.

Larril purged his mind of all the world's problems, all the causes and effects and consequences, all the ripples rushing over the world that constantly drowned his thoughts, and just let himself be still for a moment, and simply breathe. He did this sometimes to fight off the despair that constantly wore at him, clawing at his heart. Most times, he could do it and prepare himself for another day of dealing with the curse of knowledge and responsibility. Yet now, he couldn't completely clear his mind. There was one thing, a memory from his childhood, that kept playing over and over in his head. A rhyme his mother had taught him, one that most children knew:

Mind your manners, ward your heart
Finish your evil before it starts
Banish the hate, don't let it rise
In your anger, you'll draw the eyes
Of the five cursed faces upon the Moon
Wicked enough to make hell swoon

He knew, without a hint of doubt, that he had just seen one of those five faces. Yet even as the words chilled him, he knew there was something worse out there, a churning void in the Pattern, around which people and nations swirled, helpless as dust in a storm. He had felt that void for a long time. It, more than anything else, plagued him with worry. All things were connected, and everything, *everything*, was connected to this deep black pit of nothing. It was as if it were a spider, the world its web, and all the people in it merely flies. The void was a distant thing, perhaps even otherworldly, but he could feel echoes of it nearby. Another force, shaping the world around it.

Tharadis.

Dawn was breaking when the sound of creaking wheels came in through the window. Larril hadn't slept. He had sat at his desk the whole night, rolling a stone over his knuckles to keep from thinking too much. He leapt out of his chair and went to the door, throwing it open and waiting as the blue wagon came to a stop. A single Shoresman had accompanied it on foot, squinting as the sun crested the horizon.

"I suppose the Warden gave me the authority to decide what is to be done about," Larril said with a twirl of his hand, "this."

The Shoresman's eyes widened in surprise. He nodded slowly.

The door to the wagon opened, and out stepped a woman. She brushed the thick folds of her skirts straight before turning to Larril. With how pale her hair was, he had thought she was old. But when her face turned to his and their eyes met, he realized she was still young. In her late thirties, at the oldest.

Before she could open her mouth to speak, Larril raised his hand. "I don't need to know what you're about. If all you need is my permission, then that is all you shall receive." He made a shooing gesture and turned to go back inside. He could feel the weight of that pale-haired woman's gaze on his back like a burden. *One I shall not soon be rid of,* he thought.

He shut the door and leaned against it with his eyes closed, waiting until the wagon was gone before returning to his chair. And there he sat, trying to think of a way to get Tharadis to forgive him for what he'd just done.

Chapter 11: The Fensoria

It was light before Esta felt it was safe enough to leave the woods near the Face. Nedrick lay propped up against a fallen log, still unconscious. She thought he had gotten enough rest and it was time for him to wake up. So she slapped him.

His eyes shot open and he scrambled back in a panic. It took him a moment to realize that Esta was the only one there. Gingerly he touched his cheek, which was already beginning to redden, and cast her a wounded look. True, she had slapped him harder than was needed. But no more than he deserved.

"Don't worry," Esta said. "They're gone. They won't trouble you anymore."

Her words seemed to hurt him more than the slap. But he just nodded and rose slowly. She hadn't seen what was done to him, but he took his time standing. Once he was at his full height, he looked her over. "Are you okay?"

Esta sniffed. "You can't protect someone after the fact, Nedrick."

With one hand, he dusted off his backside without taking his eyes off her. "I know that. I just wanted to help."

Esta shouldered her pack. "You can help me by keeping your distance." She glared at him, waiting for him to protest.

But he studied her instead, fixing her with an intent gaze. Then he shrugged. "Perhaps you're right. With the Rift bridged, our world isn't so small anymore. Why should we limit ourselves to what's in Naruvieth?"

She should have been happier at his words. After all, she had been thinking the same thing for months. Ever since the moment the Rift was bridged, actually. But some small part of her had hoped he would've fought for her.

But who would he have been fighting? Her own doubts? She stomped away through the brush before he could see the confusion she knew was plain on her face. She didn't want to think about it anymore right now. She just wanted to get away from him.

The people back in town had already begun their early-morning tasks.

More than a few of them rubbed the sleep from their eyes. Esta wondered how any of them could be sleepy after last night, but she imagined very few people knew what had happened with those strange men. She would have to tell the Shoresmen all about it, but that too could wait. After all, those men were dead. They wouldn't hurt anyone anymore.

No one seemed to note Esta's bedraggled appearance, or even the fact that she had spent the night in the woods. But then she supposed it wasn't all that unusual for her. She had spent many nights out at the Face, and even some down in the lowlands. To the people of Naruvieth, it was just another day in the life of the strange, willful sister of the Warden.

When her mother's house came into view, Esta stopped. A large, blue carriage, led by a team of four huge draft horses—actual *horses*—sat directly in front of her mother's door. Esta wanted to inspect the horses more closely, but something about their presence here unnerved her. A black-and-white bird of prey Esta didn't recognize was painted on the door, wings tucked close to its body as it dove over a stone parapet. Two children, a boy and girl, sat in the carriage's drivers' seats. They wore odd blue uniforms—with trousers tucked into brown leather boots—and stern expressions that looked unnatural for a couple of children who couldn't have been a day over fourteen. She knew from their style of garb, as well as their unfamiliarity, where they had come from. The Accord Lands, beyond the Rift.

Within the carriage itself, she caught a glimpse of other faces. Smaller, as if they too were children. Hidden in the shadowed interior of the carriage, they glanced at her briefly.

A single Shoresman stood at the back of the carriage, leaning on his spear as he disinterestedly watched passersby. He straightened when Esta approached.

"Hi, Rod," Esta said. The young Shoresman nodded with a small but friendly smile. Esta gestured at the carriage. "Mother has visitors?"

Rod's smile suddenly seemed forced. "Best you talk to her yourself."

Frowning, Esta thanked him and headed inside.

Her mother sat at the table, holding Nina in a crushing embrace on her lap. Her eyes were red and her breath shuddered, but Nina sat impassively, absently fiddling with the painted raccoon toys tucked into her belt. No, not just fiddling. She was picking at one of the knots on the string that held the raccoons together.

An attractive woman sat across the table from them. Her skirts were blue,

46

but her blouse was a crisp white, at least where it wasn't sweated through. Her fine hair, so blond it was nearly as white as her blouse, was bound up in a small bun on top of her head. Despite the chill blue of her eyes, her expression was warm, if sad.

Esta stared at the woman for a moment before turning to her mother. "What's going on?"

The woman's voice was deeper than Esta expected. "My name is Lora Bale. I'm from a place up north called Falconkeep." She looked across the table. "I'm here to discuss little Nina's future."

Esta's heated glare did little to discomfit the woman. "Mother," Esta said, not tearing her gaze from Lora Bale. "Why is someone from the Accord talking about my niece's future as if she knew anything about it?"

Lora stood. "Come outside with me. I've already told your mother, and Nina, everything." At a quick nod from her mother, Esta followed Lora outside.

"What is this all about?" Esta asked before she had finished going down the steps.

"Do you know anything about Falconkeep?" Lora asked. When Esta didn't answer, she continued. "Falconkeep is a very old place, built before Andrin's Wall was. It even predates the sheggam scourge. You see, there have sometimes been children born with special abilities."

Side by side, they walked down the street, away from the business of town and closer to the quietude of the woods. Soon, the house and the carriage were out of sight, and only a scattering of houses surrounded them. Here, the road was more dirt than stone. Lora stopped and faced Esta. "Nina is a special girl. She is able to do things that other people, even Patterners like Larril, can't do."

"What do you mean?"

"She has a rare gift, one that can manifest in ways you or I can't even imagine. For some children, it's a special sense or ability. Others can change the world around them without the use of Patterns. They simply will the world to be different, and it is."

"You mean magic." Esta chuckled. "That's crazy. Nina's just a child."

"You're right. She is just a child. A child who can do things that other people can't, one who is undoubtedly very confused about these things and has no one to help her sort them out. That's the purpose of Falconkeep and has been ever since its founding. We're a well-established organization with a long history of dealing with the problems that can arise from this kind of situation."

Esta felt her skin prickle. "What kind of problems?"

"Have you heard of the city of Rougar?"

Esta nodded hesitantly. She had always loved stories of ancient, far-away places, and had made her father read the stories to her while he was alive. She prided herself on knowing as many of the histories as she did the myths.

But there was one story of the old world that had always frightened her, and that was the history of Rougar. "It was destroyed by some wicked creature called the fensoria. It had terrible power, and toppled towers with a glance. Three thousand people died within a day."

Lora nodded. "That's almost right. But it wasn't the fensoria; it was *a* fensoria. And it wasn't a creature at all. It was an eight-year-old boy named Harl who was small for his age and loved blueberries." Lora dropped her gaze, threading her fingers over her stomach as she slowly paced. "I've read accounts from that time, not merely the words of later historians, but those of neighbors and loved ones. That incident was what spurred the creation of Falconkeep. A group of Patterners came together to create a place where the untrained minds of these confused children could be safe to grow and flourish in their abilities. Where they could be safe from the effects of their powers." She looked up at Esta and leveled her with a hard stare. "It was also a place where the world could be protected from them."

"Even if this is true," Esta said, "I don't see what this has to do with Nina. She hasn't done anything strange. She's a perfectly normal little girl."

"Oh, she is far from normal. She has an ability, but it's one that hasn't manifested itself in any obvious way. I don't know what it is yet, but I know that Nina, just like Harl from Rougar, is a fensoria."

"I don't believe you." Esta took a step closer. "And don't you think about coming near her again." She turned to go back.

"If she doesn't come with me, she will die before she turns seventeen. Regardless of whatever threat she poses to those around her."

Esta froze.

Lora slowly walked up behind her. "It's true. For as long as their existence has been recorded, the fensoria share one thing: a short life. Even those with harmless abilities will die before they become adults. The reasons are unclear, however. Some say they become mad, corrupted by their power, and their body gives out, but no one knows for certain. All that is certain is that it *will* happen."

Esta had heard stories, usually coming up from the lowlands, of families found butchered, farmhouses burned, loved ones inexplicably swallowed by the earth. In many of those stories, the children that survived such tragedies had often become mad or vanished. People often said such children had "gone bad," as if they were fish meat left out in the sun too long and not people at all.

Esta had never considered that there was any connection between them. But perhaps there was. And as much as Esta loved Nina, she knew her niece was a strange girl. As if she knew things a little girl had no business knowing. Could it be true?

When Esta spoke, her voice caught in her throat. "And you ... can save her?"

Lora came up from behind her, gently gripping both of Esta's arms in her hands, and drew her close. "I wish I could. But I can ease her pain, give her a place where she can belong—where her *powers* belong. You see, humans were never meant to have such power. It distorts how they view the world, even alienates them from it. Madness, sadness, despair ... all of these things are unavoidable, especially for the ones who destroy everything they touch. Human beings are creatures of reason, and reason is not permitted a place in the life of a fensoria. Only madness is permitted in their lives. Perhaps Nina is stronger than others, but it is as you said. She is just a child."

Tears fell from Esta's eyes. Even the prospect of such a fate for her niece crushed her heart.

She shook her arms free of Lora's grasp. "I still don't believe you." She continued walking. "There's no way that could be true."

"I am a Patterner," Lora said. "I have ways of finding these children. That's why I was entrusted with this task."

Esta spun back to her. "If you're a Patterner, then prove it."

Lora sighed. "Very well." From a pocket in her dress, she pulled a polished wooden stick, then crouched down and, with a frown, began to etch in the dirt.

Esta felt as if she were watching a master painter at work. The strokes were graceful, yet confident, subtly varying in speed and strength. Lora held her stick delicately, with the tips of her fingers, yet it seemed she was in complete control of her every movement. It was so convincing a show of excellence that Esta thought Lora had to be a well-practiced charlatan.

At times Lora glanced over her shoulder at the line of drytrees about twenty paces behind her for long moments before getting back to her work. At times, she attacked the Pattern she was drawing with a will; at other times, it was a gentle caress. The process lasted but a handful of minutes, but by the time Lora stood with a confident and proud expression on her face, stick held at her side, it felt like Esta had been watching for hours.

Nothing happened.

"Wait for it," Lora said. "And ... now."

In a sudden rush, all of the spindly, needle-like leaves of the drytrees behind Lora fell to the ground, pushing out a wave of air that nearly knocked Esta off her feet. Lora, however, stood solid. Only her heavy blue skirts and a few strands of hair shook in the blast of wind.

Then, as quickly as the drytrees had lost their needles, new ones sprang into being, unfurling from the gnarly branches like fingers. In the span of three breaths, they were back to their original forms—save for the dead needles piled around their trunks.

Esta stared in awe.

Like any child growing up, Esta had fancied herself an aspiring Patterner. She had even gotten a couple books with Patterns recreated on their pages in exquisite detail. Yet no matter how painstakingly she recreated them, she could not reproduce the effects they were supposed to have. Because as the world changes, so do the Patterns that control it; to understand a Pattern is to understand it at that particular time and in that particular context. Being a Patterner was more than just being a well-practiced scribbler or copier. It required a deeper understanding of the nature of the world, one that was far beyond most people.

Lora's mouth formed a small smile. "Truth be told, there are few with more talent than me. Perhaps two in the Accord, and your Larril, here in Naruvieth." She began walking and put a hand to Esta's back to guide her back to the house. "Ask your soldier friend here," she said as they approached him. "He was there when I spoke to Larril. He gave me permission to conduct my business here. But I've only come to ask permission to train and protect your niece. I didn't come to take her by force."

When Esta glanced to Rod, he simply nodded, not meeting Esta's eyes.

"Come," Lora said, guiding Esta up the steps. "Say your goodbyes, and know that Nina will be safe and at home with other special children like her."

In a daze, Esta went back inside. Nina jumped out of her grandmother's arms and into Esta's. Tear's stung Esta's eyes as she held her niece. "Do you know what this woman wants you to do?"

Nina nodded against her. "She wants me to go to a place called Falconkeep because I'm a fensoria. She said it would be safer that way."

The matter-of-fact way she said it made Esta's chest ache. "You don't have to go if you don't want to."

"I know." Nina's voice dropped to a whisper. "But I want you and grandma to be safe."

Esta squeezed her even tighter. "I'm going to miss you very, very much, Neensy."

Nina returned the hug, then stepped back. "Here," she said, handing her one of the little egg-shaped raccoons. She had untied it from the rest of the raccoon family.

It was the smallest one, the baby of the raccoon family.

Esta covered her face with her hand, unable to hold her sobs in anymore. "No, Neensy. You keep it. Your mother made it for you, and she would want the raccoon family to stay together."

Nina frowned in thought for a moment, then nodded. "You're right. I think she does want that."

"I'm sure she does, wherever she is." She stood, holding Nina's head tight against her middle. "No matter how far away she is, even if she's in Farshores, she still loves you, just like I will. No matter how far we are, we will always love you. Remember that, okay?"

Nina looked up at her with a wide grin and patted Esta's belly reassuringly. "Of course."

With the last of its five new charges, the blue Falconkeep carriage trundled down the road towards the Face. Esta watched it disappear from sight through the window of her room. The grief was overwhelming, but once the carriage was gone, Esta made a decision. She rushed inside and threw her travel pack, the one she used for hunting, onto her bed and began to fill it.

"What are you doing?" her mother asked from the doorway to Esta's room. Her arms were folded tightly.

"Tharadis was supposed to be here," Esta said. "He should have handled this. Not us, and not Larril." She paused. "He deserves to know."

"How will you find him?"

Esta paused, but only briefly. "I'll figure something out."

Her mother watched from the doorway for a while, and finally nodded. "I'll help you pack."

Chapter 12: Whorls of Metal

Coruscating waves of orange light rose up out of the vast split in the earth a hundred paces from where Tharadis and Dransig stood, stretching east and west until it disappeared from sight. To Tharadis's eye, the light of the Rift was like candlelight that flickered slowly, but moved more like the ocean waves than any fire he had seen. Tharadis would think it pretty if he hadn't known just how deadly it was.

Shifting the strap of his pack, Tharadis lifted his gaze up the light pouring out of the Rift—considered as much part of the Rift as the crack in the earth itself   as it stretched upward. Its upper edges mingled with the cloudless blue of the afternoon sky, one fading into the other, so that it was impossible to tell just how tall the Rift reached. He knew it was high enough that it kept even birds from crossing over. When the Rift still seemed impassable, every few decades or so someone got the idea to try to send messenger birds through it to reach whomever might be on the other side. Ten feet into the light, and the birds fell like stones. Every single time.

"I'd prefer to keep moving, Warden," Dransig said. He looked … not old, as he had when he ceased drawing on his power. But ill. His skin was pale, his movements jerky. And … had he grown taller?

Tharadis turned his attention to the footpath in front of them. "So would I," he responded. They turned and started west, parallel to the Rift, keeping a good amount of distance between them and it. They weren't far from where the Runeway spanned it. Few people came this way, even though it was the quickest path from where he and Dransig had come. Shallow wagon tracks could be seen in places, filled with needles shaken from the trees on either side, the bulk of which grew south of the path. Tharadis was glad for the shade they cast, and he was sure that Dransig was too. Especially with him refusing to so much as pull off his gloves.

Tharadis stifled a yawn. He hadn't slept at all last night—not that they'd had much choice. Dransig's former comrades were still behind them and doubtless knew where they were headed now. There was only one way across the Rift, and that was the Runeway.

Even now, the irony wasn't lost on him. Tharadis would travel over the very thing he was trying to stop.

He reminded himself that it wasn't the Runeway itself that was the problem—only that the Council wanted to build it where they willed, the Naruvian people be damned.

There was more to it than that, however, but they were matters that Tharadis himself didn't understand—matters of Patterning. Larril had given him a document to present to the Council, outlining the troubles with the Runeway. Something about a connection to the Pattern of Andrin's Wall, but beyond that, Tharadis didn't know. And he wasn't sure he wanted to know. Thinking of Patterning reminded him of the day before, of all those dead birds … He shook the thought from his head. Now was not the time to puzzle out impossible questions.

"Do you know how this Rift came to be?" Dransig asked at his side. When Tharadis didn't immediately respond, he continued. "The moment when Andrin's Wall was finally finished, when the final stone was put into place and the Wall's magic came alive, thunder split the sky. Many thought it was the Wall failing, the sound of the sheggam tearing it down like they had done to every one of mankind's defenses until then. But the Wall held, and so did its magic. No, it was the Rift slicing across the land, coming into existence at the exact same moment as the power of Andrin's Wall."

Tharadis had heard as much before. Records had been kept from that time, and though what happened across the Rift after its formation was mostly mystery, it didn't take much to determine it was no coincidence. "What is Andrin's Wall like?"

"Can't wait to see it, can you?" A small smile touched Dransig's lips. "I don't blame you. Back when I could, I would often go out on the northernmost tower and watch the Wall until dawn. You couldn't see much of it from there, but it was the only place where you could see any of it."

Tharadis gave him a sidelong glance. "When you could?"

Dransig nodded. "Since becoming a Knight of the Eye, I couldn't look at it without it hurting me. The more I draw upon shegasti, the harder it is. Now, it's blinding. I fear to guess what would happen if I were to stare at it now." He took in a deep breath before letting it out slowly. "My time in Garoshmir will not be without its difficulties." A moment passed, and then he said, "But I am ready."

"You can see Andrin's Wall from Garoshmir?"

Dransig grunted with a nod. "Much better than … where I'm from."

They continued in silence, maintaining their quick pace. At times

Dransig would glance south, sometimes southwest. Aside from those who lived here—and, he had to admit, Esta as well—Tharadis knew the lowlands as well as anyone, and he knew the roads leading to the Runeway. They had likely taken the main road, thinking it the fastest. It wasn't, luckily. From watching the direction of Dransig's regard, Tharadis knew approximately where the Knights were, judging they were still a few hours behind them.

They came to a slight decline, and the path veered away from the Rift. Dransig's relief was palpable, and he almost seemed back to normal, as if what Tharadis had seen before was a mere trick of the light. He had to keep himself from glancing over every few steps.

"Andrin's Wall was imbued with Patterns to repel the sheggam," Tharadis said in a musing tone. "And at the exact moment, the Rift came into existence."

Dransig briefly met his eyes and nodded.

"Then wouldn't that suggest that the Rift has something to do with shegasti?"

A long silence stretched before Dransig replied. "Move the bob of a pendulum, and it begins to swing back and forth."

"And the bob peaks twice … on opposite sides." Tharadis paused. "And if the Wall *repels* the sheggam, does the Rift—"

"A question better left unasked," Dransig said brusquely.

"The answer is plain on your face."

Dransig glared at him, his jaw tight. But then he looked away, the anger seeming to leach out of him. "I suppose it's better that you know. Yes, the Rift … *affects* me. I almost didn't make it across the first time." He looked at the orange light and then away quickly, almost guiltily. "I may need your help getting across."

"Did the other Knights have the same problem?"

"No, I don't imagine they had quite the—" Dransig cut himself off. Still fixed on the path in front of him, his eyes narrowed, but he didn't say another word.

Tharadis glanced to where the embroidered Eye on Dransig's chest had been. He finally understood why Dransig refused to remove even his gloves, despite how much discomfort the noonday heat was obviously causing him. "How many do you have?"

Dransig didn't answer at first, instead his face turning so red Tharadis suspected he might stomp off ahead. But Dransig kept pace with him. As he said, he would need Tharadis's help.

"Twenty-two," Dransig finally said.

Tharadis's eyes widened. "Twenty-two? But all the other Knights—"

"Have only one piercing, yes. I'm sure you learned that in that book you plan on bartering," Dransig said in obvious annoyance. "It may surprise you to learn that that isn't even why I'm no longer with the Knights."

Tharadis shook his head in disbelief. Twenty-two. Whatever the true reason for their split, this did explain why they were so eager to catch him—and why it was so unlikely they would succeed.

No, the other Knights weren't the greatest threat to Dransig. The power within him was.

"I hope you understand," Dransig said, annoyance fading, "that this is the last time we will speak of this."

Tharadis nodded, stepping over a branch that had fallen across the road. Every muscle in his body was tense, and he found himself calculating how quickly he could draw his sword if Dransig was … overcome. "I didn't mean to pry. But like you said, it's better that I know."

Dransig harrumphed but didn't contradict him.

A short while later, Tharadis halted, raising a hand for Dransig to do the same. Then, with his knuckles, he tapped out a quick rhythm against the trunk of a nearby tree. Just beyond the bend up ahead, a similar rhythm answered—the all-clear. Tharadis nodded for Dransig to keep walking.

As they rounded the bend, a pair of Shoresmen came into view, gripping loaded crossbows. When they saw Tharadis, they snapped to attention.

"Warden, sir," said the one on the left. "We weren't expecting you until tomorrow." He looked at Dransig, his surprise turning to suspicion. "Is everything all right, Warden?"

"He's with me, Dev. No one else has come this way, have they? No one dressed like him?"

Dev shook his head. "Not today, sir. But a couple days ago we saw a man crawling off the Runeway." He gestured to Dransig. "Dressed just like this. He gave us the slip, though."

Tharadis turned. "Was that you?"

Dransig nodded, his lips pressed tight.

Dev went on. "More came over the Runeway bridge after. The lieutenant confronted them and one of them broke his leg as easily as if his bones were twigs."

"Is the lieutenant still here?"

"No. He went back on the cart yesterday. The sergeant's in charge."

Tharadis nodded, frowning. If the cart was gone, that meant the mule was too. He had been hoping they would have at least that much good fortune, but it looked as if they would only be able to take what they could carry on their backs.

Neither of the Shoresmen hid the anger from their eyes very well as they glanced at Dransig.

"I'll have you know that four of the men who hurt our lieutenant won't be going home," Tharadis said.

Dev nodded. "That's good to hear, sir."

"This man, Dransig, helped me. He had no hand in what happened to the lieutenant. And whatever you do, don't engage the others if you see them again. Just let them pass."

"Understood, sir." Tharadis could see they weren't happy with the order, even if they understood the wisdom of it. They saluted again. Tharadis saluted them back before leading Dransig past them.

It wasn't long before Tharadis felt the faint but constant breeze. It was always cooler than he expected, every time he came this close to the gap in the Rift. The footpath was swept clean of drytree needles, and even the trees themselves were barer, skeletal, as if picked cleaned by crows rather than the air rushing over the Runeway from the Accord. The edge of Dransig's brown cloak stirred, and Tharadis knew the man would be even more grateful for the cool air than he was.

Through a break in the trees, he caught sight of the guardhouse. It looked no different from one of the lowland houses—timber fortified with stone at the corners, a blue tile roof. Strong enough to withstand the winds, but little else. Tharadis hoped that "little else" never showed its face. If the Accord ever decided to send its armies across, no amount of stone corners or walls would stop them—not if the power of the Rift couldn't.

All Tharadis had to do was convince the Council of the Wall to keep their armies away while respecting the rights of Naruvian people. *No problem*, he thought wryly.

When the trail veered out past the tree line, Tharadis briefly halted as the Runeway came into view.

From this distance, it looked like a dark brown smear stretching a hundred paces beyond the Rift. It was slightly thicker in the center of its length and rounded, wide enough for two wagons to ride abreast, though few enough wagons did so with tensions between Naruvieth and the Accord being what they were. From this angle, it was impossible to look through the gap in the Rift light to the other side. It was so far—nearly two thousand paces—that in order see the Accord, one had to be practically standing on the Runeway itself, and even then, the walls of Rift light stretching up on either side distorted the view.

Or so Tharadis had heard. He had never crossed the Rift himself, had never actually been any closer to the Runeway than he was now. For some reason, the Runeway had … disturbed him. Beyond just the obvious reason that it was the source of all his troubles with the Accord. Something about it just seemed …

He shook his head and glanced at Dransig, who was standing just behind him, watching him out of the corner of his eye with a strange look. Tharadis ignored him and pushed past some brush towards the guard post.

Three bored-looking Shoresmen leaned on their pikes, staring at nothing. With the lieutenant gone, that meant two more were in the building. Tharadis raised a hand to hail them. They saluted, and one of them ran inside.

The hem of Tharadis's tunic snapped in the wind as he approached. Just behind him, Dransig had slung his cloak over the crook of his arm to keep it from whipping around, but even so, Tharadis could tell the man just wanted to unpin it and toss it away.

All five Shoresmen lined up in front of the guard post and straightened before saluting. Tharadis halted five paces from them and returned the salute. "Ah, Warden." The sergeant, a black-haired man whose face was nearly too wide for his helmet, stepped forward as the other four fell at ease. He had to raise his voice to be heard over the wind. "You found one of them. That's good. How shall we execute him?"

"No executions for this man, Sergeant Gred. I mean to see him over the Rift."

The sergeant grunted with a slight frown. "Better that than hanging around here, I guess. And his friends?"

"Will follow him home. Let them pass. I'd hate to lose any more men for no good reason."

The sergeant's face split in a wide grin. "Yeah, and who would keep you city people safe if not us?" He chuckled as one of the others standing behind him rolled his eyes. "We'll let them pass, Warden."

"Thank you, sergeant."

The man waved his hand in a dismissive gesture, as if following orders was a favor he didn't extend to every superior. "Your pack's a little light. Will you be needing some supplies?"

"Food, mostly, and an extra waterskin if you can spare one."

"See to it," the sergeant said to one of the others, gesturing for Tharadis to hand over his pack. "The rest of you, back to your posts." He turned back to Tharadis, but not without his gaze lingering a moment on Dransig. The good humor in his face was gone. "Did you hear what his people did to our lieutenant?"

Tharadis nodded. "Don't worry, sergeant. A handful of them won't be going home with the others."

A slight smile returned to the sergeant's lips, but this time it was tinged with malice. "Any idea when we should expect the rest?"

Tharadis turned to Dransig, who was already looking over his shoulder towards the main road. "As the gull flies, an hour or so." Dransig scratched his beard absently. "Though I'd wager two if they're taking the same main road I first came in on."

"You look you could rest your eyes a spell," the sergeant said, eyeing Tharadis.

But Tharadis knew better. "If I close my eyes, I know I won't want to open them until tomorrow." He had to stifle a yawn, as if his body were telling him that that didn't matter. "Once we're past the Rift and safe, we'll get some rest. But I don't want to take any chances until then." Tharadis knew they wouldn't keep their lead for long. It would doubtless take the two of them longer to cross over the Rift than it would their pursuers, but he said nothing to the sergeant, not wanting to worry him further.

Besides, who knew what waited for them on the other side?

The soldier returned with the pack, now bulging and heavier than Tharadis would like, and handed it over. Tharadis nodded his thanks to the soldier and slung the pack over his shoulder. The sergeant gestured, the corners of his mouth turned up. "This way, gentlemen."

The air cooled more as they approached, the hairs on Tharadis's arms standing up. He couldn't remember the last time he'd been this cold. He glanced at Dransig, thinking that from here on out, the Knight would no longer regret wearing so much. Dransig didn't look grateful for the cool wind, however. His brow was furrowed, his lips tight. He looked like a man marching to the gallows.

It wasn't long before they walked past the sign Tharadis had ordered built—a sign declaring that any further work done on the Runeway would be considered an invasion of Naruvieth—and the dark brown smear of the Runeway resolved into the details that Tharadis had heard described but had never truly been able to envision, so strange were the image they conjured. The Runeway was not one big solid block of metal as it appeared from a distance, but rather countless strips. Some were as long as his forearm while others were shorter, all twisted and folded together in a chaotic jumble—chaotic, at least, to Tharadis's eyes. He imagined that it would make sense to certain Patterners. And perhaps to certain madmen, as well.

The wind was a dull, constant roar, snapping at the hem of his tunic as he crouched down at the unfinished edge of the Runeway. Something about that edge put him on edge, making his stomach feel tight. He had always known that the Council of the Wall had wanted to finish the Runeway, but now, here, he could almost feel that incompleteness, as if he were staring at a bare patch of canvas in the corner of a master's painting. He looked away, wondering if everyone felt so uneasy around this thing built of Patterning. One glance at Dransig's shadowed eyes told him he was not alone in this.

The metal the Runeway comprised was dark, like iron, yet at times it gleamed with hints of a deep reddish brown, suggesting copper, or some other metal he didn't know. Tharadis had to admit that the designs the strips created were beautiful from a certain perspective. The whorls of metal were like all the steps of a dance seen at once, frozen in time.

Though it looked like a mass of knife blades melted and twisted together, Tharadis almost instinctively knew that he could brush his fingers against the Runeway's surface without so much as a scratch. He could *see* that was so. As if to prove it to some doubting part of himself, he reached forward with his left hand until the tip of his finger touched the ice-cold metal.

The cold shot through him, blinding him, seizing his lungs, turning them to blocks of ice. Pain obliterated all sense of the world, all sense of self.

Alone in the white void were the words.

The unyielding shatters
Death heralds world's end
And you shall die

"Tharadis."
He spun at the touch to his shoulder, pulling in air like a drowning man

who just breached the water's surface. The sergeant stood at his side, frowning. Dransig stood behind him, shoulders hunched under his cloak, staring at the Rift intently as if he had forgotten there were others with him.

Tharadis scrubbed his face with his hands. They came away slicked with cold sweat. He stood. The wind nearly toppled him. His head throbbed once, twice, but then the strange feeling passed. "What happened?" His throat was so dry he had to croak the words out. He gestured that he was fine.

The sergeant shook his head slowly, eyes never leaving Tharadis, as he lowered his hand. "Thought you'd decided to take a little nap after all. You sat there a near quarter hour, I reckon." He shook his head again. "But something didn't seem right. You looked … frozen. Like you'd stopped breathing."

Tharadis squeezed his eyes shut. The words were still there, hovering before his mind's eye like an afterimage of the sun. He knew without a doubt what the words were.

Prophecy.

They gave him the same feeling as the bloody words from the day before. As if … he were in a whirlpool, wind and spray lashing at his face, him frantically swimming against the current until his muscles burned, but being pulled closer and closer to that black void in the center…

Abruptly, he grabbed Shoreseeker's sheath with one hand and used the thumb of his other to push the hilt up, exposing an inch of its sky blue blade. The words from yesterday, forever burned in his memory, came to him.

Blue stands against green.

The unyielding shatters.

He snapped Shoreseeker home in its sheath and turned to the sergeant. "Thank you for your assistance. That will be all."

Something in Tharadis's tone made the man give a wan-faced but proper salute before turning on his heels and marching back to the guard post.

Tharadis turned to Dransig, who was watching him now, eyes intent. "Are you ready?"

Dransig paused a moment before nodding. "The sooner this is over, the better."

Chapter 13: The Crossing

Dransig stood two paces from the Runeway, staring at it as if it were a miles-long snake lying in wait for him. After some time—more time than Tharadis would have liked, given their situation—Dransig stepped onto the Runeway and stood there with his eyes closed.

Tharadis moved close so he didn't have to shout. "Can you keep going?"

"Do I have any choice?" Dransig opened his eyes and looked south. "It's hard to sense them, this close to the Rift." He snorted. "Hard to sense anything. I can barely feel my own toes. But the good news is, they won't be able to sense me again until they are on the other side. And anyone who's waiting for me won't know I'm coming until I'm sitting on their backs." He gathered his cloak in one arm and started walking towards the breach in the walls of Rift light.

Frowning, Tharadis followed, but it was hard keeping an eye on Dransig when the Rift was so close. He was still on the stretch of Runeway sitting on solid ground, but only a few steps in front of him, the ground dropped away, and the only thing separating him from the Rift was this strange metal road. Foolishly, he found himself imagining that it wouldn't hold once he stepped out beyond the edge, that the Runeway would choose that moment to buckle and send him and Dransig tumbling into the Rift to die—or suffer some worse, unimaginable fate.

Tharadis took a deep breath, admonishing himself to stop being such a fool, and forced himself to keep walking.

Still, once he stepped past where the Rift began, he paused. Nothing happened, of course, but it was only then that he realized he'd been holding in that breath, and he let it all out in a rush.

To either side was only the wavering, otherworldly light of the Rift, both walls stretching up so high it left only the tiniest of sliver of sky between them. Glancing down, he saw that the light even seeped up through the gaps in the Runeway. *Death, just inches beneath the soles of my sandals,* he thought, before silently admonishing himself again. The wind was much stronger here, so much so that it stung his eyes. Tharadis wiped at them, hooked his thumb under the strap of his pack, and looked to Dransig.

Twenty paces ahead, the Knight struggled forward, looking more like a man hiking up a steep incline than one crossing a level bridge.

Tharadis shook his head. If Dransig could manage, so could he. He pressed on.

Not a quarter hour passed before Dransig collapsed hard to his knees and slumped to his side. He lay, still as stone, as his cloak flapped all around him.

Tharadis himself nearly stumbled as he rushed to Dransig's side. Without a word, he tossed his pack to the middle of the Runeway, crouched, and rolled him over. Dransig's eyes and teeth were clenched tight. Sweat streaked his brow. Tharadis wasn't sure if he was still conscious or not. Either way, he wasn't going to walk on his own.

He slung the pack over one shoulder while supporting Dransig with the other. Tharadis thought that if he could support at least some of his weight, Dransig would begin to move his feet, by instinct if nothing else. But when Tharadis began to walk, Dransig's feet only dragged. Tharadis would have to carry him.

Pack now hanging in front of him, Tharadis groaned as he pulled Dransig's limp, heavy form up onto his back.

It wasn't long before Tharadis was panting, the muscles in his thighs burning. He had no idea how much farther he had to go; the sliver of sky simply stretched forward, thinning until it met the horizon. It didn't matter how far it was, anyway. All that mattered was him putting one foot in front of the other and not stumbling over the edge into the Rift. He would get there when he did, and thinking about it wouldn't change that.

Dransig started to shake. Tharadis paused, fearing the worst. Was the Rift having more of an effect on him than Dransig had originally thought?

Would Tharadis be carrying a sheggam on his back before long?

Tharadis suspected he'd have some warning before that happened. And if it did, there would be nothing he could do for Dransig. He'd be gone, a monster in his place. If that happened, Tharadis always had Shoreseeker. Or he could just toss him into the Rift.

No. He'd told Dransig he'd see him across the Rift, and that's what he meant to do. He would just have to go faster.

Tharadis turned enough to allow himself a brief glance over his shoulder. He couldn't tell how far they'd already gone, but he knew it had been long enough that they couldn't turn back now. The Knights would likely already be there. Tharadis dismissed the idea. Forward was all they had now.

"Fight," Tharadis murmured, the wind carrying the sound away. "Fight it, Dransig." Sweat began to burn his eyes as much as the wind did. He squinted, the Runeway becoming a dark blur.

The edge of Tharadis's sandal caught on one of the tiny ridges on the Runeway's surface, jolting his step enough to cause him to stumble. His knee slammed into its hard, metal surface, and a moment later, his face, with all of Dransig's weight behind it. Tharadis's eyesight flashed and dimmed, his thoughts awash in a haze of pain.

It was all he could do to roll Dransig off of his back and try to regain his senses. He took a moment to clear his head, catch his breath, and inspect Dransig. He was no longer shaking. Neither did he seem to be breathing.

Tharadis would have to recover later. He had no idea how much longer Dransig could stand to be here. With a grunt, Tharadis pulled him onto his back again and trudged forward, worry spurring him on.

The sliver of sky gradually darkened to twilight as it widened, revealing a handful of stars. Had they really been on the Runeway that long? He couldn't be sure how long he'd been carrying Dransig on his back. It couldn't have been more than an hour or two, but it felt like half his life.

Up ahead, Tharadis could see finally hints of green emerging from beyond the Rift—hints of the Accord lands.

That meant they were almost across. "Not much longer now." He wasn't sure who the words were for. Exhaustion threatened to pull him down, but he forced himself forward. They were almost across. He had to keep going. "Not much longer."

When there were only a few steps between him and his goal, two brown-clad figures stepped onto the Runeway a couple dozen paces ahead.

One problem at a time, Tharadis thought. *One problem at a time.* His mind struggled to put the pieces together. Something in his subconscious nagged at him. He should know what their brown cloaks meant. He didn't bother to think about it. He couldn't right now. All he could think about was crossing the bridge, getting Dransig and himself away from the Rift.

Tharadis glanced up at them again and saw the eyes stitched to their tabards. *Ah. Yes.*

When they finally passed the Rift, Tharadis headed right, step by lurching step, until he was no longer on the Runeway, until he could feel blades of wet grass tickle his toes. The Rift glowed five paces to his right. Tharadis didn't know if that was far enough away to loose Dransig from whatever effect it was having on him. He hoped it was, but he didn't have much of a choice—he simply couldn't go any further. He let Dransig slide off his back with a thump and dropped the pack. As soon as he hit the ground, Dransig took in a sharp breath. His eyelids fluttered briefly, but then he went still again.

Good enough. Tharadis dropped to a knee, panting heavily. He turned to the two approaching brown-clad figures, their wooden staves before them.

Trembling, Tharadis rose to his feet and drew Shoreseeker.

Chapter 14: Knights of the Eye

Y ou'd do well to step away from that one, young man," said the Knight in front. He was quite a bit younger than Dransig, though he still had a dozen years on Tharadis. Part of his thick, red beard had been braided; the rest of it was slightly matted from a lack of washing. The man's eyes were deep in their sockets beneath a heavy brow. The glow of the Rift lapped over his features like liquid firelight. The shadows cast by his steel conical helm swallowed his eyes.

Both Knights had slowed their advance once Tharadis had drawn Shoreseeker. They eyed him warily—and Shoreseeker, doubtless having never seen a sword with a blade quite like it. They could tell from his stance that he was no novice. They were likely determining how poorly he would make use of his abilities, as worn out as he was.

Tharadis tried to do the same, figure out if he even had a chance. Tried, but couldn't. He couldn't focus his mind. It took all his effort just to keep his eyes open and his sword up.

"Look at him," said the younger Knight. The tips of blond curls peeked out from under his helm. His noseguard was bent severely, and he had a nose to match it. It looked like it had been broken several times. There was a look in his eyes that Tharadis had seen a number of times before, moments before the outbreak of a brawl. It was eagerness for a fight. "He can barely stand. Let me take him."

The older man gave his companion a sharp stare. "Going for the easier prey, are you?"

"Easier than that?" The blond Knight motioned to Dransig's unconscious form. "I'll leave the murder to you." The look in his eyes turned savage as he smiled at Tharadis. "This one is *mine*."

The older one didn't seem to like his tone, but then he shrugged and slung his staff on the thong that looped over his shoulder. "Fine by me," he said. "Just don't kill him." From beneath his cloak he drew a gleaming single-edged short sword and began to slowly make his way around Tharadis, eyes fixed firmly on him.

Tharadis watched him, too—a little too long. Sensing the distraction, the

66

blond man thrust the steel-shod tip of his staff at him with a yell. Tharadis sidestepped and twisted, slapping it away. He moved too sluggishly to deflect it entirely. He avoided having his sword arm broken, but he could tell from the deep throb that it would likely bruise and swell soon. The pain wasn't entirely unwelcome. Tharadis felt his heart beat a little faster, felt his motions become a little surer.

The blond man danced back, cloak swirling behind him. He looked pleased by his quarry's performance. "Not bad," he said, nodding. "I've had better, of course, like when your mother—" He suddenly swung the staff again, and then once more in quick succession. Tharadis hadn't been fooled that time. Shoreseeker had gouged the staff, slicing off a sliver as long as his arm. With the second strike he hadn't been quite so lucky. The blood on his knuckles was proof of that.

Tharadis stepped closer to the bearded Knight, who had been close to flanking him. The Knight slowed, then stopped when Tharadis had moved directly between him and Dransig. Tharadis knew they were just trying to keep him occupied long enough to kill Dransig. With two of them, it was only a matter of time before they succeeded. Tharadis had to do something quickly before that time came. But he had no idea what to do. His mind was drawing a blank. Trying to think of what to do felt as if he were trying to catch the wind in his fingers.

There was no time to think of a solution right now. He let his instincts take over, and hoped that he had honed them well enough.

He brought his lead foot back, squaring his stance. Then he brought Shoreseeker up over his head, parallel to his shoulders, the flat of the blade facing the same direction as his eyes.

The blond man laughed. "The Fool's Salute. I've never actually seen it used before. Either you're extremely arrogant and stupid, or … well, there is no other option, is there?" His smile widened as he leaned back on his rear foot, preparing to strike again.

Without closing his eyes, Tharadis pictured a flower in his mind, one called the hearthsflame, a small orange flower that grew on the rocky slopes of the Face just north of the city. He saw it as clearly as the man before him. In his mind, it overlaid the scene before him, covering it yet not obscuring any of its details, as if the flower and his opponent were one and the same.

The flower in Tharadis's mind bent suddenly, as if propelled forward by a gust of wind.

With strokes as gentle as the brush of a finger, Tharadis brought down

Shoreseeker.

Bud. Petal. Tharadis saw both sheared from the hearthsflame, falling away slowly, as if almost weightless.

He cleared the image from his mind as the blond man fell to his knees, screaming. He couldn't seem to decide whether to clutch the bleeding stump of his right arm or the deep gash on his left cheek. The man's right hand lay on the ground two paces away, still clutching the staff as if it didn't know it was no longer attached to the rest of his body.

Tharadis turned to the bearded Knight.

The Knight backed away, short sword held in front of him. He glanced to his companion, who was still on his knees and now sobbing instead of screaming.

"You can't use that sword on me," Tharadis said. "Not unless I attack you first."

The bearded man nodded, his eyes wide. "You know more about us than you should."

Tharadis didn't think so, at least not at the moment. He hadn't even been sure he had remembered that one fact correctly. His knees had begun to shake with the effort of keeping himself upright. He hoped his opponent wouldn't notice.

The blond man had stopped whimpering. Tharadis spared a glance for him. He was now crawling on his belly towards the burning light of the Rift.

The bearded man saw this. "You opened him up pretty good," he said, his voice tense. "This is a dangerous place to do such a thing."

"I know." Tharadis began backing toward Dransig. "Mind your oath, Knight of the Eye. I don't think I have enough energy to fight him if he turns." Shoreseeker still held out in front of him, Tharadis bent to wrap Dransig's arm around his shoulders and loop the strap of his pack around his free arm.

"Bastard." Anger was plain on the Knight's face, but in his voice Tharadis heard the hint of grudging respect. The man ran to his companion.

Tharadis dragged Dransig across the damp ground toward the treeline, heedless of the bearded man's battle cry, or the inhuman screams that answered. The sounds of combat faded in the distance that Tharadis put between them, and once the trunks of the forest trees completely blocked off the light coming from the Rift, Tharadis dropped Dransig to the leaf-strewn ground, joining him a moment later as exhaustion overwhelmed him.

Chapter 15: Parting Paths

Dransig rolled to his side as he began to wake up. His mouth was dry. He opened his eyes.

Familiar trees, branches heavy with damp leaves, surrounded the clearing he was in. *Green* leaves, not the pale gray needle-like ones of the Naruvian drytrees.

He was back in the Accord. He was home.

He heaved himself up to a sitting position, pushing the ferns that had covered him out of the way. The daylight hurt his eyes. What time was it? Afternoon already?

He didn't remember much from the night before. Even thinking about crossing the Rift made his entire body throb with pain. All twenty-two of his piercings, each one a tiny sheggam bone embedded in his skin, ached as if they had been ripped out of him. Of course, that was impossible. He'd be dead if even a few were missing.

A small pot of food propped above embers simmered in the center of the clearing. A clean wooden bowl and spoon sat next it, apparently left out for Dransig as an invitation to finish whatever was in the pot. After last night, his stomach was a confusion of hunger and nausea, but the hunger won out, and he was quickly spooning the food into his mouth. There seemed to be few ingredients—beans and roots, perhaps some herbs—but combined in such a way that Dransig found himself torn between shoveling it in his mouth and savoring every morsel. His bowl was clean before long. This was, perhaps, the best thing Dransig had ever eaten.

There was still some left in the pot. As Dransig helped himself to another serving, he mulled over his situation. How had he survived? How was he still human?

The first question was easier to answer: Tharadis had saved him somehow. The man was nowhere in sight, but he had obviously been the one who had cooked.

As for the second question … Dransig couldn't recall much beyond setting foot on the Runeway on the Naruvian side of the Rift. He had felt the Rift's pull and had tamped down the shegasti within him, felt it clawing at him, threatening to burst out of his skin … and then nothing. The next thing he knew, he was here.

He kept the shegasti tamped down still. He didn't trust himself with it, not after coming so close to losing himself to it. As such, he felt every one of his years like a leaden weight on his shoulders—and it felt as if he had aged ten years since the previous day. Every one of his joints creaked as he stood. He was gasping by the time he was fully upright. He tossed the bowl and spoon next to the pack and headed up a small game trail leading out of the clearing to find Tharadis.

Small insects buzzed past him, weaving between the moss-streaked tree trunks. Birds called down from the canopy. The air was damp and smelled of soil. Dransig had almost forgotten how home had felt.

The thought was bittersweet. Dransig's life could be defined by all the times he had forsaken his different homes, moving onto the next. He was running out of places to go. Still, the Accord was as much of a home as he had ever had, and part of him was happy to be back, despite the fact that it meant he was that much closer to achieving what he came here to do.

Tharadis's tracks were clear, marching up the slope. Dransig followed them past the trees to find him on the hilltop, under the branches of a lone tree.

Tharadis sat with his legs crossed, bare sword lying across his knees, staring out at the vista. Clouds dotted the sky, casting rolling shadows over the forested hills stretching off to the horizon. It was a beautiful sight, to be sure, but Dransig's gaze was drawn to that remarkable blade.

Tharadis turned. Relief filled his eyes as Dransig approached, and he smiled. He returned his regard to the view. "It's much colder than I expected."

Dransig couldn't help but grin. "Probably colder than you've ever been in your life. And you haven't even seen winter."

Tharadis tilted his chin to the sprawling view. "It's beautiful," he said. "We have a place like this near Naruvieth, called the Wishing Well. A place of soft green grasses and clear water. A place of life."

Dransig was surprised to hear it. He had thought all of Naruvieth was the same dry gray and dusty brown. "It sounds like a lovely place."

"It is, but there's a legend about it." Without meeting Dransig's eyes, he shifted his knee to make room. Dransig slowly sat down next to him, easing onto the soft, mossy grass.

"A long time ago," Tharadis began, "three people, a mother, a father, and a baby, had been cast out of the city by the Warden of that time, a corrupt man who believed that everyone in Naruvieth belonged to him. They had been cast out because the father had called that Warden a traitor to his office, saying he was the very sort against which the people needed protection."

He paused briefly before continuing. "Knowing that executing them would turn the people against him, he banished them from the city, calling them anathema, saying that anyone who helped them would suffer an even worse fate. It was cruel enough to create greater fear of him, but not so cruel that a whipped and stricken people would rise up against him.

"So, no one helped the three of them, even though they would starve. They wandered off into the wilderness, living off the land as best they could, though the Warden's enforcers made even this difficult.

"They made it into an empty place, dry and dusty and windswept, completely devoid of living things, before they could go no further. They were blocked off by cliffs on all sides except the way they came. They were starving and too exhausted to go on.

"They had been just, good people, made to suffer because of one evil man's lust for power. And they would die because they stood up to fight against him, to fight for what was right.

"As the three of them lay down to die, each of them, even the little baby, begged the World Pattern to help them. Each of them made a wish. While the World Pattern does not grant wishes, it does love virtue, and so it shaped that place into what it is now so that they could look upon beauty before they left the world, so that they could remember life fondly. And so it has stood since then."

"That," said Dransig, genuinely moved, "is a very sad story."

"Sometimes you have to look deep within the sad stories to find the good ones, the ones that make you believe that the struggle is worth it."

Dransig turned to him. "Do you believe in that legend?"

When he finally answered, Tharadis's voice had quieted to nearly a whisper. "No. But it's a nice story nonetheless."

Again, Dransig's gaze was drawn to Shoreseeker. He hadn't gotten a good look at it that first night. Looking closely now, he found that the blade was not metal, but appeared to be ceramic of the same pale blue as the scabbard. The crossguard was made of the same stuff as the blade—indeed, they appeared to be a unified whole rather than separate pieces. Shoreseeker looked like a splinter of the sky. "The story of how you got that sword must also be remarkable."

Tharadis looked down at it and slowly rubbed his finger along the fuller. Partway down the blade, his finger caught on something.

Dransig frowned, briefly pulling in a slight thread of shegasti to sharpen his vision. A slight crack ran up the fuller. Odd. From all he had heard and seen, the blade was supposed to be indestructible.

"Actually," Tharadis said, "there's not much to tell. The day I was made Warden of Naruvieth, a man I'd never seen before walked up to me. His clothes were little more than tattered rags and he looked as if he hadn't shaved in years. I thought he was a beggar or a madman, but then he just handed the sword to me, and without a word, fell over and died."

"And you named it Shoreseeker?"

Tharadis nodded.

"That's still quite a story."

"It doesn't feel like one. Just the ending, perhaps."

Dransig nodded. *Just the ending,* he mused, *of a story that belonged to someone else.*

In silence, they watched the clouds move across the sky for a while before Dransig turned to him. "I don't know how you did it, but you got us here alive. Thank you. I'm sorry for being such a burden."

Tharadis shrugged. "I swore to bring you home."

Dransig feared to ask what, exactly, Tharadis had gone through to do that. "If there's anything I can do to repay you …"

"If it's not too much trouble," Tharadis said, "I'd like a guide to Garoshmir."

Dransig breathed in, then exhaled slowly. "I'm afraid I wouldn't be much of one. Part of my … condition demands that I travel on foot. Horses and mules don't much care for the scent of me. Not even enough to let me ride in a cart behind them." It was worse than he let on. Every horse Dransig had ever seen, even docile work horses, had tried to crush his skull with its hooves at the mere sight of him. It was far worse for him than the Knights who only had one piercing. "Perhaps our paths should part here."

Tharadis opened his mouth as if to object, but Dransig raised his hand. "Yes," Dransig said, "we're both headed to Garoshmir. But you and I both know that your responsibility lies with your people. And I refuse to be a burden any longer."

Tharadis frowned, but his expression softened. "As difficult as it's been, I wouldn't call your presence a burden."

72

"You carried me on your back, didn't you? If that's not a burden, then I don't know what is."

Tharadis chuckled softly as he stood, dusting off the seat of his tunic and helping Dransig stand up when it was clear he was having trouble.

"I hope we can meet again in Garoshmir," Tharadis said, grasping Dransig's hand.

Dransig tried to smile reassuringly, but he knew that it wouldn't happen. Only one task waited for him there.

One final task.

Tharadis watched him curiously before releasing his hand. Some of his good cheer had evaporated as he watched Dransig's face. "I hope you find whatever you're looking for," he said.

"My daughter," Dransig blurted, not meeting his eyes. Again, more softly, "My daughter."

"She must miss you very much." Tharadis clapped him softly on the shoulder and, with a small smile that Dransig couldn't match, turned and walked down into the trees.

Chapter 16: The Road to Falconkeep

The fire crackled and popped loudly in the clearing amidst dozens of trees, brown trunks growing straight up and down and leaves that were flat and green and rustled when the wind swept through them. The late evening air was so cold that Nina had to wear a blanket around her shoulders. She didn't sit close to the fire; she didn't want to sit too close to the other children, especially the two children who had come with Lora Bale, wearing their blue and gray Falconkeep uniforms. Back in Naruvieth, they had sweated in their heavy belted tunics and trousers tucked into tall boots, but once they crossed the Rift, passing into the land they called the Accord, with all its green and wetness, they looked far more comfortable than Nina felt.

This place was just so *green*. Lora Bale, the woman taking them to Falconkeep, said it was spring now, and Nina guessed she was right, from what little she knew of spring. Back in Naruvieth, there weren't many kinds of flowers, and the few they had were down in the lowlands. Only the orange hearthsflame, which Uncle Tharadis said reminded him of Nina's mother, grew near the city. But here, flowers bloomed in so many colors and shapes that Nina had lost count the day after crossing over the Rift.

She had been amazed at first, and still was a bit, but it was hard to think about that when Alicie and Vidden, wearing their Falconkeep clothes, were standing so near all the time.

There was something … *wrong*, about those two. They didn't play like Nina or the other children. Lora Bale always spoke kindly to them, a faint smile constantly on her full lips, but the only things she ever said to them were commands. And the only times Alicie and Vidden spoke were when they needed to ask a question about one of the many tasks Lora Bale had given them.

It wasn't merely that they didn't speak. They also seemed not to see. Not that they were blind, but it was more like nothing in front of them was all that interesting. When Nina met Alicie's dark brown eyes in the carriage one time, it was as if Nina had just been part of the seat. Not a person at all. She had instantly looked away, holding her Raccoon family tight against her chest.

In the days since leaving Naruvieth for Falconkeep, the other children had seemed to just pretend that life hadn't changed all that much, aside from being stuck in a cramped carriage most of the day while they put the miles behind them.

The only other girl they had picked up was Wenny, a lowlands girl who was even tinier than Nina, and probably a year or two younger. She kept her black hair in a tail, though it was barely long enough and strands of hair were always coming loose, creating a wispy cloud around her head. Nina had only tried talking to Wenny once, and the girl, whose eyes were always wide like a dog that'd been hit too many times, had run away without a word. Wenny hadn't spoken to anyone since Nina first met her, days ago.

Two of the boys, Rogert and Noil, took advantage of their occasional stops to practice fencing with narrow switches, though mostly what they did was stick out their chests and boast about their completely imaginary exploits, only crossing "blades" when they couldn't think of a tale more extravagant than their last one. Though she hadn't really talked to either boy, she did like watching them out of the corner of her eye. She didn't feel comfortable with all these strangers, so even when Rogert or Noil said something particularly funny, she did her best to hide her smile and pretend she wasn't listening.

Of the other three boys that had joined them, Thomerlin and Chrissoth were immediately drawn to each other. Thomerlin was tall and thin, copper-colored hair falling in tight coils around his narrow, freckled face. Chrissoth was a husky boy, but not fat. Just *big*. His pale features contrasted starkly with his black hair. Both seemed to find similar things entertaining: throwing rocks at trees, throwing rocks at the carriage's wheel spokes, throwing rocks at rabbits—which nearly made Nina cry, since that was the first time she'd actually ever *seen* a rabbit. She avoided them, though that seemed to draw their attention as much as not. She didn't like the way they smiled.

Only the other boy, Chad, seemed to feel totally comfortable alone. Nina liked watching him more than Rogert or Noil. Instead of riding in the carriage or up on the driver's bench with the Falconkeep children, he often opted to stroll alongside the carriage, skinny, dirty hands stuffed into his threadbare pockets, as he stared up at the breaks in the trees, smiling with his eyes closed when sunlight struck his face, chuckling silently at himself when closing his eyes too long had sent him stumbling on some upturned stone or branch. He had an unruly mop of black hair like Chrissoth and a narrow face like Thomerlin, but that was where the similarities ended. The corners of his wide eyes constantly glinted with laughter. Nina didn't really understand how that could be; unlike the other children, who were from the farms in the lowlands and thus unknown to Nina, Chad was from Naruvieth proper. While they had never spoken, Nina knew some things about him. He was an orphan, just like Nina, but unlike her, he hadn't had any extended family to fall back on. His strange, gray woolen vest and trousers—outland castoffs, no doubt, as boys in Naruvieth didn't wear such clothes—looked to be held together with hope as much as thread. Back in the city, he'd had a reputation for being the beggar who begged for odd jobs instead of handouts. And he'd always done a good job at any task given him, and could find just about anything that was lost, no matter where it had gotten to.

He was, perhaps, as famous as her uncle Tharadis.

Well, maybe not that famous, but pretty famous anyway.

While Nina tried to pretend that she didn't exist, Chad seemed to *forget* that he existed. He would simply get lost in observing things. Soon after they had set out, Chad had spent an entire afternoon getting lost in the drywoods, and Alicie and Vidden had to go find him. When they asked him why he'd left the carriage without a word, he opened his cupped hands to release an iridescent purple butterfly he had followed from the road. And when watching the antics of Rogert and Noil, Chad would laugh and clap loudly if they did something he found particularly amusing. At first, they'd eyed him with suspicion, but after a couple of days, they'd begun to grin and bow with such earnest flamboyance that Nina nearly believed their fantastic stories.

Occasionally, Chad looked at her. There was nothing in those looks that frightened or worried her. No indication that he had a purpose beyond just looking at her. As if that were all he wanted. As much as Nina hated when Thomerlin or Chrissoth looked at her, Chad made her feel even more uncomfortable. It was almost as if he really wanted to *see* her. She didn't really understand it, nor did she understand why she was so put off by his attentions. For some reason, she always found an excuse to flee when he approached. Nina wondered if Wenny felt the same way about her that Nina felt about Chad.

Now, however, as Nina was staring into the crackling fire, lost in thought, he plopped down beside her and crossed his legs, his knee only inches from her own. Out of the corner of her eye, Nina looked at him. No smile touched his lips, but his eyes were twinkling, as if *she* were some butterfly that had finally fallen into his trap.

Nina felt her heart race. This was the first time he had gone out of his way to sit so close. What was she going to do? Talk to him? Get up and leave? Neither choice seemed like a good idea, so she went for what she usually did: pretending like she didn't exist and hoping he would come around to the idea.

He didn't. Instead, he spoke to her. "Name's Chad Forder."

She glanced at him, then back at the fire.

Chad leaned back, propping himself up with his arms. "But I bet you already knew that. I've been watching you. You've always got your eyes and your ears open. I bet not much slips past you." The smile in his eyes began to spread to his lips. "I bet you know more about me than I do."

"Yeah?" she said, turning to him. "I bet you know more about me than I do about you."

He leaned forward. "I bet you don't have nothing to bet with."

Nina cocked an eyebrow. "How much you want to bet?"

The smile finally stretched across his face. He shrugged. "All right, you got me. I don't have nothing either."

Nina snorted and returned her attention to the fire, pretending to be less interested than she was. "Everybody has something."

"Really? And what do you have?"

Instinctively, Nina glanced down at the Raccoon family hanging from her belt. She had been clutching them tight; she always did. She folded her hands in her lap and decided that she didn't want to talk anymore, taking more interest in the few stars she could see in the gaps between the leaves.

Out of the corner her eye, she saw him nod. "You're right," he said. "You *do* have something. But I think that's too precious to bet. You've got to have something else."

"And what do you have?" she asked, curiosity getting the better of her.

His teeth gleamed in the firelight. "Secrets."

The skin on Nina's arms prickled. She knew what kind of secrets he meant. The kind of secrets all the children here had; the kind of secrets that none of them seemed to want to talk about. "Then I guess I don't know very much about you," she said.

He chuckled softly and snapped his fingers. "I walked right into that."

"So? Did I win the bet?"

Chad tilted his head. "You *did* know my name already, didn't you?"

In her loftiest Esta impression, Nina lifted her nose and said, "I've already forgotten it."

"Nice try. Tell me something I don't know."

"There's a graveyard up ahead." Nina glanced out into the night.

Chad turned to look, but there was nothing to see. Nina couldn't see it either, but she just … knew it was there.

His head swiveled back around, the touch of a frown on his brow. "Been out this way, have you?"

Nina didn't answer. He knew she hadn't. None of them had.

Chad grinned. "You've got secrets too, don't you? Well, we've all got secrets. I'm guessing yours is why you're here. Just like me. Just like the others."

"What's your secret?" Nina asked. She figured the more this Chad was talking, the less she'd have to. She already regretted saying as much as she had.

"It wouldn't be much of a secret if I went around telling people, now would it?" Although Nina still didn't quite trust this boy, she decided she did like his wide, toothy grin. The glint in his eyes seemed to say that Nina was included in the joke, and not the butt of it. Despite herself, she was smiling right along with him.

He stood, dusted off the seat of his pants, and with a sideways glance at the others, leaned in close to whisper with his hand cupped against his mouth. "I'll do better than tell you. I'll show you." With that he crept towards the fire, where the others were seated. Rogert and Noil, exhausted from their play, barely glanced up at him. The Falconkeepers didn't even acknowledge him with a glance. Chrissoth and Thomerlin sat with their backs to Nina, silhouetted by the fire. Chad gave a little wave and crouched down right behind Chrissoth's bulk, disappearing into his shadow.

Nina gaped, astonished at his boldness. Was his special ability getting beaten for acting so foolishly? She didn't know what Chad was trying to prove, but the one thing he had proved was that he was stupider than he looked. Once Chrissoth turned around, or even glanced to the side, he would see Chad sitting there, hiding in the large shadow he cast. Chad might as well have called him fat and spared himself the waiting. Either way, Chad would earn himself a thrashing.

Nina watched, waiting for that fateful moment. How could Chad could sit so still for so long? Was that his special ability? Sitting for a long time?

If so, it wasn't much of a skill, but he managed to be doing an impressive job of it. Chad was so still that Nina couldn't even tell he was there, hidden in Chrissoth's silhouette.

Someone tapped her on the shoulder. Nina spun with a loud yelp.

Chad stood behind her, grinning his wide grin as if he had expected her reaction.

Nina looked at him, then at Chrissoth and Thomerlin, who were now scowling at her, then back at Chad. "How—"

He raised a finger. "I said I would show you. That's what I did. Never said I would tell you how I did it."

Her voice dropped to a sharp whisper. "But, but that's impossible! You were in his shadow! If you'd moved, I'd have seen it!"

"Well, if it's impossible, how am I standing here?"

Nina had no idea. But she understood then that he *had* shown her what he could do. She just couldn't make sense of it.

With an exaggerated sigh, he took his seat next to her again. He crossed his ankles, leaning back on his elbows. She watched him and waited. He was only trying to look calm and cool, but she knew he was aching to tell her as bad as she was aching to know.

Finally, he leaned over and whispered. "There are places that other people can't go. Places in the shadows. No one else can see them but me. No one else can go in them but me." He met her eyes then. "I can walk in and out of the shadow world."

A … shadow world? Chad didn't give her the chance to ask about it. Abruptly he stood up and sauntered over to the fire. "What's that in the pot?" he said to no one in particular. He peered in. "Stew, huh?" He snatched up a bowl and scooped some into it.

Nina doubted he would talk with the others nearby, and her grumbling stomach was demanding her attention, so she scooted over to the fire and silently filled her own bowl, only once catching the amused glint in Chad's eyes before it was gone.

The next day, it rained.

Fat droplets splashed on the sills of the carriage. None of the Naruvian children sitting inside wanted to close the shutters, not even when Lora Bale, crowded in the carriage with them, stared malevolently at the wet seat fabric nearest the windows. Even Wenny stared at the downpour with open interest.

It wasn't the first time Nina had seen rain, of course, but she'd never seen it quite like *this*. When it rained in Naruvieth, it did so sparsely, intermittently. Here it was like someone had filled a bucket with the sea and was dumping it on their heads. The trees and ferns around them were alive with motion, rocking and swaying with each rain drop that struck them. Nina had never seen so many things moving at once. It almost made her feel a little sick, but that didn't stop her from wanting to keep watching it.

At the front of the wagon there was a narrow slot with a board slanting over it, shielding it from the rain, though some came in there too. Through the slot, Nina spied Vidden and Alicie, hunched in the driving seats, wearing large hooded oilcloaks. They looked miserable, hunched over like that, though Nina was jealous. She desperately wanted to walk outside in the rain, but that would mean speaking up, drawing attention to herself.

She glanced at Chad, sitting across from her with his legs folded up beneath him. He must've felt her look at him, for he tore his gaze from the outside to meet her eyes. And, as if he could read her mind—and who knew that he couldn't?—he grinned.

Nina grinned back. "Mistress Lora Bale," Nina said, turning to the woman. All heads swiveled at once to look at Nina. She felt herself flush at all the attention, but it was too late to back out now. "Is it all right if I walk next to the wagon? I'll make sure to keep up."

Lora Bale raised an eyebrow, mouth set in a thin line. "I don't have any extra oilcloaks, child. If you catch a cold, you'll have only yourself to blame."

"I know."

"Well." Lora Bale sighed. "As long as you understand the risks, I don't see why not. Make sure you stay in sight of the carriage."

Before Nina could respond, Chad shouted, "Thanks!" and burst out the door. Nina followed him out, slamming the door shut behind her. They sprinted into the foliage, cold mud sucking at their bare feet. Nina almost went back for her boots, but that would mean looking at the others and that would spoil the moment.

They careened into a patch of ferns taller than they were. Chad seized a stalk of one and snapped it off. Nina followed suit.

"There," he said, holding the wide frond over his head. "Now we can stay a little dry at least."

Nina looked at his mud-spattered knees and then down at her own, thinking there was little danger of them being dry anytime soon. Still, at least they were making an effort to be sensible, even if the fronds didn't do all *that* much.

Making sure to be where the two Falconkeepers could see them, Nina and Chad walked close to each other.

"How much longer do you think it'll be?" Chad asked quietly. Almost to himself as much to Nina, it seemed.

She shrugged. "I'm just glad we're not on that stupid road."

"The Runeway?" Chad eyed her. "Why don't you like it? It seems pretty neat to me. All that metal … more metal than a thousand blacksmith shops will ever see."

Nina didn't answer. In truth, she didn't like it because Uncle Tharadis thought there was something wrong with it. She trusted him more than anyone else, and if he didn't like the Runeway, Nina was sure he had a good reason.

Chad launched his fern into the bushes and stuffed his hands into his trouser pockets with a thoughtful expression, letting the rain fall onto his head. "I wonder why we aren't taking the Runeway. It's got to be faster, don't you think?"

"I don't know." Nina held on to her fern. It *was* better than being totally soaked. "Maybe this way is safer?"

Chad grunted doubtfully. "I heard the Accord's got guard posts along the Runeway with lots of soldiers. If there are any bad guys around, they probably won't be on the Runeway. They'd be hiding in the forest, where we are."

"Huh." Nina didn't know what to make of that.

Back at the carriage, Alicie called their names and told them to come back. The carriage was stopped, and Vidden was feeding apples to the horses, whose drenched manes clung to their necks. All the children were still inside—Thomerlin and Chrissoth staring at Chad and Nina with clear envy—but Lora Bale was crouched down in the mud with the folds of her skirts piled up in her lap to keep them off the ground. She had a floppy straw hat on her head and appeared to be studying a patch of grass near the wheel ruts. As they got closer, Nina expected her to be inspecting animal tracks or something of the like, but Nina didn't see anything like that. Just regular grass, the blades bowed with the weight of the rain.

Abruptly, the woman stood and turned to them. All the warmth was gone from her face. "Get into the carriage. No arguments. Alicie," she said, turning to the Falconkeep girl. "On the roof. Hurry."

Teeth bared like a snarling wolf, Alicie vaulted up on the roof as Nina and Chad clambered in. Lora Bale shoved Vidden over to make room for herself on the driver's seat, took up the reins, and snapped the horses into a trot. Nina could hear Alicie stumble up on the roof as the carriage lurched into motion. Lora Bale snapped the reins again until the horses were nearly galloping.

The carriage seemed to find every rock and root, jarring Nina's teeth as the trees, ferns, and bushes whipped past them. Unable to contain her curiosity any longer, Nina poked her head out the window and looked behind them, ignoring the rain smacking the back of her head. The other children quickly joined her, heads hanging out the windows to catch a glimpse of the road behind them.

First one, then two more riders shot out of the foliage and onto the tracks thirty paces behind them. Uniformed soldiers, like the Shoresmen in Naruvieth, but they were wearing gray and white, with gray cloaks whipping behind them. The rear two had crossbows slung to their backs, and the one in front was shouting and holding up his sword, but Nina couldn't hear the words over the rain and the thunder of hooves.

Nina felt her heart thumping wildly, her breathing uncontrollably fast. What did these soldiers want? They weren't criminals or anything! They were just a bunch of children!

The boards of the carriage roof creaked as Alicie shifted her weight. Nina had almost forgot she was there. She glanced up, but from this angle, Nina could only see the top of the other girl's head. Alicie's eyes were fixed on the lead rider. A thin, low-hanging branch lashed the girl's back, but she barely flinched, so intent she was. Alicie raised her arm and pointed it at the rider.

Nina turned to look back at him.

It was hard to make sense of what she was seeing at first. She had thought that maybe the rain in her eyes was making her see funny things. She remembered the time when the hem of her favorite dress, the light green one, got snagged on one of the pricker bushes growing along the Face, but Nina hadn't noticed and yanked a large bit of string loose. She tried pulling the string free from the thorns, but only ended up pulling more string loose. No matter what she tried, it only got worse until nearly a hand of fabric was missing from the bottom of her dress.

Like her dress had done that day, the man *unraveled*.

It started at his sword hand. Flesh and glove leather alike were stripped away from bone by an unseen force in a sudden mist of blood. The man screamed and dropped his sword as the ribbon of skin and muscle fell away from the bones of his arm in a spiral. The ribbon got tangled in the galloping horse's legs and the sudden jolt of the horse's powerful legs yanked the ribbon—as well as the bloody bones of his forearm—clean off. In the space of a breath, the man's other hand, his chest, his legs, even his face began to unravel, and his scream died away as his throat was no more.

Nina wanted to scream, but she vomited all over the door of the carriage instead. She felt hands, gentle hands, pull her back inside, hold her face. It was Chad. He made soothing sounds like Nina was a spooked mule, but they weren't working and it was so hard to breathe and why did that man just fall to pieces like that and why oh why couldn't she just wake up and end this nightm—

A hard slap threw Nina's head against the wall of the carriage.

"Thomerlin! What do you think you're doing?" Chad shouted.

Thomerlin's voice. "She should be thanking me."

Strangely, Nina felt a little better, even though her cheek stung like mad. She turned to face them. "It's okay, Chad." Then to Thomerlin. "Thank you."

Both boys, standing hunched under the low ceiling, sat down. A smirk of vindication spread across Thomerlin's face.

Through the slot, Nina could see Lora Bale twist around in the driver's seat to look back at Alicie, still on the roof.

"Well?" the woman asked. "Are they gone?"

Alicie didn't answer. At least not with words.

She laughed.

Hearing that laugh made Nina's stomach churn even worse than seeing what had happened to the rider. Nina met Chad's eyes then. He reached out and seized her hand. "Don't worry," was all he said.

Nina, not caring what the others thought, nodded and didn't let go of Chad's hand until they stopped later that night.

Chapter 17: Traveler

Esta crouched behind a thick cluster of ferns at the forest's edge, peering through the gaps in the fronds to the cluster of houses scattered about in front of her. Sheep and goats milled about in large pens between the houses, occasionally bleating. Seeing them made Esta's mouth water. There were more birds than boars north of the Rift, and Esta was no archer—she didn't even have a bow, nor did she know how to make one. She'd had to resort to eating berries for the past two days. Luckily, she'd avoided poisoning herself, but she wasn't one to count on luck. She needed real food.

Hungry as she was, Esta couldn't very well spear someone else's goat in broad daylight. She leaned her spear against the trunk of a tree, pulling the leafy green branches down around the spear to obscure it. She hid her pack as well at the base of the tree. Her mother had given her some coins, which Esta had divided into three handfuls—one in her pack, one hanging from the purse on her belt, and a smaller one sewn into the inside of her dress. A young woman traveling on her own could never be too careful, which was why she also kept her knife, the blade as long as her forearm, sheathed at her hip and in clear sight at all times.

Her mother had insisted she bring some Shoresmen with her, but Esta knew that they would just tell her to stay home and let them deliver the message to Tharadis themselves. Which was, admittedly, the sensible thing to do, but doing the sensible thing was often merely an excuse to avoid doing the *right* thing. Esta couldn't help but think that she was partly responsible for Nina having been taken, that she hadn't fought hard enough. She also knew that Tharadis had been too trusting when he'd let Larril decide what to do with Lora Bale's request, and it was only right that she upbraid him in person, rather than try to convey her anger in a letter.

Besides. It wasn't every day that one had an excuse to travel north of the Rift. Realizing this was such a weighty motivation shamed her, but only a little. The only thing more important to Esta than getting out of Naruvieth was the safety of her family, and this trip served both ends. If anything, her feelings only proved that she had made the right choice in coming on her own.

With her thumb hooked over her belt an inch from where her knife hung, Esta walked out into the well-trod dirt path winding between the houses. She kept her pace steady and her back straight with a cool, disinterested expression on her face. She was a stranger here and didn't want to give the impression that she was a criminal. Nor did she want to invite the attention of actual criminals.

As she passed the first house, she caught sight of a woman sitting on the wooden fence surrounding the goat pen behind that house. The woman was thin, the hands poking out of her long sleeves nearly skeletal, but the woman's cheeks drooped as if she'd once carried far more weight. She sat on the fence with her knees spread like a man with her forearms propped on them, hands dangling. Her hair, pulled back into an approximation of a tail, was the same color as the dirt that smudged her face. She seemed to be staring in the general direction of the goats but not at anything in particular, eyes as unfocused as her jaw was slack. Her gaze sharpened when she finally spotted Esta.

"Who're you?" the woman asked.

Esta stopped, studying the woman. It was hard to judge her age; Esta couldn't tell if the woman was as young as she was or as old as her mother. "A traveler. Heading for Garoshmir."

"On foot? Alone?" The woman snorted and looked back at her goats, which looked to be in even worse shape than their owner. "Good luck with that, eh."

"I … was hoping I could have some food," Esta said, cursing the hesitation in her voice.

The woman eyed her again for a moment before sliding off the fence and crossing the distance between them. "What've you got to trade? I ain't helping no freeloaders."

Esta drew a copper coin out of her waist pouch and held it up. "It's a Naruvian stamp, but it's money just the same."

"Naruvian, eh?" The woman beckoned her over. Esta kept her thumb hooked near her knife as she met the woman at the corner of the fence and handed her the coin. The woman turned it over in her hands and looked up. "This'll get a half loaf of black bread. Nothing more." Her eyes fell to the purse at Esta's hip.

"Do you have any dried meat?"

"Aye, and proper boots to keep you from catching your death. But only

85

if you've got silver in there, too."

"All right, a silver then." Esta held out her hand.

The woman shook her head and pocketed the copper. "I'm keeping this, too."

Esta dropped her hand, feeling her face flush in anger. She waited, but the woman showed no sign of budging. "Fine then," Esta said. "A silver and a copper. But I want some information. Tell me the quickest way to Garoshmir. And show me what I'm buying before you expect to see another copper from me."

The woman didn't argue any further, but instead disappeared into her house. A short while later, she returned with a cloth sack and a pair of worn boots. The woman loosened the sack's drawstring, allowing Esta to peer in. It wasn't much meat, and the bread looked more like a quarter loaf than a half, but just the sight of it made Esta willing to part with all her money. She hoped she kept such thoughts from touching her expression. Nodding, she took one of the boots and pressed the sole to the bottom of her sandal. They would be a little snug, and a couple of the seams looked ready to burst already, but they would protect her feet from the dampness that covered the grass every morning better than her sandals did.

Esta pulled out a silver coin and held it up. "And Garoshmir?"

The woman stared at the coin as if it were more than she had seen in one place. "Two silvers and I'll guide you there myself."

Esta paused. It would be nice to have some company, if nothing else. The woman seemed to be shrewd and grasping, but Esta didn't really think she would rob her. Not so long as Esta knew where she lived. She fished out a second silver coin and handed both to the woman. "What's your name?"

"Meedith."

It was an odd name, but Esta supposed her name might sound odd to people from the Accord. "I'm Esta. It's a pleasure to meet you."

Meedith merely grunted and handed over the goods Esta had bought. "Easiest way to Garoshmir is to head straight up the Runeway. It points straight as an arrow right towards it." Meedith shook her head. "But that's not the way we're going to take, and you're wise to avoid it. It's crawling with highwaymen, and the checkpoint guards don't bother with patrolling it much. Caravan's the best way to go, but there ain't no caravans 'round here."

Esta nodded as if all this were already known to her, but in truth she had strayed from the Runeway because there was no game or food growing anywhere nearby. Hunting in the lowlands around Naruvieth was second nature to her, but the Accord lands were just so ... *different*, not to mention vast, that Esta had found herself more or less lost. It was only by luck that she had stumbled onto this tiny village.

Meedith jabbed a thumb over her shoulder. "I'm gonna put my goats away in the shack and tell Ord next door to take care of them for me. He owes me one." Meedith shuffled off, muttering, "More than one. Three or four, more like."

Esta went back to the forest's edge to retrieve her pack and spear before meeting Meedith in front of her house. Meedith, her own lumpy sack slung over one shoulder, eyed the spear. "You know how to use that thing?"

"I've hunted and killed more than a dozen boars with this."

Meedith snorted and started walking north along the path. "Boars is one thing. But they can't use words. It's men, clever men with their clever tongues, that you have to watch out for."

Chapter 18: Clever Men

As night fell, so too did a deep chill that burrowed into Esta's bones. The fire was hot against her face, her arms, and her shins, but the heat only seemed to warm the surface of the skin, not touching the night's deathly cold that had wormed inside her. Anything covered up didn't even get the superficial benefit of the fire's heat. Every night Esta had spent north of the Rift had seemed colder than she thought possible, and this night coldest of all.

Meedith's face poked out of a bundle of ragged blankets across from Esta. The woman's eyes glinted in the firelight as she watched Esta's obvious discomfort. "You would do yourself a favor to get a cloak, eh?" Meedith chuckled. "Me, I prefer blankets myself. The rattier the better. Cloaks make you look like you got something to rob."

"Yeah?" Esta couldn't keep the challenge out of her voice. "And what about someone with neither?"

Meedith's homely face split apart to reveal teeth. It took Esta a moment to realize the woman was smiling. "If sense were coin, you'd look a beggar indeed."

Esta harrumphed but didn't argue, staring at the fire instead. She had nothing to say in her defense. She pulled her knees tight against her chest and wondered how Nina was doing right now. Was she, too, huddled up with strangers around a fire in this cold night? Esta knew she herself was willful and headstrong—she had spent much of her life being berated for this, by both men and women in Naruvieth—and knew she could rely on herself to some degree, no matter what happened. Nina had no such comfort. She was still a child, and no matter how caring and friendly a person Lora Bale was, she was no substitute for Nina's family.

But perhaps Nina's youth would help her in the short run, too. Children tended to be more trusting than adults, certainly more than Esta was. Maybe that trust would keep Nina from feeling so lonely so far from home. Perhaps, in time, Nina would forget that she'd had a family at all before Lora Bale came and took her away.

No. Nina wouldn't forget because Tharadis would get her back. They would be a family once again. No matter who, or what, Nina turned out to be.

Even if she destroys Naruvieth, just like fensoria have done to their hometowns in the past? a part of her asked. Esta had no answer. That possibility was too horrible to contemplate. Maybe Tharadis would know what to do. She hoped he would.

"You're worried about someone," Meedith said, startling Esta from her thoughts. She'd almost forgotten the woman was there. "I can see it in your eyes."

Esta glanced up and searched the woman's expression for mockery. But there was none. She looked genuinely sympathetic, at least as far as Esta could tell. "Yes," she admitted. "Someone I care about is in trouble, and the only person I can trust to help her is heading to Garoshmir."

Meedith nodded as she shifted in her bundle of blankets. "I lost a son, once. He was nothing more than a wee boy. Stood about yea high." Her thin hand protruded from the blankets, held up the height of a five- or six-year-old, before disappearing back into their folds. Meedith smiled, warmly this time, her eyes focusing on nothing. At least nothing in the present. "Name was Nathan. He liked to cut switches and whip the goats into a frenzy so bad they'd break through the fence. A little bastard he was, but I loved him still. He liked to climb trees, too, and he often fetched eggs out of hawks' nests and brought them home for breakfast. I switched him like he was a goat himself, but he just kept on doing it, grinning like a cat layin' a dead rat at his master's feet." Meedith fell silent as her smile faded.

Esta inched forward and prodded the embers with a stick, sending up a cloud of sparks, before tossing the stick on the fire. Her spear was next to her, the sharp end pointing towards the fire but far enough that she wasn't worried about it catching. She waited a few moments longer, but curiosity got the better of her. "How did you lose him?"

Meedith took a deep breath and let it out in long sigh. "Nathan had a younger brother. Called him Owly. He always walked around, dazed and big-eyed." Meedith met Esta's eyes and tapped her temple. "He wasn't all right in the head. Quiet, he was, and seemed to look at things but not really see them. Liked to follow his mammy's rules and always made sure everyone else did, too.

"Especially Nathan. One time, I said, 'Boy, if you don't quit crawling up those trees, I'm gonna set one on fire with you in it!' I wasn't telling truth, of course. I would never do that to one of my boys, but I wanted them to *think* I would." Meedith shrugged. "So that's why I said it. Didn't mean much at the time, but I wish I never had.

"Owly heard me. Simple as he was, he didn't know I didn't mean true. One day, I saw him follow Nathan out once. Next thing I knew, the forest was afire. Nathan never came home. Owly did, had soot in his hair. Asked him what happened, shook him, even slapped him some. But he didn't say nothing. Not then, not ever."

"Where's Owly now?" Esta asked.

Meedith stared at the flames, face still as if she hadn't heard Esta's question. Esta was almost glad for the silence. She hadn't actually wanted to ask the question and didn't know why she had. She could guess the answer anyway.

Bushes rustled. Both Esta and Meedith jerked upright and turned towards the noise. Esta snatched up her spear when she caught sight of two large forms, each bigger than most of the men in Naruvieth, lumbering out of the shrubs and darkness.

One of them, a bearded man with a battle axe resting on his shoulder in the casual manner of a logger, nodded in Esta's direction as he approached the fire. The one crashing out of the bushes behind him stood slightly shorter with bulging eyes, grinning at Meedith. His gloved hand was on the head of a warhammer hanging from a metal loop on his belt. Both were soldiers, with matching uniforms, belted gray tunics with a single wide white stripe stretching lengthwise, mail shirts underneath. Matching gray cloaks hung to the turned-down tops of their worn-in brown leather boots. Their flat-topped helmets had noseguards, but the bug-eyed man's was crooked, as if he'd been in more than his share of fights. His nose, bent in the opposite direction as the noseguard, only added to the impression.

"Good evening, ladies." The man in front inclined his head to Esta, studying her intently. His regard of Meedith was even more intense. "I must say I'm surprised to find you this far from your farm, Meedith. Milking goats no longer suit you?"

Meedith was huddled down in her bundle of rags, eyes fixed on the bearded man. He stared back a moment before shrugging and easing himself down next to the fire with a heavy groan. He joined them as if they were friends and not strangers. But then he knew Meedith, didn't he?

"What I wouldn't give for a drink right now," he murmured, combing his gloved fingers through his unruly brown beard as he stared into the fire. He glanced up at Esta so suddenly she started. "You wouldn't happen to have … No. No, of course you wouldn't." He sighed and studied the fire again.

Esta wouldn't share with him even if she had a barrel of wine. One brief meeting of Meedith's eyes was all the confirmation Esta needed—these were precisely the kind of clever men she'd warned her about.

The other soldier stood back away from the fire, watching them with his bulging eyes. Meedith in particular. His gray cloak was draped to cover everything from the neck down, giving Esta no view of his hands, though his posture was taut as a coiled snake ready to strike.

Without taking his eyes off the fire, the bearded man said, "We lost a man not two days back. Chasing monsters. Monsters of the worst kind. It was … well, I just don't have words for it." He tugged loose a few blades of the damp grass at his side and held them out in front of him. "He just fell to pieces, right in front of my eyes." He let the blades of grass fall through his fingers one by one.

"We had nothing to do with it," Esta said. "Obviously we aren't monsters."

He raised his eyebrows, thick and wild, just like his beard. "Oh, no doubt of that. For you, at least," he said, pointedly referring only to Esta before leveling his gaze on Meedith.

"Why are you telling us this?" Esta pressed.

The man shook the damp from his cloak. "I'm tired of death. So, I'd rather you quit edging toward that spear, girlie."

Esta halted, fear rushing through her. How had he noticed? *Fool*, she chided herself. *He's a soldier. Of course he'd notice a threat.*

The man turned a weary gaze back to Meedith. "And you. Off your farm with a pretty thing in tow." He shook his head. "When will you ever learn, Meedith?"

"Don't listen to a word he says." Meedith's eyes flicked between the two soldiers. "They may look like fine men, what with their uniforms and all, but believe you me. They're liars, brigands, and worse."

Beneath his beard, the man's face split in a grin as hard as cold iron. "You wouldn't be the first one Meedith sold to the Garoshmiri brothels, girl. The third, actually, by my reckoning. First one didn't last two weeks before she was wearing the red dress." Still grinning, the man drew a finger across his throat.

Esta tried to suppress a shudder but failed.

Meedith's expression went from wariness to red-faced anger in the space of a breath. "Still you flap your mouth, spewing lies, Ander. Still you—" Suddenly Meedith leapt to her feet and sprinted away from the fire.

Esta gaped in surprise but only for a moment. She scrambled to her feet and snatched up her spear, but before she could bring it to bear, the man called Ander, standing now, chopped it out of her hands with a quick swing of his axe. The blow hadn't touched her, but she felt it through the spear, leaving her hands ringing with pain.

Ander shook his head with a disappointed sigh as he slung his axe on the metal loop fastened to his belt. "Last time I help anyone," he muttered softly. He turned toward the trees, cupping his hand by his mouth. "Lannod! You get her?"

The other man, Lannod, answered by dragging Meedith out of the trees a few moments later, his fingers tightly entwined in Meedith's hair. When the woman tried to claw her way free of his grip, he simply tightened it. Meedith's face scrunched up in pain, her hands held in front of her as if she still wanted to fight but knew it was no good.

"Now, now, Meedith," Ander said softly. "None of that."

Eyes burning with rage, Meedith lowered her hands.

Ander nodded approvingly. He hooked a thumb in his weapon belt. "Now, just because I don't trust you doesn't mean I can arrest you. Not without more proof than I've got. But that doesn't mean I'm just going to let you hurt someone, either."

Meedith opened her mouth to speak, but whatever she was going to say was cut off in a sharp yelp when Lannod tightened his grip again. She blew out her cheeks she was breathing so hard. Where there was anger in her eyes before, now there was only hate.

"Take her home," Ander said, jerking a thumb over his shoulder. "Make sure she stays put. And hurry back."

Lannod nodded and began guiding the now-silent Meedith back toward her house. Esta watched them disappear into the woods, then her eyes settled on the bearded face of the man before her, heart pounding so loudly she suspected he could hear it too. She was distinctly aware that the two of them were now alone, with no one around to hear her scream. "What are you going to do with me?"

He raised his eyebrows. "With you? Well, I suppose it's too late to take you to the Waystation tonight, so that'll have to wait till morning." He eased himself onto his back near the fire again, propping his head up slightly with a forearm while he drew his cloak over himself like a blanket. He took off his helmet, revealing dark hair matted with sweat, and rested his head on it before closing his eyes. "Running through the forest at night isn't a good idea. There are worse things than Meedith out there. And I wouldn't blame you if you don't sleep, things being what they are and all. One of us should keep watch, and well, you've already decided to stay awake, haven't you?" He cracked open an eyelid at her. "And if I don't wake up tomorrow morning for whatever reason, you'll find that the rest of the Way Patrol might not be so friendly." He closed his eye again.

When Esta picked up her spear, Ander didn't stir. He knew as well as she that she wouldn't touch him. She sat down at the base of a tree at the edge of the firelight, knees drawn close with her spear lying across her lap. She fingered the shallow gash Ander's axe had put in it. The image of her skull with the same gash flashed in her mind. It made her stomach churn.

She wondered if leaving her home like some stupid, willful child had been the best idea. The tears running down her cheeks were all the answer she needed.

Chapter 19: The Waystation

It was near dawn when the pounding of heavy footsteps woke Esta.

Blinking in half-sleep, she clambered to her feet with her spear in her hands. Ander was already standing and looked like he'd been awake for hours. Though he too held his axe, his stance wasn't that of a man expecting a fight. More like one waiting for news.

Lannod staggered into the clearing, clutching his leg. Strips of cloth were tied around his upper thigh, but even in the dim pre-dawn light, Esta could see a large, dark stain spreading from the makeshift bandages. His face was twisted with pain.

In no great hurry, Ander went to Lannod's side to help the wounded man to the remnants of the fire, little more than embers now.

"What happened?" Ander asked, crouching down next to him. He shook his head. "Never mind, save your breath. She got away from you, didn't she?" He gestured at the wound. "More than that, I'd say."

Lannod puffed out his cheeks and nodded sharply.

Ander stood. "And now she's on the loose." He sighed, scrubbing his hand through his beard, making it even more unruly. "You can still ride, can't you? Come on, up you go." Lannod gritted his teeth as Ander pulled him to his feet.

"What's your name, girl?"

It took a moment for Esta to realize Ander was talking to her. "Esta."

"You'll ride with Lannod here. Don't worry; he'll be in front."

Esta stood in shock. Ride with *him?* She looked to Lannod, expecting him to leer, but he seemed to have forgotten she even existed. As the two men shuffled toward the treeline, with Lannod's arm draped over Ander's shoulder, Esta realized that she was still standing there, gaping at their backs. "Shores take me," she muttered and hurried after them.

The two horses were hobbled only a couple minutes' walk away. Just out of earshot from the campfire, Esta realized. She didn't like the fact that Ander had kept them a secret from her. But any suspicion she felt was utterly overwhelmed by the sense of amazement rushing through her as she stopped to stare.

The two horses stopped their snuffling of the grass and raised their heads at the approach of their owners. They stood well higher than Esta, their creamy coats dappled with large dark spots. Their manes, so silky they shimmered, were colored the same way. They were incredible. Beautiful.

"Until only a few days ago," Esta said, "I'd never even seen a horse."

Ander and Lannod shared a glance. "Where you from, girl?" Ander released Lannod to head over to the bags sitting on the saddles stacked nearby and pulled out a brush of some kind. He eyed her as he ran the brush over the horse's back. Lannod shuffled over to the saddlebags to fuss with them, his back kept to Esta.

"Naruvieth," she said. "Looking for my brother." She took a step forward, but Ander raised a hand to halt her.

"Careful. Let them get used to the smell of you first. These are battlehorses. They'll bite and kick anyone they don't trust." He continued brushing. "Saw a man lose his face once. *Chomp*, and most of the skin was gone. He screamed for nearly an hour before he bled to death."

Esta nodded. It seemed impossible that these magnificent creatures could be capable of such brutality, but she'd read the histories. Horses trained for fighting were often as fierce as their riders.

Riding sidesaddle, Esta soon learned, was tricky. Especially when clinging desperately to a man who was wounded and liked to grumble wordlessly to remind you of the fact. She didn't like the way Lannod smelled, either. Though after traveling as much as she had, she doubted she had any room to talk.

Fortunately, Ander kept them at a slow pace—a walk, Esta reasoned, based on what she'd read—but for the first half hour or so she was certain she'd nonetheless be bounced off the horse to fall flat on her face. After a while of staying ahorse, however, she loosened up a little and found that riding became a little easier once her back wasn't as stiff as a statue's.

The sun was well over the horizon, if still partly shrouded by clouds, when Esta caught sight of a squat stone tower in the distance. The trees had thinned as they rode, revealing jagged green hills scarred by jutting rocks. Yet despite the wildness of the terrain, a flat copper ribbon cut through it in sheer defiance: the Runeway.

"How's that leg?" Ander called over his shoulder.

Lannod winced as if he'd forgotten about it until Ander mentioned it. He grumbled again, getting a chuckle out of Ander.

"Worse than Caney Forks, eh? You couldn't walk for three weeks after that." Ander chuckled again before his voice turned serious. "Can't have you walking on it like that, Lannod. We need you hale. You're going to stay at the station. And don't fight me on it," when Lannod opened his mouth, presumably to do just that. "I'm pulling rank here."

When they got close enough that Esta could make out the shapes of men standing atop the roof of the drum-shaped tower, Ander sawed his reins and raised an arm. One of the helmeted men on the tower followed suit. Ander kicked his horse back into a walk with Lannod's mount not far behind.

A red-haired young man wearing the same colors as the two Way Patrolmen, though lacking any sort of armor, rushed out of a rickety wooden building abutting the tower when the three of them neared with a mounting block tucked under his arm. He took the reins and helped a wobbly Esta out of the saddle.

"Make sure they're well-watered," Ander told the young man, adding with a growl, "and don't touch the saddlebags." The young man, a stableboy it seemed, saluted awkwardly before leading the mounts toward the wooden building, chatting the horses up as if they were long-lost friends.

"Well, girl," Ander said, "you have two choices while I report in. You can either follow Lannod and watch him scream and soil himself while the medic sews him up. Or you can hang around the stables."

It wasn't a hard choice. Scarcely a choice at all. "The stables." Esta silently cursed at herself for saying the words so breathlessly.

Anders face shifted under his beard. She realized he was smiling. "I figured as much. Tony, the stablehand, is better with beasts than people, especially pretty, young women like yourself, and would likely soil himself if you talked to him. Better just to watch him work, I think."

Esta nodded, idly wondering who among the Way Patrol *wasn't* prone to soiling himself, and jogged to the stables to poke her head through the open side door. She grinned like a little girl who'd just tasted sweets for the first time and suddenly decided that she really did love the smell of horses. Even more than she loved the smell of books about horses.

"Well," Ander said when he appeared some time later, startling Esta while Tony nervously instructed her on the finer points of currying. "It seems this brother of yours passed by some four days ago. Carrying an official summons from the Council of the Wall." He raised one of his bushy eyebrows. "You never said he was the Shores-damned Warden of

Naruvieth."

Esta handed the curry comb to a now-gaping Tony. "You never asked. Are we ready to go?"

Ander swept his arm out with a shallow bow, his dark eyes never once leaving hers. "By your leave." She could tell by the way his face shifted under his beard that he was smiling again.

Esta ignored him—he was mocking her, wasn't he?—and scratched the brown gelding she'd been currying under the chin, eliciting a snort. "Stay out of trouble, you hear?" she told the horse. Silently, she added, *And I'll try to do the same from now on.*

She turned back to Ander. "Lead the way."

Chapter 20: Through the Gates

In the days since the rain had come, little had happened, but much had changed. Nina could feel a strange tension in the air. Rogert and Noil no longer boasted during their swordplay, and their sparring had become fiercer, more like real fighting than playing. Noil had throttled Rogert after getting a bleeding welt on his cheek from a swipe of Rogert's switch, and Thomerlin of all people had had to pull them apart.

Nina herself didn't get out of the carriage much unless Lora Bale commanded it. The woman seemed not to notice the change in all her new charges. Either that or she didn't care. Nina didn't know which it was and her mind was too muddled to even begin to puzzle it out.

The rain had washed away the vomit from the side of the carriage, but to Nina, it felt as if the stain were still there, hidden under the lacquered blue wood of the carriage's door, as if nothing could ever wash it away. The vision of what had happened to that soldier was burned in her memory. Even the wordless whispers of the Raccoon family, clutched close to Nina's chest at all times, couldn't soothe away that horrifying image.

It wasn't until the carriage trundled out of the forest and into a land of rolling green hills and distant rocky peaks that the sickening feeling begin to fade. Nina was beginning to realize just how vast the Accord really was—and just how puny Naruvieth was in comparison. She had lost track of how many weeks it had been since she left home. Now more than ever, she wished she could go back to that day and tell Lora Bale no. Nina didn't care what would happen. She just wished she had never left home.

Though Nina apparently had power, going back in time was not something she could do.

She sighed as she stared out the window. The downpour had only lasted a day, but the dark clouds hadn't gone away, only letting the sun peek through every once in a while. A small village, only a handful of small wooden huts, passed by. A farmer in shabby brown clothes stood among the rows of vegetables, watching the carriage impassively as he hoed the ground.

He was completely unaware of who—or what—was in this carriage.

Fensoria.

Monsters.

Nina was starting to realize why she was feeling so bad. It wasn't just the horrible things done to that man. It was that the power Alicie had used was the very reason Falconkeep existed—to keep monsters like Alicie away from normal people.

But Alicie wasn't the only monster. They all were.

Nina started to cry, and Chad was there with his arm around her, just like the other times she had been like this. And it was more than a few times. Even Thomerlin and Chrissoth didn't bother the two of them anymore. Whenever Nina met their eyes, and that wasn't very often these days, they only looked at her sadly. And that just made it worse.

As much as Nina wished she were still home, she knew why her family had sent her away.

She wished she'd at least had a chance to say goodbye, a real goodbye, to Uncle Tharadis. But maybe it was better that when he'd last seen her, he'd thought of her as just a little girl, and not a fensoria. A monster.

Nina wiped at her eyes and dried her hands on her dress before touching the faces of Mother Raccoon and Father Raccoon, tracing her fingers along the lines of their smiling features. The Raccoon Family was the only family she had left, it seemed. At least they'd never need to send her away.

As twilight fell, gravel crunched under the wheels of the carriage as it came to a halt under a sheltered overhang jutting out of the side of a wooden structure. Nina heard the snort of horses aside from those pulling the carriage; the structure was a stable. A couple of stable hands, a bit too old to be fensoria, rushed out of the building to slide blocks under the wheels and remove the horses' harnesses, but not before bowing and murmuring greetings to Mistress Lora Bale.

"All right, everyone," Lora Bale called out cheerfully as she slid out of the driver's seat and onto the gravel. "Who'd like to come see your new home?"

The five of them filed out, none moving any faster than was necessary. Nina, the last one, clung to Chad's vest as they shuffled out. He smiled briefly over his shoulder but said nothing.

Just beyond the stables was a massive fist of stone rising high into the sky.

Falconkeep.

The walls were high, far higher than any building in Naruvieth, and they looked sturdy enough to withstand a tidal wave, though there was little risk of that this far inland. The tops of the walls weren't flat, but had short gaps at regular intervals, looking like teeth. A pair of blue and gray banners hung from the gaps, and on the banners was the same picture that was on the side of the wagon: a bird soaring over a stone tower. Nina had learned that the bird was called a falcon, though no one, not even Lora Bale had ever seen one. They were supposedly birds from the old world, from before the sheggam scourge and Andrin's Wall.

Between the two banners was an arched gate huge enough for two carriages stacked on each other to pass through. The squeal of grinding metal came from the gate as it slowly rose, revealing wooden spikes at the bottom that looked like the fangs of some beast. Nina shuddered and looked away from them.

Vidden and Alicie jogged ahead to join two rows of children of various ages and sizes that stood rigid in their Falconkeep uniforms, like soldiers lined up in front of the gate to honor important guests. The pomp and silliness of it all—*Us! Important guests!*—almost made Nina forget what this place was and why she was here. As she got closer, however, she saw the same expression, or lack of one, in their faces as in Vidden's and Alicie's. These were children who had given up on dreams of home.

Aside from the dozen that stood outside the wall, there were thirty or so inside the walls standing in a half-circle. These children had no uniforms, but were dressed like Nina and the other newcomers, in whatever clothes they had brought with them. Once Nina and the others were beyond the gate, standing in the courtyard with the uniformed children pushing their way in behind them, the gate began to lower.

One of the children in the half-circle, a tall boy with short-cropped brown hair and eyes so big they looked like they would fall out of his head, began to fidget.

Then he ran for the gate, screaming.

Shocked, Nina followed him with her eyes.

Instead of ducking under the still-lowering gate as she expected, he ran straight into the stone wall.

The gate had vanished.

Nina spun, searching everywhere. She knew it was still there; she could *hear* it. But she couldn't see it, not a trace of it. Neither could the boy who tried to escape.

Still screaming frantically, he clawed at the stone as if his fingers could find purchase and carry him over the wall, but they only left streaks of red where his fingernails broke. In no hurry, two girls in Falconkeep uniforms began to drag him away. He thrashed in their grip, not intent on hurting them, only on getting to the wall.

With her hands on her hips, Lora Bale shook her head, tsk-ing. "You disappoint me, Thello. You know the rules. Unless I deem you ready, you cannot leave."

Gone was all the pleasantness that Nina had seen in Lora Bale's face before this. Nina knew, with sudden certainty, that that had all been a mask. A lie. The true woman was the one standing here. Lora Bale's eyes were cold as the ocean's depths, and just as deadly.

She turned to the two girls. "Take him to the stones."

The boy, Thello, began shrieking even more maniacally at these words. He punched at the girls' backs, tried to trip them, but they handled him easily. His energy was flagging even as he became more desperate. Tears fell from his red-rimmed eyes as he and his captors disappeared through a heavy wooden door in a square building off to the side of the courtyard, though his screams didn't fade until long after the door was shut.

All of the children without uniforms stood still, hands folded in front of them, heads bowed as they stared at the ground. Several had tears on their cheeks. One sniffed quietly. All of them made Wenny look boisterous by comparison.

Take him to the stones. Something about these words had made them look even more scared than before that boy tried to run off. Whatever these stones were … everyone was utterly terrified of them.

Nina glanced over her shoulder, trying once more to see the gate. But it had already crashed back into place; even if she could see it, she couldn't go through it. She was stuck here.

At her side, Wenny started to cry.

Lora Bale leveled them with a glare and raised her voice. "Everything I told your parents was true. You are here because you're a threat to everything you love. You are, each and every one of you, abominations. You are something that should not be. But rather than killing you abominations, as is their right, I have convinced your parents to abandon you. In time, they will move on. Perhaps even forget about you."

She paced slowly, staring at every face. Nina felt her breath catch when Lora Bale's cold eyes met hers. "If you love them, this is what you will hope for. You are nothing. No, worse than that. Your very existence is *evil*."

101

She halted in her pacing. "But that doesn't mean you aren't useful. Yes, I have use for you. Which is why I have claimed you as my own. Not as my kin. But as my property. Don't you ever forget that that is what you are, and all you shall ever be. Keep that in mind, and you may yet see the outside world again."

She turned to the other children, those in uniform and those without them. "Well?"

All the children bowed to the five newcomers, intoning in unison.

"*Welcome to Falconkeep. Welcome home.*"

Chapter 21: Ritual of Joining

Gaspard Rikshost sat on the small reed cot with his legs crossed, wearing only a rough-woven tunic and a rope belt. He gently breathed in the cloying air of the tiny, underground room, emptying his mind of distractions. He closed his eyes; he didn't want the sight of the meager plate of seasoned radishes and strips of dried rabbit meat to remind him just how hungry he was. He imagined the food was part of the test, though he had no way of knowing for certain.

No one outside of the Sentinels themselves knew what exactly happened in the Ritual of Joining, when a man put himself at their mercy to see if he would be judged worthy to join them.

Gaspard spent years training for this moment. He had risen through the ranks of Swordmaster Kourick Sandranios's select group of pupils to become, in Kourick's own words, the best he had seen in two decades. Once, Gaspard had run fifty miles—without stopping. He hadn't slept and had only eaten what he could forage from the trailside. His body was lean and well-muscled and, in the words of many a young Garoshmiri woman, very fine indeed.

Yet his training extended beyond the physical: he had trained his mind as well. He had apprenticed with the great architect, Light Thassoum. With him, Gaspard had built the Temple of Undiriath, now touted to be one of the greatest monuments to an apoth in the whole of Garoshmir, if not all the Accord. He had learned mathematics and natural philosophy, and had even become a novice in the Holy Order of Undiriath once the temple had been built. Though he felt he had developed a sufficient degree of humility in the Order, Gaspard knew that many considered him to be one of the greatest living specimens of man alive today.

He knew all of this, knew all of what he was capable of, and still …

Still.

The Ritual of Joining filled him with dread. In truth, it terrified him.

Great men, Gaspard knew, had attempted to join the ranks of the Sentinels in the past. Some of them had become greater still, by succeeding. The current captain of the Sentinels, Rannald Firnaleos, was one such great man. None of the others were poor soldiers either, even if they hadn't risen to the prominence of their captain.

Many more great men, however, failed. And everyone who failed had died in the process.

That was the reason no one knew what went on in the Ritual of Joining. Those who lived did not do so to tell about it. Every Sentinel was sworn to secrecy, and in the thousands of years of the Sentinels' existence, not one had ever violated that trust.

A small twitch had developed in Gaspard's left cheek as he sat there, otherwise motionless. That usually happened when his nerves got the better of him. He tried to school his body to stillness, but it simply wouldn't listen. He breathed in deeply, and exhaled.

Twitch.

He cracked open an eyelid. The food sat there, tantalizing him. Someone had come in and set down a ceramic cup full of clear water next to the wooden bowl. He hadn't heard anyone enter or set the cup down, yet there it was. Suddenly Gaspard realized just how parched his throat was.

No. Discipline. He would not be tempted. He prided himself on how he could resist such temptations in the face of such a test. That was how he had achieved all that he had. Through discipline.

Twitch twitch.

He slapped his cheek to still it. Then he sighed and let his hand drop back into his lap, shaking his head. Foolish to give in to such a thing.

He tried to summon the courage to face this. He wouldn't have asked to undergo the Ritual if he didn't think he could do well, so why was he so worried? He had done everything humanly possible to prepare for this day. What did these men, these Sentinels who had survived the Ritual of Joining, have that those who failed didn't?

Did Gaspard have it too?

He drew in another breath, this one shuddering, and blew it all out quickly. The door creaked, and he opened his eyes.

A man stood there in the flickering light of the candle that lit the tiny room. Gaspard was unsurprised to discover that the man was a Sentinel, wearing an instantly-recognizable yet rarely-seen dress uniform. Cloth-of-gold piping trimmed the angular purple jacket, along with brass buttons marching in two columns up its breast. Black trousers were tucked into knee-high leather boots which shone like obsidian. A thick gold stripe descended from each hip to disappear into a boot. And perhaps the only insignia that the Sentinels wore, a mother-of-pearl belt buckle shaped and riveted like a small shield.

The man's freckled cheeks jutted out from beneath sunken eyes. His head had been shaved closely not long ago, and orange stubble covered it now. He wore no hat or cap and had no facial hair to speak of. Though his body was at rigid attention, he regarded Gaspard with a withering look of contempt.

"Refusing to eat?" he asked.

Gaspard could barely croak a reply in the face of such a barely-concealed admonishment. "I have no need of it." He decided not to rise to the bait, yet knowing that they had expected him to eat the food almost sent him scrabbling to the floor to shovel it into his mouth. He stayed seated with every ounce of willpower within him. He had sat here in this room for three days now, with no food or water. His own sense of discipline demanded that he continue to do so until the Ritual was over.

The expression on the Sentinel's face, or lack thereof, did not change, yet Gaspard could sense a surge of disapproval within the man. "Suit yourself. Are you finally ready?"

Two other Sentinels had come each day to ask him the same question. Gaspard had suspected it was a part of the Ritual, a part of the trial to see if he was suitable to become one of them. He had said no both times, thinking that perhaps they expected humility to join them, but each time they had merely left him alone, taking the bowl of untouched food with them.

Though perhaps this part was not a test. Perhaps it was a genuine question. Gaspard wasn't sure. He knew one misstep could send him to the fate that all the other failed Sentinels found.

He took another breath to calm himself, but he wasn't sure if it had any effect. He wasn't going to die today. If he thought he would, he wouldn't have come at all.

"Yes."

The Sentinel grunted. "Follow me, then."

Chapter 22: The Test

V ery few people ever saw the underhalls of the Sentinel compound, but, Gaspard noted, there was very little to see. The long hallway curving ever deeper into the ground beneath the Keep was made of the same stone bricks as the tiny chamber he had waited in as preparation for the Ritual of Joining. The only structural difference was the arched ceiling. There weren't many doors, and all of those they did pass were closed. Pitch torches sitting in sconces flanked the hallway, occasionally popping as Gaspard and the Sentinel leading him passed. The ginger-haired man hadn't said a word since leading him from the chamber, though Gaspard suspected that wasn't part of the Ritual. It seemed the man just didn't like him.

Gaspard forced himself not to care about that. It was just another challenge to overcome, a puzzle he could solve later, once Gaspard himself was a Sentinel. Someday, he would earn the respect of these men, one way or another. Now, he had other things to worry about.

Unconsciously, Gaspard rubbed at his cheek, but stopped once he realized he was doing it. At least it had stopped twitching. The last thing he wanted was to make a fool of himself in front of the Sentinels during the Ritual. *Well*, he thought, correcting himself, *the last thing I want is to die.*

The last four men to undergo the Ritual had doubtless thought the same thing. None of them survived.

Palpable dread began to build in his gut. He took a deep breath. *No. I will not die today.*

I will not.

Suddenly the Sentinel stopped in the light of a torch and turned to face him. Gone was the cold derision in his face, replaced by something Gaspard hadn't expected to see. Sadness.

"Are you sure you want to go through with this?" the man asked. "You have a chance to turn back now. I'd take it if I were you."

Gaspard lifted his chin. "You went through with it."

"You're right," he said. "I was a fool once, just like you. Not a day goes by when I don't regret it. Take my advice and turn back."

Gaspard knew this was all just part of the Ritual, something to make his resolve slip. It wasn't the first time Gaspard had heard words like this. His initiation to the Holy Order of Undiriath had been similar. The whole goal of ritual initiation was to break down an individual and reform him into something the organization could use. Gaspard knew the best way to achieve that was by having the initiate face his fears.

Gaspard took a deep breath. "I have faced death before, sir. I am not afraid of it."

The Sentinel chuckled quietly and shook his head. There was no joy in his laughter. Without meeting Gaspard's eyes, he asked, "You want to know what I truly fear?"

Gaspard frowned. "What?"

For a moment, he thought the man wouldn't respond. But then he answered in a soft voice, "Fools like you."

The Sentinel turned away and wiped at his face. With his back to Gaspard, he pointed down the hallway. "There's the door at the end. I'll follow you in."

Gaspard slowly stepped past him, but the man kept his face turned away.

A large wooden door, trimmed with steel plate, stood at the end of the hallway. There were no handles, knobs, or hinges that Gaspard could see. He briefly glanced over his shoulder back at the Sentinel, who stood just beyond the light of the nearest torches. He said nothing, made no move to help. Gaspard turned back to the door. *Just as well*, he thought. *Whose Ritual of Joining is it, anyway? Mine, or his?*

He put both hands to the door and gently pushed.

To Gaspard's surprise, the door didn't swing in to the left or right. It slid *backwards*, gliding without noise or friction, into a room untouched by the light of the torches, a room blacker than anything Gaspard had ever seen. There was no floor that he could see. No walls, no ceiling … nothing. Nothing but that door sliding forever backward into inky darkness.

A sensation like little shards of ice pricking him formed beneath his skin. With a *thump* so deep it was felt more than heard, the door stopped moving, frozen in a tableau of eternal night.

Gaspard stared, disbelieving. He couldn't move his feet. Where would he put them, anyway? There was no floor beyond the threshold. Just … nothingness.

He heard the Sentinel step close to him, and heard his voice, whispered close to Gaspard's ear. "The time for turning back has passed," he said.

"Don't make me draw my sword."

Gaspard took a sharp breath and forced his mind to work. The Sentinel behind him had no doubt done the same thing, gone through the same experience. He had seen this same blackness, stepped into it, and lived. Gaspard suddenly realized he didn't know the man's name.

He turned. The Sentinel's face betrayed no emotion, was as hard as the stone wall behind it. "What's your name?" Gaspard asked.

"Arrion Metsfurth."

Gaspard closed his eyes. Major Metsfurth, second in command only to Rannald Firnaleos in the ranks of the Sentinels. There were only a few men with the same facial features and hair coloring in the Sentinels, and Gaspard would have guessed him for any of them before the Major. Gaspard cursed his own impertinence. He would do better, and he would make this man proud.

"Major Metsfurth," he said. "There is no need to draw your sword. I … I just need a moment."

"Fear is not generous," said Metsfurth. "It never gives you what you need, least of all time."

Gaspard nodded at this. *Do it. Just do it.*

He lifted his bare foot, leaned forward, and stepped.

The impact of his foot against something solid startled him. He still couldn't see anything beneath his foot, just that shapeless blackness, but there was something solid there nonetheless. It was smooth and cold. If he didn't know any better, Gaspard would have assumed the floor to made of obsidian, but even that would reflect light. He took two more steps into the room and then turned around to smile at the Major.

The hallway was gone.

Gaspard stared at where the hallway had been. It had vanished soundlessly. Completely.

There was only Gaspard and the door.

He sank to his knees, fear enveloping him. He felt as if he had been swallowed into a nightmare, a dark dream of infinite loneliness and meaninglessness. He was completely and utterly cut off from the world which he knew; he was far away from home, never to return. He was as good as dead.

No, no, no. It's just an illusion. You're still in the Sentinel compound. The ground is there. See? You can feel it beneath you. You're not alone, you're not alone, you're not alone.

He fought back a cry. He fought, and he won. He stood. Still, he had to stifle the quivering in his gut.

To his left, a small orb of icy blue light appeared as if from nowhere, revealing the hints of a human form behind it. The orb, Gaspard realized, had been drawn from the figure's pocket and was now held in its hand. The figure was standing on the same black nothingness that Gaspard stood on, but was doing so as if such an act were a normal occurrence. The figure felt no fear that Gaspard could see.

As expected. The figure standing there, holding the orb of light, was a Sentinel.

The orb's light rose in intensity, casting its glow farther to reveal dozens of other figures standing in a circle around Gaspard, yet no light touched the floor they stood on, nor the ceiling—if there even was one.

Though Gaspard recognized the men around him as Sentinels, it was only because of their purple and gold coloring. The uniforms were completely alien to him, not at all like the dress uniform that the Major was wearing, and nothing at all like the armor they normally wore. From the neck down to the toes was a dark purple cloak, trimmed in cloth-of-gold embroidery so elaborate and complex he couldn't stare at it for more than a couple of moments without his head spinning and his stomach turning, even in the weak blue light of the orb. Their steel helmets were nearly as unsettling, looking like a gallery of terrors, each one sporting a number of protuberances that reminded Gaspard of insect heads.

The faces were the worst, though. Mother-of-pearl masks, expressionless, glimmering coldly in the blue light of the orb. The light didn't reach the eyes hiding behind the masks.

The one holding the orb was tall and broad-shouldered. This one stepped forward.

"Many people despise fear." His voice was deep and carried well. Gaspard knew this voice, famous as it was. It belonged to none other than Rannald Firnaleos, Captain of the Sentinels. "Many even fear it. They see it as a weakness, a vice. And indeed, it can be such, but only so long as it is not understood. Fear often obscures the truth of the world around us, causing confusion and doubt. But it can tell us a great many things about ourselves. About the limits of our endurance."

Rannald began to pace in a circle around Gaspard, its unsettling eyeless gaze upon him. Gaspard looked straight ahead. "All of us assembled here today have seen the limits of our endurance," said Rannald. "All of us have touched the void beyond it. All of us of have survived the ordeal."

Rannald completed his circuit and halted directly in front of Gaspard. "And all of us wish we had chosen death instead."

He lifted the orb closer to Gaspard's face. The light was near blinding, but Gaspard didn't flinch or close his eyes. Soon, all he could see was the icy light of the orb; all of the looming figures had vanished beyond his sight, the bright light obliterating everything else.

"Why," came Rannald's voice, "do you wish to join our ranks?"

Gaspard had done his research. Everyone said that whenever someone was in dire need of help, the Sentinels were there, no matter the jurisdiction or the laws at play. Rumor had it that a Councilor of the Wall had even been cut down by a Sentinel for attacking his servant. It was this that defined the Sentinels in the public eye, and it was this that Gaspard admired the most about them. "I wish to protect the weak against the strong."

"Hmph. The weak. The strong." Rannald's voice was filled with scorn. "I'm strong. Am I a villain?"

"No. Of course not."

A pause. Then suddenly the light vanished, leaving only the memory of its glow burnt into Gaspard's eyes. He heard two quick steps and felt two large hands grip his arms. Rannald's masked face leaned close to Gaspard's ear.

"Evil itself is a weakness in the hearts of men. Do you wish to defend evil against me, boy?"

"I—" What could he say? Didn't he want to be a defender of the weak? He had always thought so, but Rannald's words had the ring of truth to them. Even more importantly, Gaspard didn't want to upset him any more than he already had. "No," he said, lamely.

Rannald stepped away from him. "At least you have the sense to know when you are wrong. We do not care for such things as strength and weakness. They are meaningless in the moral realm. Sometimes good men are strong, sometimes they are not. The same is true of the wicked. We strive to defend, not the weak, but the *innocent*. Because sometimes the innocent may be strong, but not strong enough."

He produced the orb from within his cloak again and knelt down to set it into a recess in the floor. Blue light spiderwebbed out from the orb across the inky black floor, illuminating the rest of the Sentinels in detail, traveling in a flowing, script-like design. Gaspard realized that it was more than a design.

It was a Pattern.

Rannald regarded him. "I see you recognize what this is, if not its purpose. Let me tell you of that purpose. The Ritual of Joining has two parts. The first part is the test, and it is by use of this Pattern that we can perform it. The second part of the Ritual is the oath. Everyone survives the first part. Very few survive the second. Why that is will be made clear to you if you choose to undergo the Ritual."

"Choose to … you mean, I can back out now? I can still leave?"

Rannald nodded to his left. Another Sentinel stepped forward and drew his sword, then spun it to offer the hilt to Gaspard.

Rannald said, "No. You cannot leave. You know too many of our secrets. But you can choose to forgo the test." He gestured to the sword. "By taking your own life first."

They were simply trying to scare him. Or were they? What did he mean by, *very few survive the second*? What was so dangerous about taking an oath? Gaspard shook his head. "No. I have no reason to kill myself before having even tried."

The Sentinel holding the sword sighed and sheathed it. "Very well," he said. Gaspard recognized the voice as belonging to Major Metsfurth. The Major stepped back into the ranks.

Rannald stretched out his arm, pointing behind Gaspard. Gaspard turned. The Sentinels behind him parted, making a path.

"There," said Rannald, "lies your test."

The filaments of light along the path revealed a large box hovering just above the floor. It looked very much like a coffin.

Gaspard had to remind himself that all these men had survived the trial before he could get himself to take the first step and walk to the box. The lid was already open on its hinges. He looked in. It was padded and lined with silk of a color he couldn't quite make out, though it looked to be the color of wine. Or blood. He glanced at the masked faces, but saw nothing in them, of course. There was no help to be found here. And no other way out.

He climbed into the box.

Gaspard could no longer see anything but the faintest outline of the lid above him. But once it was shut by unseen hands, even that was gone.

Chapter 23: The Oath

For several moments, the Sentinels stood in silence, watching the box in apprehension. Only when Rannald removed his ceremonial helmet and mask did any of them relax.

Major Metsfurth did the same, revealing a bleak expression. "You talked to him, Arrion?" asked Rannald.

Arrion shrugged. "I tried. Just another fool who thinks he can do anything."

Rannald nodded and sighed. "So you think this is his first trial?"

"His first real one, though I doubt he would tell it that way. He's accomplished, to be sure, and likely would have gone far if he had chosen a different path. But I don't think he has any idea what he's about to go through."

Rannald snorted. "Did any of us?"

Arrion's face grew bleaker. "Perhaps."

Rannald looked around at the men assembled before him as they, too, began to remove their masks and helmets. While no one truly knew how the magic of the Ritual worked—none of the men were Patterners, and outsiders were not allowed down in the underhalls to study the chamber—Rannald had his suspicions, and they were generally shared by the others. Each of them had one thing in common: they had lived through something horrible. Some of them, like Rannald, had seen war and survived. Others had seen dreams crushed, love die, lived through something that forced them to wonder if life truly were preferable to death.

Rannald closed his eyes, his hand moving to the empty scabbard hanging at his hip. Even touching the scabbard was enough to send flashes of memory jolting through his mind like a bolt of lightning, momentarily stunning him with remembered screams of the dying, screams caused by his sword.

He had already survived his first trial before coming to this chamber for his own Ritual of Joining. When he had climbed into the same coffin as that young man Gaspard, Rannald had already lived through his fears, and relived them every night in his dreams, causing him to wake screaming and weeping. The worst the Ritual could do to him was bring those memories back into focus, into stark clarity, and make him remember what it was like to wield a sword.

Yes, he had survived. But it was a near thing.

Arrion turned at the sound of scratching coming from the coffin. "That didn't take long."

"To us," said Rannald. "To that boy in there? It likely felt like days."

"Still," Arrion said, frowning. "Usually they last a little longer." Then, as if the implications of that finally dawned on him, he sighed and drew his sword. "Here we go again."

One of the men was already standing by with a bucket of water and a rag, and another pair with a stretcher—out of sight, of course. They were always there, even when the potential recruit looked promising. Because one never knew how a man would react until he had actually gone through the Ritual.

Soon came whimpering from the coffin, and then cries for his mother. It was always the same. Everyone seemed to have the same kinds of reactions and in the same order. Rannald wondered if that was just the way people thought, or if these were the kinds of reactions the magic tried to induce. He tried not to think about it too much; just hearing it over and over and over was enough for him to realize he just didn't care.

The whimpering quickly turned into pitched screaming, the scratching turning into punches in the desire to escape. While it was true that the magic wouldn't kill him, it also wouldn't stop him from injuring himself. The confines of the coffin prevented the potentials from damaging themselves too much, but Rannald had seen more than his fair share of broken fingers and toes during the Ritual.

Rannald nodded at a pair of men, who moved into position behind the lid. Everyone re-affixed their masks and helmets. The time was near.

The blue filaments of light running along the floor suddenly turned yellow.

"Not very long at all," muttered Arrion under his breath, adjusting his grip on the sword. Rannald turned a reproving glare at him, but said nothing.

The two men opened the lid.

Gaspard flung an arm over the edge of the coffin and pulled himself up, gasping and wide-eyed. He looked years older, though Rannald knew it was only the pain in his eyes that made him look so. His hair was soaked with sweat. Bloody scratches covered his face and shoulders—scratches caused by his own fingernails. His tunic had been ripped apart, and a small strip of scalp had been laid bare and bloody. He looked at them with the wildness of an animal beaten within an inch of its death, seeking nothing but escape from the hell it had just lived through. He looked at them as if they were both the cause of all his suffering, as well as his only hope for salvation.

Rannald felt weary. He was so, so tired of seeing this.

"You now know what it means to fear," he said, projecting his voice. "To suffer. To lose. It is something that few people truly experience, even though many of them believe their lives have been nothing but hardship. If anyone—"

Gaspard rolled over the edge of the coffin and fell hard on his back. The men who had lifted the lid rushed around to help him up, but he struggled as if he didn't realize they were there. Once he had finally regained his feet, he rushed over to Arrion, who rested his hands on the pommel of his sword, its tip against ground. Gaspard fell to his knees and grabbed Arrion's cloak in his fists, his eyes filled with tears and pleading.

"Kill me, please!"

Arrion turned to Rannald. "He will not kill you, Gaspard," said Rannald. "That is not what we are here to do. We are only here to give you a choice, and it is a choice of the sword. But you must take that sword yourself."

"Get up, man," said Arrion harshly. "Show some dignity."

Gaspard looked as if dignity were some alien concept he had yet to discover. Still, he stood, eyeing the sword with a combination of repulsion and eagerness.

Rannald continued. "You have seen the inner reaches of your soul. You have seen the limits of your endurance. You now have a choice. Use this sword to vanquish your fear, to slay it, to see what lies beyond the limits you have discovered within yourself. Or use it to slay yourself, to protect yourself from any further pain. It is a choice that rests on a question. Which do you fear more: life, or death?"

Gaspard moved to answer that question. He snatched the sword from Arrion's hand, spun it, dropped the pommel to the floor, and leaned onto the blade. With the sound of steel grating on the bones of his ribs, the point pierced Gaspard's chest and came out his back. He fell to his side, eyes lifeless and blood pooling around him.

Without a moment's hesitation, the body was loaded onto the stretcher and the blood mopped up. The men had no need of instructions; they had done this often enough. Gaspard's body would be returned to his relatives, along with a brief, prewritten note expressing sorrow for their loss. Rannald would sign the letter, and then he would wait for the next dewy-eyed youth to show up on the doorstep of their keep with no fear or understanding of death, ready to throw his life away.

Rannald picked up the orb and swiveled the bottom half. The blue light vanished, as did the illusion of darkness that obscured the details of the rather ordinary, stone-walled chamber. The others began filing out, but Arrion hung back. He removed his mask. His eyes showed concerned.

After a moment, Rannald removed his own mask and smiled to allay his major's concerns. "I just wish these young men would stop coming here."

Arrion smiled back, but it looked genuine. "If you didn't, we wouldn't follow you."

Rannald nodded, but he said nothing as he followed the rest of his men out.

Chapter 24: Councilor of the Wall

N ot the knees," Councilor Yarid said from the cushioned chair he lounged upon. "I want her to be able to walk, after all."

Jordin, his manservant, stood with his back to Yarid, holding the cane in his hands. Without turning to his meet his master's gaze, he nodded slowly before resuming. The crack of cane meeting flesh echoed off the stone walls of the small underground discipline chamber. To her credit, the woman servant—what was her name again? Yarid found it hard to remember their names sometimes—didn't cry out. Only muffled whimpers escaped her lips as she hung by her wrists from the rope in the center of the room.

Yarid took a sip of tea, focusing on some insignificant spot on the opposite wall. Just because he understood the necessity of such beatings didn't mean he enjoyed watching them. He wasn't a monster.

Well, at least no more than anyone else.

The woman hadn't done anything wrong. Neither had Jordin. But Yarid occasionally needed to remind his servants of the hierarchy in his household, to remind them of their places.

Yarid's place, of course, was at the top.

Nothing reminded them of this as effectively as a good beating. That is, nothing except for a good *unearned* beating.

"Enough," Yarid said with a waggle of his fingers. With perhaps a little too much haste in his movements, Jordin returned the cane to the rack with the others. Two other servants, who had stood one either side of Yarid's sofa, rushed to untie the woman. Once she was free, she rubbed her wrists and wiped the tears from her eyes before stepping before Yarid.

"How can I serve you, master?" she said, eyes lowered.

"Refrain from bleeding on my carpets for a start." He handed her his empty cup. With a bow of her head, she took the cup and headed up the stairs, wincing with each step. Yarid watched her disappear from sight and stood, flipping his thick brown braid back over his shoulder. Turning to the other two servants, he snapped his fingers at the chair. "Take it back upstairs." They complied, and Jordin fell in behind Yarid as he, too, went

116

back upstairs.

Back in his room, Yarid walked to the window. Gray clouds filled the sky without a break in sight. A few raindrops trickled down the glass. Not enough to warrant a change of wardrobe, but enough to be a bother.

Outside his window, beyond the courtyard of his manse and the tall iron fence encircling it, Garoshmir was subdued. Relatively few people were out for the time of day, though anyone from a smaller city would have still called it bustling. Yarid understood Garoshmir better than them, better than even most of those who had grown up here, as he had. Few people knew what Garoshmir wanted like he did. That was how he had become such an important figure in the political landscape not only of the city, but of the whole of the Accord lands. No one wielded as much power as the Councilors of the Wall. And no one held sway in the Council like Yarid.

At least he had that to look forward to. The Council was meeting today, late in the afternoon. He wasn't sure what time it was now, but he suspected that he had a couple of hours before he had to go. The midday bell had yet to toll.

He stood there, slippered foot tapping impatiently as he decided what he could do until then.

The problem was that many of the tasks he would normally perform in preparation for the council session he had delegated. A stack of reports sat on the desk in the study adjacent to his bedroom, sealed against prying eyes. They had been put there by Jordin. An array of messengers delivered them to the side door of the manse, where Jordin collected them and brought them here. Doubtless he thought they were mere missives keeping Yarid informed of general happenings throughout Garoshmir and beyond—which was, in its own way, true, but only a fraction of the truth. This stack of reports was the prime of the pump of rule in this city. It held all of the secrets of its most powerful citizens. Jordin wouldn't suspect that, considering how cavalierly Yarid treated them. Jordin was a professional, and likely wouldn't even start to consider their contents, much less arrive at the truth of them.

Yarid went to the study and sat down in his maple desk chair, delicately carved with exquisite scrollwork, and cracked open the top report, which was sealed with blue wax. He didn't even bother to read his reports in secret. Doing so would arouse suspicion, and Yarid believed that the best secrets were those in the open. So did many of the Councilors, heads of merchant houses, and other quality people, apparently, but at least Yarid knew how to have an open secret remain that: a secret. The fact that his stack of reports was as large as it was proved that few of his rivals had that skill.

This particular report outlined the worth of seashell necklaces in Garoshmiri copper ghellia, a typical trade report that was innocuously dull and appropriate to one such as Yarid, but it said much more than that. As Yarid deciphered the message encoded within the report, he learned that the governor from the seaside city-state of Twelve Towers, Shad Belgrith, was on her way to Garoshmir to petition the Council. Belgrith had been the primary architect of the Runeway and had supplied the Council with many of the Patterners required to build it. She herself had a seat on the Council of the Wall, but despite that, she had never once shown her face in Garoshmir. All of her correspondence had either been written or conveyed by a proxy representative. Now, it seemed, she was coming in person. Yarid wondered what she wanted.

Wealth and power were the obvious answer, of course. Belgrith had expended significant resources in providing the means to create the Runeway, and who knew how much she paid just for the development of the underlying Pattern itself. But how that desire for wealth and power manifested itself was what intrigued Yarid.

Perhaps she was coming in regard to the little hangup involving the people of Naruvieth. Yarid found their protest amusing. What was not amusing, however, was the Council's response, which was little more than hand-wringing and waiting. They simply stopped construction while they figured out how to handle the situation. And while the partially-constructed Runeway had fulfilled half of Belgrith's promise—that the Rift separating Naruvieth from the lands of the Accord would be spanned, thus opening up new avenues of trade, and some other nonsense about changing the course of history—it could not make good on its much more alluring promise of bridging all of the Accord lands with a travel Pattern so advanced it stumped the best Patterners the Academy had to offer. Even Tirfaun, arguably the most talented Patterner not affiliated with the Academy, was disturbed by just how advanced the Runeway was. Each step down it would be as good as five, meaning travel from one location to the next would only take a fraction of the time. That was the true lure, one that left nearly every member of the Council, and the trading houses in their pockets, drooling. In trading, a deal that took only a fifth of the time was as good as five times the profits—or much greater, as things that would perish during an extended journey could be moved much farther. Wealth would simply grow like magic, and at a truly unprecedented rate.

Now *that* was changing the course of history.

But that was only part of it. As surely as wealth trickled out of Garoshmir, so did law and order—a particular export that was the Council's specialty. The dispersal of laws and their subsequent enforcement required time and resources, but with the completion of the Runeway, such obstructions would become trivial. The Council's influence would grow exponentially, and when the Council took credit for the Runeway's construction—they were, after all, the ones who permitted its existence—the people would be more willing to bear a tax increase with their newfound windfall. It was the perfect arrangement: the Council gained in influence, and the people welcomed it. Would that all political maneuvers were so elegant and symmetrical.

However, none of that mattered so long as the Council allowed Naruvieth to interfere with the construction of the Runeway. It was a ridiculous situation, and it angered Yarid every time he considered it. Naruvieth was sending a representative to the Council to speak on his city's behalf. The man called himself the Warden; supposedly he was their leader, but from what Yarid had heard, he had very little real power. Hopefully he would travel by Runeway. Even though, being unfinished, it wouldn't get him here any faster than mundane means, it would show precisely the sort of monumental undertaking he was interfering with. It would give him some perspective before the Council ate him alive and spat him back to his little backwater town. Then, finally, civilization would be able to continue.

With a practiced flick of his wrist, Yarid tossed the report into the low-burning hearth to his right. The paper burned quickly; flashpaper was one of the requirements Yarid held his contacts to. No sense in leaving his messages vulnerable to being recovered for enemy eyes. This way, only the most talented Patterners could reconstruct the message, and Yarid had already ensured that they had no reason to do so.

The rest of the reports weren't nearly so interesting, and had a difficult time keeping him engaged. Sometimes being Councilor was tedious work. As he stared at the smudged handwriting of one of his least educated spies, rapping his fingers on the herringbone pattern of his mahogany desk, Yarid wondered what Tirfaun was doing right now.

While he could not match the Academy's most powerful Patterners in terms of ability—being, perhaps, only the third most powerful—Tirfaun was the one whose company Yarid actually enjoyed. Tirfaun had been disgraced several years back, something to do with illegal acts and children, and had been subsequently cut off from the attention of all quality persons in Garoshmir—save for Yarid, of course. Yarid was not quite so picky in his allies, and he found that on certain things, he and Tirfaun had similar views. While he wouldn't go so far as to call Tirfaun a friend, Yarid did consider him more than a mere acquaintance or political tool. It may have been nothing more than companionship by convenience, but Yarid had a mischievous streak, and Tirfaun had nowhere else to go and nothing else for which to use his powers, save getting himself in trouble. He was bored more often than Yarid, which meant he was likely doing nothing at the same time as Yarid.

As if his master's wishes could be fathomed from a distance, Jordin was already standing at the door, hands behind his back, deep-set eyes forward. Out of sync with the latest fashions, of course, Jordin still wore his musty gray trousers that cinched below the knee, below which were his white socks. While it wouldn't do to have a mere manservant dress like the upper echelon of society, Yarid couldn't have the man looking like that, especially since he was the one responsible for Yarid's own wardrobe. It had been Jordin who had discovered that robes had supplanted trousers as the new norm for the fashionable elite, and Yarid had been among the first of his peers to profit from that discovery. It was good to have a manservant be relatively unobtrusive, but Yarid preferred if he could do so without being offensively old-fashioned. Older fellow that he was, Jordin was still Yarid's manservant, not one belonging to the so-called Greater Council. He should at least look the part.

Yarid indicated the man's outfit with a curt gesture. "I want you to go to the market and buy yourself some suitable clothes. But first see if Tirfaun is anywhere to be found. Begin by looking in any particularly dark gutters."

"At once, Councilor." Jordin bowed smartly, turned on his heel, and left.

After nearly an hour of staring blankly at the fire as it dwindled to glowing coals, Yarid had his peace once again disturbed by Jordin's silent arrival. "What is it?" he said more sharply than he intended.

"Tirfaun awaits in the downstairs sitting room, my lord." Jordin bowed himself out of the room.

Yarid had nearly forgotten what he had been sitting around waiting for. He had finished his missives quickly, impatient to do something else. Giddy at the prospect of mischief, he rose from his seat and dashed down the hall, his slippered feet whispering against wood floors.

Tirfaun's thin frame was hunched down on the least comfortable couch in Yarid's downstairs sitting room, as was his custom whenever he arrived. It was a beautiful piece, its trim elegantly carved with images of mermaids coupling with dolphins, but it was hardly worthy of the name *couch*; nothing was ever really couched upon it. Its cushions were as thin as rugs, but they were better than sitting on the floor. Barely. Tirfaun claimed to like the couch the best, but Yarid doubted that. No one could honestly like sitting on that thing.

The aging Patterner lifted his bedraggled face when Yarid entered the room, his thinning gray hair disheveled. The beginnings of facial hair had begun to sprout on his face again, though it was peppered with black rather than simply gray. Yarid wondered when the man had bathed last. With his stained green smock tied around him with a battered piece of leather, he looked absolutely disreputable. Yarid couldn't help but grin.

Tirfaun raised a hand. "Before you say otherwise, you know it's not good to see me. I'd rather you not embarrass yourself."

"Why, I had no intention of lying to you, Tirfaun." It was a little ritual of theirs, though Yarid sometimes suspected that Tirfaun really meant his half of it. That was part of its charm. Yarid took a seat on the couch nearest the one on which Tirfaun sat, perched near the very edge, hands folded in his lap. A rounded table stood between them; within a breath Jordin had set two steaming cups of red tea on it. Yarid could tell by the smell that a bit of rum had been added to Tirfaun's.

He waited patiently while Tirfaun took a sip and grunted in appreciation. The Patterner settled back into his horrible couch and they stared at each other.

"Well?" Yarid asked.

"Well what? You invited me here."

"And you know why." Yarid leaned forward, resting his elbows on his knees. "What do you know that I don't?"

Tirfaun took a draught of his tea, deeper than the polite sip he had taken, and settled the cup in his lap with both hands wrapped around it as if drinking in the warmth of the cup as much as the liquid inside. His gray eyes were troubled. Yarid could barely contain his anticipation. The more troubled Tirfaun looked, the better the news, more often than not.

Judging by his expression, the news he was sitting on was going to be monumental.

Yarid couldn't begin to imagine what it could be. Most of the reports he had read portended a rather uneventful day. Even the arrival of Twelve Towers' representative was remarkable only in its rarity; Yarid was sure nothing interesting would come of it. Just more of the same.

Could it be Councilor Nangrove? Yarid had very recently heard hints of her daughter Jilliana's infidelity, which was scandal enough—the daughter's husband was himself a Lesser Councilor named Jacobs, who had strong ties to the Rafter's Guild, who, in turn, were opposed to the construction of the Runeway since the very beginning since it would disrupt their control over trade. Rumor on the street was that Councilor Nangrove regretted shipping her daughter off to such an unpopular Councilor and had been considering forging a new alliance. Unfortunately, she couldn't do that with her daughter married to Jacobs, and the marriage couldn't be nullified unless there were sufficient cause, namely, an affair. There was also the risk that Jacobs wouldn't press for divorce—he had benefited from the pairing as much as Nangrove and continued to capitalize on it. There was also the risk that the Rafter's Guild wouldn't touch the daughter for fear of their own reputation, which was of critical importance now.

It was a veritable mess, and it was just the sort of thing Yarid loved meddling in. If he had information that no one else on the Council had, he could stir things up with his own signature style before anyone was the wiser.

Yarid shifted in his seat as he continued to stare at the silent Patterner. If it weren't for his eyes being open and staring deeply into his tea, Tirfaun would have appeared asleep. Yarid's patience was becoming frayed, yet he kept his complaints to himself. Patterners were another sort of creature altogether, and Yarid had found that he couldn't play by their rules and hope to get anywhere. So he waited.

"Water seeks lowest ground," Tirfaun said, almost to himself, almost too quietly to be heard. "As it always does. Such is the way of Patterns. The world simply works as it does, and we are its innocent bystanders, its victims. The least fortunate among us can see exactly which path the water will take. We watch, and can do nothing, and we drown just the same. We, alone, know the horror that is fate."

Yarid stared, mouth agape, as Tirfaun drained his tea in one inelegant gulp. This wasn't like Tirfaun at all. Yarid had expected gossip, rumors, tangible things, things that only a man of Tirfaun's particular and peculiar talents could know. Not philosophy. Still. Yarid had never seen him in this state. Perhaps he hadn't noticed it in his excitement, but thinking back, Yarid realized that Tirfaun was even more disheveled than usual. For the first time in as long as he could remember, Yarid was at a loss as to what to do.

Finally, Tirfaun met his gaze. The older man's eyes had become frighteningly lucid. "Water seeks lowest ground. Well, a hole has opened up in the earth, and the water can't help but go down, sweeping us all along with it. We will fall for all eternity. There is no bottom to this pit." He shook his head. "I have always suspected this. Now I know it. Worse, the time is near. It's on its way here as we speak."

"Who is it? What is it?" Yarid nearly leapt out of his seat. Tirfaun was not one to embellish or gloat about the things he knew. He was horribly genuine, which is something Yarid had always warned him about. It made him susceptible to manipulation. But Yarid wasn't one to let opportunities slip by, and if Tirfaun was going to be predictable, Yarid would predict him. When Tirfaun became dour, it could only mean dour things were afoot.

It was in such times that great opportunity could be found.

Jordin set another steaming cup of tea in front of Tirfaun. At the first sip, he frowned. No liquor. Even so, it seemed to calm him. Yarid felt relief, and then gratitude towards Jordin. Sometimes he suspected his manservant had arcane powers himself, what with how well he could read a person.

"I'm sorry I mentioned it," Tirfaun said in apparently genuine contrition. "I shouldn't have said anything. There's nothing you or anyone else can do about it." He shot Yarid a warning glare, as if to tell him to stay away from it. Unfortunately, Tirfaun was not the manipulator that Jordin was—at least not of people. He should have known that the best way to get Yarid interested in something was to tell him that he shouldn't. Of course, there remained the possibility that Tirfaun *did* know that about Yarid, in which case it wouldn't hurt to indulge the man. Yarid's interest was piqued anyway.

It seemed as if Tirfaun wanted to draw out the suspense. "Enough of this," he said. A dark smile stretched across his face. "I assume you've heard about Councilor Nangrove?"

Yarid's smile matched Tirfaun's. He let his concerns of the moment vanish. "Shall we go have some fun then?"

Chapter 25: A Little Harmless Mischief

Yarid crossed the street, nearly tripping in his boots and trousers. He didn't feel comfortable wearing common clothes such as these, with their scratchy cloth clinging to his legs, but he couldn't very well ride over to Councilor Nangrove's manse in his own carriage, announcing his actions to the world. No, what he and Tirfaun were doing had to be done discreetly.

There was, of course, the danger of being caught. But making sure that didn't happen was half the fun.

He had stolen the clothes from one of his own servants. Jordin had cleared out the servants' quarters so that Yarid and Tirfaun could leave the premises through the servants' gate, and Yarid had taken that opportunity to take the clothes then. Jordin had been there all the while, eyeing him disapprovingly. It wasn't like it was truly stealing, though. After all, Yarid *did* pay the man's wages. And who would he complain to? The Council of the Wall?

The air was filled with the low din of pedestrian voices and the scent of horse droppings. Tirfaun walked up ahead, given a wide berth and judgmental stares by the generally well-dressed passersby of the Central Avenue. He had his hands stuffed into his grubby pants pockets and his small satchel slung over his shoulder. Yarid had suggested that they not walk together at first, since doing so would likely draw more attention than not. The truth was that Tirfaun attracted attention wherever he went; he wasn't the type to really blend in anywhere, so Yarid had hung back to use Tirfaun to draw attention away from *himself*.

Despite the fact Tirfaun was naturally one of the most conspicuous humans alive—especially here in the Council District, where there were few enough beggars—he was a master of disguise and evasion. That he was an outlaw in four cities—including Garoshmir, which he usually considered his home—but could walk freely in any of them was testament to this.

That was what the satchel was for. To anyone who looked through it, it would look like nothing more than an ugly sack filled with needlework. Strange needlework, but no one short of an Academy Patterner would see anything amiss in the little squares of fabric stitched with strange designs. However, if you found yourself in trouble and pulled out the right thread and tossed the square in the path of your pursuer, you would find yourself free and in the clear.

Your pursuer would find himself ... somewhere else.

Yarid had seen Tirfaun work his needlework magic a handful of times, and it was truly a wonder. Once, a city guard had spotted them pilfering some melons from a merchant stand and gave chase. Tirfaun had used one of his little squares. Once the guard stepped past the square, he veered sharply to the right and smashed his face into a brick wall, as if he hadn't noticed his own feet turning him in that direction. The man had lost the use of his right eye and could hardly speak now. Yarid, in a public show of good will, had sent a basket full of the stolen fruit to the guard's house as payment for his valiant service. His family was very grateful.

Unfortunately, not every one of their little excursions ended in excitement. Sometimes they went exactly as expected, putting Yarid in a sour mood. And since he usually went out with Tirfaun in the hours before a Council session, he sometimes had to suffer a series of boring, meaningless events strung together like some poorly written tragic play. He hated such days.

Today wasn't going to be like that. Yarid knew it. This wasn't just some random tomfoolery. They were acting against a Councilor of the Wall this time, one of the few in the Accord who could call herself a peer of Yarid. And though Nangrove had the wits of a dog and a face to match, she held quite a bit of influence. Perhaps Yarid and Tirfaun were doing the world a favor by knocking her off her pedestal.

Yarid kept his head low and his shoulders slumped forward as he followed Tirfaun, adopting the same servant's posture that he had on their previous outings. A light drizzle fell from the bleak, gray sky. He loathed rain, but at least it gave him a pretext for the hood, which he had pulled up to cover his rather conspicuous hair. He was more worried about his face, however. Tirfaun had given him one of his needlework Patterns, which Yarid had pinned to his shirt. It was designed to tweak the image of Yarid's face, making it seem just a little bit *off*. Yarid didn't doubt Tirfaun's Patterning ability, but knowing that a bit of cloth was all that kept him from being recognized made him nervous.

Up ahead, a gray-and-green carriage trundled up the Avenue, heading straight towards Yarid. Two dappled mares, paragons of their breed, pulled the carriage. Yarid recognized the colors. The carriage belonged to none other than Councilor Jacobs. The windows weren't shuttered, despite the drizzle.

Yarid resisted the impulse to bolt. But if he didn't, the carriage would pass right by him, giving the Councilor a chance to spot him clearly. Yarid knew the wisdom of taking precautions such as the Patterned face disguise, but he honestly had no idea it would be tested today.

He took a deep breath, kept his eyes forward, and kept on walking.

The carriage passed by him, its wheels splashing in the shallow puddle formed in a dip of the paving stones.

Yarid glanced into the window—and locked gazes with Councilor Jacobs. Yarid could almost *feel* Jacobs' deep-set eyes pick apart the lie concealing his face, could sense Jacobs' inborn desire to leap off his seat, to point at him and cry out his name.

Yet Jacobs' gaze fell from Yarid's just as easily as it had found it, completely without recognition.

Against his better judgment, Yarid paused and watched the carriage roll away.

And grinned. *Tirfaun, you magnificent bastard.*

Yarid turned and trotted to catch up.

Trellises, forged from black iron, flanked the curving Central Avenue at regular intervals. The vines that enshrouded their lattices bore no flowers despite the season and were now merely shrubby, green things that did little to improve the atmosphere of the Council District. Today, no one stopped to admire them; instead, aside from the people riding or strolling along the Avenue, small crowds had gathered in the parks that separated the Councilors' estates. Large canvas tents had been erected to keep the misting rain off the instruments being played by musicians. As well as to keep the delicate coifs of the present Councilors from becoming damp, of course.

Yarid had been to many such parties and hosted quite a few as well. They were, in fact, as important as the Council sessions themselves, if not more so. Here was where deals were made, alliances formed, concessions made, and conspiracies hatched. One could say that the Council sessions were merely the by-product of parties like these, a show for the lessers explaining the deals that had already been brokered.

Yarid didn't frequent the parties as often as others, though. He didn't need to. His power was consolidated, and most of his communication was written. His influence was almost mechanical in nature; he set things in motion, and they acted according to his will and predictions. Yarid half suspected that if politics were Patterning, even Tirfaun would defer to him.

He smiled wryly as he passed by. Tirfaun was up ahead, standing by a trellis with his arms crossed, waiting with a frown. When Yarid was within earshot, Tirfaun jerked his head in the direction of the party. "Care to join your friends? You were watching them with what one could only call envy."

Yarid chuckled at Tirfaun's attempt to rile him. "Envy … I wonder what that feels like." He shook his head, still grinning. "Politics is not breaking bread. It is breaking eggs. Stirring the pot." He glanced to the party in the park, his grin hardening. "They're still learning to boil water, and I am a master chef."

"A cooking metaphor." Tirfaun raised an eyebrow. "Thanks. Now I wish I'd brought lunch. We could stop over there, grab something to eat. I'm sure they wouldn't mind."

Yarid grabbed him by the sleeve and pulled him along. "I assure you, we'll have our fill soon enough."

Councilor Nangrove's estate was nearly opposite the Avenue, on the eastern curve. Unlike Yarid, hers was on the outside edge of the curve. She was on the Greater Council, having reached the age at which one was automatically wiser than the younger generation and thus afforded the title "Greater." Having seen the Greater Council in action, Yarid knew it to be a misnomer. And though he rarely felt envy for anyone on the Lesser Council, he *always* felt it for those on the Greater. He hated that they were privileged merely for having creaky joints and liver spots.

Such privilege manifested itself in many ways, including the size of their estates and manses. Since the Greater Council estates were along the outer edge of the Avenue, they were, by necessity, much larger than their Lesser Council counterparts, which were all crammed together inside the Avenue's loop with the parks. This was often justified by the fact that many among the Greater Council had also served among the Lesser Council in their younger days, and their rewards should match the effort spent. No mention was made of any particular *achievements* from said time, of course. Such was too much to ask.

The rain finally let up and breaks in the clouds began to reveal hints of sunlight as Yarid and Tirfaun neared the Nangrove estate. A handful of wealthy children played sailball in a park along the way, surrounded by pike-wielding soldiers with round shields on their backs, pretending to be surreptitious in their guardianship but fooling no one. Tirfaun had lingered to watch a moment, a gleam in his eye. Yarid had gripped his arm tightly, practically dragging him from the spot. The soldiers would be little problem for a Patterner of Tirfaun's skills, but Yarid didn't want him to get distracted. Much as Yarid complained about moralists, even *he* had his limits. Children were certainly beyond those limits. Sometimes he feared to think what Tirfaun did when Yarid wasn't there to shepherd him.

"This way," said Tirfaun, jabbing his thumb in the direction of a narrow pathway winding through a garden near the estate.

"You're sure?" Yarid hadn't heard of any breaches in the wall surrounding the estate.

Tirfaun gave him a look.

Yarid raised his hands. "Sorry I asked." He waved him on. "Please, lead the way."

They passed only a pair of gardeners along the brick pathways winding between the shaped hedges and ivy-wrapped statues of nude instrumentalists, trapped in various poses of performance. As bare of flowers as the gardens were, it was understandable why there were few people around to appreciate them. The rain likely hadn't helped encourage visitors, either.

After a few twists, side paths, and obscured entryways, Tirfaun led him into a narrow, teardrop-shaped dead end, completely surrounded by thick hedges that were twice as tall as the two of them. Yarid looked around, but there wasn't much to look at. "Is this where you take your dates?"

Tirfaun flashed him an amused glance before crouching down in the center of the dead end, his fingers brushing the bricks. "Perhaps." Yarid remembered the park nearby and suppressed a shudder. He decided he'd rather think about the task at hand and stood behind Tirfaun, watching him.

Yarid could tell that the bricks had been shifted from their original placement. Clean red surfaces were exposed in places, a contrast to the dull brown parts that had been exposed to years of weather. And though in other parts of the walkway the bricks fit together tightly, here they were loose, bits of damp earth exposed here and there. Judging by the familiarity with which Tirfaun began his strange little ritual, this place had been prepared for a Patterning.

Yarid saw what Tirfaun was doing, even if he couldn't make sense of it: each flick of his finger shifted bits of dirt around, sometimes drawing a light line of mud along the bricks' surface, sometimes doing nothing but rolling a tiny clod over. Tirfaun did all this wordlessly, eyes focused intently on his strange task, jaw tightly clenched. Yarid had seen him Pattern before, and sometimes it was an extravagant affair, heavy lines scraped into the earth with a specially designed metal rod. Other times, like this, it was subtle. Yarid suspected that this was the purer of the two. Purposeful Patterning, devoid of any showmanship.

The shift was as subtle as the Patterning. Dead ahead of them, leaves in the hedges almost seemed to *grow* away from each other, forming a part in the hedge like curtains being drawn by invisible hands. By the time Tirfaun looked up from his task, a hole had formed at about eye-height, exposing a gray stone wall.

It was a few moments before Yarid realized he was gaping. He shut his mouth. "Is that the Nangrove estate wall?"

Tirfaun nodded, looking as spent as if he had run a mile. "Three of the stones are loose. Mind pulling them out?"

"Not at all." It took a few prods to find the loosened stones, but once Yarid had pulled them out and set them aside, he had a clear view beyond the wall. Yarid clucked his tongue and shook his head. "I take back everything bad I've ever said about you."

Tirfaun joined him at the hole, hands on his hips. "Everything?"

"Well, all the things you've heard at least." Yarid leaned forward a bit to peer through the hole, but not too far. The hole was nearly as big as his face and he didn't want to expose himself. It wouldn't do to have a pair of faces sticking out of walls this early in the game. Someone might raise an alarm and spoil their fun.

Luckily, there weren't too many people around this part of the Nangrove estate. They didn't have much of a view, however. He could barely see the tops of two windows. The stables stood directly between their hole and the manse. Apple trees flanked the stables, blocking much of the rest of the estate.

"Couldn't you have picked a better spot?" Yarid asked without looking at him.

"No," said Tirfaun, amusement in his voice. "I couldn't have."

Bemused, Yarid glanced at him then. Tirfaun was twirling a leaf between his fingers, smiling as he stared fixedly at the stables. Tirfaun spoke. "They'll come any minute now. Watch for them. They vary their meeting times. I bet they think they're so clever, that no one would ever figure it out." Tirfaun shook his head. "Didn't even require any Patterning to find *that* pattern. Pathetic, really."

Yarid didn't know who *they* were, but Tirfaun's cryptic words made the stable a lot more interesting. If something were to happen in there, Tirfaun was right: he couldn't have picked a better vantage point. The door to the hayloft was open, the winch-operated platform that lowered the hay to the ground swinging gently in the light breeze. It was highly doubtful that anyone in the city would see what happened in that hayloft—unless, of course, they happened to be peering through a hole in the perimeter wall.

Which was quite a bit more visible from the stables. "Uh, Tirfaun."

"Mm?"

"If someone did come to the stables, would they see us?"

"Most likely."

"Can you do something about that?"

"Perhaps." Tirfaun made no move, however.

"*Will* you then? Please?"

Tirfaun released a long-suffering sigh. "Fine. I've never been one to neglect the needy." He crouched down and began drawing a new design on the bricks, using the leaf he had been twirling as a pen and the dirt as the ink. "I disguised your horrid face already; I can do it again. It's not much different from that." He paused, looking reflective. "I guess I've given the world *two* reasons to thank me today."

"How remarkably charitable of you, though my face was already obscured. Now, you're just disguising the disguise."

"Ah, thank you. I was almost worried I was on my way to redemption."

"No need to worry. We're here, aren't we?" Yarid said with a sweep of his arm, indicating both their hiding spot and the Nangrove estate.

Tirfaun grinned wryly as he finished. Once he was done, he stood slowly. There was an audible popping sound in his knees. He grimaced. "Well?"

Yarid looked through the hole again. Rather than merely being open space, there was now a foggy sheen between them and the view beyond. "Not bad, though not your best work either."

Tirfaun grunted as he took his place at Yarid's side again. "It'll have to do."

They waited, but not for long. A handful of servants in Nangrove's orange and blue began to spread out near the stable, peeking under bushes. Some disappeared into the stable. *Looking for spies,* Yarid realized. It was a little paranoid, but then the paranoia was justified, wasn't it? He grinned. *It just isn't enough in this case.*

130

No one even looked at the wall from where Yarid and Tirfaun watched. Once satisfied there were no lurkers, the servants left, including those in the stable. Yarid counted to make sure. As he did, he noticed the servants were all younger. He had seen Councilor Nangrove's closest servants before and recognized none of them among those that were here. *Interesting,* he thought, shifting his feet to get more comfortable.

A few moments later a young woman appeared and Yarid rocked back on his heels. Jilliana, daughter to Councilor Nangrove and wife to Councilor Jacobs. Why was she here, at the stables? And why had she searched her own mother's estate as if it were enemy territory? She wore a form-hugging green dress trimmed with white lace at the ends of her long sleeves. Red curls were bunched over one shoulder, tied together with a turquoise-beaded leather strap. She glanced around nervously, dry-washing her hands. It appeared that she wasn't as convinced of her solitude as her servants were. Yarid's breath caught as her gaze fell over them. She frowned as she studied the hole where Yarid's and Tirfaun's faces were. Yarid soundlessly reached over and gripped Tirfaun's sleeve tightly but made no other move.

A noise he couldn't hear made her spin suddenly toward the stable. A young man stood at the edge of the hayloft, looking down at her. His chest was heaving as if he had been throwing bales of hay around, and likely he had been. His white shirt, opened nearly to his naval, clung to his chest with sweat. His blond hair was damp, too, slicked back from his forehead. His skin was darkened, as if it had sought the sun at every opportunity, in contrast to Jilliana's pale complexion. They watched each other for several long moments but said nothing. Then the stable hand vanished back into the hayloft. Jilliana glanced over her shoulder, her gaze falling upon their hiding spot once more, but she strode toward the door on the first floor, tension in her posture.

Did the stable hand have some sort of hold over her, some information about her alleged indiscretions? Or was he the *source* of such allegations? Yarid felt sweat dampen his palms.

"He chokes her," Tirfaun said at his side, voice low though they were too far to be heard anyway. "She likes to be choked. A little anyway."

She didn't immediately close the door when she went inside. Instead, she first lit a glass lamp and hung it from one of the support posts, casting shadows throughout the room. With one more cautious glance outside, Jilliana shut the door.

A moment later two shadows appeared in the hayloft, forms entwined among stacks of hay. Yarid couldn't quite tell who was who in the darkness, but the one on the bottom moved more sensually. Probably Jilliana. They shifted positions slightly, the young man's head seeming to disappear between her thighs. His hands pushed the dress up slowly, Jilliana arching her back. Though he couldn't see much, Yarid suddenly wished he were alone. What would it feel like to wrap his fingers around a woman's throat? Choke her? He found his fingers clenching at the mere fantasy of it. Maybe he could make an alliance of his own with Jilliana.

Dress removed, the stable hand's hands found her neck. His head rested on her stomach, but Yarid couldn't see where he was looking—into her eyes? It didn't matter. All that mattered were the hands.

Jilliana tensed, seeming to struggle—though not with him. Rather with herself. Arms spread wide, she kneaded the hay with her fingers. She shuddered visibly.

Yarid was entranced. The implications of this were staggering. "Jacobs isn't clever enough to set this up on his own," he muttered, mostly to himself. "He must've had help from the Rafting Guild. Discredit Councilor Nangrove's daughter, and you discredit Councilor Nangrove. And get a pretext for divorce in the process. *If*, of course, anyone finds out before Jilliana wises up." Someone would likely insist on visiting the Nangrove estates unannounced. If not during this particular liaison, then during another. As Tirfaun said, the pattern of their meetings wasn't that difficult to figure out, and likely known by the Guild. It could've even been arranged by them.

"Politics, politics, politics. Is that all you see in an opportunity like this?" Tirfaun crouched down again and began drawing something new with the stem of his leaf.

"No." Yarid sounded pathetically defensive even to himself. He watched Tirfaun for a moment. "What are you doing?"

"Nothing political. You wouldn't be interested."

"Shores take you, *tell me*."

Tirfaun paused and peered up at him. With a little smile, he held the leaf up for Yarid to take. "Fancy yourself a Patterner?"

"Of course not. I wouldn't have the slightest clue what to do."

"Just this." Tirfaun mimed the motion with the leaf an inch above the ground. It was simple enough, hardly more than a straight line.

Yarid hesitated. "What will this do?"

"Just what you wanted," Tirfaun said. "It'll break some eggs."

Yarid stared into those shadowed eyes of his, wondering how much he could *really* trust this man. Well, there were many different kinds of trust, one for each situation, and there was one thing Yarid *did* trust Tirfaun to do. And that was make the day a little more interesting.

He took the leaf in his hand.

"Come on now." Tirfaun swirled his hand in a hurrying gesture. "The longer you wait, the less likely it'll work."

Yarid took a deep breath. Held it. Then, before he could talk himself out of it, he drew the line and dropped the leaf as if it were a viper.

It was done. Whatever Tirfaun had wanted him to do, he had done it. It wasn't like he could've changed the outcome, whatever it might be— Tirfaun did what he wanted to do.

Besides. It wasn't like there were any children around. Whatever happened, Yarid wouldn't have *that* on his conscience.

Once he caught his breath, he spun back to the hole and watched. He half-expected the stables to be ablaze, or a sudden gust of immensely strong wind to rip the roof off and expose the lovers within for all Garoshmir to see.

But there was none of that. Jilliana and the stable hand were still in the loft, the movements becoming more urgent. Yarid thought he could make out the stable hand's hoarse moans, but the sound was too quiet to be certain.

Then it stopped. The stable hand's body was frozen in place, but Jilliana's was still moving. It took Yarid a moment to understand. These were no longer the sensual motions of lust. She was struggling, her hands pulling at his, legs thrashing.

"Jilliana?" came the young man's voice from the loft. "Jilliana!"

He stood quickly, yanking Jilliana up by the neck. He began to shake her—violently, panic-stricken groans coming from his lips. "*Jilliana!*" It was almost as if he didn't know he was killing her—or he simply didn't know how to stop.

"I can make vines grow," Tirfaun muttered at Yarid's side, "twist among themselves, grip things. Hold them there forever. All it takes is a little understanding of the fundamental nature of reality and a little dirt on some bricks." He chuckled quietly. "All told, fingers aren't so different from vines, you know."

"You're a monster, Tirfaun." Yarid's voice was flat. It wasn't a condemnation, but an observation.

"Well, today, *we* are the monster."

Yarid nodded, transfixed by the scene in the hayloft. The stable hand suddenly lurched into the daylight, stark naked, dragging the blue-faced, limp body of Jilliana behind him. She was dead already. The stable hand, still unable to let go of her neck, was frantic, almost insane-looking. He stood on the ledge, glancing side to side.

Then he stepped out into the open air.

The corner of the platform caught his face as he and Jilliana fell. The platform jolted wildly, straining the winch. The stable hand spun halfway before he and the body of his lover thumped to the ground. The right half of his face was crushed. His eye was missing. He wasn't moving.

Still watching through the hole, Tirfaun swept his foot backward, obliterating the Pattern they had made.

The dead man's hands finally released Jilliana's throat just as servants ran to their bodies. Someone shrieked.

"Put the bricks back in," Tirfaun said. "Quickly."

"Why?"

"Something I neglected to mention when we started. There's a Patterner in the Nangrove manse who felt everything we did." The amused gleam in his eye returned. "So, you might want to hurry."

An hour later, they leaned against an alley wall deep in the Merchant District, panting heavily.

Yarid listened for footsteps. "I think we lost them," he said.

"Good." Tirfaun opened his grubby sack and counted his needlework scraps. "I only have two more of these."

Soldiers had been posted at the garden's entrance—nearly two dozen of them. It had taken drawing half of them into the garden and a few improvised Patterns along the way to escape them. Yarid had brought them into the Merchant District with the other soldiers quick on their heels. He knew their trail would go cold here if they continued to search.

"I can't believe you did that, Tirfaun."

"I know. That's why I did it."

"You're a real bastard, you know that?"

They rested there, catching their breath, and then they began to laugh.

The second afternoon bell tolled.

"Ah." Yarid pushed himself off the wall and started walking toward the alley entrance. "Time for me to go to work. I have the remains of the civilized world to run."

Tirfaun waved half-heartedly. "Don't work too hard now."

Chapter 26: The Killing Tool

Rannald Firnaleos gripped the wooden practice sword in one hand and a small buckler in the other, chest heaving as his three opponents circled him. Though sweat covered his bare chest and soaked his curly hair, he was grinning. Two bruises purpled his torso. That was more than they usually got on him. Even if Rannald had only held wooden swords in the years since becoming captain of the Sentinels, he knew his skill hadn't decreased. Which could only mean his men were getting better.

Rannald stepped to the side, never dropping his guard. The wicker mat which covered the floor of the Sentinels' sparring room was unevenly made, with broken bits poking up here and there to bite into their bare feet. It was made this way intentionally, to better simulate the distractions one faced in battle. As he stepped, a sliver of wicker stabbed into the sole of Rannald's foot. He twitched in pain but kept his focus on the three that remained standing. The four he had already bested, clutching their various bruises and sprains, were standing by the lower-ranked Sentinels gathered around the edges of the room to watch their Captain.

Rannald watched as a glance passed between the man to his right and the man directly in front of him. A moment later, the strike came from the right. A distraction; Rannald passed under it. The true attack would come from in front. It came fast, but not fast enough—Rannald deflected it with his buckler, rapping his own sword against the man's knee. The man cried out, but only until Rannald's knee took him in the chest, knocking the wind out of him.

That was five down, but Rannald didn't wait for the next attack. He pressed forward to the man on his left, exchanging a quick flurry of blows before sweeping the legs out from under the man on the right, who landed hard on his face. It was one of the lessons Rannald continually drove into them. The sword was merely one tool among many, and the warrior who hadn't mastered them all had weaknesses.

The remaining two launched into a coordinated attack—another thing Rannald had taught them. A sword couldn't be everywhere at once, but two swords working in concert could be in twice as many places. Rannald's grin widened as he deflected the flurry of blows with sword and buckler. He even had to backpedal a couple steps.

Once he had them lulled into a false confidence, he went on the offensive. In a heartbeat, both of their swords flew from their hands, with the span of Rannald's wooden blade at both of their necks. His two final opponents, both clutching their wrists which Rannald hoped he hadn't broken, took to their knees, yielding the battle to him.

The room erupted into applause.

Rannald chuckled to himself as he tucked the practice sword under his arm and bent to pick up a rag to wipe down his face and chest. He knew the applause wasn't for him. It was for the two that had lasted the longest against him. Rannald shook the hands of those two, and the others who had fallen earlier, as everyone funneled out of the sparring room, leaving Rannald alone.

He didn't feel alone, however. His gaze traveled up to a fixture on the wall, a wooden oval with words inscribed along its bottom edge: "*We fear not.*" Above the words were two pegs, and resting on the pegs, a sword with a large amethyst in the pommel.

Rannald's sword, Guiding Light.

He didn't want to admit it to himself, but his hands ached to hold that sword. It had been—how long? Five years, since he had held his sword? It felt much longer than that. Though he taught his men that a sword was merely a tool, he knew Guiding Light to be much more than that to him. It was his friend. Perhaps even his very soul.

And he had given it up for love.

Sherin.

Rannald felt eyes upon him. He turned towards the door, and as if thinking her name had summoned her, there stood his wife.

Though it wasn't a very warm day, the pale blue dress she wore was sleeveless. Only a thin linen shawl hung over the crooks of her elbows. A wide leather belt, studded with silver, hung over her hips and met in a large turquoise clasp below her stomach. The folds of the dress followed the contours of her body closely. Stately, elegant, yet leaving no questions as to beauty of the one who wore it.

Her brown hair, parted on the side, was pulled tight against her head and tied into a tail. Some would call the look austere, but Rannald knew that wasn't right. It was … tempered. As was all of Sherin. She wasn't the same wild-eyed idealist he had fallen in love with. She had changed in their years of marriage. Still full of life and passion, but she had grown. Matured.

To Rannald's eyes, she had become even more beautiful.

She looked at him towering above her, stripped to the waist and covered in sweat. He could see the desire in her dark brown eyes, the desire to come to him, but she remained where she stood. Those eyes filled with sadness as they stared at him.

Rannald knew why. Carelessly, he tossed the practice sword away. It clattered on the wicker mat.

She smiled then, though it looked forced. "I thought you'd be here." The sadness didn't leave her eyes. It never seemed to, of late. It was as if she was beginning to realize the truth of Rannald, a truth that he had long since known: no matter how much physical distance there is between him and his sword, it will always be with him in spirit.

The pain of knowing he could never truly be good enough for her was as ever-present in Rannald as was the sadness in her eyes.

He smiled, though it too required effort. He continued to wipe down his shoulders, if only to give his hands something to do. "The Council in recess?"

She nodded. "I thought we could have lunch together."

Sherin didn't come into the room. She never had. So he went to her. As he always did.

Rannald didn't want to keep her in the Sentinel compound any longer than he had to, so he instructed her two aides to take their baskets to the small garden on the other side of the high stone wall separating the compound from the rest of the city.

Once they passed under the portcullis, Sherin hooked her arm through his. "You should probably wear a shirt when escorting a Councilor of the Wall to lunch." He could hear the smile in her voice.

"You're right," he said. "But you aren't just any mere Councilor. You're the wife of Rannald Firnaleos."

She pinched his arm, chuckling. A little sharper than a playful pinch, but he endured it nonetheless with a chuckle of his own.

They sat on a stone bench, a small mat loaded with food between them. Sharon told the aides to enjoy themselves until the next hour bell. The aides hastily disappeared onto one of the footpaths curving between the hedges.

Rannald and Sherin ate in companionable silence for several minutes until she spoke. "People have been talking about Gaspard Rikshost. About how he had been planning to join some secret order within the city." She took a deep breath without meeting Rannald's eyes. "His body was returned to his family this morning."

Rannald picked up a salted plum and put it in his mouth, chewing slowly and saying nothing.

"He was a promising young man," she continued. "Top of his class at the Academy. He was even a favorite for becoming a member of the Lesser Council once he came of age." She placed her hands in her lap. "They say he died of a sword to the heart. That it ... may have been self-inflicted."

"A tragedy," Rannald said. "May his journey to Farshores be filled with peace."

Sherin shook her head slowly. "He is only in Farshores because a sword killed him."

Rannald had been there. He watched as the young man fell onto the sword. He had killed himself; the sword, as Rannald always said to the Sentinels, had merely been a tool.

He knew Sherin wanted him to admit that the young man had been trying to enter the Sentinels. That he had died before Rannald's eyes. But Rannald wouldn't tell her. He had sworn an oath to his order to keep the Ritual of Joining a secret. He couldn't answer her unspoken question and still deserve to call himself a Sentinel. Or a man at all. His integrity wouldn't allow it.

So he said nothing.

Sherin nodded as if she had expected his reaction. She stood, and her aides, having apparently sensed Sherin's intentions, returned to gather up the remains of the picnic.

"Goodbye, Rannald. I will see you at home."

Rannald reached forward to brush her hand with the tips of his fingers, but she was already out of reach, walking away with her two aides in tow.

Sitting on that bench, Rannald thought of the Sentinel oath carved into the fixture holding his sword: *We fear not*. It wasn't entirely true—a Sentinel could, and often did, feel fear. But he was not threatened by it. It was an obstacle, something to overcome. But not something he was helpless before.

Rannald knew that a fear had been growing within him, one that was beginning to overwhelm his ability to resist.

More than anything in life or death, he feared losing Sherin.

Chapter 27: Someday

Erianna Vondallor sat in the corner of the carriage, hands folded in her lap, looking out the narrow window as the world passed her by. Trees, hills, and, just out of sight to the north, Andrin's Wall all rolled by smoothly. Too smoothly, to her eyes.

She had been Shad Belgrith's servant for most of her life and had been by her mistress's side nearly every day. But that hadn't granted her many opportunities to travel out of Twelve Towers. Shad didn't leave Twelve Towers often, and did so even less as of late. Ever since the sheggam came.

Still, Erianna knew what it *should* have felt like to travel by carriage. The wheels were supposed to catch every hole and rock and stick on the road, jarring her teeth every few minutes. This stillness, the relative silence … it was eerie. Like traveling in a dream.

Only it wasn't a dream at all. The feeling was simply the result of riding over the perfectly flat plane of the Runeway.

"Erianna." Shad sat in the opposite corner of the wagon, elbow resting on the windowsill with her chin propped up on her fist, eyes watching the landscape roll by. "Something to drink."

"Of course, mistress." Erianna opened a small compartment next to her seat, pulling out a decanter of Pattern-chilled wine and a ceramic mug. She poured the wine and handed it to her mistress, her eyes lingering a moment too long.

It was hard not to stare. The changes in Shad ever since the sheggam emissary had given her his … *gift*, were subtle. Perhaps too subtle for others to see. But Erianna had bathed, groomed, and dressed her mistress more times than she could count, and knew her mistress's appearance far better than she knew her own. The drab paleness of her skin could have belonged to a sick person. Erianna would have written it off as such if she hadn't seen what the sheggam had done to her.

The white smoke creeping over the tiles, rushing into Shad's piercings, Shad writhing on the floor, screaming …

The decanter clinked loudly as Erianna returned it to its place, drawing a frown from her mistress. Erianna folded her hands in her lap, hoping Shad

140

didn't notice the shaking that the memory had brought on.

Shad took a slow sip of her wine before returning her attention outside.

Erianna restrained the urge to exhale and cursed herself for letting her emotions get the better of her.

Odd, that. She had never had much of a problem holding in her feelings. Shad had beaten that impulse out of her at a young age, when they both had been in their teens, after Shad had officially assumed the governorship. Since Erianna no longer had a real outlet for her emotions, they had begun to wither away, until there was only duty left in her heart. Duty to her mistress.

Slaves had no room, and no need, for anything else.

True, slavery had been outlawed years ago, ever since the rebellion in Caney Forks, but Erianna knew that one still could be a slave while being called something else. And she had no illusions as to what she was to Shad Belgrith.

It hadn't bothered her, not for a long time. Duty had no need for freedom. Duty needed only itself.

But that had changed when the sheggam came to Twelve Towers.

Duty had given way to fear, which began to wriggle and gnaw in her gut like a bloated worm. She had continued to obey, just as she always had, but she also began to wonder. About her mistress and about herself. About a great many things.

Beyond the creaking of the carriage axles, Erianna could hear the faint sound of marching from the two companies of Twelve Towers soldiers arrayed around them. Occasionally she caught sight of them through her narrow window, breastplates and pikes gleaming in the intermittent sunlight.

Beyond them was the forest, filled with ferns and shadows and twisting paths. A place a lone woman might be able to run and escape.

Erianna cursed herself for a fool for even considering the notion. The soldiers of Twelve Towers were the most disciplined and obedient in the Accord. None of them would hesitate to cut Erianna down if Shad commanded it.

And even if she could get past the soldiers, Orthkalu, an actual *sheggam*, rode in the wagon behind them. Erianna knew he had powers far beyond those of a normal human—perhaps even beyond those of a Patterner. The way his face was hidden in the hood of his cloak, as though the light were afraid to touch him … Did she really think she could escape him, too?

Maybe. For a few moments, at least. And for those few moments before Orthkalu tore her limb from limb with his massive taloned hands, she would be a free woman.

Would it be worth it?

Erianna had to think long and hard about the answer. She almost felt that it *would* be worth it.

Perhaps a better opportunity would present itself, one that didn't end with her dead. Now was not the time, she knew, no matter how much she wished it were.

She would flee her mistress. Someday.

Shad Belgrith turned abruptly, startling Erianna from her thoughts, to knock on the wall between her and the driver. "Stop the carriage." Turning back around, she frowned again at Erianna. "Something the matter, Erianna?"

"No, mistress," she said, feeling the heat rush to cheeks. "I suppose I was distracted. Forgive me." Once the carriage came to a halt, she opened the door, climbed out, and took Shad's hand to help her down the steps. Three officers dismounted and strode toward them in case Shad had orders to give, but she dismissed them with a wave and started walking toward the wagon behind their carriage.

Orthkalu's wagon. Erianna's heart raced as she turned her eyes to it.

It was enormous, rising to nearly twice the height of the carriage. Tall enough for Orthkalu to stand up in it comfortably—but why would he need to? Shad had built it to his specifications, even ensuring it was windowless so no one could see inside. And it was heavy, borne on six wheels and pulled by four huge oxen. Apparently, horses wouldn't go near it.

Erianna didn't believe the wagon was for Orthkalu alone. Something else was in there with him. She couldn't imagine what, but even wondering made her shudder.

What was so horrible that even a sheggam would hide it?

"Would you—" Erianna stammered, taking a step toward the wagon. "Would you like me to accomp—"

"No," Shad said, striding forward without turning back. "I know you don't like our guest. I'm sure he knows as well. I don't want you to offend him any more than you already have."

Erianna swallowed. "I understand, mistress. I will wait in the carriage." If she had offended their guest, she would be beaten, she knew. But not until they returned from Garoshmir. Shad had said she would need her there, that she would need Erianna's pretty face. But for what, Erianna had yet to learn. Something to do with Shad's meeting with the Council, she imagined.

She watched as Shad ducked under Orthkalu's strange staff, set lengthwise in a rack above a small door in the side of the wagon. Shad pushed the door in and slid into the wagon's dark interior before letting the door shut behind her.

Erianna loosed a long, shaky breath, glad her mistress wasn't there to see it. Shad was likely taking another "lesson" from Orthkalu, as she called it. Erianna didn't know what her mistress was learning, but she believed it had something to do with keeping her human. For now.

Erianna walked back to the carriage. She could feel the eyes of one of the officers on her as he lingered nearby. She wondered, foolishly, if the man could read her thoughts. She was glad he couldn't. She was glad he didn't know what she was now planning to do.

Someday, she thought as she climbed into her seat. *Someday*.

Chapter 28: Garoshmir

Tharadis stood at the top of a tall, boulder-strewn hill overlooking the sprawling city of Garoshmir. A panoply of wood and tile roofs of every shape and color poked up over the crenellations of the curtain wall surrounding the city. Tharadis would become an old man before he could count every building here. Five of Naruvieth could fit within these walls with room to spare.

Yet for how surprisingly vast Garoshmir was, he stared at it for only a brief moment before something else just past the city drew his attention away, forcing him to draw a sharp breath.

At first, he had thought it a line of low-hanging clouds obscuring the horizon, but it was too close, its lines too distinct.

Andrin's Wall.

It stretched out of sight to the east and to the west, dwarfing the city before it. For all that Tharadis could see it, he found it difficult to fully focus his attention on it. His gaze wanted to slip past its white surface, focusing on the trees along its base or the clear morning sky above it. After a few moments of trying, he made himself stop and rub his eyes. Any longer and he would give himself a headache.

It would almost be worth it. He had never seen anything so incredible. Not even the ocean filled him with such wonder. How had human hands created something so monumental as this? It was hard to tell, but with Garoshmir's wall as a guide, he figured the top of Andrin's Wall reached over two hundred feet high. If the stories were to be believed, Andrin had finished building it in less than six months—six months of pitched battle with the sheggam vanguard. Yet, with the help of his Patterners and Crafters, he had done it. Against all odds, he had built his Wall and saved mankind.

Emotions suddenly seized Tharadis, overwhelming him. Without this wall, the world would have been a very different place—likely a terrible place. Humanity would have been vanquished and enslaved. Tharadis would never have lived. Neither would those he loved.

But thanks to Andrin's Wall, none of that came to pass. Tharadis bowed his head, feeling immense … *gratitude*.

Once he had wiped his cheeks dry, he headed down the hill toward the city. His pack, lightened of the supplies he had used, bounced against his back. Off to his left, through breaks in the trees, he caught sight of the Runeway. He had avoided it as much as possible on his way here, only using it when hitching a ride with a merchant or farmer driving a cart over its disconcertingly flat surface. It was strange how something so similar to Andrin's Wall in scope and scale could provoke such a different reaction in him. Perhaps it had more to do with those building it than the thing itself.

The Runeway terminated just south of the city gate, its tip rounded like a finger. From the maps Tharadis had seen, the entirety of the Runeway was shaped like a sword stabbing southward. The parts resembling a sword's crossguard jutted southwest and southeast, curving around until they neared Caney Forks on the western coast and Twelve Towers on the eastern. The unfinished tip of its blade pierced the barrier of the Rift, into Naruvian lands. This part, then, was akin to its pommel.

Tharadis exhaled slowly. Hopefully, when he was finished with all of this, he wouldn't have to worry about the Runeway any longer.

Peeking up above the rooftops in the northern part of the city was a large, squat dome, a needle of stone rising up in front of it. That would have to be the Dome and Spire, where the Council of the Wall held their meetings. Tharadis decided to head there first. After all, if he got this business about the Runeway cleared up quick enough, he might not even need to get a room at an inn. He smiled at the thought of getting back home that much sooner and made his way toward the city gate.

Plush red-and-yellow carpets ran down the center of the hallway that curved along the outer wall of the Dome and the Spire. The arched ceilings were high—high enough for pikemen to march through. Similarly arched windows with clear glass ran along the outer wall, letting in the day's dreary gray light. Shaded sconces provided the rest of the light, though Tharadis had heard that the Dome and Spire had special lighting that didn't even require a flame. Perhaps the claims were exaggerated, or maybe they weren't so common as to light the Supplicant's Hallway.

Most of the people standing in line with Tharadis seemed to be commoners—farmers, artisans, laborers, and the like. The more well-dressed supplicants had the humble poise of servants, standing in for their masters' needs, though a couple wealthy people stood in line fidgeting impatiently backed by a small retinue of hangers-on. Judging by the hunched shoulders and heavy gazes, Tharadis guessed that nobody wanted to be there.

Tharadis fought to keep himself from fidgeting. How long had he been waiting in line? By the angle of the daylight streaming in through the windows, he guessed he'd been standing here, inching forward every few minutes, for well over two hours. He couldn't believe how many people wanted to talk to the Council. What business could all these people have with them? Whenever someone had come to Tharadis for Warden business, it was usually because someone had been robbed, beaten, or killed. He supposed with so many people living together that crime would be more of a problem. But this much?

"Next," called a clerk without looking from his ledger book.

Tharadis realized with a start that he had reached the front of the line. *Finally*. He stepped in front of the table. "I'm here to see the Council of the Wall."

The clerk sighed, as if this were the worst possible thing Tharadis could have said to him. "On what business?"

"The Runeway."

"Trade and guild issues? Land use issues? Labor issues?" Annoyance crept into the clerk's voice. "You'll have to be more specific than just 'the Runeway.'"

"Land use issues, I suppose."

The clerk sniffed. "The Council won't be convening to discuss land use issues for another four days. I suggest you return then. Next!"

Tharadis raised his hands. "Wait a moment. My name is Tharadis, and I'm the Warden of Naruvieth. I was summoned by the Council of the Wall."

The clerk snorted, a smug grin spreading over his face as he finally looked up. "Yes, I'm sure you ..." He trailed off, frowning as he looked Tharadis over. When he spoke again, his voice was small. "Do you have your summons?"

Tharadis pulled it out of his belt pouch and handed it over. The clerk unfurled the small paper, eyes widening and face reddening as he scanned it. Slowly, almost reverently, he placed it back in front of Tharadis. "I ... apologize, Your ... ah, Your Majesty." He stood, bowed twice, and began shuffling backward with his hands raised in a placating gesture as if Tharadis had threatened to strike him down. "Please wait a moment. Just ... please wait here." The clerk dashed off.

Tharadis tucked the summons back in his belt pouch and waited some more.

The clerk returned with a woman dressed in similar garb, though her gray robes were ornamented with slashes of red silk. The stiff tilt of her chin suggested she was the clerk's superior. She smiled at Tharadis, though he could tell it was forced. "Sir Warden Tharadis, welcome to Garoshmir. We are preparing quarters for you and your retinue as we speak. Could you tell me how many servants and soldiers need quartering?"

"I came alone. And just 'Warden' or 'Tharadis' is fine."

The smile cracked, but the woman recovered with a bob of her head. "Of course, of course, Sir Warden." She aimed a dark glance at the previous clerk, who had hurriedly sat at his table and began speaking to the next supplicant. Returning her attention to Tharadis, she swept her arm toward a corridor leading out of the Supplicants' Hall. "Right this way."

Tharadis didn't move. "Are we going to see the Council now?"

"This is the way to your quarters. They should be ready by the time we arrive."

"It's midday. I'm not tired." He rested a hand on his hip. "But I am growing impatient. I came a long way to get here. A lot of that was on foot. I'd like to see the Council now."

She smiled again, though this time it was indulgent, as if he were a petulant child begging for a treat. "I understand you came a long way, Sir Warden. The Council has every intention of hearing your concerns. But it will take some time to notify them of your presence. They will also need time to prepare themselves for your presentation as well. As inconvenient as it may seem, our procedures are designed to ensure problems are resolved as quickly as possible."

Prepare themselves? Tharadis sighed. He had the feeling that no matter what he said, he wasn't going to see them today. "How long will all of that take?"

She hesitated. "Possibly three days. More likely four."

Tharadis closed his eyes. So much for making it home early. It almost felt as if the World Pattern were conspiring to keep him here longer than he liked. Although he was kept from his responsibilities back in Naruvieth, he had to remind himself that his goal in coming here was to keep the Accord from continuing with the construction of the Runeway. He supposed that a delay in them hearing his case was simply more time they weren't building. Resigned, he opened his eyes. "Fine. I'll be back in four days. I *will* speak to the Council then."

Her answering smile held a hint of relief. Apparently, she was as glad to be done with this as he was. "I will see to it that they are informed."

"Thank you." Tharadis stopped himself just as he was about to leave. "Are there any books on prophecy here in the city?"

"Prophecy?" A slight frown creased the woman's brow. "If you're looking for stories about them, there are a few booksellers in the city."

"I'm looking for something more … academic."

She shook her head. "I'm afraid the books on prophecy at the Academy library are only open to students and faculty."

The Academy library. He would have to figure out how to get in there. Fortunately, he had a few days to think about it. He nodded in thanks and turned to leave.

Chapter 29: Penellia

A stiff breeze carried the scent of brine and sulfur through the branches of the long-needle pines. Penellia Varan didn't flinch at the sudden stink wafting off Twelve Towers, even though her mount twitched her reins and snorted. Not even a small part of her wanted to wrinkle her nose in disgust at the scent; it was just another data point, another fold in the Pattern she had been following for much of her adult life. A Pattern that slowly but inexorably led her here, to Twelve Towers.

She let her horse crop some tall yellow grasses growing up through the rocky earth while she peered over the tops of the trees. The top of the hill gave her a clear vantage of Twelve Tower lands, if not Twelve Towers itself—she was still too far, the morning air too foggy for that, even if the wind did intermittently bring its distinctive aroma. She wouldn't see the Towers until almost nightfall, and then only if the sky cleared somewhat. Still, she was content to mark her progress. Every step along the path to truth was another small victory.

She twisted in her saddle—hampered in the act by her large girth—at the sound of her assistant Stem's horse climbing the hill, leading the pack horse behind them. Stem's eyes were glazed with exhaustion, and his horse looked no better. The boy's—well, young man's, she supposed—lean frame sagged in his saddle, hands barely gripping the reins. If the boy were half as competent in the field as he had been in the Academy's classrooms, he would listen to Penellia when she told him to rest. Instead, he often complained that he followed a normal human being's sleep schedule, and not Penellia's—suggesting that she was not normal. Or perhaps not a human being.

True, Penellia caught short naps in the saddle or on cushions of moss on the roadside whenever her mind began to get overworked, rather than sleeping through the night, but that was because her best inferences were done when her senses weren't flooded with stimuli. She hardly thought such behavior disqualified her from the human race. It merely meant she was an intellectual. She was, after all, a High Patterner of the Academy, a title not given lightly. Or given at all to anyone living, aside from Penellia herself.

149

Of course, being *of* the Academy didn't necessarily mean *at* the Academy, a distinction her comrades often forgot. Just three days ago a messenger from the Academy trotted up on a lathered horse, the boy himself winded. A roll of parchment from the administrators of the School of Patterning, screaming as well as written words could about untaught lectures, unfiled paperwork, unattended meetings. They had even insinuated that if they had the power to do so, they would have dropped her to mere Patterner—as if the position of High Patterner were a favor doled out by the Academy staff. Penellia had thanked the messenger profusely, saying that it was a good thing he had come with that message because they had just run out of dry tinder. The boy had looked stricken as he turned and rode back the way he came, but surely, he must have been used to the recipients of his messages not always taking kindly to their contents. If he wasn't, he would soon be, or be wise to find another occupation.

The Academy shouldn't have wasted the poor boy's time. They *knew* Penellia was on the cusp of a grand revelation and was far too busy to bother with petty things like administration. They also knew that if the Academy burned to the ground, Penellia wouldn't give a damn. She would merely secure a new source of funding for her research and continue on with her life's work.

Stem's horse slowly walked up beside her, hooves clopping as if the beast were half-asleep and half-dead. Stem swayed slightly in his saddle as he craned his long neck forward, brushing the unruly mop of thick brown hair out of his eyes so he could squint at the eastern horizon. "Are we there yet?"

Penellia hissed through her teeth, swallowing a retort. While she had devoted the last twelve years of her life to a single intellectual problem, her patience didn't usually extend to other people. Not everyone else had the same goals that she did, or worked at the same pace, a fact she often had to remind herself of. Sometimes out loud, repeating several times.

"Why don't you check the map?" she said as calmly as she could. His quick glance told her that it wasn't calm enough to fully mask her irritation. Still, he bent his will to the task with little more than a mutter of complaint. Having him bungle through his saddlebags to find it would give her a few minutes of peace to observe and to think.

Penellia closed her eyes and slowed her breathing, letting the sounds of the world fill her mind. The cry of a hawk, echoing off the jagged mountain peak on her right, the sigh of wind rustling through pine needles, the delicate patter of hooves. And there, ever so faintly, the burble of a shallow creek twisting through the rocky, hilly lands. Sometimes the world felt so *alive* that Penellia allowed herself to forget her task for a few moments and bask in its vitality.

Patterners didn't have heightened senses compared to regular people, as many suspected. They were simply trained in the Academy to isolate and focus their senses to better collect information about the world. Such information, after all, was where all Patterns could be found. Merely collecting information was not enough; much of it was noise. Sorting through it all, determining what was relevant, was an even more important skill that Patterners learned.

Her training had gone far beyond what the Academy could offer. That was the problem with being the very best; you could only go so far with the teachings of others. If you wanted to progress, you eventually had to teach yourself.

She focused on each sense one at a time, shutting off the others. When she went through this process, others observing her often thought she was in some state of meditation, as if she were some sort of charlatan mystic, shutting out the world for the sake of pondering her navel and misleading others with pleasant-sounding prattle. That couldn't be farther from the truth, but she supposed that was why she was the only living High Patterner. Other people simply didn't have the intellectual discipline to question the world and accept the answers.

She finished, as she always did, with sight—the most useful of the senses. She tucked the strands of gray hair that had come loose from her braid behind her ears since even the slightest obstructions could interfere with her observations. She took a deep breath, let it out. Body prepared, she focused her mind.

Tiny details that she hadn't noticed before became glaringly obvious. Tiny fissures in the rock at her horse's feet, the faint shadows cast by protrusions in the mountain's face, the fall of a pine needle, the way the moss grew on a log at the trail's edge, a trampled fern.

Strange. Trampled by what? It didn't look like the hoof prints of the deer common in these parts. Sensing something subtle in the way the detail caught her attention, like the plucking of a guitar string slightly out of tune, she rode down the side of the hill to get a better look at it. Stem followed.

At the base of the hill, she slid out of her saddle, booted feet thumping to the ground. She was briefly glad for the softness of the patch of soil beneath them; it kept her knees from jarring too much. Without comment, Stem took her mount's reins in hand as she took a knee a couple paces from the trampled fern, heedless of the dampness of the ground soaking through the leg of her leather trousers. She wasn't one of those women who wore skirts or dresses or those foolish Naruvian long tunics; what practical purpose could such garments possibly serve? All they did was draw attention to the fact that most women were little more than stones with painted faces, willing to tumble down any hill of a man's choosing—so long as the tumble wasn't too rough. Penellia had no respect for such aimless beings, and certainly not for their frippery.

She glanced over her shoulder at Stem, who happened to be staring at precisely nothing in particular. Penellia sighed. Men, it seemed, were no better than women.

Ignoring the despondency that naturally arose when one contemplated living amongst other people, Penellia returned her attention to her task.

Some of the tracks were clearly made by men: they were bootprints. Large men, taking long strides. Most likely soldiers, though most of the Twelve Towers men were now headed to Garoshmir with Shad Belgrith. Thanks to the strange geography—and geology—that gave Twelve Towers its name, it was highly defensible. Few men would be needed to garrison the volcanic, sulfur-spewing Towers, and few men had been left. In spite of the wealth that Twelve Towers enjoyed thanks to its prime coastline, few people hungered for control of it. The people there were reportedly almost as strange as their mistress, Shad.

These bootprints were odd in how large they were. Large soldiers were rarely left behind for unimportant jobs, since they could carry thicker armor, if nothing else—but their haphazard order showed a lack of discipline. They were not the bootprints of a crack unit.

Penellia cocked her head as something else caught her attention. Animal prints. Made by something also quite large, not quite as heavy as a bear but heavier than a normal man. A series of slight indentations suggested claws, and the innermost toe on each foot was set back.

She had never seen such prints before.

A chill ran through her, prickling her skin.

"Should I set up camp here?" Stem asked.

"Quiet, fool." Penellia leaned forward and touched a print with a finger, letting the sensation envelope her. Her pulse quickened as she considered the implications. One of the most basic things a Patterner learned, particularly if she considered field research, was the various foot- and hoofprints to be found in the wild. While the Accord lands were not small by any measure and had only grown with the recent bridging of the Rift, they were totally isolated. There weren't many creatures that could make tracks like these. And with Andrin's Wall shutting the Accord lands off from the rest of the world, nothing new could come in or out.

Or at least that's what the world was led to believe.

She stood and dusted the dirt and bits of moss off her knee. *This* was significant.

But how? It wasn't immediately obvious to her. She had spent nearly the entire year—since the crossing of the Rift to Naruvieth—sitting on the beach on the western shore, watching the waves. Not idly, of course; nothing she ever did was idle. The waves carried with them traces of things that otherwise could not be found in Accord lands.

Traces of Patterns from beyond Andrin's Wall.

As grateful as Penellia was that the Wall kept out whatever nasties it was intended to, it was perhaps a bit *too* effective. The magic that powered the Wall was like a knife that severed the Accord off from the rest of the world, just as surely as the Rift had previously severed Naruvieth off from the Accord. And while it was impossible to *sail* the Restless Sea, it was not impossible for a skilled High Patterner such as herself to read the bits of Patterns that managed to survive from beyond the Wall.

Nearly a year she had sat there, watching. Waiting. She was used to collecting information bit by bit and piecing it all together, but while she was struggling to find sense in the shredded remains of Patterns that survived the Restless Sea, the revelation finally came crashing over her like a tidal wave.

Head east, to find rotten lands. Look within.

It was a Pattern so clear she knew she could not mistake its meaning … but one that had also alarmed her. Patterns so earth-shatteringly clear simply did not come from nature. She initially suspected that she was being thrown off the trail by another Patterner, someone who worked them rather than read them. But no one in the Accord had the power to create what she had seen, not even that twisted bastard Tirfaun or the crazed Lora Bale from Falconkeep. The Pattern *must* have come from beyond Andrin's Wall. What that meant, she was not yet sure.

Yet it *was* a lead to something great; this much she knew. She doubted, though, that it was merely some new creature. That was just another piece of the puzzle.

With a grace that belied her size, she swung back up into the saddle. Stem didn't bother to hide his grimace; he had doubtless been hoping they would rest more. Penellia paid him no mind. Instead, she cast her attention to Andrin's Wall, felt it pulsing through every twitch of the Pattern. No, it had not been breached, this much she knew. The Wall's magic could not suffer a breach and remain intact. If anything ever damaged Andrin's Wall and its attendant magic, the whole thing would come down in a pile of rubble.

She wondered about the Restless Ocean—could someone, against all odds, have crossed it? She frowned as she thought, her horse picking its way through the trees. No, she decided. Even *Patterns* were shredded to bits by its wild waves. It was so violent that even fish larger than a sea trout died in the passage. Nothing as large as whatever made that footprint could have crossed the Ocean.

She was looking in the wrong places. The problem with Pattern reading, however, was that to find the truth, one couldn't simply go with a gut instinct. One had to consider all the possibilities and rank them according to probability. There were no instincts when it came to true understanding, only diligent study.

Perhaps there was something in the Pattern she had read in the waves, something more she had missed.

Head east, to find rotten lands. Look within.

Lost in thought, Penellia nearly jarred her teeth when her mount unexpectedly leapt over a fallen log. She cursed the beast loudly, but its only response was a flick of its ears. She glanced back to see if Stem was making a mess of himself trying to do the same, but he rode over it with little ill effect. As she caught sight of him, her attention was drawn to the end of the fallen log, a couple paces from the trunk it had come from. It was ragged, looking like it had been chewed. Penellia knew that hadn't happened, of course. The tree had likely just died, fallen, and had been partially consumed by the elements, like any other fallen tree.

She halted her horse and looked closer. Insects, ants and beetles and others she didn't have names for, swarmed out the of the end of the log, from tiny holes where they burrowed. Burrowed, into the rotted flesh of the dead tree.

Look within.

The pieces of the puzzle all snapped together in her mind in a single instant, filling her with dark dread. An image of vermin swarming out of holes, reeking of rot, consuming the land. Killing, slaughtering, destroying everything within their reach.

"Astral Sea," she muttered. "The sheggam. They're already here."

Ignoring a bewildered Stem, Penellia turned her horse and galloped east, knowing she had to put a stop to it but not knowing how.

Chapter 30: The Shadow Box

Nina crouched in the corner of a cold stone hallway, brush in hand, scrubbing as hard as she could. She wasn't sure how long she'd been scrubbing this particular spot. She wondered how much longer until the stone wore away beneath her brush. But she wasn't about to move from that spot, not until the tall blond girl wearing Falconkeep blue and gray standing behind her told her to move.

The sound of her own scrubbing wasn't all that she heard. Other children were doing the same thing down the hall from her, but Nina couldn't see them—not that she would look up from her task to do so. There wasn't a speck of mold or filth to be found in this hallway, but it had been made clear to Nina that not even the *opportunity* for mold to grow would be allowed. This was a special hallway, they said, though they never told her what was special about it. It looked like any other hallway in Falconkeep.

But to Nina, it was special in that it was the only place she ever saw now. She began her work before dawn and ended after sundown, and never did they light torches here. Nor was light allowed in her sleeping quarters. She was taken from there in darkness and guided back there in darkness. Even her meals, which Nina was forced to down quickly or risk going hungry, were given to her in this hallway. This bland stretch of gray stone was all she knew now.

A hard swat to the side of her head knocked Nina off her feet. "Good work," said the Falconkeep girl. "Get up and move to your right. Hurry now." Nina did as she was told, ignoring the stinging pain in her ear. She had quit bothering to wonder why praise was coupled with punishment. She had quit bothering to wonder about anything anymore and simply went about her task with a show of effort, though she knew it mattered little. She had fought back at first, but she soon learned it didn't help. Nothing did. The strikes would come or they wouldn't. What Nina did had nothing to do with it.

Her mind drifted. Where were Rogert and Noil? She hadn't seen them since that first night, when they'd all been separated. Chad she saw on occasion, but they were never alone long enough for Nina to talk to him.

But when she met his eyes, the sparkle that had always been there was gone. She could tell that his mind hadn't left him yet, not like the children that had been here longer. But he wasn't the same boy that he'd been when Nina first met him.

She suspected that she wasn't the same either.

Bristles from her brush broke off. Nina stared at them, not slowing her work, but unsure what to do. Pick them up? Her job was to clean this spot, but she was only making a mess of it. She decided that she would wait until the Falconkeep girl told her what to do. She did her best to ignore the broken bristles, but they nagged at her attention until tears filled her eyes.

Only the gentle clacking of the Raccoon Family at her waist kept Nina from screaming and going mad, the way she'd seen one of the other children do. No matter how badly she'd failed some task or how rough the punishment, they'd never touched the Raccoon Family. It was Nina's anchor to the ground; without it, she knew her mind would simply float away and become one of the clouds that she no longer saw. Sometimes she wanted to throw it away just to get it over with, but those moments were rare. The Raccoon Family was her, and she was the Raccoon Family. She could never throw it away.

The hours dragged on, filled with nothing but the ache in her arms and her back and the ever-present sound of brushes on stone. Judging by the angle and color of the light coming through the narrow slit high in the wall, it was late afternoon when Nina heard the clack of boot heels marching in rough unison up the hall, echoing ever louder as they approached.

Even when the pair of strangers stopped right behind her, Nina didn't look up from her work. She hadn't been told to.

But she could hear the whispers of danger from the Raccoon Family.

The hairs on Nina's arm rose in alarm as she felt the strangers' eyes bore into her back silently. Something was different about this. Usually there was only one person watching her, if not the blond girl, then someone else. But now there were three. There were never three.

Rough hands grabbed Nina, yanking her to her feet. A black woolen sack was pulled over her head. Nina wanted to scream, to fight back, but she was just so tired. She hung limp as the hands dragged her down the hallway.

At the end of the hallway, they picked up her feet as well, the two strangers carrying all her weight down a curving staircase. Nina didn't know about this staircase; it had never been part of her route between where she slept and where she worked. As they descended the steps, the weak light that had filtered through the sack vanished, leaving Nina in total darkness. They were taking her deeper into Falconkeep.

She didn't know how long they carried her. It could've been all night, or it could've been a few minutes. But they finally came to a room that reeked of mold and worse things, and Nina hoped beyond hope that all they wanted was for her to scrub this room too.

Her feet were lowered to the ground. A moment later, Nina heard a flint being struck. A weak light, perhaps a lantern or a candle, flared to life, but still they kept the sack over her head. Her feet were gathered up again, but they didn't carry her far. Gently they lowered Nina into a box so small that she had to bend her knees a little to fit inside.

"Keep your eyes closed, vermin." Nina recognized the voice. It belonged to a girl she knew, but for some reason she couldn't remember her name. Nina did as she was instructed, squeezing her eyes shut until they ached, as the girl and the other stranger removed the bag from Nina's head.

Alicie. That's whose voice it was.

Alicie and the other one—likely Vidden, she thought—slid a plank of wood over the box, brushing against Nina's knees and blocking out the light entirely.

"Don't move or make a sound until we tell you to." Alicie's voice was filled with menace. Nina kept herself as still as possible, daring only to breathe.

Something scraped over the wood. Then something heavy and metallic smashed into the lid. Shudders ran through the whole box with each impact.

Nina bit her lip to keep from crying out, to keep Alicie from getting mad at her. She remembered the man in the woods, how that man just fell to pieces when Alicie had looked at him. Nina didn't want the same thing to happen to her, but she was also frightened, terribly frightened, and she wanted to scream and cry all at the same time.

The smashing continued around the edges of the lid, and it wasn't until it was halfway done that Nina realized that the metallic sound was a hammer hitting a nail. They were nailing the lid shut.

Tears burned at Nina's eyes, yet still she did not cry out or move. She was too scared. She clutched the Raccoon Family tight to her chest, so tight that it hurt her ribs. But she didn't care. She just wanted it—everything—to stop.

Finally, the hammering did stop. Then Nina faintly heard footsteps getting quieter and quieter until there was silence. The two of them had left

Nina alone in this box, and they still hadn't given her permission to move.

Nina no longer worried about that. She screamed, pounding the lid until her hands hurt and her throat was raw, and even then she didn't stop.

She heard a voice. It was so faint that Nina was almost sure she'd imagined it. Nina fell silent then, listening for that voice, for any hint of salvation.

Nina.

She was sure she heard it then. It was a voice, a real voice, but it wasn't coming from outside the box. It was here, with her, inside the box.

I'm here with you, my Nina. I'm here with you, my love.

Tears fell from Nina's eyes. It was the Raccoon Family. It wasn't just the faint, wordless whispers she normally heard, the subtle suggestions. Nina heard an actual voice.

She wiped at her cheeks, drawing in a shaking breath. "Mother? Is that you?" she whispered.

I'm here with you, my love, came the voice. *I know you're afraid, but you're not in danger.*

Nina sniffed. "I'm not?"

A pause. *Not right now.*

New tears fell from Nina's eyes.

I'm sorry, my love. I didn't mean to frighten you. They aren't going to hurt you, but you have to get away from this place.

"But I don't know how. Mother, please. You have to help me get out of here."

Another pause. *Someone's coming.*

The voice fell silent, and so did Nina. She listened hard, willing her heart not to beat so loudly, but the stupid thing wouldn't listen.

Silence. Utter, total, black silence.

Then the bottom of the box disappeared, and Nina fell through darkness.

Chapter 31: The Shadow World

Nina fell onto a rough stone floor. The impact of it knocked the wind out of her. Hadn't she been in that tiny box just a moment before? Where was she? And how did she get here? She struggled to get her breath back for several agonizing moments, but once she did, she staggered to her feet and looked around.

She was in a cave-like tunnel. There was no light source she could see, but she could faintly see herself and the details in the stone, which glistened softly as if its rippled surface were made of dark, smoky glass. The tunnel disappeared not far off, or at least it seemed to until Nina realized that it just turned. Where was she? How did she get here? She didn't know how she knew, but she could feel in her very bones that she wasn't in Falconkeep anymore. The air was cool and damp, with a faint scent that she couldn't quite place. Almost like a musty book, but bitter, somehow.

"Hey."

Nina spun and stared at the apparition standing before her. She was so confused it took her a moment to realize that she was looking at a person. A very familiar person.

Standing with his hands stuffed in his pockets, Chad grinned at her with that familiar sparkle in his eyes.

Nina gaped at him, unbelieving, before launching herself at him, nearly bowling him over. They grappled as much as embraced, Nina sobbing her relief like a river breaking through a dam.

"Whoa, there," he said, but he only held her tighter.

"Did they, did they do the same to you?" Nina asked between gasps. Her voice sounded strange to her ears, as if she were talking with a mouthful of cotton.

She felt as much as saw him shake his head. "No, they pretty much left me alone. I just sat in my room most of the time, eating with the kids in uniforms. No hard work, no boxes."

Nina sobbed even harder at the unfairness of it all. "Why me, then?" She pushed herself back and looked up at him, hardly able to see him through her blurry, watery eyes.

"I think," he said, "that they needed to … to hurt you. To get you to do whatever it is that they think you can do." He shook his head. "Remember my secret? The one that I showed you on the road?"

She nodded.

"Well, I'm pretty sure they know about it too, and that's why they let me be. Only the kids who haven't shown any special abilities are the ones they're treating badly. I think maybe they're trying to scare those kids into being special. I overheard Lora Bale talking to herself about it—trust me," he said, eyebrows raised, "she's crazy, that one. But I heard her talking about breaking kids. Breaking their minds. Like their minds are nutshells, and she's trying to get at the good stuff inside."

A hundred questions flooded Nina's own mind. "Lora Bale? You've seen her? I haven't seen her at all since the first day."

Chad nodded, that familiar grin spreading across her face. "You'd be amazed the places I can go."

Only then did Nina understand where they were. The realization chilled her. "This is the shadow world." She frowned. "But I thought only you could come here."

"Me and whoever I want to bring."

"Can you get us out of here?" She seized his vest in her fists. "Can we leave Falconkeep?"

His grin faltered. "I tried. But I think whatever Lora Bale did to hide the gate, she's doing to me here too. She's a Patterner, and a strong one too. I tried finding my way out of Falconkeep, but I just kept circling back on myself."

Nina felt her hope crumble. She let go of his vest. "We're stuck here then."

"Nina. I need to know. What can you do?"

She flinched from the weight of his gaze. *I'm just a normal girl,* she thought. *There's nothing strange about me.* But that was a lie, she knew. She remembered what Uncle Tharadis always told her: in the end, liars only end up hurting themselves. Doubly so when lying *to* themselves.

Nina sighed. "I don't really know. I can … hear things."

Chad nodded sharply. "Like the graveyard. I remember now. You knew there was a graveyard, but you hadn't even seen it yet." He tilted his head, studying her. "What do you hear?"

She shrugged. "A voice. Sometimes it's from places where people used to be." She looked down at the Raccoon Family looped over her belt. "But usually the Raccoon Family is the one talking to me."

Chad nodded again as if that was what he was expecting to hear. "Lora Bale mentioned something about the Raccoon Family. She said no one was supposed to touch it. She called it something, a … I think she said 'talisman.'"

Nina didn't know that word. She didn't understand any of what was going on. Why was Lora Bale doing this? Why couldn't she just leave them alone?

"Did something happen in the box, Nina?"

"Yes." Her voice was very small. "I heard words this time."

"Whose words?"

"My mother's." She felt tears running hot across her cheeks again. "She died a long time ago. I never heard her voice before, but I know it's hers."

"I believe you." He grabbed her hand and they started walking down the tunnel. Strange, faint images passed by them under the surface of the glassy stone, flitting away as soon as Nina tried to focus on them. Curving walls of cut gray stone, small, shadowy forms crouched over menial tasks. She was catching fleeting glimpses of Falconkeep.

Noises filtered into the shadow world as well—short, clipped voices; footsteps as if she heard them underwater. The images flitted by them much faster than they were walking, and Nina thought that every step here might be worth more than one step in the real world. Sometimes the images changed so suddenly that her stomach lurched. She stared at the back of Chad's head. How could he be so comfortable in this bizarre place?

Nina jerked to a halt. Chad turned to her. "I can hear something," she whispered.

He nodded. "What are they saying?"

"It's … quiet. I can't really tell."

"There's a fork up ahead." They continued walking, the strange sound getting louder with every step.

They came to the fork. Nina nodded to the right, and that's the way they walked. She couldn't make out what the noise was, but the louder it became, the more her stomach tightened. There was something wrong about the noise. It wasn't words, like she'd heard in the box. There were no pauses, no changes in tone. It was just one long noise that never seemed to end.

She stopped again. "It's getting quieter."

"Take me back to where it's loudest."

When they got there, Chad nodded. His face paled noticeably as he studied the image in the wall. Nina couldn't tell what it was at all, but Chad seemed to recognize it. Perhaps he'd been here before. He glanced at Nina, opened his mouth as if to speak, then closed it again. He turned back to the wall and rested the tips of his fingers on its surface. They sank into the stone a little. He twisted them, almost like he was turning a door handle. Blackness rippled out from his hand and then they were walking through it.

Nina realized they were back in the normal world when the noise suddenly changed.

It was screaming.

Relentless screaming. Unending screaming. It was so terrifying that she wanted to crouch down and cry, or even go back into the shadow world and never leave again. Instead, she slowly walked forward, her grip tightening on Chad's hand, deeper into the room.

It was dark, but flickering torchlight from the adjacent room came through the open doorway, casting a rectangle of light across the stone floor and filled the room with a soft yellow glow. In the center of the room was a simple wooden table with no chairs. Shallow scrapes and gouges, surrounded by brown stains, were etched in places near the edges of the table about halfway down its length. Fingernails had made them. Nina shuddered, turning away from the table as they walked towards the other side of the long room.

They finally came to a row of shelves bolted into the far wall. Nina covered her ears with her hands, but it did nothing to cut out the sound. *Fight it*, she said, taking a ragged breath. Rounded objects of different sizes sat on the shelves. Chad took one off the shelf, ran his fingers over it.

"Stones," he said, though his voice was quiet against the torrent of screams. The word echoed dully in her mind until it triggered a memory from the day they were brought here.

Lora Bale's voice echoed in her memory. *Take him to the stones.*

Nina pulled her hands from her ears and snatched the stone out of Chad's hands. She ran her hands over the contours carved into it. A nose, ears, eyes wide in terror, mouth frozen in an eternal scream … She'd seen this face before on that same day. On the face of the boy who had tried to flee and was taken to the stones.

No. He had *become* one of the stones.

"What are you doing here?" barked a low voice behind them

Nina and Chad both spun. Standing in the doorway was a familiar form. Vidden stepped into the room, a large river stone clutched in one of his hands.

Eyes burning with anger, Vidden lunged for them. Veins of unearthly red light pulsed in his palm.

His fingers caught only air as Chad tackled Nina hard. She braced herself for the inevitable impact with the wall, but she fell right *through* it, collapsing onto rough but glassy stone. They were in the shadow world again. She spun to see Vidden's arm reaching through the inky blotch on the wall. Chad staggered to his feet, stabbed his fingers into the blackness, and *twisted.*

The blackness vanished. A faint roar of pain echoed through the tunnel as Vidden's arm, severed at the elbow, fell to the ground at Nina's feet. The red light slowly faded from Vidden's hand.

Chad helped her to her feet. "We can't stay here anymore," he said. "We have to find a way out *now.*"

Chapter 32: The Path to Prophecy

Nestled between a hedge garden and a fishpond on the western side of campus, the Academy Library was shaped like a collection of boxes stacked on each other haphazardly. Dark vines crept up the walls of red brick, obscuring nearly the whole exterior. Only the peaked windows and the tall, arched entryway were clear of the vines. Tharadis stood in front of the building, clutching his pack to his chest.

"Do I really want to do this?" he asked himself in a whisper. A small group of students walking past him, wearing their brown robes, gave him a frown. Maybe it was because he was talking to himself. Or maybe it was how he was dressed. He wasn't interested in the robes that most people in this city wore—how did anybody get about in those things without tripping over themselves?—but had opted for leggings to wear under his tunic, a style he noticed that no one else had adopted. The leggings had drawn their share of stares, but at least he was a bit more comfortable in the cool, damp weather.

In his pack was *First Night, Last Night*. The book reminded Tharadis of Dransig, of how the Knight never really got a chance to read his own order's history. He wondered how Dransig was doing now. Had he made it to Garoshmir yet? Had he found his daughter? A part of Tharadis hoped he hadn't. From the look on Dransig's face when they parted ways, it wouldn't be a pleasant meeting. No, when Tharadis had looked in the man's face, he had seen the eyes of a man resigned to a dark fate.

Or so Tharadis had thought at the time. Perhaps it would simply be that: a man meeting his daughter after a long time. Either way, Tharadis doubted he'd run into the man again, and would likely never learn what happened.

He opened his bag once more and peered in, silently asking himself again if he wanted to give up his book. After making his decision, he slung his pack over his shoulder and walked into the library.

"Excuse me."

The librarian, a red-haired woman only a year or two older than Tharadis, looked up from the heavy book she had buried her nose in as he approached.

The reception desk she sat behind was a massive oak affair, trimmed with scrollwork and narrow brass plates wherever there was a corner. She pushed her wire-framed spectacles higher up her nose as she sized up Tharadis. She didn't seem to particularly care for what she saw. "Can I help you with something?"

Judging by the tone of her voice and her cocked eyebrow, the "something" she could help him with was finding the exit. Tharadis wondered what about him could provoke such a reaction, until he realized that her eyes had gravitated to Shoreseeker's hilt peeking over the edge of her desk.

"Yes. I'm looking for any books you have on prophecy."

"I'm sorry, but the section on prophecy is off-limits to the public." She went back to perusing her book. She flipped a page as if he wasn't still standing there.

"What if—" Tharadis took a deep breath. "What if … I have experienced one myself? A prophecy, that is?" The admission wasn't an easy one. It was difficult for him to even admit it to himself.

Without lifting her eyes, she said in an irritated tone, "Then write it down. Maybe it will be included in the prophecy section someday."

"I see. What will it take to be admitted?"

"Well," she said, finally looking up at him. "You could always cut me down and battle your way in. Otherwise, you're not going in. The prophecy section is very off-limits." She leaned back. Tharadis noticed a large, almost fist-sized orb hanging in a brass fixture chained around her neck. He had never seen anything like it. He could see tiny specks of refracted light hidden beneath its green, glassy surface. When the woman noticed where he was looking, she cleared her throat.

Tharadis met her eyes, face reddening as he realized where she thought he *might* have been looking. "So," he said, clearing his own throat, "no one can go into the prophecy section? What's the point of even having it?"

"I never said no one can go in. Anyone who isn't the public can go in."

Tharadis hesitated, hooking his thumb under the strap of his satchel. He had hoped he wouldn't need to use this, but he was running out of options. Still, even if it did get him admitted, it didn't mean that he would find anything of worth. It would be an expensive gamble if he lost. "What if I were a contributor?"

"Only contributors from the Academy or one of the temples would be considered, and then only if they had special clearance from the Council."

Again, she flicked her gaze to Shoreseeker. "And what, pray tell, could you contribute anyway? Mayhem? Destruction?"

He smiled, willing it to not be as tight as it felt. "A book, of course. A very rare and valuable one."

She smirked briefly, but a hungry gleam entered her eye. She obviously couldn't resist the idea of a rare book. "I'll be the judge of that." She leaned forward and waggled her fingers at him. "Let's see it."

Tharadis took a deep breath. He had to remind himself that the book itself wasn't what was important, but rather the knowledge inside. He knew this book inside and out; keeping it wouldn't help him, but trading it for more knowledge might. He drew out *First Night, Last Night* and gently set the old book on the desk in front of her.

For several moments she didn't move, but just stared at the leather cover with a mixture of skepticism and awe. Using a flattened end of a thin brass rod to keep from touching it with her fingers, she lifted the front cover. The book creaked as its binding shifted.

Her breath caught as she scanned the faded writing on the first page. "It could be a forgery."

"It's not the original," Tharadis said. "But Belliceos was the scribe who copied it."

"If that were true—" She flipped to the back cover with her brass rod and leaned further until her nose was only a couple inches from the cramped writing on the last page, frowning intently. After several long moments, she closed the book and leaned back, pulled out a linen kerchief from her breast pocket, and dabbed at her forehead. "It appears to be authentic, though it may take weeks to be absolutely certain of that."

Tharadis didn't have weeks. He was about to protest when she stood and walked around the corner of the wall near her desk, leaving the book where it lay and Tharadis standing there. Was she going to take the book or not?

He didn't have to wait long to find out. She came back around the corner holding a sheet of white paper. Without looking at him, she sat back down in her chair and placed the piece of paper on the book's cover. She then pulled out a small glazed ink pot and a narrow wooden brush topped with a tuft of horsehair.

"Uh …"

"Don't worry," she said. "It won't actually seep through the paper into the book."

She seemed to know what she was doing, but Tharadis couldn't help but feel a bit of apprehension as she dipped the tip of the brush into the inkwell two times and made her first stroke.

Tharadis was entranced by the easy grace with which she made the first mark. It started off thin, under the slightest pressure from her delicate wrist, and quickly developed into a wide swirl. Suddenly the line changed direction, crossing an earlier curve, then slowly curling back in on itself. Though her next motion lifted the brush from the paper, it felt as if it were a continuation of the last motion. The next figure she drew was more angular than the last, a square overlaid with a looped pattern that resembled the curve of a snail shell. Each abrupt change led to a different form from the last until the entirety of the sheet was covered in layers of strange designs, right to the very edges.

Even so, not a drop of the pure black ink went anywhere she hadn't intended. Whatever was in that ink pot was very thick, which was doubtless why the library assistant was certain there was no doubt of seepage. Still, Tharadis believed that the finished result had more to do with the skill of the artist than with the materials. If it had been a different ink, she would have adjusted her technique to suit it. She was a master at her craft; there was no doubt about it. What Tharadis couldn't determine was exactly what her craft was.

Once she was finished, she rested both hands next to the book, still holding the brush between her fingers, and stared intently at the paper.

Tharadis didn't know what she was looking for; he couldn't make any sense of the designs, if there was any design to them at all. Still, he decided that she must have been looking at something, so he focused his eyes on the center of the image.

After several long moments, it was still a jumbled mess. It didn't represent anything in the real world, at least not any objects that he had ever seen. He blinked twice and looked away. It took him a moment for his eyes to readjust, but then he turned to look back at the design.

Something shifted.

He frowned, turning his head for a different perspective. He knew that the ink was drying, but it seemed as if the various markings were moving ever so slightly, bending around each other, appearing as though there were space between markings that were directly overlaid on one another, at once sinking into and bulging out of the flat sheet.

He had heard of such things before: designs meant to trick the eye. Illusions. They were supposed to be difficult to construct, and he had never seen one himself, at least not one that actually created the desired effect. That must be what he was looking at now. It seemed as if he hadn't given this librarian enough credit. If a librarian was all that she was.

She leaned back and blinked, as if returning from a trance. "It's real, all right. Matches Belliceos's style down to the letter."

"How is an illusion supposed to tell you that?"

She turned to him as if just realizing that a person was still standing near her. "Illusion? What did you see?"

Tharadis shrugged. "Nothing, really. I'm just not sure how this," he waved his hand at the paper, "was supposed to tell you anything."

"You're not supposed to be sure," she said, voice inflected with a hint of irritation. She snatched the paper off the book, ripped it down the middle, and held first one half, then the other, over a candle until both were ashes, which she then swept into a bin tucked beneath her desk. "All that matters is that I believe this book is authentic." She paused. "And I think, if you really are willing to part with it, then the least we can do is show you to the prophecy section." Gently she ran a finger along the spine. Then she looked up at him, guarded curiosity alight in her eye. "Any specific prophecy you're interested in?"

"I'm more interested in general theory."

"Hmm." She stood. Her expression was filled with obvious skepticism. "Well. Not too many people are interested in that, truth be told."

She eyed him a moment as if waiting for him to comment, perhaps even divulge why he was interested in prophetic theory. Tharadis smiled politely.

She sniffed and started walking briskly. "This way."

Tharadis had always thought that his set of books back in Naruvieth was rather impressive, but it was a pitiful sight compared to the Academy Library's collection. Scores of freestanding shelves crowded the massive main room, yet even those paled in comparison to the number of books shelved along the walls of the first floor. The second floor, connected to the first by a single staircase that split the library into two halves, appeared to be mostly alcoves where people studied, though even there were more shelves. A number of mezzanines and elevated sections were interspersed through the first floor, creating a maze of short stairways and narrow passageways between shelves that had no design that Tharadis could discern. At least no *sensible* design.

They walked down an aisle between two rows of long tables, each made of a single wide plank of darkly stained wood. Spread out among the tables were a number of brown-robed students, some of whom were huddled next to small towers of books or stacks of scrolls, occasionally interrupting their reading to scratch a note or two on a sheet of parchment. Others leaned back in their chairs with ankles crossed, casually perusing a single volume, lazily flipping a page now and then. One raven-haired girl's head rested on her folded arms without even the pretext of an open book next to her. She merely sat at the table and slept.

As Tharadis and the librarian passed, her eyes flicked open. Frowning, she lifted her gaze and flatly studied Tharadis. A few others turned to silently regard him, and then more. Soon everyone sitting at a table was staring at him, curiosity and puzzlement in their eyes.

The hairs on Tharadis's arms lifted. While the library was relatively quiet, there were enough small sounds to mask his steps, muffled as they were by the long carpet running between the rows of tables. Yet that didn't stop anyone in the library from knowing he was there.

Even the librarian glanced wordlessly over her shoulder as he walked behind her.

When they passed the last table, everyone went back to their studies— or their nap—as if nothing had happened. Tharadis released a breath he hadn't realized he was holding.

"You sure like to make an impression, don't you?" asked the librarian.

Tharadis regarded the back of her head. "What do you mean?"

She chuckled softly. "If you didn't notice back when I was checking the authenticity of your book, I'm a minor talent when it comes to Patterning. What you did back there …" She lifted her hands and let them flop back at her sides.

Tharadis didn't quite know what she was talking about, but he suspected what she was implying. "You think I have some Patterning ability."

She dropped back a step until she was walking at his side and seemed to seriously ponder his question. "I'm no adept, but I have learned a thing or two. Perhaps 'ability' is not quite the right word. More like, 'effect.' Though maybe you do have some ability, and it's latent and you're using it only subconsciously."

Tharadis didn't like the sound of that. Though it did help explain why a prophecy had been keyed to him.

She studied him out of the corner of her eye as they walked. "You're the Naruvian, aren't you? The one who came to petition the Council."

He smiled at her. "Yes. My name's Tharadis."

She nodded and looked ahead. Instead of giving her own name, she said, "I've heard of you. Everyone in the city has by now." She gestured for them to turn at the next corner.

Tharadis wondered how true that was. He hadn't been trying to draw attention to himself. He had even left his headband in his room today, though he supposed Shoreseeker declared him Warden just as much, if not more so. Still, he had seen more than his fair share of strange looks. He wondered if it was simply him not fitting in rather than anything to do with Patterning. The possibility of having some latent ability, some "effect" as she called it, frightened him. It meant that he wasn't in control of himself. He might even be a threat to those around him.

He realized with a start that they had been winding through rows of shelves and had even gone down a flight of stairs while he'd been lost in thought. He stopped and rounded on the librarian, who had come to a halt a step behind him.

"What is this?" he demanded. "Why haven't you been leading me to the prophecy section?"

She studied him through her spectacles with her head cocked, red hair draping over one shoulder, brow furrowed in a thoughtful frown. Her hand drifted to the large orb hanging from her neck, stroking its glassy surface in an unconscious motion. "You have no idea how we got here, do you?"

"How could I? I've just been following ..." He trailed off. "No," he whispered. "I'm the one who was leading us here." A chill ran through him. "But I don't even know where here—"

"The prophecy section." The woman gestured to a door down the narrow corridor just in front of Tharadis. "We've arrived."

Tharadis stared at the door, unwilling to meet her eyes. Was she playing him for a fool? Or had he really led them here? He finally turned back to her. "How?" he asked, his voice quiet.

She shrugged. "Consider it a test. If you hadn't been keyed to a prophecy, you would have never found it on your own. The library has an interest in making sure only those who have business studying prophecy can access this section."

"And if I hadn't found it? You would have just taken my book without honoring our agreement?"

"I was fairly sure you would find it. That's why I agreed in the first place."

Tharadis drew in a deep breath and exhaled slowly. "So ... what you're telling me is that the library's entire floor plan is a Pattern?"

"Of course it is. That's what we do here." She gestured to the door again. "You going in or not?"

He hesitated. His head was already beginning to ache, and he hadn't even started learning about prophecy yet.

But ignorance was precisely his problem. And he wouldn't solve it by waiting any longer. "All right," he said, striding for the door.

"Alyssa," she blurted.

Tharadis stopped to look at her. "I'm sorry?"

"Alyssa. It's my name. I'm the Academy's chief archivist. Sorry if I was rude to you earlier." She looked away as if she regretted speaking. A wavy strand of red hair came loose. She stuffed it back behind her ear and gestured him forward. "This way, then."

He turned to hide a small smile as he walked to the door and opened it.

Chapter 33: Books and Words

Tucked away in the depths of Academy library, the prophecy section of the library was an oasis of stillness in an already silent sanctuary. The section was kept in its own compact room. The smell of the air here, filled with dust of history, was intoxicating. Alyssa loved the place; quiet though the library was, she often came here to escape even the sight of other people. Books and words, those were the things that made sense to her. People were an enigma.

None more so than this man, this … Warden. Yet in spite of that, she found herself feeling at ease in his presence. Flustered and frustrated, which was to be expected, but still strangely at ease.

To him, Alyssa imagined that many of the books collected here were hardly worthy to be called such: some of them were short stacks of coarse vellum, only a dozen pages or so, with two scraped hide covers bound together by a braid of aged leather. Others were scrolls, stacked in diamond-shaped cavities, and still others were merely loose papers, flattened and stacked in a haphazard manner in shelves of their own.

Tharadis entered the room slowly, his eyes taking it all in. Then he circled around the single table in the center of the room to the shelves with the scrolls. He pulled one out, unrolled it, and scanned it quickly. He put that one back and looked at another. "These are just … random designs. They don't look like prophecies at all."

"That's how all prophecies look to the people they're not meant for." Alyssa shrugged. "To you and me, just a bunch of nonsense, scribbles. But prophecies are keyed to specific people. Only those people can read them."

Tharadis nodded. "That's what Larril told me, too. I thought I was losing my mind when I read those words on the wall. There was a crowd of people there, but I was the only one who could read them." He paused a moment with his fingers resting lightly on the scroll. "Prophecies are Patterns, aren't they?"

"Yes," Alyssa said, "but I know what you're going to say. Patterners have tried to crack prophecies in the past, and while they often think they get one right, their assumptions always turn out to be wrong."

Tharadis glanced up. "Why is that?"

"Do you know much about cryptology?"

"Codes, right?" He shook his head. "I haven't studied it. I've only heard the term." A smile spread across his face as he added, "I was pretty good at riddles when I was young, though."

"Codes can be quite a bit more complex than riddles, although some of the same principles apply. There's one particular kind of code that is impossible to crack, even by Patterners." Alyssa straightened her back as she adopted a lecturer's tone. "It's called a Vayan cipher. It's made when the key used to encrypt the message is longer than even the message itself. What do you think happens when that is the case?"

Tharadis lifted one hand while he pushed the scroll away with his other hand. Alyssa paused as he sat in thought, his eyes flickering across the wood grain of the table, as if he were counting in his head. Or studying the grain itself. "They would get a number of false solutions that were indistinguishable from the correct one."

"That's ... that's entirely correct." She had prepared to launch into a deep explanation of mathematical uncertainty and false positives, but found the wind stolen from her sails. It was *supposed* to have been a rhetorical question.

Tharadis stood and began to pace. "So, each prophecy is keyed to its intended recipient." He paused, then wheeled on her. "Couldn't a Patterner reverse engineer the key? Study the person, figure out how the prophecy was keyed to them?"

"If only it were that simple. You would have to *completely* understand the recipient's Pattern, which is next to impossible. Most Patterning is done by understanding only *part* of an object's Pattern. In principle, it's actually rather crude, which is why it often seems more mystical than scientific to laypeople."

"But prophecies are unique in that they require total knowledge of a person's Pattern."

Alyssa nodded. "That's right."

He folded his arms and stopped pacing, one thumb stroking his chin. He was staring directly at Alyssa. His study of her was so sudden and intense that she had to turn away. With her fingers, she combed some of her hair over her ears so he wouldn't see how red they doubtless were becoming.

In truth, she didn't mind the intense scrutiny. And she berated herself for it. This man was a foreigner, and an important one besides. And he was making her head all muddled with his questions. She wasn't in any condition to be so drawn to him.

And yet, she found she was no longer thinking about prophecy or Patterning. So she was utterly startled when his next words were, "How can I understand you?"

She glanced up at him. "Excuse me?"

"Perhaps I misspoke." Then, suddenly, he smiled to himself as if to some private joke. The smile was gone as quickly as it had come, replaced by the same serious expression as before. "I mean, how is it that we're speaking the same language?"

She frowned. "What do you mean?" She knew exactly what he meant, but she couldn't believe that *he* did.

"Well …" He started pacing again. "Our lands have been separated for over six hundred years, with no contact at all. That's a long time, long enough for the meaning of words to change. A few changes to start out with, to be sure, but these changes would compound over the years. Like," he held out his hands in a helpless gesture as he struggled to find the words, "like a story, told over and over and over again, never once written down, never once checked against its source. After enough time, the story changes so drastically that it becomes unrecognizable. It becomes a different story entirely." He pointed at Alyssa. "Our language should've behaved the same way. Since the appearance of the Rift, Naruvians haven't been able to check the meanings of words with the people of the Accord. Yet I understand you as if we grew up in the same town. As if the language we speak hasn't really changed in over six hundred years."

Alyssa groaned as she dropped into a chair across from Tharadis. "I can't believe this!" She threw up her hands in exasperation. "Did you know that I studied at the Academy for over five years before they taught me that? And I really struggled with it. I nearly had to quit the Academy for something you figured out in," she fluttered her hand, "a few idle moments." Her eyes started to burn. *Oh no. Don't cry.*

Tharadis sat down across from her and took her hands in his. "Alyssa. I'm grasping at smoke here. I'm not here to make you feel foolish. I'm here because I need your help. So, please … I beg you."

Alyssa stared at her hands in his. Tharadis's hands were calloused, the hands of a swordsman. Not the hands of a scholar. He was right, of course. Even if he did have some good guesses, she knew that relying on guesses was a dangerous way to live. She pulled back one of her hands and wiped at her eyes. "I … I will do my best to help you." She met his eyes.

He smiled.

Quickly, she pulled her other hand away, stood, and rubbed her palms on her robes to rid them of the sweat that had mysteriously sprung into being. "Anyway," she said, trying to distract herself from the memory of her hands in his, "yes. Language. You want to know why it hasn't changed. Well, it has. But not as much as it could've."

She sat back down. "You see, language is a description of the world we live in. We create words to keep track of our ideas. They're a little like signposts."

Tharadis nodded. "I'm following you."

"But the strength of our language is dependent on the precision of our definitions. If our definitions are sloppy, we could be using the same word, but talking about completely different things."

"That makes sense." Tharadis nodded again, then stood. "So you're saying that our language was specifically created from the bottom up, with more accurate definitions, to reduce miscommunication. Which had the added effect of making it more resilient to change over time." Then, as if to himself, he muttered, "Very resilient, it seems. It must have been a Patterner, or group of Patterners, who created it."

Alyssa stared at him. How was he *doing* that?

"How long ago did they create it?" he asked.

Alyssa shrugged. "Over eleven hundred years ago. A number of wars had broken out over simple diplomatic misunderstandings, so a cabal of Patterners came up with it as a means to world peace." She shook her head. "They failed in that regard, but they did a good job of coming up with a clear language. It was adopted almost everywhere."

"And when were the first prophecies?"

"We don't have any going back past the Sheggam Scourge, and few older than four hundred years here in the Accord. Everything older than that had been destroyed. But the first confirmed prophecy was …" She trailed off. *Shores take me! Could it be true?*

"Alyssa. When?"

Her words sounded strange, as if someone else were speaking them. "Just over a thousand years ago."

Tharadis nodded, as if he had expected her to say that. "They weren't merely making a new language. They were creating a language based off the World Pattern." He slapped his palm on the table in excitement. "That's

176

what prophecy really is. It's the World Pattern speaking to us."

Chapter 34: Analysis

Alyssa stared at Tharadis from across the table as he silently paced. She had studied at the Academy for years, ever since she was old enough to call herself a young woman. Even before then, her childhood had been directed towards one goal: entrance to the Academy. And though her own skills as a Patterner were quite limited—she could only do a few things well, though she was the very best at one of those things—she was still able to become an archivist at the library at a very young age. She had nearly unlimited access to everything the Academy published, and she was trusted with the highest-level secrets.

Yet never once in all her years attached to the Academy had another spoken of a connection between the Patterned language everyone spoke and prophecy. Had they kept it from her? Her, the archivist, responsible for the preservation of the Academy's knowledge?

Or had they even known at all?

She found it impossible that they hadn't. After all, it seemed so obvious in retrospect. But Alyssa herself hadn't made the connection and had never heard anyone else voice the suspicion.

Except for Tharadis.

"The question remains," he continued, "what is the World Pattern trying to say?"

Alyssa finally found her voice. "I suppose you can start by telling me the prophecy you received."

Tharadis paused, eyeing her. "All right," he said, "but I have one more question. This Patterned language … it's still capable of containing flaws, isn't it?"

"Yes," Alyssa said, feeling like she was a lost ship that had found familiar waters, "it is. It has to allow for individual context. So it's still subject to change, only less so."

Tharadis nodded and pointed at the table. "From where I'm standing, I see a table. From where you're standing, you see the same table. But it looks different to you, because you're on the other side and sitting down. I'm over here, standing up. We see the same object but are looking at

178

different details because of our perspective."

"That's right. That's one of the strengths of our ability to form concepts. It's flexible to a certain degree, to allow for changes in perspective. Otherwise I would see a table and you would see something that wasn't a table, even though we were both looking at the same object."

"But," Tharadis raised a finger, "that flexibility can also lead to other problems, such as vagueness and ambiguity. No matter how resilient our language is, we can't get rid of those because we need the ability to account for context."

"That's true." Alyssa cocked her head to the side. "You don't understand the prophecy, do you?"

Tharadis smiled. "No. It's ambiguous, and it's vague." He sat down. "All right, I'll tell you."

He took a deep breath before letting it all out. Then he said:

To the land of the dead, one must go
To find what was lost
Blue stands against Green
The unyielding shatters
Death heralds world's end
And you shall die

Alyssa listened to the flow of his words, enraptured, carried along against her will with her eyes half-closed. The words were evocative, beyond the mere meaning of the words themselves. They had no meter that she could identify, but still, it sounded like poetry. No, more powerful than that. She suspected that it was a quality of the prophecy itself, its inherent Pattern.

Yet as she opened her eyes, the words began to haunt her with their meaning.

Alyssa cleared her throat. "I can see why you were hesitant to tell me about it," she said, "and why you are so desperate to learn about prophecy."

Tharadis nodded, his face grave.

"Some parts were ambiguous," she added hesitantly, "but others were … not so much."

"That last part worries me."

"Yes." Alyssa rubbed her palms on the thighs of her robe again. She didn't want to think about that. "But who is this 'one' it mentions?"

179

"Well, if it's not me, then it has to be someone I know. Or will know. Otherwise, why give the prophecy to me?"

"Perhaps," she said, "but we don't know the purpose of the prophecy. It may be telling you something you need to know in order to change something. Or it could just be something to torment you for some purpose beyond your understanding and control. Or it could just be something that has nothing to do with you. Lots of true prophecies have been given to people for no apparent reason. It's a mistake to think of the World Pattern as a person, with some sort of stake in the outcomes of what we humans do or don't do."

"Normally, I'd agree with you." Tharadis leaned forward with one hand on the table. He tapped the table with a finger on his other hand. "But, again, the ending. What if the World Pattern did have a stake in this one? If *all* is destroyed, then wouldn't that mean the World Pattern, too?"

"I suppose, but does a rock care if someone takes a hammer to it? Of course not. It just does what a rock does, and it doesn't care or act to preserve itself."

Tharadis straightened. "Rocks can't speak. And if they could, we would have to consider whether or not they were capable of thought."

Alyssa shook her head. "That's still all conjecture."

"True. But there are some things we can be certain about."

Alyssa's face brightened. "Such as?"

"This 'one' mentioned in the prophecy has at least one true choice open to him."

Alyssa thought over the words again carefully, she but couldn't see a choice in them at all.

Tharadis smiled. "'The unyielding shatters.'"

"That's not referring to the 'one,' but to 'Blue.' Whatever that is."

Tharadis reached for the hilt of his sword. Instantly, Alyssa scooted her chair back in a panic, glancing towards the door. Why in the Abyss had she sent the guards away?

But then he drew it and placed it on the table.

She had expected a steel blade. She had not expected a blade that looked like it was made of a sliver of the sky itself.

Blue.

Entranced, she reached out and touched the blade. It wasn't slick, like metal. It almost felt like fired clay, but even that wasn't quite right. She had seen ceramic knives, and they were rare and incredible things. But nothing at all like this.

She ran her finger inside the fuller and frowned as she felt the tiniest tug on her skin. She pulled her finger back and squinted.

Inside the fuller was the tiniest of cracks.

The unyielding shatters.

"And blades do not yield," Tharadis said, as if reading her thoughts. "Only those who wield them."

Alyssa's mind reeled. She looked up. She wanted to believe that this man was a charlatan, trying to trick or deceive her.

But she *knew* Patterns swirled around this man like a maelstrom. It didn't take a trained Patterner to see them; they were obvious even to her. From the book he brought, to how he found the prophecy archives, to all the connections he made without—she begrudgingly admitted—much help from Alyssa at all. The man was a whirlwind of destiny. It would have been strange if the World Pattern *hadn't* tried to speak to him.

Still, the words troubled her immensely. If they were true, and if Alyssa understood them, then it could only spell their doom. And there was no escaping it.

"This, this is big." She stood up so fast that she knocked her chair over. "I have to tell someone. The Headmaster. I can't deal with this."

"Alyssa."

She froze.

"Who is this prophecy for? The Headmaster? Or me?"

As she mulled over the words, the beating of her heart slowed. "Okay." She righted the chair and sat back down. "It's strange, but I feel better knowing that you're going to take care of it. And stranger still that I'm willing to admit it to you."

"Thank you." Tharadis sat back down. "Now, I need your help with the beginning."

"Right." She took a deep, quavering breath. "'To the land of the dead, one must go.' It seems to me that the one would have to die. Which makes sense, given that the prophecy explicitly states that later on."

Tharadis frowned. "But why say it twice? Especially when it's so explicit the second time." He shook his head. "No, I think we're missing something. I think that passage is ambiguous."

"Hmm. Yes." They sat in silence.

It hit Alyssa like a blow. She leaned in. "'*Land* of the dead.' That's it. That's what's different. It has to be the important part."

Tharadis stood and raked his fingers through his hair again. "Shores take me," he whispered. Then he laughed, though there was nothing joyful in that laugh.

"Tharadis," Alyssa said softly, "you have to go to where all dead souls go. You have to find Farshores."

Chapter 35: The Second Line

You know," Tharadis said, grinning with his hands on his hips, "there's something funny about that."

Alyssa couldn't imagine anything funny about a prophecy telling someone they had to find Farshores. She merely blinked at him wordlessly.

His smile widened. "I don't even believe in Farshores. I don't think it really exists."

"I don't think that's funny. I think it's …"

Sad.

Alyssa's mind went to the next line in the prophecy.

To find what was lost.

She studied his face. His smile wasn't genuine at all, she realized. It was a mask.

A mask hiding pain.

To find what was lost.

"Tharadis," she asked hesitantly, "what about the next line?"

She saw tiny cracks form in his composure.

Tiny cracks, like the one running up the fuller of his sword.

Alyssa pressed on. "What was lost?"

Slowly, Tharadis pivoted on his heel, turning his face away from her. His answer came low, hoarse, so quiet it was almost inaudible. "Everything."

His sadness was so tangible, so absolute, that Alyssa wasn't surprised to find tears filling her own eyes at his answer.

Tharadis raised one hand to his face, head bowed, as he raised the other to ward Alyssa off as she rose from her chair. "Thank you for all you have done for me today," he said. "I'd like to call on you for help again sometime, if I may."

With her sleeves, Alyssa dabbed at her face. "Of course."

With his face still turned away, he grabbed his sword from the table, slid it into the scabbard at his hip, and walked out without another word.

After a few moments, Alyssa began the mundane task of cleaning up the scrolls. She managed to stack three in her arms before casting them aside, throwing herself on the table, and weeping as she'd never wept before.

Night had fallen, yet traces of twilight still clung to the horizon. Tharadis walked down the steps of the library, carefully placing one foot in front of the other. He focused on the simple act of walking. Focusing on that was all that kept him going.

He couldn't think about anything else. Not yet, not until he was alone in his room.

He passed inns along the way. Light leaked out from beneath doors and through shutter slats. So did sound. From nearly every inn he passed, Tharadis could hear laughter, singing, talking, and in some, guitars and flutes.

When he had first come to Garoshmir, he had reserved a room in a local inn rather than taking up the offer given to him by the Council of the Wall, to stay in one of the apartments in the Dome and Spire set aside for visiting dignitaries. He knew that such apartments came with lavish furnishings, food, and servants, all of which would be paid for by the citizens of the Accord. He knew he had no right to their money, so he had brought his own to spend on lodging. Yet as he passed inn after rowdy inn, he knew that he couldn't stay in the room he had originally planned to.

Mere solitude wouldn't be enough. He needed isolation.

He headed for the Dome and Spire.

When he arrived, Tharadis showed the guards there his summons. Moments later, a clerk came trotting toward him, smiling and bowing his head. With a sweep of his arm, the clerk showed Tharadis the way to his apartments, and then proceeded to lead him there, chattering all the while. Tharadis grunted at the man occasionally, which seemed to placate the clerk's need for a response to his endless stream of words. Tharadis paid little attention to anything the man said. He was still too focused on putting one foot in front of the other. Only when the man mentioned something about servants did Tharadis utter a word: "No."

When they finally reached the room, Tharadis shut the door on the clerk's face. A few moments later, Tharadis heard the clerk's footsteps fading as the man walked away. Tharadis let out a quavering sigh.

Finally, he was alone.

The room was dark and silent, save for the sound of Tharadis's own breathing. Moonlight filtered through gauzy curtains that reached the floor, presumably leading to a veranda. It gave enough light for Tharadis to make his way to the massive four-poster bed pushed up against the far wall without cracking his knees on any of the small tables and sofas scattered about the room.

He lay down on the soft bed. He didn't get under the covers, cold as the Garoshmiri night was; he had never felt comfortable covered in blankets. The bed was massive, much too big for a single man. He stretched his arm across the covers. He felt their coldness sink into his hand.

A cold bed. Cold as death.

Like a dam breaking, the feelings Tharadis had fought to control roared through him, drowning him, obliterating all thought of the present and dragging him back to the past.

Back before the Rift was bridged.

Back before he was made Warden.

Back before he had lost it all.

Chapter 36: Hearthsflame

It was a simple enough design. A few sweeping curves flowed out from a single point, swirling and branching, layered upon themselves, all of which was encapsulated in a perfect oval. Tharadis was proud of that; he had worked on sketching ovals for a very long time.

The design was his obsession. It reminded him of a flower that grew only in the driest, most shadowy places of the Face. The flower was called hearthsflame for the soft red color of its petals. It had no uses that anyone had discovered—no medicinal properties, and while it wasn't dangerous, it was bitter and left one feeling like he had been punched in the gut for a day if eaten. Although no one paid much attention to this seemingly useless flower, Tharadis found himself drawn to it. Some days, he would hike down some of the hidden game paths on the Face just to see it. Seeing such a beautiful flower persevering in such harsh conditions had always made him feel emotions he couldn't put names to. The mere contemplation of such a flower had sometimes even brought tears to his eyes.

Ever since he had first seen hearthsflame, Tharadis had been compelled to draw it, to capture and retain and immortalize some fragment of its essence, as if failing to do so were some great injustice to the world. So he had always drawn his design, ever since he was a boy, to remind himself of the flower, even if no one could see or really understand what it was he drew. All they saw were the lines.

Hunched down near the footpath that led down to his brother's house with a stick in his hand, Tharadis etched the final line in the flat patch of dirt. Sometimes other young men his age would scoff at him for playing in the dirt like a child, but what Tharadis did was more important than listening to them. He still worked as hard as any of them, sometimes harder, but he still made time for this. It was profoundly important to him that every once in a while, he was reminded of this flower.

There was a rhythm and an order to its design. He had to lay the foundation, which was a strong heavy line curving across the center. From there, each subsequent line had to be placed at the right time, as if ridges of one needed to overlay those of an earlier line. Such details mattered to him,

186

though he supposed it was his own peculiar need than any inherent importance in the design. Still, that was the way he always did it.

Occasionally, he even made improvements to the design. It always seemed perfect every time he saw it, as if it captured the spirit of hearthsflame exactly, but sometimes he would look at it from a different angle and could see something to make it even better. He didn't know how he judged such an abstract design to be better, and again marked it up to being an affectation of his.

This was one of those times. The line representing the third stamen could be turned the other way, providing a counterpoint to the direction of the first two. Once he had finished it, he rocked back on his heels to study it and was pleased by the change.

"It's beautiful," he heard from behind him.

Startled, he jumped to his feet and spun. "Oh, Serena. Shores, you scared me." He chuckled softly. "Thank you, by the way." He cocked an eyebrow. "What are you doing out of the house?"

"Living my life," she said, leaning on the crutch she sometimes used. Her straight black hair hung around her face, the tips touching her belt. As always, her deep brown eyes seemed to swallow him whole. Once his eyes met hers, it was hard to look away. He felt a bit guilty for staring so intently at his brother's wife, and quickly glanced somewhere else. His gaze joined hers in regard of his design, and for some reason, sharing that with her felt just as private. His guilt grew and he chose some sage brush to focus his attention on.

"It's … a flower, isn't it?"

He nodded. "Hearthsflame." He had never told anyone else what it was.

She nodded as if it was what she had expected. "I've always seen you drawing it, but I never thought to actually take a look at it." She turned and smiled at him. "I'm glad I finally did."

He didn't know what to say.

She turned and began walking back to the house she shared with Owan. The crutch tucked under her left arm took as much of her weight as either of her legs. Still, she didn't complain. "My husband send you to tend to me?"

Tharadis picked up his woven sack and slung it over his shoulder. "Duty calls," he said. "But no, not exactly. He said you never needed tending, but that the house, the laundry, and the kitchen might while he was gone." Tharadis hung back a few moments while she made her way back toward the house. He didn't want to walk at her side. It didn't seem right for him to, so he followed her a few steps behind.

Her answering laugh, low and throaty, was one Tharadis could never tire of. "Well," she said, "I guess he respects me somewhat, if that's what he said."

If she had been there, she wouldn't have believed that. Tharadis's brother had said the words with contempt well-masked, but not well enough for Tharadis to understand how his brother truly felt about his wife. She had taken ill two years back, shortly after their marriage. Tharadis hadn't been told the specific details—he could guess, but always regretted it when he did—but Serena had gotten hurt by something that shouldn't have hurt her at all. No one had thought anything of it at the time, with some of the men in town blaming "women's moods," but it happened again later. And again.

And it only got worse as time went on. It wasn't long before people began to recognize that Serena wasn't merely a fickle and snivelly young woman, but that there was something genuinely wrong with the way her body experienced pleasure. Owan couldn't even massage her feet without causing her to cry out in pain. The best healers in Naruvieth had examined her but could find no way to cure her condition.

Her life became a test of endurance. She didn't want to be touched, not even by her own husband. Simple pleasures that other people took for granted, such as scratching an itch or combing her hair, were exercises in agony. Of course, she felt any normal hurts no less keenly than anyone else.

But as her condition worsened, Serena only seemed to get stronger. With each new challenge, her resolve to overcome it hardened.

Tharadis wondered just how hard she could get before becoming too brittle to sustain any more. Was there a limit to how much she could take? Would she decide she had had enough one day? What would happen then?

What would she do?

It was on days when he wondered this that his drawing of the hearthsflame consumed him the most.

The setting sun was an orange egg settling into the nest of drytrees that towered behind Owan and Serena's house. A thin curl of gray smoke rose from the brick oven out behind the house. She had built the fire on her own, then, despite the healer's orders to go easy on herself. She probably had chopped the wood herself, too. Tharadis swore to give her a scolding about that but smiled when he realized just how useless it would be. He might as well scold the hearthsflame about growing where it did. It would have the same effect.

And why should he scold her for doing something that made him feel happy? No, he wouldn't scold her. But he would make sure to chop enough wood for her before he went back home.

Owan had built his house outside town, on a small ledge on the side of the plateau upon which Naruvieth was built. The path leading down was steeper than the switchbacks on the Face, and so Serena didn't have many opportunities to go into town. Ever since Owan had been made Warden of Naruvieth three years ago, he would often be gone for long stretches of time. Tharadis often took it upon himself to bring down a few days' supplies for her. She wouldn't hear of it when he said he would pay for them with his own money. She didn't want charity, or even gifts, so he let her pay him back for everything he brought, though sometimes he snuck in a few extra trinkets, jade hair clips and opal-headed pins he was sure wouldn't hurt her to wear, frivolous things, without telling her. She never complained about those.

He could have sworn something green like jade pinned her hair behind her ear. Seeing her wear it made him happier than he could account for. He tried to shake himself of the feeling, failed, and focused on following her into the house.

It was a cozy place, its single large room given the appearance of three rooms by sheets of canvas that stretched up to the conical ceiling. Tharadis had read in one of the old books his father had given him that it was a holdover from when the remnants of mankind were on the run from the sheggam, never settling down and living in tents. Times had changed, and more buildings, particularly those of a more official function, had actual walls separating the rooms within, but people had grown used to seeing canvas dividers in their homes. Owan and Serena's house was big enough for them, and a baby, should one ever make its way into their lives, but with only her in the house, it seemed an empty, lonely place. Maybe that had more to do with the expression on her face, one which she only ever seemed to show Tharadis, one that she was too proud to show in front of anyone else. He wasn't even sure if she knew just how alone she looked when it was only him around.

He wondered how she looked when she was truly alone. He wondered if she cried.

With her crutch under one arm and a broom in the other, she swept up the remains of a clay cup she had apparently dropped. Her left hand trembled, from what Tharadis didn't know, but her face betrayed nothing.

Tharadis tried to blame the way she felt on Owan, though it wasn't completely fair. Things between husband and wife would have been normal if Serena hadn't been afflicted with her condition ... but did that really matter? She was who she was, and if she struggled to hold on to something meaningful and good in all aspects of her life, even those that hurt, Owan wasn't doing the same. She, at least, had an excuse for bitterness, if she ever felt it; she was the one suffering. But what excuse did Owan have?

Without glancing up, she said, "I know that look on your face." He could see the faint traces of a smile on her face.

Tharadis realized his fist was clenched and relaxed it, letting out a breath. "More highwaymen, I take it." He made a noise in his throat. "We don't even have any highways."

"Then I think the appropriate term would be criminal."

"Crime in the farms is no worse than it's ever been." He shook his head. "It's the second time this week he's been gone. How long will it be this time?"

"Tharadis," she said softly, finally looking up at him. "I have my own way of dealing with this, and he has his. It has been harder on him than you can possibly realize, and he hasn't given up on me yet." The smile on her face blossomed rich and full, and even the hearthsflame couldn't rival it. "He has his own kind of strength, and he's kept his faith."

Tharadis mumbled something about stoking the fire and rushed out the back door. The clutching feeling in his lungs and dampness in his eyes must have had something to do with the smoke, though he was glad she wasn't there to witness it.

He was able to take his mind off that as he focused on cooking. Enjoying good food was one of the few bodily pleasures in which Serena could partake of, and Tharadis could admit he had more than his fair share of talent. Whenever he cooked, he was able to refuse her payment for the ingredients with the excuse he had every intention to eat what he had prepared, and she was welcome to anything that was left, since it would otherwise just go to waste. She had laughed the first time she had heard that one. It was the last time she had brought up repayment when it came to dinner.

He always brought a few spices from his personal stash and would quiz her over what he had used. While she typically loved what he cooked for her, she didn't have quite the discerning tongue he did, though her tasting skills were improving the more he cooked for her.

She gave as good as she got, though. She was a thoughtful, discerning critic and offered suggestions as well as praise. While at first, she merely mentioned what she thought was wrong with a dish, she had recently begun to offer suggestions on what could improve it. Though Tharadis's parents sometimes ate what he cooked for them, they didn't give any more constructive feedback than "It was good," or "Why don't we try the lamb instead next time?" Serena gave him what he needed to feed his passion for cooking.

He was halfway through skinning a root on the wooden cutting board when he realized he was in love with her.

He paused, only briefly, before continuing to skin the root. The skins would be good for sweet bread, which he decided to bake later on. He pushed them off to the side before cutting the root into very thin slices.

It didn't matter—it couldn't matter. Serena had been right. Owan had his way of dealing with things, she had her way of dealing with them, and Tharadis had his own. If she could live with her affliction, if she could endure such agony daily, then he could deal with a little pain of the heart. She had taught him that.

The creaking of wood announced her leaning against the door jamb, watching him work. He didn't turn to look at her in acknowledgment of her presence. He continued cutting, crushing, and sprinkling. The ingredients sizzled and popped on the cast iron skillet atop the oven.

She took a deep, heavy, sensuous breath and let it out in a joy-laced exhalation. "Is that black cardamom?"

Tharadis stopped what he was doing. Swiveled his head. "You can tell that from over there?"

Her eyes widened. Again, that heartrending smile. "Am I right? Is it really in there?"

With a practiced flip of his wrist, Tharadis tossed the knife in the air. He caught the blade as it spun with his right hand, and extended the handle towards her, resting the knife on his left forearm, bowing deeply at the waist with one foot extended.

"It appears," he said gravely, "that I am now the student."

He felt her move close to him, felt her hand rest on his shoulder. His whole body tensed, yet he kept as still as possible. He didn't know what she was doing, but his mind spooled out endless possibilities, many of them

191

wild and gloriously improbable. Here they were, alone in the clearing behind her house, far from town … her touching him.

She took the knife by the handle, flipped it around, and placed the handle back into his hand. She bent forward, and he could feel her breath on his neck as she whispered in his ear.

"Nice try. Get back to work, master chef."

For some reason Tharadis couldn't figure out, Dalton Threed just wouldn't let him into the kitchen of his restaurant, called Sunflowers. He had had no compunction about hiring him most days, mostly for menial, back-breaking labor, but whenever Tharadis asked for a chance to prove what culinary skills he had, the portly restaurant owner, whose fleshy face wore a continual mask of stubble no matter how frequently he shaved, would cast Tharadis a suspicious look out of the corner his eye and mumble to himself about trusting skinny people with the preparation of food before walking off to wipe down the bar.

Sunflowers had been an inn many years ago, one of the only ones in Naruvieth, but few enough people stayed overnight in town that didn't already live there. The farmers that came in to market to sell their crops of drymelons and tanglewort and whatever else would deign to grow that year often had friends or relatives in town to stay with, and visitors beyond them were impossible, what with the Rift being what it was. No, there was little reason for another inn, but people always needed to eat.

When Dalton's father Ballow willed the Sunflower Inn to him—"best thing he ever did for me was die," Dalton would say with a sharp nod that set his jowls to shaking—Dalton used his shrewd mind to convert it to a restaurant—and to Farshores with anyone who wanted somewhere to sleep. He had built a reputation for serving the finest food money could buy because, of course, Dalton had found the greatest chefs money could buy. Though Tharadis found the man to be somewhat of a slob and bastard in his personal life, Sunflowers set the standard for eating-only establishments, and several others popped up since then but could never reach the stature of the original.

Tharadis hoped to own Sunflowers one day, or, better yet, start his own restaurant. But first, he had to start small, and prove what he was capable of. Even if that start was very, very small, he would do it.

He hadn't realized just how small that start would be.

Tharadis was almost glad when Owan went off on one of his adventures, because then it gave him an opportunity to do what he loved most: cook for someone who could appreciate it. He didn't know how long the path toward becoming a chef would be, but it felt like he had already achieved all of his dreams whenever he saw the look in Serena's eyes as she tried his newest culinary creation. So, when he discovered that his brother's wife would be alone again this night, he felt more enthusiasm than was appropriate.

Over the month and a half since the night of his revelation, he had since learned how to subdue his feelings and desires. Serena was his brother's wife; he had to accept that and move on. In a way, being around her, seeing her live and enjoy living despite all the trials she endured daily, gave him the will to deal with the situation that was. Being with her was a problem that provided its own solution. He could live with that, bittersweet as it tasted.

Tharadis finished all of his tasks early. Dalton was impressed, if not altogether surprised, but still managed to dodge the question of when Tharadis would be allowed in the kitchen. "Cooking is women's work," he said, though he didn't sound like he believed it. Especially since Dalton himself was known to occasionally cook the finest fish anyone had ever tasted. Tharadis was wearing him down. Grinning like a boy half his age, he took his day's wages from Dalton's thick fingers—"never let a fool like that near my kitchen," the man grumbled—and sprinted off to market.

The sun was high in the sky as he walked the footpath to her house, the canvas bag slung over his shoulder, bulging with goods. Once he realized how he felt about her, he had stopped bringing her gifts. She never said anything about it, but he suspected she knew more about how he felt than he did himself.

She sat with her legs crossed in front of her in front of the house, staring down the slope. Beyond the trees a few leagues was the sea, little more than a gray line barely distinguishable from the sky. She was staring in that direction, though she didn't seem to see it. Or anything at all.

Her raven hair, flashing red when it caught the sunlight just right, was bound up with one of the last hair clips Tharadis had brought her, shaped like a tiny silver comb with a small agate in the center. It was barely clipped to anything, and much of her hair had come free and was now dancing listlessly in the breeze sweeping over the treetops. It was shorter now, barely brushing her shoulders when the wind stilled. It almost seemed as if her hair had been hacked at with no precision at all, as if she had simply tried to rid herself of the hair that almost seemed to define her.

She turned her head to indicate the spot on the ground next to her but didn't meet his eyes. He sat as she did, legs crossed, and settled his bundle in his lap. His eyes searched the view for something worthy of his attention, but the woman at his side pulled at him. He continued searching.

"Why a hearthsflame?" she finally asked.

He turned. In her lap her hands rested limply, but Tharadis could see something within them: a wilted yellow flower, called a dunblossom. They were common, but fragile. They were used in the mourning ceremony, when a body was committed to the seas in hopes that someday, the soul that once resided within it would reach Farshores.

He breathed in sharply when he saw it. He didn't like this, her sitting by herself, contemplative, holding a wilted flower that symbolized death. Her dark brown eyes, he noticed, were unfocused, liquid, and slightly red around the edges. "It … well," he began, "it perseveres. No matter what. No, it *flourishes*, not in spite of its harsh surroundings, but because of them. And it never gives up its beauty." He suddenly felt foolish, as if he had stripped down naked in front of her. But then the feeling washed away as soon as it had come as he watched her lips curve into a faint, beautiful, yet somehow tragic smile.

"It perseveres," she said. Coming from her, it sounded like a benediction.

A tear fell from her eye, rolled down her cheek, and clung to her chin. Reflexively, Tharadis raised his arm to wipe it away, but halted just as his hand left its resting place on his bundle. He clenched his fist and let it drop to his side.

"You know," she said, "I've never seen a hearthsflame. I mean, I've seen it at the market. It's a pretty flower, but … it's never stood out to me before. It's always just been another flower. Severed from its roots and stuffed in a basket." Her breath came raggedly. "But I've never truly seen it where it flourished." He felt her eyes upon him. "I've never seen it … as you see it."

In the silence after her words, his pulse pounded in his ears. The hairs on his arms stood, the flesh beneath them tingling as if a being with feathered feet walked across them. There suddenly wasn't enough air in the sky to fill his lungs. But none of that mattered. All he could see was her eyes, liquid brown, the raven locks that fell around her face, the depth of her skin's tan. All he could hear were her words, echoing endlessly in his mind. All he could taste and smell was the scent of her, the delicate perfume of hearthsflame, though he knew none grew here. She enveloped all of his senses. She was the world.

"Serena—"

"Take me to them," she said. "Take me to where the hearthsflame grows."

With one of her hands gripping his upper arm and the other behind his neck, he lifted her by her waist to her feet. They were fatally close to an embrace. Her could feel her trembling. Back before their teenage years, before the affliction had taken her, Tharadis remembered how she would sometimes bite her lip to keep from crying. Now, tears fell freely down her face as she struggled not to bite her lip. That would only compound the pain she was in.

She stood only a moment before her knees gave out. She fell into his arms, sobbing and shuddering.

"Don't touch me," she whispered as her embrace only tightened. "Don't …"

His arms held her up as much as they simply held her. She felt slight in his arms, though she had always had such … *presence* before. As if by willpower alone she commanded the seas themselves to do her bidding. Now, to see her so vulnerable, so weakened … it shook him.

She kissed his neck and clutched him ever tighter. There was no romance in it, only purest gratitude. The scent from her hair filled his nostrils and it was—

"Black cardamom," he said, somewhat shocked. "You've been cooking without me."

Some moments passed. Still she shuddered, but said, "It was either that or starve. Owan can't even boil water, you know."

"Still?" Tharadis clucked his tongue. "A shame, that one. A disappointment to the whole family."

Serena shook again. This time, though, it was with silent laughter. "And you know what? I'm pretty good, too."

"Hmph."

"I'd watch out if I were you. The competition will eat you alive."

Tharadis couldn't help but laugh at that. When he subsided, he had to wipe the tears from his eyes. He could feel her throaty chuckle against his chest.

"Where's your crutch? I'll go get it for you."

"It's gone."

"Gone?"

"Mmm. Mixed in with firewood somehow. I wonder who put it there."

"I see."

She nestled in closer to him. "You made that for me, didn't you?"

"Yes."

"You should have used wood that wouldn't smoke so much."

"Had I only known." Gently, so lightly that she could barely feel it, he ran his fingers through her hair. To get to the Face where the hearthsflame grew, they would have to ascend the path to the main plateau—not an easy trek, even for someone healthy—cross through half of town, and hike down some of the steeper goat paths.

There was no way she could make it, even if she was at her best and still had her crutch. "Well, there's nothing for it. I guess I'll just have to carry you."

"Tharadis." Her voice was quiet. "You know I can't ask that of you."

"Whether or not you ask it, the answer is always yes."

He waited for her to nod before scooping up her legs. She winced, but schooled her face to calm. "All right. Let's go."

She watched his face the whole way. He didn't dare watch hers back, not when she needed him to focus on the path ahead, where one tiny stumble could send her crashing to the ground. Even though not being able to look at her was a challenge, feeling her gaze upon his face was reward enough.

The streets of Naruvieth were thronged with people. It was still high heat, but business was business and wouldn't go away just because you broke a sweat. It was as crowded as Tharadis had ever seen it. People clotted the streets, and even a couple arguments broke out because people were stalled from reaching their destinations. Despite all that, the crowds parted around Tharadis as he carried Serena. A few of the faces in the crowd he recognized. He caught glimpses of their scandalized expressions out of the corner of his eye. He stared straight ahead, ignoring them as best he could, focusing on his goal instead. Besides, at that moment, only one pair of eyes mattered to him.

With the sun beginning its western descent, the Face was blanketed in long shadows. Even so, the flowers would be impossible to miss. Descending the goat paths along which they grew was a task, holding Serena as he was. There was more skidding on his butt than walking, and a few rocks went up the bottom of his tunic. One or two lodged themselves where Tharadis would rather they not be, and he had to accommodate his stride to suit his awkward situation. Serena laughed a little. She had earned the right, he supposed. He laughed, too, and endured. He would adjust himself soon enough, but he would have carried on this way until the end of time if he had to.

Of course, he certainly wouldn't prefer that.

Serena released his neck with one of her arms and pointed. "There!" He had never heard so much excitement in her voice, or anyone else's.

He would have missed them if she hadn't pointed them out. True to their nature, they grew out of a split in the rock, with nothing but sand for soil. The vibrantly green stalks, though thin, stood erect, their warm red petals open, reaching desperately for the sky, for the light of the sun. A few rays touched them briefly, and they were triumphant.

"Put me down, please. On my feet."

He did. And as if she were any other woman, she stood straight and tall, and stared in unfettered and naked awe.

She wept.

She laughed.

She turned and drew his face to hers, touched their lips together briefly, and said, "Thank you."

Tharadis did not carry her home. But he did walk by her side the whole way there.

It was long past dark. No man who cared for propriety would be in a married woman's home at this hour, especially not with her husband camped miles away, chasing bandits through the wilderness. Tharadis cared nothing of propriety, and everything of Serena.

She reclined in her cushioned rocking chair. In her hands was a small lump of gray wood that she was whittling. She frowned as she did, though it seemed to be a little more than concentration to cause that expression. When he had first seen her take up the hobby, he had been worried about her causing injury to herself, but she was defter with that little knife of hers than he was at cooking. She had been at it for some time, working at it here and there, and had a few more irregular lumps of gray drywood in a basket next to her chair of roughly the same size. He wasn't sure what she was making, but it was vaguely egg-shaped. When he asked the last time he was here, she said she wasn't quite sure yet either, but that perhaps it was actually an oval, with a flower blooming inside. A flower that only the two of them could see.

Tharadis sat on the rug, legs folded in front of him, leaning back as his arms propped him up. A single oil lamp sat on the table next to her, filling the room with more warmth than illumination. The silver clip sat next to the lamp, its hammered surface shimmering in the flickering light.

Serena set her wood and knife in the basket and began to rock back and forth in her chair, staring out the unshuttered window into night. A change came over her, a look of acceptance. A thin yellow blanket covered her legs, though it was warm enough without it. A black and white moth fluttered in the air before her, catching her attention briefly before dancing out of sight.

"My husband won't touch me anymore." Her voice was emotionless, flat, without inflection. She continued to rock in her chair. Though she and Tharadis were exactly the same age, born less than a week apart, she looked older now, like someone who had experienced the worst life has to offer and grown weary of it. "Not even if I beg him to. He won't even hold my hand. The body, I've discovered that it can endure much. But the heart … the heart is a fragile thing, prone to breaking. And it doesn't lend itself to mending quickly."

A cicada sawed its whirring song outside. Tharadis turned to watch the stars flicker in the firmament. Like most nights, the sky was cloudless. He wondered what it would be like to feel rain on his skin. Freshwater ran in streams that cut across the lowlands nearly all year round, but Tharadis couldn't remember the last time water actually fell from the sky. It had happened when he had been little, but he didn't remember it.

"He told me what he really thought of me. He said I was a leper, and that my skin would begin to rot. He told me that he left me alone so much because … because he was worried he would get sick, too." That hesitation was the only emotion she betrayed. Her face was a mask. "If he would only slap me, or shake me, anything at all, it would be better than this. But he's afraid to hurt my body with even the gentlest touch. Even if he must watch my soul wither and die, he refuses to cause me a little discomfort." Her eyes focused sharply on Tharadis. "Do you know what sustains me?"

His gaze met her eyes briefly, then sank to the floor.

"Your cooking."

He smiled faintly. "I'm not *that* good."

"You are. But it wouldn't have mattered if you weren't. That you cared enough to do it, that you treated me like a woman and not brittle blade of grass, that you cared more about my thoughts and ideas than about my pain … those things are the nourishment I need."

The moth landed on his knee before Tharadis saw it coming. Two black dots stared up at him from its wings like frightened eyes, blinking as the moth quickly flapped them.

Serena stopped her rocking. "Those, and knowing that you love me."

The moth flew off his knee, circled about in a seemingly senseless fashion, but eventually found its way out the window to join the cicada.

"Is that so wrong?" he asked the night.

"You haven't been listening."

"I have," he said. "But someone had to say it."

"Tharadis."

"Good night." He rose to leave, but he didn't take a step to the door. He couldn't move his feet. They were fixed where they were. *I can leave at any time,* he told himself. *Any time I want to. They're my feet.*

He could have left at any time, but he chose to stay instead.

Tharadis turned back to her, and when their eyes met, no words were spoken, but they both moved as if one mind. Serena rose from the chair and eased herself onto the bed. Tharadis was there with her. Serena's hands took his, her fingers entwined in his, and pulled them close to her ears until he had no choice but to straddle her hips with his knees. Every muscle in his body grew tense, quivering with anticipation. His hands, pinned to the thin mattress, couldn't help him now, so he slowly lowered his face down to her chest. After he had unfastened the button on her dress, he blew softly on the exposed skin of her breast. He felt her shudder beneath him.

Suddenly worried, he glanced up at her face and saw tears streaming down her cheeks. But then she said, "Don't stop."

He didn't. He knew that stopping now would hurt her more than it would him.

Tears continued to fall down Serena's face all through the night. She wept as Tharadis had never seen her weep. But Tharadis knew that it was a bodily pain, a pain she had learned to endure.

Her soul would know nothing of pain then. He swore he could feel it soaring through him.

As dawn finally broke, her back arched, her toes curled, her fingers reached desperately for the sky, for the light of life. A few rays of the sun's light touched her briefly, and she was triumphant.

Two days later, the door to Sunflowers slammed open. Tharadis heard it from where he sat on the kitchen floor, scrubbing a pot with a handful of sand. It was not what he had in mind when he asked Dalton to let him work in the kitchen, but it was a step forward. Ignoring whatever the disturbance had been, he put his mind back to his task.

"Where is my brother?"

Tharadis froze. A few grains of sand fell to the floor.

"He's, ah, in the kitchen, Warden."

Tharadis set the pot aside and stood, dusting his hand off on his tunic.

Owan stepped into the kitchen. His square face betrayed nothing, though there were a few drops of blood clinging to his short beard. A wound, and fresh.

Owan towered over him, and always had. Though this was Tharadis's twentieth year, Owan made him feel as if he were thirteen again.

The sword he always wore, the sword of Naruvieth's Warden, gleamed with deadly promise in the etched steel-covered sheath at Owan's hip. Another sword was tucked under his arm. He lifted his arm to let that sword fall to the ground, then kicked it disdainfully to Tharadis.

"That's ... Father's sword."

Owan nodded. "That's right. He died protecting this city, protecting *you*, while you ..." He scrubbed at his beard, wincing briefly when he touched the wound on his chin. His eyes turned savage. "I want you pick up that sword and follow me to Westing Fields. You're going to learn how to use it, and I'm going to teach you."

Shores take me. Father. Dead. His father was dead. The thought was mere words, a rattling in his mind. Mother would be crying. So would Esta. She was too young to have to learn about things like this.

Father.

He picked up the sword. It wasn't as ostentatious as his brother's, but it was a fighter's sword. Father had been a fighter. Tharadis clutched it to his chest. His mind was empty. All it could conjure was a single question: "Why?"

Owan turned to the door. "So you won't be defenseless when I kill you."

Chapter 37: The Duel

Tharadis was on a knee in the short yellow grass, desperately trying not to clutch at the wound in his side. The strike had glanced off his rib, a finger's width from killing him. The pain was searing.

It would only feel worse if he touched it, so his fingers hovered near it, trembling. He compromised by wrapping his fingers in a sweat-drenched fold of his tunic.

Owan stood twenty paces away, impassively wiping the edge of his blade with an expensive lace kerchief, looking as fresh as if he had just woken up, as if he hadn't spent the afternoon battering his younger brother.

It wasn't the first time Owan had scored his flesh. Sometimes he would go for days without hurting Tharadis. Sometimes, Tharadis imagined he could see a flash of sympathy in Owan's eyes if the gash was deep enough. Owan's face would be filled with something harder when Tharadis looked again.

His father's sword lay in the grass at Tharadis's feet. Mastering himself, mastering the pain, he gripped the hilt with his free hand and stood.

The Westing Fields were one of the few places south of the Rift where grass grew heavily. It was relatively flat, though pocked with sand gopher dens. Tharadis had found many of them with his feet, twisting his ankles in the process. One or two he had found with his face.

Trees surrounded the fields, separating them from the rest of the plateau. Hardy shrubs dotted the grounds, though many of those had been cleared. The tawny grass no longer grew here in the places where children usually played.

Months had passed since Owan had told Tharadis he would kill him, but only in the past few weeks had Tharadis been able to stand his ground—at least against his own ineptitude. He had never been much of a fighter, though he had gotten himself in a few scuffles when Esta found herself the subject of teasing. Those had been more Tharadis drawing a line. Never had it been a matter of life and death.

Owan had pledged to take his life. Tharadis knew Owan intended just that.

At least when Tharadis had proved himself worthy to die on his blade.

Tharadis sighed, wincing at the pain this caused him, and tossed Father's sword back in the grass. "I'm done with this," he said, turning. "I'm done with you." He began walking toward the dusty footpath that led into town.

To his surprise, he heard Owan slide his own blade back into his scabbard. "Fine," Owan said. Then, as if the thought just occurred to him, he added, "Aren't you interested in why your audience hasn't come?"

Tharadis paused. From the beginning, people had come to watch. Few people knew what was going on at first, thinking that since their father had died, Owan was training him for the Shoresmen, or at least that it was some harmless sibling rivalry. As the brutal lessons continued, they had come to realize it was something else entirely. Many stopped showing up, though a few came every day, curious.

One person, however, had not come once. Tharadis hadn't seen Serena's face since that night.

She was who Owan was referring to. But Tharadis would not be baited further. He continued walking.

"Wouldn't you at least like to know how she's doing?" he asked, the very soul of calmness. "If you stay with me for the rest of the afternoon, I will consider telling you."

Consider. Which meant that he wouldn't. Still, it was tempting to hope, but he knew better than to believe Owan would err on the side of mercy. Though he claimed to not want to hurt his wife, Owan had a cruel streak in him.

"I have to work tomorrow," Tharadis said, though Dalton hadn't been asking about him. "And so do you, presumably. If you still call yourself Warden."

"Oh, I do." He could hear Owan's slow and measured footsteps as he walked up behind him. "Warden of Naruvieth. Righter of wrongs. Defender of the innocent. Avenger of the betrayed."

"I'm not the one who killed our father."

"True." Never once had Owan admitted why he wanted to kill Tharadis. There was no need. There was only one thing Tharadis had done that would ever warrant Owan's desire for his blood.

But why hadn't he taken it? Why this farce with training him for the sword? Owan had even taken to paying for Tharadis's needs while he trained, seeing as it took up all the hours Tharadis would have had to work. Tharadis had refused his brother's money at first, but Owan wouldn't take it back. He had said he wanted Tharadis to focus on what was important—his death—rather than his pride. His lessons on the Westing Fields had only reinforced that.

Was there more to what he wanted? He said he wouldn't kill him in cold blood. Perhaps there was truth to that, but Tharadis couldn't shake the suspicion that there was more to it.

It was that more than anything else that made him go back up and pick up his father's sword.

"Good," Owan said, though his voice didn't betray any pleasure. He drew his own blade, eyes intent, and crouched into a defensive position. "Now. Come at me."

The sun sank beyond the horizon to the clash of steel.

At one point during the day, one of Owan's men had come by to report that there was nothing to report. Over the past few weeks, Tharadis had heard—mostly by listening in the marketplace, since no one would talk to him about it openly—that crime had plummeted. Neighbors were settling their disputes without the help of the Shoresmen. No one thought of it as a good turn, for everyone understood the cause: people were deathly afraid of Owan.

Some called it obsession. Others, speaking in whispers, called it possession. Ever since the formation of the Rift, not a Naruvian had seen a sheggam with his own two eyes, but the tales from older times were fresh in everybody's mind. The sheggam were the beasts that mothers used to frighten their children into obedience; they were shadows in the dark of night that filled the hearts of brave men with crippling fear. They simply couldn't understand why a man who was once considered so honorable would suddenly be seized by the notion to beat and humiliate his own flesh and blood. At least not without blaming it on a sheggam curse.

It wasn't merely that, though. Owan wouldn't sleep in his own home at night; he would simply wander off in some random direction and return by morning. A few people had seen him do it, though no one dared go to his home while he was gone. Days would go by before anyone would see Serena. Those were the worst, when Tharadis was sure that Owan was venting his frustrations out on her. It was always a relief when she had been spotted in town, but she was never there when Tharadis was. He heard she had taken to using a crutch again. A few people remembered the day when she had been carried across town by her husband's brother and knew the cause of Owan's obsession was nothing supernatural, nothing beyond the understanding of normal men.

Normal men could understand a jealous rage just fine.

When the last traces of twilight vanished, Owan dropped the tip of his sword. "Enough for today."

It was all Tharadis could do to keep from collapsing where he stood. Sweat slicked his hair and stung his eyes. Every breath was a gasp. A dozen nicks and scratches bled through the fabric of his tunic. It was almost to a point beyond mending. Each cut burned as if the steel were still in him. The red moon was full in the sky, providing some light, but it was still darker than Tharadis was used to while sparring. Owan's blade had had no trouble finding *him*, however.

Owan took a drink from his water skin and, after a moment of eyeing Tharadis, tossed it to him.

"You want me to end this. I know, little brother. It wouldn't be difficult, you know."

Tharadis wiped his mouth. The water was almost as hot as the air, but was as welcome as a second chance at life. "Right. All I have to do is die on your blade."

"No, of course not. Though that's one way." He walked to Tharadis and took the skin back. Fireflies danced around them. Owan stared up at the sky. Tiny points of light reflected off his eyes. His voice was calm, yet there was an undercurrent of pleading in it. "You can beg for my forgiveness."

Tharadis paused to consider it. It would be a simple thing to do. He could just say a few words, and this whole messy business would be behind them. Things would go back to the way they were before.

Tharadis remembered those moments leading up to the night everything changed. He remembered Serena holding the dunblossom in her hands, the look of utter bleakness in her eyes, shrouding the spark of life which had always seemed to glow so brightly. He knew he had saved her in a way Owan never could, or would.

Tharadis sighed. "I cannot ask you for forgiveness," he said. "That would assume I feel guilty about what I've done. I could tell you that, I could say those words, but it would be a lie. I can't regret what I've done. That would be betrayal."

"And what you did to me wasn't?"

"I … I don't know if I believe it was. At least, not my betrayal."

Owan turned to look at him with more puzzlement than accusation in his voice. "You blame her?"

"No, Owan," said Tharadis quietly. "I blame *you* for your pain."

"I can't say I'm surprised." Owan turned to walk away. "Whether you're ready or not, tomorrow is the day you will die. Prepare yourself."

Tharadis knew Owan wouldn't have told anyone—sometimes it seemed he had forgotten the world existed, and could only see Tharadis with a flat, emotionless gaze—but that stopped no one from figuring out that today would be the day. People filled the fields, from shopkeepers and tanners to even some farmers from the lowlands. A few small children, boys mostly, pushed up against the legs of adults, eyes wide with morbid fascination. A handful of the more business-minded vendors from town wove through the press, selling hot food. Some people Tharadis didn't even know, and many he did. Dalton was there, standing among the crowd circling around the area Tharadis and Owan had taken to be their unofficial sparring grounds, but he wouldn't meet Tharadis's eyes.

He didn't expect his mother to show up. The pain of losing her husband was deep, and the fact that Owan planned on taking a son from her as well would be difficult to bear. Tharadis scanned the sweating faces of the crowd as the sun crawled higher in the sky and was grateful not to see her there. She might not have been able to stop Owan from this, but at least she didn't sanction it.

He looked for another face in the crowd—Serena's. He wasn't sure he wanted her to witness this either, but he did want to see her face one last time. He saw nothing of her before Owan stepped into the ring.

The muscles beneath his crimson tunic were taut as cords ready to snap. He had shaved off his beard, save for a single patch of black on his chin. Tharadis wondered why that looked so familiar—Owan had always kept a full beard—when he remembered that it was how Father used to wear his own beard when both Tharadis and Owan were children.

Not wanting to get slashed to pieces, the crowd gave them an ample berth. They were close enough to see the action, while far enough away that Tharadis couldn't hear some of the more quietly spoken words through the general murmur. As much as everyone wanted to witness the spectacle, no one wanted to be skewered by an errant sword thrust.

This would be no formal duel. The opponents would not bow to each other with their blades pressed to their foreheads. There would be no third party to moderate. There would be no interference from the law. The man primarily responsible for upholding the law was already here, breaking it.

There would only be swords and sweat and death.

Tharadis considered walking away. He didn't mind being called a coward; it was better than dying to appease his brother's hatred. That wasn't what stopped him from leaving. It was Owan's empty gaze, one utterly devoid of anything resembling passion. He didn't look forward to killing Tharadis. He wasn't fueled by rage, rage that would dissipate over time. No. Owan meant to kill him, one way or another. He would try to kill Tharadis today, whether or not Tharadis sought to defend himself. It was merely something that had to be done.

Tharadis knew that all those months of training hadn't tipped the balance in his favor. But if he had to die, he would die fighting.

Before Tharadis even knew what was happening, Owan had his sword out and rushed him. The tip of his blade was coming too fast, he had no way to parry it, so Tharadis stumbled out of the way as he dragged his father's blade free of its sheath. Owan stepped back to shake his head.

"You disappoint me, brother." When Tharadis was back on his feet, sword held out in front of him, his breathing panicked and fast, Owan pressed the attack again. Tharadis could only parry. Owan was simply too fast and too skilled. The few openings he left were closed as soon as Tharadis recognized them. Owan unleashed a flurry of blows faster than he ever had before. Defense was all Tharadis had, and he knew it wasn't enough.

Still, none of Owan's strikes connected, not even for a glancing blow. None of them seemed to have been pulled, but Tharadis suspected Owan was good enough to fake a genuinely deadly assault. If he truly wanted to kill him, he would without hesitation. All of this was for show. But why? What was he holding out for?

Tharadis didn't dare relent in his defense. Perhaps this was merely a test. If it was, Tharadis had no intention of failing it.

Then, just as quickly as they had started, the rain of blows stopped. Owan let the tip of his blade sink almost to the grass as he watched the crowd off to Tharadis's left.

Tharadis himself wasn't sure he wanted to take his attention off his brother long enough to see what had caught Owan's eye. But when he caught a glimpse of sable hair, the edges of which flashed red when the sun hit it right, he couldn't help himself.

Serena was there.

Tharadis didn't know what he expected to see if she should come—pain, despair, the emptiness he saw in her eyes that day, the same emptiness that would frequently visit Owan's expression—but it certainly wasn't what he saw when she looked into his eyes.

Happiness.

It stunned him. If Owan had walked over and stabbed him then, Tharadis wouldn't have even noticed until his heart stopped.

She was, somehow, happy.

It wasn't fleeting, ephemeral contentment or momentary pleasure or even a reprieve from the pain that always haunted her, but pure, unrestrained happiness.

She was beyond beautiful. It took him a moment to realize that the wreath of flowers woven throughout her hair was hearthsflame. Her hands rested on her belly, which Tharadis was surprised to see was bulging slightly.

A child.

My child.

"Now you know," Owan said quietly. His face was stricken. "Now you know why only death can come of this."

Tharadis lowered the tip of his father's sword, pitching his own voice so no one other than Owan could hear it. "It doesn't have to end this way. You can walk away from this. No one has to know who the father—"

"They *will* know. They will know *I* am the father."

"Fine. But don't do this."

Frustration warred with disbelief on Owan's face. "You're willing to give up everything over this?"

"Of course not," Tharadis said. "Death gains me nothing I wouldn't already have in life, however meager that may end up being."

Owan smiled sadly. "You have an odd way of trying to convince me." The smile withered. "But I'm afraid you'll fail, no matter what you say."

Tharadis tossed the sword in the grass. "Then you'll just have to execute me for a criminal. I will no longer be a part of this."

Owan's eyes fixed on the sword lying at Tharadis's feet. "Our father's sword." He looked up, cocked his head to the side. "Have I told you how he died?"

Tharadis folded his arms. "No. You didn't."

Owan nodded and stepped closer. "I hadn't trusted you for quite some time, not with how often you went to my house when I was gone. So I had one of my men stay behind to follow you, just to make sure nothing ... out of the ordinary, happened. He came as soon as he could and told me what he heard that night. I was in a fit, of course. Father tried to calm me down." He shrugged. "He tried to hold me back from doing what needed to be done. I ran him through."

The words were like a fist in Tharadis's stomach. "*Liar.*"

"No, brother. It's true." Owan lifted the sword in his hand. The Warden's sword. "I pierced his heart with my sword. Ask Rellin. He watched me do it. Our father died at my hands."

"You're just telling me this because you want me to fight you."

"Of course. But that doesn't make it any less true."

Tharadis bent to pick up his father's sword and felt his rage boil through him. Tharadis stared at the blade, at the scratches and dings. An old sword, for an old man. An old man who never had a chance, who never thought his own son could raise a weapon against him. He died, likely disbelieving Owan's fury and what it would cause him to do.

A senseless death.

Without quite knowing what he was doing, Tharadis raised his sword over his head, the blade sideways, parallel to his shoulders. For some reason, it just felt right to hold it that way. Natural.

"Ah." There was a touch of amusement in Owan's voice. "The Fool's Salute. I can't imagine where you learned that one. It seems fitting, though, doesn't it? A couple of fools, trying to kill each other." He raised his own sword to mirror the salute, then brought it down and thrust toward Tharadis's heart.

And was deftly parried. The tip of his father's sword pierced Owan's leg. First stroke.

Owan cried out, backed away, favoring the wounded leg. His eyes widened in surprise, then narrowed. "Interesting." He winced as he began slowly limping in a circle around Tharadis.

It was misdirection. Owan sprang forward, lightning-quick, his sword a bolt of death. Tharadis parried it easily. Owan avoided his previous mistake and didn't lean into the thrust. Had he, his shoulder would have been skewered.

Why the hearthsflame? Serena had asked on that day when this all began.

Because that's what drove him.

It drove him now.

With his sword, Tharadis began to draw.

The design was firmly fixed in his mind. Each cut curved out from a single point fixed in his vision, swirling and branching, layered upon each other. There was a rhythm and an order to his cuts. Each subsequent stroke of his sword had to be made at the right time. It was a design he had drawn a thousand times before, one he had perfected in his mind and in his wrist. He had never drawn it with a sword, had never needed to, but he found that it wasn't all that different from what he had used in the past. Neither dirt nor paint was his medium now; blood was. Owan's blood.

Tharadis proceeded to create his masterpiece.

Their roles were reversed. Owan was no longer the teacher. No, he was the one learning a lesson now.

He would learn that the hearthsflame refused to yield to death.

Tharadis's wrists were numb with the ringing shock of steel on steel. His muscles burned as if liquid fire flowed through his veins, yet he dared not—could not—quit. The design trumped all. The hearthsflame was the expression of the universe. Tharadis merely realized that expression in physical form.

Owan couldn't stand against his relentless assault. His face was streaked with sweat. His hair clung to his skull. Blood seeped through his tunic from a dozen cuts. With each barely-deflected stroke, his movements became more sluggish, weaker.

The flower was done. Tharadis completed the design by creating the oval, whipping Owan's sword from his hand in the process. The Warden's sword flipped once, twice, and flopped to the ground at Serena's feet.

The tip of their father's sword hovered at Owan's chest as he fell to a knee.

Fury pulsed through Tharadis in a torrent. It took all of his willpower to keep his sword hand from shaking. "Do you relent?"

Owan's panting slowed. "I'm sorry, brother." Owan smiled sadly. "I've never been good at much of anything except killing. Not much of a husband, a son, or a brother. I've done a fair job as Warden, though, I think. For a little while, anyway. But that's all." His smile faded. "I can't do this anymore, Tharadis. Be the better man. Be everything I could not."

Owan gripped their father's blade in his hands, twisting it so as to wrench it out of Tharadis's hands. Tharadis saw what he was doing and tightened his grip, but that was just what Owan had wanted him to do. Owan threw himself forward and, weighted against Tharadis's grip, the sword pierced his heart.

The night air by the sea was balmier than up on the plateau, where the city lay. Clouds of insects buzzed around, unnoticed by the people gathered around the lacquered canoe. The shadows cast by flickering torches stabbed into the wet sand were all that moved. A crowd nearly as large as the one that had witnessed the duel circled around the canoe, hands folded and heads bowed.

Only Tharadis, his mother, and his little sister Esta stood at the canoe's side. Tharadis rested a hand on Esta's shoulders. She gripped the gunwale tightly in her own small hands but didn't cry. Their mother, however, leaned forward, hands on the canoe's side and tears in her eyes. The shroud, covered with dunblossoms, only came to Owan's neck. His face looked like their father's had in death. Tharadis knew how broken she felt inside. But she held her head high and, though she cried, radiated a strength that endured. Perhaps she, too, knew of the hearthsflame.

Serena. Tharadis closed his eyes briefly. *Where are you?*

He had wondered if she would come. As Owan's widow, she had an honored place here among the family of the deceased. But she had disappeared utterly since his death. Rellin, the ranking officer of the Watch, had sent search parties out to the lowlands yesterday. Esta, who had recently determined to cause as much trouble for her mother as possible, tried sneaking along with one of the search parties and almost got lost herself. Rellin was kind enough to deliver her, kicking and screaming, back to their mother's house personally.

Rellin. Tharadis had asked him about what had happened with Owan and their father on the day that he died. What Owan had said was true; he had had Tharadis followed, and when he found out what happened, flew into a rage. Owan had immediately tried taking *his own* life, and their father had stopped him. But Owan would not be stopped. They struggled. Father died.

Owan had been crushed. It had been an accident, but he was responsible, nonetheless. The guilt consumed him more absolutely than his grief at losing his wife's heart, and he knew he was not fit even to take his own life.

But Tharadis, Owan had believed, could be. If only he were a little stronger.

He could even be Naruvieth's Warden.

Rellin had not asked Tharadis to take the position. But he made it very clear that Rellin himself was only the acting leader of the Shoresmen and had no designs on being anything more. And the other Shoresmen who had seen the duel had no qualms with Owan's unspoken suggestion.

Tharadis had yet to give him an answer.

Larril, Naruvieth's sole Patterner, strode out of the crowd to stand near the canoe. He had changed out of his typical red tunic for one of coarse, undyed fabric that was nearly the length of a robe. His deep eyes were even wearier of the world than usual. Once he stood next to the canoe opposite Tharadis's mother, he raised his hands to address those gathered.

"Here lies a man sworn to protect us," Larril called out. "A man committed to the safety of all in Naruvieth. Though no man is perfect, perhaps we should look at the comforts we enjoy and the security we feel as testament to this man's worth. He was many things to many of us. Some of us knew him as family. Others only as the sword held high in defense of justice. But all of us knew him, and all of us were touched by him in some way. Let us now reflect on this man's life as it was."

He stepped away as Tharadis circled around to the other side of the canoe. He brushed his fingers along the hilt of his father's sword, laid atop the shroud. Both he and his mother lifted the canoe up from the small wooden platform it rested upon. It was surprisingly light, considering that Owan was not a small man.

Larril said, "And so we commit the body of the man toward its journey across the Astral Sea in search of a better place, in search of Farshores. May it meet the spirit there and be united once again."

Tharadis and his mother waded out to their knees. The sea did indeed look like a sea filled with stars as its gently lapping waves reflected the clear night sky. Once the canoe reached the end of the Calmness a few miles out, where the churning Restless Ocean began, its journey would end. It would never reach Farshores, or any shores for that matter. It would be thrashed to pieces, and its remains and the remains of the man wrapped within it would be pulled into the dark depths.

Death was not the beginning of some new journey. It was merely the end of one.

The canoe drifted across the water, becoming indistinguishable from one of the wavering points of light reflected from the sky. Soon it was lost to sight.

"What will you do about your brother's child?" His mother's voice was muted with sorrow. It wouldn't carry to anyone else, save perhaps Esta and Larril.

"I will protect her."

"Her?" His mother turned to him.

After a moment, Tharadis realized he was answering two questions at once. "Or him, whatever the child turns out to be. But I will make sure that this world is safe for her." *For my child.*

For Serena.

"Then you'd better get to work, Warden." His mother's steps sloshed as she walked back to shore.

Though she couldn't see him, Tharadis nodded.

When he turned, he saw everyone beginning to disperse and return to their homes. Standing there waiting for him, hair black as night, was the woman he loved, carrying the child they had made inside her.

She had come back at the last, to see her husband leave her life forever. Her wet eyes met Tharadis's, and then she, too, turned to head back to her home.

Tharadis let her go.

Chapter 38: The Wishing Well

It seemed as if an eternity had passed since Tharadis had last seen Serena's home. He hadn't known what to expect. Would it look exactly the same as it had months ago? Would it have fallen into disrepair, a product of her despair at losing her husband to her one-time lover? No matter how he imagined it, the one possibility that hadn't occurred to him was, of course, the reality. Seeing it as he walked around the bend in the trail with a wicker basket full of food tucked under his arm, he couldn't help but smile at seeing how wrong she had proved him. Serena's stubbornness was unmatched.

The house had been re-roofed with new shakes, freshly cut by the look of vitality in the bright red wood. It looked like madrona. Leave it to Serena to fell and split one of the hardiest of trees by herself while pregnant. Tharadis saw her in his mind's eye, legs spread apart, sweat soaking through a thin linen shift, determination burning in her eyes as she swung her long-handled axe awkwardly around the bulge of her belly as if defending the world against a horde of sheggam invaders, merely to fix a roof that didn't really need fixing.

Tharadis chuckled to himself when he heard the distant sound of wood being split and realized he could probably see such a scene with his own eyes. He left the basket on the table inside the house and went out the back door toward the sounds of chopping.

Dry, gray moss crumbled like ashes beneath his sandaled feet as he stepped into the drytree thicket behind Serena's house. A scattering of clouds, rare any time of the year, scudded across the sky, sometimes muting the light that streamed through the narrow, needle-like leaves. The air was still, and the wood was silent saving the falling of Serena's axe and crackle of Tharadis's footsteps. Here and there forest creatures, small rodents or mottled gray lizards scurried away at his approach, and the odd bird took to wing as he passed by.

Tharadis felt oddly naked without his father's sword at his hip. He kept wanting to rest his hand on the hilt that was no longer there. He still wore the studded leather swordbelt over his embroidered green tunic, though it felt extravagant compared to the loop of woven hemp he used to wear before he began training for the sword. He supposed that once he was truly Warden, he would have to get himself his own sword, but for now, the Watch's dulled practice swords would have to do.

The chopping stopped. Serena must have paused to take a break. Try as she might to prove otherwise, she had to share her body with another person who required energy, too. It wouldn't be good for the baby if Serena to worked herself to death.

Not the *baby.* Our *baby.*

Tharadis halted as the truth of that suffused him. He was going to be a father. He and Serena would bring new life into the world.

He had known it abstractly, but not until that moment had he realized just how that would change his life—change him. His future rolled out before him like the unfurling of a golden carpet, glittering in the sunlight. He hadn't been sure he'd been ready, that this would be something that he could handle, what with all the change he had been dealing with in his life. At times, he felt overwhelmed, though most of the time it was just a subtle anxiety he felt, one that he could only name as fear of the unknown. The events that would shape his future were still unknown, but at least one thing was certain—he would be a father.

Sweat prickled his skin as the enormity of that responsibility, responsibility for the life of someone else, swept over him. He stared at the ground ahead of him and started plodding forward, scarcely aware of his surroundings as his thoughts came to the forefront of his focus.

Then he heard voices. Voices of men, raised in anger.

Tharadis broke into a trot and drew his sword—or tried to, until he remembered he didn't have it. He cursed himself for a fool as he crashed into a clearing.

His gaze passed over the prone trunks of two madronas, red wood bursting out through its bark. Serena stood much as he had imagined her, though her black hair, skeins of it clinging to her face, had been cut off at her shoulders again. And in her wild eyes was as much anger as fear.

With white knuckles, she adjusted her grip on the long haft of her axe. Her teeth were bared in a snarl as she warily circled around the two men in the clearing with her. She looked as much like a mother boar protecting her young as Tharadis had ever seen a person.

Tharadis recognized the two men with her. Trandsull and Forrigan, two Shoresmen, wearing mail shirts over their tunics, as if they expected there to be danger, though Tharadis couldn't imagine what they expected. Both wore tired, almost resigned, expressions.

Both had their swords out.

What were they doing there? He couldn't see any threats that would have the two of them baring steel. And why were they staring at Serena? Their presence here was so shocking that Tharadis almost couldn't believe it. He didn't at first, until the reality of the situation settled over him.

"We aren't going to judge you, woman," Trandsull was saying. His dark red beard had gone scraggly in recent weeks. His eyes looked dark against his wan skin. "We don't care what you've done. The Astral Sea will deliver you to Farshores or they won't. It's not for us to say. But we can't let the seeds of your crime bear fruit."

"Child of blood," Forrigan muttered, almost trance-like. His blue eyes looked glazed, unfocused. "Child of blood."

Serena didn't say a word. Her eyes were fixed on the two of them. Though she circled them, they stood in place, turning as she moved. Each step took her slightly farther away from them. Angry as she was, she knew she couldn't take on two trained swordsmen.

A small part of Tharadis's mind tried to make sense of what he was seeing. It was impossible that Shoresmen, men sworn to protect the innocent, would threaten Serena for any reason. Another part of him knew that these two men were among the contingent who had fervently opposed Tharadis's rise to the role of Warden of Naruvieth, at least until their cries of outrage found no ears that would listen. They had been Owan's men to the bone.

Owan, who had, in their eyes, died because of his slut of a wife and his traitor of a brother. Owan had either told them, or they had figured it out.

They were going to kill Serena

They were going to kill Tharadis's child.

That small, skeptical part of him that believed there had to be a reason for this died in a firestorm of rage. That small part of him screamed as flesh dripped from its bones until nothing was left, nothing but swirling tornado of blazing, white-hot anger.

Tharadis took a step. A leaf crackled beneath the sole of his sandal.

Without turning from his quarry, Trandsull made a quick gesture with one hand. Forrigan spun to face Tharadis in a two-handed attack stance. It was then that Serena saw him.

She saw what was in his face and staggered back.

In a break from discipline, Trandsull turned his frowning gaze briefly in Tharadis's direction before quickly snapping back to Serena. "Ah," he said. "Tharadis. Well, we may not judge the tramp and her get, but you are another story entirely. You are not fit to be Warden. You are precisely the sort that Naruvieth needs protection *from*. Which is exactly what we're here to do."

A fanatical gleam shone in Forrigan's eye as he held the tip of his broadsword at a level with Tharadis's chest. "The child of blood must die. Blood-soaked, hate dripping, child of blood must *die*."

A cold calm came over Tharadis. The scorching fury didn't relent, but it became focused ... purposeful. The red that had suddenly clouded his vision rolled back, revealing the scene in clarity. In a flash, Tharadis knew what Forrigan would do once Tharadis stepped forward: the man would dip the tip of his blade and swing upward as he lunged, attempting to catch Tharadis off-guard. He doubtless expected Tharadis to attempt to throw his arms in front of his face—typical, for an unarmed man to try to block any blows to his face while leaving his abdomen open to a fatal strike. Failing that, Forrigan would step back, preparing a true thrust, then a feint. Step to the left, attempt to trip Tharadis over the roots of the fallen tree, slash, backslash, thrust, back up a step, feint, thrust.

The realm of all of Forrigan's possible moves blossomed open for Tharadis like a flower. Everything suddenly looked so simple. How did Forrigan possibly think he could defeat Tharadis?

The path of Forrigan's attack, the progression of his forms could be seen in the position of his feet, the twitch of his left thigh muscle, barely perceived, in the strength with which he gripped his broadsword, in the rise and fall of his chest and the space between heartbeats. There was something wrong with the way he was breathing, some sort of sickness in his lungs; Tharadis could see that, too. Forrigan would compensate by shortening his movements.

Tharadis would kill this man. He would do so easily. Forrigan wasn't swordsman enough to defeat him. He wouldn't surprise Tharadis, even if he should somehow change his mind in his attack. Tharadis could see everything, *everything*. No matter what Forrigan did, Tharadis would be prepared. Tharadis could predict every single movement Forrigan's body would make, anticipate it before he made it. Nothing could stop him from killing this man.

Nothing.

Tharadis took another step and sprang forward. He had choreographed this dance in his mind before he made the first move; it was merely a performance. Forrigan wasn't a dim-witted man, but he was a man obsessed with *something* ... Tharadis didn't take the time to wonder what. He only used that knowledge to determine the best way to kill him.

The first upward slice was fast, as Tharadis had suspected it would be, grazing the sleeve of his tunic as he leaned to the side. It had been close, but he knew it would be. Going unarmed against a trained swordsman was never an easy thing, even if Tharadis's success wasn't assured. Every motion Tharadis made would have to be precise; the slightest error would mean death, death for him, death for the woman he loved, death for his unborn child.

He could not, would not fail.

The blade found air three more times, then it was stopped as Tharadis seized the man's wrist, twisted, pivoted on his feet. Forrigan dropped his sword, watched as the bones in his wrist snapped, and screamed. The scream was cut short in a yelp of surprise as Tharadis yanked him around and flipped him over his back. The wedge-shaped edge of the madrona stump crushed Forrigan's spine as he landed on it, forcing the air from his chest with a sharp gasp.

Tharadis snatched the sword from the air and reversed his grip, quickly reassessing Serena's situation. Now that he was armed and Forrigan taken out of the fight, he could focus on the true threat: Trandsull.

Ten paces away. Back at an angle to Tharadis. He was roaring, mid-thrust, spittle spraying from his mouth. Serena was in the wrong position to defend herself; her axe was raised high, evidently to defend against his last strike. Trandsull's sword would rip through her belly, killing her, killing their child.

Tharadis couldn't make it in time, not if he ran as fast as he could. Even if threw the sword at his back ... no, that wouldn't help, it would just push him forward, make him kill her all the ... Why couldn't he see it like he had with Forrigan?

Tharadis had no time to think about it. He spun the sword around, launched it like a over-large throwing axe ... and hoped.

The sword's blade flipped end-over-end. Time slowed.

The tip of the sword flying through the air nicked the back of Trandsull's knee and sailed past to disappear in the foliage. Something snapped. Trandsull's knee buckled and the man jilted to the side.

Still, the edge of Trandsull's blade found flesh.

The head of Serena's axe descended.

The man watched, bemused, as the axe fell. Watched, as it caved in his face like it was an overripe melon.

The sword dropped from his dead fingers.

Serena's eyes rolled back. Tharadis ran to catch her before she fell to the ground, unconscious.

"Hey," came a gentle voice.

Tharadis's eyes snapped open. His head jerked up. Everything around him was dark, wreathed in shadows by the weak light of two small candles. Serena, was she—

"Shhh. It's okay."

Tharadis turned to look at her face. It was pale, but she was smiling from where she lay on her bed. She ran her fingers through his hair, and he felt the tension in his muscles melt away.

He must have fallen asleep, exhaustion having finally claimed him. He'd been tending her all day. She hadn't once woken up. The wound she had taken at her hip was shallow, and he had cleaned it and stitched it up as best as he could, worried that it had somehow been infected, though he had no idea how that could have happened so quickly. Serena seemed feverish from the moment she passed out. As he carried her back to the house, he hoped it was just her pregnancy, or the shock. She looked better now, and he released the breath pent-up inside of him.

He was sitting on the floor next to her bed, legs folded up beneath him. He straightened one with a grimace. Though he hadn't planned on falling asleep at her side, he wondered at his lack of foresight for not even moving a rug to where he now sat.

When he realized just whose fingers were laced with his, all of his worries fell away. He turned to stare at Serena's face, wide-eyed in amazement.

She laughed. "That's not an expression I had ever imagined on your face."

He looked at the swell of her belly, mere inches from his nose.

"Shores ... you're really—"

"Yes, Tharadis." She ran her fingers through his hair again, bringing a tingle of pleasure up his spine. "We're really going to be parents."

He turned to regard her. "I was sure that you—"

"Shush. Come here, idiot." She pulled his head to her breast. "I just needed some time to think about things."

Tharadis nodded against her and closed his eyes. The months without her felt like a nightmare from which he'd just woken. Unreal, unimportant, fading from memory. He wondered how he had lived so long without her, without even bothering to see her, to see how she was. The feel of her, the smell of her ... he knew it was all he needed, all he would ever need in this life.

"I'm sorry," he said.

"Nonsense. You're here now."

"I'm sorry nonetheless." He squeezed her hand. She squeezed back. "Those men today."

She shifted her body slightly. He could feel her eyes on him. "You heard what they wanted."

"I did. But I didn't believe it."

"Believe it. It's real."

He grunted in agreement. "Perhaps 'understand' was the word I meant."

"I guess I'm glad you can't understand them." She jabbed him playfully in the shoulder. "It means there's hope for you yet." He could hear the smile in her voice.

He looked at her, voice grave. "How are you? Really?"

The playfulness wilted from her eyes, yet she forced herself to smile. "I've been awake for a little while, and I've had time to think about what happened." Her smile withered as she looked away. "I killed someone today. I've never had to do that before. I know I should feel something— shame, horror. Something bad. But truly, all I felt when I saw that man dead, dead by my hands, all I could feel was relief. Relief that I was alive, that you were, that our baby was, and that he was not." She met his eyes. "Does that make me a bad person?"

"No," he said, and meant it. Whatever apprehension she had felt melted from her face then. He understood her completely. He felt the same way. Those dead men didn't matter; they had chosen their fates. Serena did matter, and her safety was all he cared about. "And ... what about everything else?" he asked.

It was then that Tharadis could feel the tentativeness in her touch, as if his body were a thatch of stinging nettles.

He didn't pull away. His touch she could bear, he knew; him pulling away, she could not.

"Hungry," was all she said.

The food he cooked for her was the best he had made in some time, though it was a simple meal of fried vegetables and carp, freshly-caught. It had little to do with the food itself. Merely being around Serena made the world come alive, made his senses sharper.

"You were incredible," she said between bites. Her face was near rapturous, and she made no effort to hide it. Her voice, though, betrayed some concern. "You've been practicing."

Since I killed your husband. Tharadis fought to dismiss the bitter thought. It was difficult, but he managed when he glanced up from his meal into her eyes. She loved him, of that there was no doubt. It was his own guilt he was feeling, not any condemnation from her.

"I have," he said. "But, honestly, I couldn't say exactly what I felt. Everything just … seemed to add up for me." He took another bite. "It didn't last long, though. I almost didn't save you."

"But you did." She smiled and reached across the table to touch his hand.

He smiled back. "I wouldn't have it any other way."

She stared at his hand as she absently ran a finger across it. "In the morning, I want to take you somewhere." Tharadis could see the words cost her something, but what, he had no idea.

He nodded after a moment. "I'll come get you after dawn."

"I thought you were done with your foolishness." She pushed her chair back a ways and stood, one hand on her belly. "You'll stay here with me tonight. Just to sleep, mind you." Her voice dropped to nearly a whisper and she glanced away. "I know how you get, you know." She tried to smile, and failed.

She was in pain. More pain than she had ever been in before. He could see it in her words, in the way she held herself. He wondered if it was just the natural progression of her affliction, or if her pregnancy had somehow worsened it.

She got undressed and climbed back into bed, pulling the blanket up to her chin. She rolled over and smiled as she reached a hand out to him. "Come to me. Hold me."

He went to her and held her through the night.

"Where are you taking me?" Tharadis asked, bemused.

With the corners of her mouth turned up in a slight smile, Serena had been gently tugging him along by the hand all morning, since before the

220

sun had risen. The people of Naruvieth had scarcely begun to stir as they had walked through the city, starting their daily tasks bleary-eyed yet with customary eagerness. Tharadis had always thought that those who woke up the earliest were always the most enthusiastic in their work. He had often seen this translate into success.

But they hadn't stayed in the city any longer than to trade a coin for a pair of small pastries, which they ate while walking the streets. Wherever they were going, Serena was in a hurry to get there. And she hadn't told him where she was taking him, no matter how many times he asked. In fact, she hadn't said a word to him since she poked him in the chest to wake him up and said, "Get up. It's time to go."

At times, he had to trot to keep up with her or risk losing his grip on her hand. Pregnancy wasn't slowing her down; neither was her condition. If anything, she only seemed more spurred on than usual. While descending the Face, she had crashed through some overgrown thorn bushes barelegged, with only her sandals and her vermilion dress hemmed just above her knee for protection. Her black hair, half of which was done up in a tail, bounced above her shoulders with each tromping step. Tharadis had known Serena since they were children. They used to go on adventures and sometimes got themselves in trouble, though never with any regrets. It almost felt as if they had gone back to those simpler days.

"Let's rest," she said once they had reached the edge of the drytree forest. She leaned against the gnarled gray trunk of one the drytrees and took a pull from the waterskin slung over her shoulder, glancing at Tharadis with a glint in her eye. Then she handed the skin over and wiped the sweat from her brow as he drank.

"Rest time's over!" She snatched the skin from him before he had gotten a mouthful and bounded into the forest with it. Tharadis took off after her with an inner promise to wrestle her to the ground once he caught up, pregnant or not.

But she was quick. Several times she had disappeared from sight, only to reappear long enough for him to get a sense of where she was. Occasionally, all he had to go by was the rustle of her passage or, once or twice, her teasing laughter. The forest thickened the deeper they went, blotting out much of the light. Tharadis found himself tripping on roots more often than he would ever admit.

Finally, he broke into a clearing. Serena was there, biting into a small apple so red it was almost purple, holding another apple just like it in her other hand. "Here," she said, tossing it to him. "No luck hunting for our lunch, what with all the game you scared off."

He grinned at her as he bit into his apple.

When they had finished eating, Serena crossed to him, took his hands in hers, pressed her lips to his. At first, it was tentative, but then the kiss turned fierce, desperate, fingers twined together into knots, squeezing and tightening. The sensation of pressing against her rippled throughout his body as he felt her tongue meet his. He felt as if he was a part of her, and she a part of him. It was a union unbending, eternal, unyielding.

When she broke away, more winded now than at any time during their morning trek, Tharadis noticed the tears in her eyes.

"Come," she said quietly.

They walked west out of the clearing, and Tharadis suddenly knew where she was taking him.

People often feared what they didn't understand, which was why so many stayed away from the Wishing Well. Tall cliffs surrounded the place on all sides but one, which was itself shielded from casual visitation by rough ground and the thickest part of the drytree forest. Tharadis knew why Serena had wanted to leave so early now; it was past noon by the time they arrived, and it would likely be dark by the time they returned home.

The place still shocked him, even though he had been here a few times before. It was so unlike anything else south of the Rift, so unlike anything else he had ever known. It was how he imagined the world looked north of the Rift.

It was green. Vibrant, brilliant green.

Green grass, green leaves on the trees, green moss growing on boulders. Two waterfalls poured out of nooks in the cliffs, sending up clouds of mist that drifted across the water. They emptied into the basin of the Wishing Well, filling it with fresh water, clean enough to drink and clear enough to see the deepest parts nearly thirty feet below. No one knew where the water came from, as it was impossible to climb the rugged cliffs and follow it to the source. Those few that had tried had gotten turned around and confused, and eventually gave up. Some said that the Wishing Well existed as a result of a fold in the Pattern, and that no one save Patterners should try to plumb the depths of its mysteries. Yet even Larril threw up his hands in frustration and promptly changed the subject at any mention of the Wishing Well. He was among those unsettled by it. Perhaps the most unsettled.

Tharadis couldn't understand their feelings. He was in awe of the place.

From the grassy area that ringed the basin extended a tiny isthmus, barely wide enough for two people to walk across side-by-side, which led to a grass-covered mound in the center. It was for this that the Wishing Well got its name.

Tharadis didn't believe in Farshores, but if any place in the world came close to paradise, it was here.

Serena removed her sandals. Tharadis followed her lead and removed his own. It was as much to feel the springy, damp grass under his toes as it was because the place felt hallowed.

As they walked together towards the island in the center, Tharadis felt a prickling on his skin, the tiny hairs on his arm standing on end. He watched Serena sidelong. She faced forward, calm yet intent, eyes fixed on the destination. He wanted to ask her why she had brought him here, but he knew she would tell him in due time.

Once on the island-like mound, she eased herself down to sitting with her hands in her lap, legs folded in front of her. Tharadis sat down next to her, and once he draped an arm over her shoulders, she leaned back until they were both lying down. A sleek blue bird with bright orange bars slashed across its wings, a kind of bird never seen outside the Wishing Well, swooped past them with a chirp.

"I've learned how to deal with what's happening to me," she said in a strangely flat voice, as if she were talking about someone else. "As much as I can, I suppose. Some things … certain things are too painful to bear. I don't like admitting it. It makes me feel weak to say it aloud, as if I'm not trying hard enough, but it's the truth. I think I've just gotten better at hiding the pain, from myself and everyone else, than truly dealing with it."

Tharadis didn't say anything. Serena was not like other people, who often liked hearing soothing lies. She was smarter than that, more honest with herself. It was one of the things he loved about her.

She took a deep breath and shuddered as she let it out. "The healers say there is no question that I will die when I have our child. The pain of it will kill me." She turned to bury her face in the crook of his arm. "I believe them. No, I knew it was true before they even told me."

Tharadis stared up at the empty sky. He knew he should say something, but words couldn't form in his head. He wasn't even sure he understood what she said. It almost sounded like she was talking about a world without her.

She clutched his tunic tightly and began to silently weep. He pulled her in close. "I'm not going to let anything happen to you, Serena."

"Tharadis," she whispered. "It's already happening. You're going to have to get used to it. It's just the way things are ... the way they are going to be."

He doubted it. Things like that just didn't happen. Serena would be fine; she was strong. She had kept two steps ahead of him all the way here. There was no way this could get the best of her. Everything was going to be—

Time seemed to pass at a strange, jerking pace once her words crushed his understanding of the world. He wasn't even sure what he had done, but some time must have passed since he lost track of himself, judging by the position of the sun. It was as if he had lost consciousness while he kept on talking and moving around, like a sleepwalker. It didn't feel like he was ever really asleep, though, just as if his mind rebelled at everything around him.

The brief touch of Serena's fingers to his cheek brought him back to reality.

She was sitting on the other side of him now, though he couldn't recall how she had gotten there. That he could lose so much control ...

He took her fingers and kissed them. Her eyes were wide. "You scared me there for a moment," she said.

"Serena," was all he could manage.

She nodded. "You've heard the story about how this place was named, haven't you?"

He blinked at the change in subject and felt tears roll down his cheeks. He tried to focus on her question. "I believe so, though it's been a while." He wondered what this had to do with anything, how it could be important in light of the news he had just been given, but he waited for her to go on.

She hooked a strand of hair that had come loose behind her ear. She rested a hand on his chest. "Three people, a mother, a father, and a baby, had been cast out of the city by the Warden of that time, a corrupt man who believed that everyone in Naruvieth belonged to him," she began. "They had been cast out because the father had called that Warden a traitor to his office, saying he was the very sort against which the people needed protection."

She paused, no doubt remembering Trandsull's words, but then continued. "Knowing that executing them would turn the people against him, he banished them from the city, calling them anathema, saying that anyone who helped them would suffer an even worse fate. It was cruel enough to create greater fear of him, but not so cruel that a whipped and stricken people would rise up against him.

"So no one helped the three of them, even though they would starve. They wandered off into the wilderness, living off the land as best as they could, though the Warden's enforcers made even this difficult.

"They made it into an empty place, dry and dusty and windswept, completely devoid of living things, before they could go no further. They were blocked off by cliffs on all sides except the way they came. They were starving and too exhausted to go on.

"They had been just, good people, made to suffer because of one evil man's lust for power. And they would die because they stood up to fight against him, to fight for what was right.

"As the three of them lay down to die, each of them, even the little baby, begged the World Pattern to help them. Each of them made a wish. While the World Pattern does not grant wishes, it does love virtue, and so it shaped this place into what it now is so that they could look upon beauty before they left the world, so that they could remember life fondly. And so it has stood since then."

She bent to kiss him lightly, a mere brushing of their lips. "This is where I want to have our baby. Here, in the Wishing Well."

With all the strength left within him, he nodded.

"Help me with this." She untied her belt and struggled to pull her arm out of her sleeves.

"Are you sure?" Even as he asked, he helped her out of her dress. He already knew the answer.

When she lay back against the grassy slope of the hill, he kissed her lips, kissed her breasts, kissed their child in her belly. He could have sworn he felt a kick. He began to remove his own tunic.

"Yes," she said, breathless. "Let me see beauty once more, so I can remember life fondly."

There you went to have our child, two weeks later. The people I trusted the most, my mother, my sister, Rellin, and two healers helped you walk all across town. The healers said it was dangerous, but you didn't care. Screaming in pain at each contraction, you walked, or let us carry you, but you would not change your mind. You would have your baby at the Wishing Well.

The baby crowned almost as soon as you lay down on the island. You insisted on a water birth. The healers did what you asked.

I held your hand as they delivered our baby. Your hand shook and was soaked with sweat, so much that I almost couldn't hang on. But hang on I did. I would never let go, not as long as you needed me.

You screamed. Oh, how you screamed. It tore my heart apart to hear your pain, to know how much you suffered. But I wanted to know. I wanted to be there with you. I wanted you to believe that maybe the load you carried could be lighter if someone was there to carry it with you. I wanted you to know that you weren't alone.

You looked so pale, so thin, yet when it was finally over, when you opened your eyes to see the face of our daughter, I saw all the love in the world there. More than I ever saw when you looked at me. I couldn't possibly be jealous of what I saw in your face. All I could do was rejoice that anyone could ever feel that way, that such an expression was even possible. I was in awe of you then. And I was in awe of our daughter, that she could do such a thing to you.

You smiled and said, "Beauty, one last time." You let go of my hand, and you were gone.

The world changed in a great number of inconsequential ways. That same day, I just so happened to become Warden in truth. Rellin said that I had lost something precious, so I knew what it meant to protect. He said I became a man that day. He said I was ready.

In front of a crowd of a thousand people, I swore to protect the people of Naruvieth from injustice and violence. I also swore to protect your child … the child of my brother.

That was a day of shame.

I sometimes wonder if I should have claimed her as mine and defended her against anyone who thought her unfit for life, as if my transgression were hers too. Rellin told me that not claiming her would appease the men who still supported my brother. He asked me what it would be like if I lost her, too.

I had failed to protect you back then. I guess I didn't believe I had what it took to protect her, either.

The only thing that mattered to me from that point on was our daughter. Nina is amazing. If only you had gotten a chance to know her. She is your daughter utterly and totally; all she got from me was my ears … which is fine by me. She's a wonderful, good-hearted little girl. You would be proud of her.

Some have said there is balance in the World Pattern, that her birth is the balance to your death. I know that's not true. Her birth was a result of something we chose. She is our daughter. She does not belong to the Pattern.

The responsibility for what happened to you … that, that was the Pattern.

That's the problem with the story of the family and the Wishing Well. The Pattern doesn't care about virtue, about truth or love or justice. It lets the best among us die for no reason.

I made a wish that day at the Wishing Well, the day our daughter was born. I wished I would see you again.

But the world took you from me anyway.

And I don't know that I can ever forgive it.

Before Tharadis knew it, bars of daylight streaking through the slats in the window shutter were moving over his face as he lay in his cold bed in Garoshmir. He hadn't slept at all. His memories, the memories of all he had lost, saw to that.

He pushed himself up to a sitting position, then stood and crossed to a basin filled with cool water. He splashed it on his face and dried himself with a rag. He felt more awake. Serena was gone, true … but he still had a job to do. It wouldn't do for him to fall asleep in the middle of it.

Forcing his memories back into the shadowed corners of his mind, Tharadis left the room to get ready. It was time to speak to the Council.

Chapter 39: Flight from Falconkeep

F inding a way out of Falconkeep was proving impossible. Nina and Chad trudged through the shadow world for a long time. Daylight never came to this place. All she ever saw were the images in the walls, and she could never tell day from night in them.

The shadow world was a maze, but Chad navigated it with confidence. Or at least he seemed to. But as time wore on, she saw his confidence begin to crack, replaced by a worried frown. No matter how confident he seemed, they couldn't find a way out, and Nina could see it was wearing on him as much as it was her.

They often snuck into the kitchen, filling sacks with food before dashing back into the shadow world. No one saw them. Luckily, Falconkeep was large enough that it was impossible for the Falconkeepers to look for them everywhere at once.

But they couldn't stay in the shadow world forever.

The two of them sat hunched with their backs against the rippled stone. Nina was holding a piece of hard cheese in her hands, nibbling it thoughtfully, while Chad was working on a piece of bread.

She paused, cocking her head to look at him. "How did Vidden reach through?"

Chad finished chewing and swallowed before speaking. "I can't just walk in and out of the shadow world. There are doors in the shadows. I have to open them, and I have to shut them. If I don't, then other people can come in too. That's how you're here."

Nina frowned. "But what about in the room with the …" She trailed off. She didn't even want to mention the stones.

A shadow of the old Chad came back as a small smile spread across his lips. "I'm very good at opening the doors."

Nina went back to her cheese. Chad must be good, to have opened it so fast. Once they were finished, they brushed the crumbs from their hands, slung the sacks of food over their shoulders, and continued looking for a way out. However, Nina soon found that the two of them weren't even looking at the forks in the tunnel or the images in the walls anymore, only where they were putting their feet.

"Nina," Chad said softly. "Can you hear your mother?"

She shook her head. "Not since the first time." Not since she'd been in the box.

She shivered, remembering that awful place. But there was something about it that seemed strange. "My mother told me someone was coming. Then you pulled me here." She looked at him. "Was there anyone else nearby?"

Chad shook his head. "No. I checked. Alicie and Vidden were the only ones down there, and I waited for them to leave." His eyes widened. "Your mother must've been talking about me."

Nina nodded. "Which means she can see in here." She paused a moment. "But why doesn't she help us?"

"Maybe she can't speak to us in here for some reason." Chad shrugged. "I don't really know much about ghosts."

Ghosts. I can talk to ghosts. Now that she thought about it, she knew that's exactly what her ability was. Realizing this made her feel a little better. As if she understood what she needed to do with herself.

Once she got out of Falconkeep, that is.

If she ever got out of here.

Hopelessness overcame her. She squatted down, trying to bite back the sobs and failing utterly. Chad was there, standing by her side. "Hey," he said, his own voice betraying tears. "We'll get out of here. I promise."

"Mommy," Nina whispered. "Mommy, where are you?"

She heard something. Far in the distance.

A voice.

Nina shot to her feet. "I heard her!" She started running. "This way, come on!"

She thought of the stones then, those screaming voices, trapped there forever. Those were ghosts, too. They were stuck in that room. Ghosts couldn't be everywhere all at once. Maybe they could only be in one place. And maybe Nina's mother was just somewhere else, looking for her.

She ran up steps cut into the glassy stone, around bends, through narrow gaps and down passages that seemed to wrap around on themselves as Chad struggled to keep up with her. The passages followed no pattern that Nina could see; the twisting tunnels certainly didn't match the layout of Falconkeep. Every step of the way, she heard her mother's voice calling, getting louder, and when it got softer, she doubled back.

It wasn't long before she found herself running in circles. "This way," Chad said, waving her to follow. "I think I know where she's leading us." Nina followed him, and sure enough, her mother's voice was soon louder than ever before, whispering her name.

They came to a place where an image shone through the wall, an image of a place Nina hadn't seen but knew nonetheless. In this room she could see the ghostly flicker of a candle, as well as the shape of a box a little bit shorter than she was. It was the same room where Chad had freed her. It was where her mother had last spoken to her. Perhaps her mother believed Nina was in there still.

Chad pressed his fingers into the image, darkness flooding out from them like spilled ink. He met Nina's eyes, and with an encouraging nod, he pulled her through the darkness and back into the real world.

Nina took in a sharp breath as she stepped onto cut stone, the air tasting drier and smokier than in the shadow world. Her eyes took in details that her mind had only guessed at before, when she'd had the bag over her head: the box resting atop two barrels, herbs hanging racks on one wall, a bench with the candle on the other. A large bag of nails sat near the candle, its contents spilled out carelessly. The hammer they had used was nowhere in sight. The candle was nearing the end of its life, wax pooling around it, the uncertain flame casting shifting shadows across the room.

The voice of Nina's mother was silent. "Mommy?" she whispered.

She heard something else. The soft scrape of boot leather on stone.

Heart pounding wildly, Nina stepped back toward the shadow she'd come through, but it was solid stone now. Chad must've already closed the door to the shadow world.

Chad. Nina glanced to the side where she expected him to be, but he was gone. Nina was alone in there, with only one door leading out of the room.

Someone stepped into that doorway, wearing the blue and gray of Falconkeep.

Alicie.

Nina pressed herself against the wall, willing herself to disappear, but Alicie's eyes were fixed on her as if Nina were the only thing in the world. A tight, joyless smile spread across the other girl's face.

"They don't think Vidden will make it," Alicie said, her voice flat. She stepped into the room, arms loose at her side. "He got lost in the passageways, bleeding everywhere. He was nearly dead before anyone found him." She chuckled. "All of us can do special things, *amazing* things, but not a one of us knows how to fix a simple wound like that. Healing isn't something that matters much here."

Nina slid across the wall, trying to put distance between her and Alicie, but ended up in the corner as the other girl slowly closed the distance between them. Alicie lifted her arms once she reached the box in the middle of the room, resting them on the lid she herself had hammered shut.

"Not that it matters," Alicie continued. "Vidden had a couple of years left in him at most. Likely fewer." Without touching the wood, Alicie moved her hand over the box's lid. A thin ribbon of wood peeled away from it as if an invisible blade were shaving it. Her eyes never left Nina's face. "He's fortunate, you know. It's one of the rules of Falconkeep. It's forbidden to kill yourself. The best you can ever hope for is someone else killing you." Her smile widened. "Lucky for you."

Alicie's smile vanished as she thrust her hand out.

Nina screamed as burning pain erupted in her wrist. Twin lines of blood oozed as her flesh slowly parted, cut like a ribbon.

Through the agony, she caught a glimpse of a shadowy form behind Alicie. Alicie shrieked as the form grabbed her hair, yanking her down.

It was Chad. His face was twisted with rage, so twisted that Nina scarcely recognized him. He raised his other hand, closed in a tight fist, the sharp ends of nails sticking out from between his fingers.

Before Alicie could raise either of her hands to attack him, Chad repeatedly punched his fist into her throat, nails ripping it to bloody shreds. When Alicie's arms fell limp, Chad let go of her hair. Alicie's body slumped to the ground.

Chad tossed the bloody nails away and squatted down next to Nina. "I'm sorry," he said. "I was too late to stop her."

Nina shook her head, eyes blurring from the tears. "You stopped her just fine."

"I … I waited too long." He glanced down. "I was scared."

"Me too."

Chad's face paled as he inspected her arm. Two cuts corkscrewed around it. They looked shallower than they felt. "I think I know where some bandages are," he said.

Nina shook her head and ripped a strip of cloth from the hem of her dress. It wasn't clean, but at least it would stop the bleeding. She didn't want to end up like Vidden. "We've got to get out of here." Though she knew she wouldn't see, Nina glanced around the room. "Mother, are you there?"

I'm always here, my love.

Tears spilled from Nina's eyes in relief. "How do we get out of here?"

The voice was silent a long moment. *Your friend walks in the darkness. Is that where you were before?*

"Yes."

Good. Let your hands be your guide. A twisting of the air can trick your eyes, but it cannot trick your hands. Trust your hands to get yourself through the darkness. When your eyes and your hands do not agree, then you'll know you're on the right path.

A twisting in the air … an illusion? That must be how Lora Bale was keeping them there. "That will get us out of Falconkeep? Then what?"

Head northeast until you see the city. Our family waits for you there. I will do my best to warn them you are coming, but they aren't special like you. Your father may heed me, though.

Her father? Wasn't her father with her mother in Farshores? Nina let the odd comment pass, mind overflowing with enough as it was. "Thanks, mommy. I love you."

I love you, too. More than life itself. Now go, my dear. Go and do not stop.

The sound of running boot steps reached them, getting louder. Chad grabbed Nina's hand and quickly the two of them disappeared into shadow.

Chapter 40: Insects

A swath of daylight fell across Marinack's wings. The subtle heat from it occasionally caused the skin stretched across them, the color of boiled pork, to quiver, but Marinack didn't flex her wings as she would've liked. She didn't want to risk waking any of the ferals again. It had been a chore taking care of the last one that had woken up and escaped. Not because she had had to kill it—that brief surge of ecstasy she felt as its blood poured over her claws had been the only benefit of the ordeal—but because she had had to dispose of it and the human bodies it had left in its wake, all without being detected. That was why Marinack was here: to make sure that the Patterner Orthkalu's plan wasn't fouled by the unpredictable nature of the feral sheggam hibernating below her.

Their hibernation was the result of some Pattern made by Orthkalu; Marinack had no idea how it functioned. She only knew that the Pattern's hold over them was tenuous. If it hadn't been, there would've been no problem to begin with. Ferals tended to live up to their name. They were barely more than beasts, hardly capable of conscious thought—they were too overwhelmed by the Song of Pain to function as well as the warriors, or even the smokers. It wasn't until they created their own harmony that the Song of Pain was reduced from a maddening cacophony to a mere susurration of constant gnawing, a constant, endless scraping of the nerves that was as much sound as sensation. Only then could the rudiments of thought form.

None of the sheggam were fully immune to the Song of Pain, though. Sometimes, Marinack herself would have to flex her wings and fly just to fight back against the Song of Pain, scratch the itch that never went away, or risk going as mad as the ferals. That was what had happened the last time, and was why one of them had escaped, but there was nothing to be done for it. She had needed to get out of that cloying pit Orthkalu had sentenced them to.

Comfort, even in the relative sense, was an alien concept for the sheggam, but Marinack was really beginning to appreciate its absence. She was crouched on the cold, wet stone of her perch, completely surrounded by a rough tube of fungus-spotted natural stone—though everything about it seemed so unnatural. It was too dark, its edges too gritty and sharp.

And the constant smell of *rot*. There were no corpses she could see that would have caused this kind of stench, no traces of any life anywhere in this pit. Nor had they seen any as their army made the long trek through the hot, barren tunnels that led here—had there been, the ferals would have killed it. The stench seemed to come from the very air, or maybe from the stones themselves. The smell had been present ever since they entered the ground back in Sheggamur, wafting up in vents. She hadn't been able to decide if she hated it, or if it comforted her. It was both foreign and familiar, nostalgic and nauseating. In the end, though, she decided that she hated it. Anything that confused her so much was a plague unto itself.

She scraped her claws against the stone, gritting her teeth against the harsh sound she herself had made. Even her teeth itched. Every muscle in her body ached to break free of this prison of waiting. She knew she couldn't. Timing, Orthkalu had said, was everything, and only Marinack could make sure things went as planned. Only she could be trusted.

That trust was all that separated from the beasts below her.

However, there were circumstances that could change the timing. Discovery was one. That was why Marinack had killed that feral and cleaned up its mess. Only the ruler of these reeking stone towers, a human woman named Shad, knew that Marinack and the ferals were down here. If anyone else knew that sheggam had burrowed under the Hated Wall, they would collapse the tunnels, or flood them. Orthkalu had set up several Patterns that acted like tripwire alarms, keyed to Marinack's hearing. Again, she didn't know how they worked, only that it wasn't mere proximity that would set them off—thousands of humans lived around these stone towers, swarming about them like insects. No, it was something closer to discovery. If someone was on the verge of merely *knowing* that the sheggam were here, Marinack would hear a clear, sharp sound. She could then signal the ferals to awaken and begin their rampage.

Marinack often found herself straining to listen for that sound. Orthkalu could do things that she couldn't believe or even begin to understand, but he, like everything in this world, wasn't perfect. What if he had made a mistake with this Pattern? What if a human had discovered them, but Marinack hadn't heard the sound? What if she *had* heard it, but mistook it for something else?

Uncertainty wormed through, and it had for days. With nothing else to do, she listened, cursing the ferals whenever they twitched or yelped in their sleep.

Now, the pressure was almost too much to bear, almost greater than the burden of her responsibility. She was becoming convinced that timing was meaningless to Orthkalu, that it was all about *control* with him. Besides, what difference would a few days matter? They would kill humans no matter what, and the humans were helpless to stop it.

Narrowing her eyes, she looked up. It was late morning, judging by the brightness. Not the best time to stage an attack, but the humans were doubtless fat with complacency. They had been protected by the Hated Wall for centuries; there was no way they were ready for a sheggam invasion from beneath one of their own cities, even in daylight.

Despite every instinct screaming at her to rouse the ferals and fly up the tube and out into the sky, she waited. And waited. And waited.

Her patience was finally rewarded.

A clear chime sang through her mind, drowning out all other sounds, and then faded away.

It was time.

Marinack let out a roar that tore at her throat, one that echoed madly throughout the tube. Feral eyes, alight with sudden hunger, flashed open. The warriors and the smokers that had come with them also roused, but without the mindless ferocity of the ferals—their eyes were hungry, but not without sense. As the echoes of Marinack's bellow began to fade, the ferals, too, let out a roar. Their voices created a Song of Pain of their own, one that would haunt the humans as much as it did them.

The ferals wasted no time, bounding up stone protrusions, climbing easily with their claws crunching into the stone, making holds where there were none. Marinack took a moment to savor the sight. It was magnificent to watch—muscles flexing beneath pale skin, a horde of bodies flooding up the walls of the tube, bent on nothing but the rending of flesh. It wasn't long before the first of the ferals reached the end of the tube and crawled over. She couldn't hear the screams of the humans here, in this tower of stone and stench, at least not yet, but Marinack knew it would only be a matter of time before the screams of the injured and dying would be heard from shore to shore.

The itching in Marinack's teeth finally overwhelmed her. A few beats of her wings, and she was above the rim of the pit, airborne. Below, a handful of the ferals began to tear each other apart in their haste to taste blood. Marinack let them, and pulled back her lips to expose her sharp teeth. A few dead ferals wouldn't make a difference. There were plenty more where they came from.

The wind whistled in her ears as Marinack flew out of the tube and circled about, eyeing the ferals as they overcame the human settlement on this tower. Destruction spread below like the ashes of a paper held over a candle flame—slow, but relentless, absolute, and irreversible. First handfuls of humans fell, then dozens, then hundreds. The panic spread even more quickly. Marinack had circled only twice before the pandemonium spread to the second tower. Soon, all twelve of them would be overcome.

Marinack longed to join the fray, but a more powerful urge overcame her. As she turned her head west, the chime filled her head again. The ones who had discovered the presence of the sheggam were still out there. The desire to kill them, to tear them to pieces, throbbed through Marinack's body—likely the result of Orthkalu's Pattern, but Marinack didn't mind. The yearning for blood felt almost as good as feeling it wet her claws.

She could feel how close they were by the changes in the sound's pitch. They were close—*very* close. Marinack could see farther than most birds, and though the sunlight hampered her greatly, it wasn't long before she could pick out two figures on horseback, briskly riding along a lightly wooded trail.

Quivering with anticipation, Marinack pulled in the tips of her wings and prepared for the dive.

"What's wrong?" Stem asked.

"Quiet, idiot." Penellia pinched the bridge of her nose with her eyes closed. Then she sighed. She almost apologized, but she didn't want Stem to think he could suddenly become impertinent with his questions. She did, however, soften her tone somewhat. "I'm not sure what's wrong. Something …"

Something in the Pattern she had been tracing. A fold, deliberately placed. And subtle, too. Only a few Patterners alive today were capable of something like this. Yet the flavor of this fold in the Pattern tasted all wrong to her. Its signature was impossible for her detect. It was far too … alien.

Which only meant that her prior suspicions had been correct. She snapped the reins and led her beast on, Stem following suit after a moment's hesitation. Their mounts carefully picked their way down a slightly stony slope wending through the trees. Tall ferns whipped at Penellia's knees, but at least the morning mist had burned away. She was tired of being in the saddle and wanted a bath. She told herself that she would take one once she arrived at Twelve Towers and sorted this mess out, but she knew it was only a comforting lie.

The sheggam. Here, in the Accord.

How?

The real question was how to deal with them. If they truly were here, they must be hiding in Twelve Towers, in the hollow pillars of volcanic rock themselves. They were there; that's all that mattered. They hadn't yet made themselves known, but that could change at any moment. Penellia had to do something before it was too late, but she couldn't decide what action to take until she learned more. She had to go to Twelve Towers and see for herself.

The trees ahead thinned, and Penellia could finally catch glimpses of the nearest of the towers. They were closer than she had thought. The cylindrical stone formation was squat. Signs of human habitation spiraled up its steeply inclined sides: walkways carved into its sides; light, wooden structures attached to them; a network of scaffolding holding it all together. It bustled with activity, more than she had expected given Twelve Towers' current ruler's penchant for control.

Historians had long wondered why the founders of Twelve Towers had built their city on the sides of the towers, rather than at their bases. Some had thought that it was more easily defensible, but that was simply not true: the collection of structures wrapped around each tower was so precarious, so close to the brink of collapse, that shoddy construction workers could be as dangerous as saboteurs. A committed siege would devastate Twelve Towers, high ground or not. No, Penellia had studied the people alive in Andrin's time, the same time Twelve Towers had been settled. They were weary and beaten, but they had also survived the greatest threat ever to face humanity. Many of them were filled with ambition, ambition that even the sheggam hadn't crushed—something that Penellia could scarcely imagine, particularly in this age of mediocrity. Penellia imagined that the founders of Twelve Towers had decided to live on the towers' sides simply because of the practical and engineering challenges it presented. Such challenges would seem like nothing to those who had fought the sheggam and lived to tell about it. Building Twelve Towers would have been nothing short of a celebration of their own survival.

Penellia would have loved to take a moment to marvel at this rare showing of human ingenuity, but the odd feeling she had gotten when she had stumbled into that fold began to grow into a headache, pulsing more heavily with every passing moment. It was getting hard to think. She called them to a stop again and leaned against her saddle horn, staring at her mount's neck, to catch her breath.

Something was very, very wrong.

Stem craned his neck and shielded his eyes from the sun. "I see something. In the sky. Flying."

"As opposed to swimming?" Penellia snorted. "Considering there are only a few forms of creature capable of flight, I'm wagering it's a bird." Sometimes she wondered how she had survived this long with Stem at her side.

Stem's nose wrinkled up as he squinted. "No, I don't think so."

Not a bird? Penellia didn't like the sound of something flying that wasn't a bird. She lifted her head. The sky was bright, and she could only make out a silhouette. But Stem was right. It was too large to be a bird.

It was coming from Twelve Towers. Headed their way.

She realized what that fold in the Pattern had been. An alarm.

"Shores take me." She spun her horse around and heeled it into a hard gallop. "Stem, ride! *Ride!*"

Chapter 41: Patterns in the Dirt

The pounding of hooves jarred Penellia's teeth. For once, she wished she had brought a sturdier mount, one used to galloping through rough terrain. But how could she have known that she would need one?

How could she have possibly known that the only thing between her and death would be the speed of her horse?

Leaning low in the saddle and clutching the reins desperately, she glanced over her shoulder. Thankfully, Stem had heeded her advice for once and was riding right behind her. The expression on his face was so serious, so fiercely determined that Penellia had almost thought it was someone else.

She caught a glimpse of shadow not far behind them and moving quickly. Foliage and tree branches slapped at her face and arms, and slowed her horse, but Penellia was grateful nonetheless. She feared to think what would happen if they reached open ground.

She steered her horse toward thicker vegetation, careful not to ride into an area wide enough to allow the beast to fly beneath the tops of the trees and reach her and Stem. Soon, though, she could see the shadow at her side, keeping pace with her horse. It would only be a matter of time before it descended.

A *flying* sheggam! The histories had never mentioned such a thing. They had always been vague, unfortunately, allowing the imaginations of the generations since to fill in the gaps. Penellia wished they had been more academic back then, but she couldn't rightly blame them now. She was quickly learning how fear filled the mind, making her think of only one thing: escape.

The path was rugged, and her horse was already blowing. She couldn't keep up this pace, not without killing her horse. And what if Stem's horse fell first? Would she stop to help him, or would she take the opportunity to ride on while her pursuer was busy? She honestly didn't know what she would do, and that scared her. Not because she would leave him to die, but because she was thinking about what she would do to save him.

239

The wing-shaped shadows on the ground next to her flapped once, and then again. The sheggam was soaring, barely using any effort to chase them. No matter how far Penellia and Stem rode, the sheggam would follow them with ease. They had no chance of outdistancing it.

Only one thought rang out in her head, like the tolling of a distant bell: *I was too late, I was too late, I was too late.*

Out of the corner of her eye, she caught sight of a thick patch of vegetation. She rode toward it. Her horse slowed, but she spurred it on and they crashed through it. Suddenly she was falling; at the same time, she heard something snap. Her horse screamed and fell out from under her.

For a few moments of confusion, Penellia was airborne, slowly spinning. When she finally crashed to the ground, all the air rushed out of her lungs. She clutched at her chest, struggling to breathe, eyes watering against the pain. A few paces away her horse thrashed and screamed, one of its legs bent at a sickening angle.

Mere seconds passed before she drew in her next agonizing breath, but it felt like an eternity. She rolled off her back and scrambled to her feet as best she could, and started running, each step ringing oddly, leaving her horse behind. Perhaps it would distract the sheggam long enough to buy her escape. The late morning sun warmed her back—she was no longer under the cover of the trees.

She was standing on the Runeway. It stretched off to the northwest, its dark metallic surface gleaming dully.

She spun, panicked, looking for something to hide behind. She had been running the same direction she had been riding—which was now *away* from the trees. Here, where she stood, there was nothing to hide behind. She briefly considered going back to the tree line, but that was where her horse was. If her horse was to serve as a distraction, she wanted to get as far away from it as possible. Still, her head pounded, clouding her thoughts. Where was Stem?

The frantic clang of horseshoes on the surface of the Runeway answered her question. She turned and saw him riding toward her. The sword he kept packed away for scaring the odd highwayman, which until now had been merely for their own assurances rather than any practical benefit, was unsheathed and in his hand, gleaming. He rode tall in the saddle, fear absent from his eyes. Skinny, young, stupid Stem, now looking to Penellia like some hero out of legend. Relief flooded her at the sight of him, and tears filled her eyes. She almost believed that he could save them.

Almost.

The shadow once again passed over her just as Stem slid out of his saddle and began running towards Penellia. A thump behind her announced the creature's landing. Penellia turned to see what she faced.

Pale skin stretched across its wings. Its wide, elongated face was more like a dog's muzzle than a man's. Muscles packed its wide, hunched shoulders. Penellia could see the slight bulge of breasts under its ratty mail shirt. A female? Penellia couldn't tell; there was nothing else to indicate the creature's sex.

Greasy, black hair hung around its head in clumps. Solid crimson orbs, with only the slightest hint of yellow indicating pupils. Watching Penellia as if she were an annoyance, less than an insect. In any other creature, they would have been seductively beautiful, but in this *thing*, they only seemed to highlight its monstrosity.

Along its arms was a ridge of bony protrusions, skin stretched across them. They were heavily scarred, and Penellia realized they were likely as deadly as its claws.

A sheggam, standing before her. "I can't believe what I'm seeing," Penellia muttered, unsure of whom she was speaking to.

Stem gripped Penellia's arm tightly—she hadn't heard him approach—and then pulled her behind him protectively, the tip of his sword held out in front of him.

"What are you doing, you fool." There was no scorn in Penellia's voice. Only pleading. "You'll get yourself killed."

She felt the quivering in Stem's grip. He was shaking with fear, but his voice was steady. "Yeah," he said. "I'm dead either way. I can't fight this thing. But you can, if I buy you time."

"What?" But then she knew what he meant: she was the most skilled living Patterner in the Accord. She had spent the most recent part of her life only reading Patterns, but it wouldn't take much to remember how to work the other half of her magic.

"Go," Stem shouted, pushing her back. "Go!"

Penellia stood a moment, speechless, before she saw the sheggam surge forward.

She ran.

Once past the edge of the Runeway, she fell to her knees. The ground here was dry, but not as sandy as she would have liked. It would have to do. She swept away the largest of the stones and brushed the earth as flat as she could with a single swipe of her arm. Then she grabbed a stick and started drawing.

At first, the Pattern eluded her. She merely drew preparatory symbols, the kind she practiced a thousand times when she was still a student at the Academy. These she could do without thought. But once it came to the important part, to the strokes that would create a Pattern that could change the world around her, her mind went blank. Still, her head throbbed. And though she forced herself to focus on her task, she could hear the sounds of Stem's fight. She could hear his frantic shouts, his panicked breathing. The beast was toying with him.

Stem, she thought, her throat tightening. But the name triggered something in her mind. There were patterns found in nature, that even those with mundane training could see—especially in living things. Things like plants.

Stem. Branch. Leaf. Flower. A cascade of images and connections formed in her mind. She understood the Pattern her imagination made. She set to making it real.

Sharp, quick gestures, varying in speed and intensity. Some were deeper in the dirt, some shallower. The Pattern she created was simple, but it was a work of beauty.

She realized that it wouldn't only kill the sheggam. It would kill Stem, too.

Stem's sudden scream finished wetly. Penellia could hear him breathing, but she didn't look up. *Please, Stem. Live just a little bit longer.* She hated wishing for his prolonged suffering, but each moment the sheggam was distracted helped her chances. And as Stem said, he would be dead soon anyway.

Only a few more strokes, and the Pattern would be complete. Only a few more strokes, and his pain would end.

Only a few more—

A wet, ripping sound. Stem was silent. Against her better judgment, Penellia glanced to the side. The sheggam tossed Stem's limp body—no, only *the top half*—away, discarding it like so much trash, and stalked toward Penellia, crimson eyes fixed on her. Penellia hurried to finish the Pattern.

The stick caught on a root hidden in the dirt. It snapped.

No.

Quickly, she finished the last stroke with her finger.

She turned as the sheggam reached for her with blood-soaked claws.

An unseen force, like the footstep of an invisible giant, yanked one of the sheggam's wings down, pulling the sheggam back. The other wing folded in a way that looked *wrong* to Penellia's eyes—accompanied with a satisfying snap. In a choked voice, the sheggam screamed in agony and began to thrash about blindly. It wasn't dead, but nor was it coming for her.

Grinning, Penellia rose to her feet, wincing when she put her weight on her right ankle. She must have twisted it. Favoring that leg, she walked over to where Stem's sword had fallen and picked up it. Mindful of the sheggam's thrashing, Penellia walked over to its head and held the sword over it.

"See you in Farshores, bitch." Penellia drove the sword down with a crunch.

The sheggam went limp.

Penellia fell to her knees, suddenly overcome by exhaustion. She had done it. She, a fat scholar, had killed a sheggam and survived. Stories would be told about her for decades. She laughed and wept, utterly overwhelmed.

Stem's horse stood a ways off, wary and watching. At least it hadn't run off, though she wouldn't have blamed it if it had. She might be able to make it in time to warn the Council if she left now.

A rustling in the trees drew her attention.

Her skin prickled as she turned. Worry turned to abject horror.

Hundreds—no, *thousands*—of the sheggam burst out of the trees, running on all fours, most of them naked, snarling like dogs.

A half dozen pairs of crimson eyes turned her way. The beasts' paths veered towards where Penellia knelt, helpless.

As they leapt for her, she took one final look at Stem's dead face. *See you in Farshores, Stem.*

Soon.

She felt regret, then terrible pain, then nothing.

Chapter 42: To the Hall

The road to the Dome and the Spire, which housed the Council Chambers, was bumpier than usual. The wheels of Yarid's carriage seemed to seek out every loose paving stone there was and slam into it with a vengeance, even jarring Yarid's teeth once or twice. He decided he knew what the Council's first order of business should be—fixing this road. Or maybe second, after the Runeway. But it should definitely be on the agenda. It was an important road after all.

The drizzle had finally stopped, and the sun had come out through breaks in the clouds. Yarid took the opportunity to throw open the shutters and lean with one arm hooked over the narrow sill, gazing impassively at the thickening crowds on the street in the growing warmth of the sun. It was still early yet, but the Council session was getting closer, and more and more people usually had business in the Council District around this time. Yarid liked to arrive early at the Council Hall for a number of reasons, not least of which was the fact that his carriage wouldn't be crammed wheel-to-wheel with other Councilors' carriages along the way. Some of the blunter and stupider Councilors loved taking such opportunities to corner people since there was nowhere for them to go, sometimes for several minutes at a time. It was tacky and boring, and so Yarid had decided long ago to avoid putting himself in those situations.

But as a particularly boxy yellow carriage, led by a team of ill-fed horses and trimmed in garish orange, trundled up next to his, he realized he might not be so lucky today.

"Councilor Yarid." A round, grinning face with narrow-set eyes slowly leaned in to fill the other carriage's window.

Yarid stifled a sigh. "Minister Aelor. I certainly didn't expect to run into you like this today."

"Yes, and I'd wager you didn't *want* to run into me today, either." Aelor combed his sausage fingers through the curly, black mess of whiskers he insisted was a beard. A bad habit of his, and one he engaged in often.

Yarid pasted an ingratiating smile on his face. "Nonsense. I've always got time for the Minister of Disasters."

"It's Minister of Disaster *Relief*." Aelor shook his head, nearly tossing off the small tassled hat of his office. "I can't believe how shoddy your memory is. I have to remind you of this every time I see you."

"Ah yes, I apologize." Yarid bowed his head slightly in a mimicry of contrition. "At least I remember the important things."

Aelor's gaze sharpened as he bared his teeth in a fierce smile. "I hope you're referring to the matter of the small debt you owe me."

"Indeed I am. I look forward to the time when I am finally able to offer what is owed."

Aelor's chuckle was high, like a tiny dog's frantic barking. He gripped the edge of his window as he leaned forward. "Of course you are. No one, not even a mighty Councilor of the Wall, wants to be indebted to a Minister of my standing."

That much is true, thought Yarid, *because you stand as high as a worm.* "I hate leaving my balance sheet like this. I just wish I could be of more use to you, Minister."

"Well." Aelor sat back, apparently satisfied with Yarid's level of groveling. "I too dislike the status of your balance sheet, Yarid. I shall think of something you can do to settle the score soon, perhaps." He watched Yarid, eyes narrowed. "Or you could share some more of your information. That would go a long way towards balancing the scales, and it will help me decide how I shall make use of the favor owed."

Yarid feigned thoughtfulness for a moment. "I may have some information coming soon that will be of use to you, Minister. I shall let you know the moment I have confirmation."

"See that you do. Councilor."

"Minister."

Aelor waggled his fingers, and his coachman lashed the reins. In a few moments, they were out of sight.

Yarid had no leads he wanted to share but had just wanted to get rid of the Minister. Aelor was a stupid man, his mind shielded from reality by sycophants. He thought himself far more powerful than he was—but to his credit, he did have influence where no Councilor, not even Yarid, had any due to the separation of powers outlined in the original Accord agreements.

But stupid, greedy men like Aelor were easily manipulated. All you had to do was get in their debt and pay them back in a way that benefited you greatly and them not at all. Which had been Yarid's design from the moment he first laid eyes on that pompous fool. He had no need of the man yet, so he would continue to string him along for the time being. Once Yarid found a use for him, he would yank on the string.

And the minister who fancied himself a fisherman would find himself in the water, boat capsized, circled by the very sharks he thought to make his dinner. *I just hope you taste better than you look.*

Yarid nodded to one of his servants, who then knocked on the panel behind the coachman's seat. The snap of reins sounded, and the carriage lurched into motion.

The Dome and Spire was so-named for what would appear to be, to the architecturally inclined at least, a melding of disparate ancient styles. This was to represent mankind's mixed heritage; after all, the beginning of the Accord was Andrin's army, which consisted of soldiers from wherever they could be found, and a host of civilians of a similar lack of shared origin. Since no one culture could claim what would become the Accord, they decided they *all* could. And thus, a building with such confused aesthetic elements as domes and spires was built, declaring to all that the pure blood of nobility and royalty was a thing of the past, and we were all mutts now.

But the exterior was hardly the most important aspect of the Dome and the Spire. In its heart sat the Council Chambers. The Chambers, a vast half-circle of a hall lined with tiered alcoves, was heart to more than just the Dome and the Spire—it was the heart of all human civilization. Proclamations issued here flowed like blood to all the other cities in the Accord, giving them life in just the same way. The Councilors were the ones holding that heart in their hands, squeezing it to pump that lifeblood. In a very real way, that was Yarid's job—to make sure that all the Councilors squeezed in concert. Otherwise, everything they did here was in vain, and human civilization would begin to wither and rot, from the extremities inward.

As carefree as he often was, Yarid could not help but feel that he walked upon hallowed ground as he treaded the curving hallway, servants silently trailing behind him. The carpets beneath his slippered feet gave him a charge of motivation, as if merely walking them was enough to change the fate of the world.

Once he reached his own alcove, the alcove used for the two Councilors representing Garoshmir, one of his servants slid the door open for him. Nodding for them to stand outside the door, he stepped into the relative darkness of the Council Chambers. His alcove was on the third tier and, like the others, held two chairs—one for the Lesser Councilor, and one for the Greater. Yarid's chair was empty, but the other one was already occupied.

Without a word or sideways glance, Yarid sat.

"You know," came the voice from the other chair, tremulous with age. "I asked your man Jordin where you were earlier this week. He covered for you beautifully, with more skill than half the Councilors would have."

"Of course he did, Councilor Gorun," Yarid said. "He speaks with me every day. One would think I would rub off on the old fellow."

"You don't deserve him."

"Truer words have never been spoken. He vexes me daily."

Yarid glanced over at his Greater Council counterpart. Gorun sat heavily in his chair, as if he bore the weight of rule all by himself. His chin was lowered, nearly resting against his chest, white beard splayed across his breast. He was the very epitome of advanced age. Yarid supposed that could be an advantage, since advanced age was often associated with the power of the Greater Council. Yarid thought it just made the man look slow and ineffective.

Gorun's gray eyes stared out from beneath thick eyebrows. "Well? Where were you?"

"Minding my own business, as always. Perhaps you should follow my example."

Gorun looked away and stared at the flat wall opposite the alcoves. "A man doesn't sneak out the servants' entrance in disguise if he intends to mind his own business."

Yarid's fingers tightened around the arms of his chair, but he kept his voice level. "Watching me, are you?"

"No." Gorun's chuckle was coarse and grating. "I simply spend my days cloistered in my manse, cataloguing the breaks in my hip."

"I'm not sure what offends me more. Your watching me, or your admitting it."

"You spend too much time with that Patterner. He is a foul creature, and your friendship with him only weakens you."

Yarid shrugged. "What good is brandishing a weapon if it isn't coated in blood from time to time? The other Councilors are afraid of Tirfaun because he's one of the only things they can't possibly control."

Gorun glanced back at him. "And you think you can?"

"Control him? No, not really. But I understand him, which is its own

247

kind of control."

"Be careful, Yarid." Gorun used his name like a stern parent would, as if Yarid's very existence were an admonishment unto itself. "You court disaster."

"Court disaster? No, my old friend. You have it all wrong. I'm done courting her." He leaned forward and jabbed his own chest with a thumb, and his voice lowered to a sharp hiss. "Disaster spreads her legs for me time and time again. She lays at my feet when I snap my fingers. She continues to beg for scraps at my table though she has never once gotten any. That bitch is *mine*."

Gorun clucked his tongue and shook his head. "Then I hope, for your sake and everyone else's, that you pull out in time. Abyss take me if I ever witness the spawn of such a union."

"Then may the day arrive sooner rather than later." Yarid stroked his chin, affecting an abstracted expression of deep thought. "Hmm ... the child of disaster. Maybe if I offered such a child to Tirfaun, I'd have an alliance for life?"

Gorun turned to him, his wizened face a study in shock. *"Shores*, man. Is nothing sacred to you?"

Yarid's own face froze. For some reason, he couldn't summon a retort.

Luckily, Gorun apparently hadn't expected one. Nor did he wait for one. Again, the old man shook his head. "Sometimes I wonder if you're up to the task of governance. Sometimes ... Sometimes I wonder if you care about the vocation at all."

"Yes, governance is *very* serious business." Yarid flashed his most winsome smile and threw his leg over the arm of his chair in a fruitless effort to get comfortable. Though he put on his typical playful air, his conversation with the wrinkly old dung heap had stirred up his ire. The worst part was he wasn't certain why. He fidgeted with a loose thread on the cuff of his sleeve for more time than it was worth and resolved to beat one of his servants later. Yarid quietly blew out his cheeks and glanced around the room for something else to grab his attention. He suddenly regretted the decision to come here as early as he had.

As much as he didn't want to talk to Gorun anymore, Yarid wanted to hear his wheezing echo across the relative silence of the Council Chambers even less. So he decided to strike up another conversation.

Luckily, he was spared that exercise in dullness. At that moment, a few of the lesser functionaries trickled into the Council Chambers: messengers, clerks, scribes, assistants, and the like. Some of them would likely be familiar faces, having served in their positions—and never rising above them—for as long as Yarid had been a Councilor himself. Most, though, were quickly replaced. The floor of the Chambers, or the Pit as he sometimes thought of it, was often filled with a blur of faces that weren't worth remembering.

The balconies were another matter entirely. Yarid not only recognized the faces of the Councilors, but he knew everything there was to know about them as well, even things that they didn't know about themselves. Though the functionaries had their functions, they were merely the grease that allowed the gears of power to turn.

Gradually, the dozen lights built into the flat wall opposite the balconies began to brighten. It was meant to be a subtle thing; they brightened so slowly that unless one watched them or expected the change, they wouldn't have noticed it all—until, inexplicably, the room seemed brighter. It was at once an unobtrusive convenience as well as a display of wealth and power. Most of these functionaries were doubtless still using open flames in their homes and offices for lighting. Nothing at all like the softly glowing globes ensconced in the Chambers of the Council of the Wall.

Similar lighting devices were found in each of the balconies as well, though these were manually adjustable by a small silver lever on the wall behind the chairs. The lever was a thin bar of metal affixed to a thick slab of oak lacquered white, which was covered with an incomprehensible design, this too made of polished silver, developed by a Patterner. The very nature of the pattern changed with the position of the metal lever and was specifically tied to the light in this alcove. Such a Patterning was considered state of the art, or had been before the Runeway anyway, though Yarid didn't see what all the fuss was about. Granted, they were clever, but they were cleverly doing a job that men had already been doing, albeit more crudely, for millennia. Yarid was more concerned with the glow of prestige they brought rather than the admittedly weak light they produced.

It wasn't long before more Councilors began to filter into the room. This was one of the other reasons Yarid liked arriving early; it gave him a chance to see each Councilor when their emotions were rawest. Few people thought to school their expressions before they reached the seats in their respective alcoves. It was a brief window through which Yarid could spot plots and strategies, thus allowing him to adjust his own as needed. He smiled as the portly Councilor Nangrove shuffled into her alcove. Framed by frizzy red hair, her round face had a haunted cast to it, her green eyes hidden in shadow. Yarid couldn't see from this distance, but he imagined a quiver to her lips. It was all very quaint and precious.

"You did something evil, didn't you," said Gorun, one eye prised open and staring wetly in his direction. Yarid started. He had thought the old man was dozing, perhaps even finally dead, not busy reading his thoughts. Yarid silently chastised himself for being so readable. It was a good idea to take Gorun seriously, falling apart at the seams though the man was. Much of the power Yarid now had was the legacy of what Gorun himself had accumulated. It was wise to remember that.

Yarid flipped a hand dismissively. "Don't be so old-fashioned, Gorun," he said. "Leave the moralizing to the priests while the rest of us deal with the real world."

Gorun said nothing, merely shook his head and resumed his corpse imitation.

Yarid pointedly resumed his study of the Hall's newcomers. Odd. While there were constantly two Sentinels guarding the Hall's main entrance in at all hours of the day, there were rarely any others in attendance. Now, however, Councilor Firnaleos's husband, Rannald, stood at her side as she settled into her Lesser Council chair. He wore the Sentinel's rarely-seen dress uniform, rather than the breastplate and helm of the two guards down in the Pit. The gold-trimmed purple jacket fit his broad shoulders rather well, Yarid had to admit, and was rather sharp, in a stuffy sort of way. The man was a match for his wife Sherin, whom Yarid had always found physically attractive. Though he had resisted any impulse to attempt to bed her. While her husband carried around that ridiculous empty scabbard at his hip, the other Sentinels did not—and who knew how they would react to such a slight? More importantly, however, Yarid didn't want her bodily fluids staining his sheets. Her self-righteous stupidity might be catching.

Still, that didn't stop his gaze from lingering on her face. He had always thought her heavy-lidded brown eyes were a study in seduction—one that was often spoiled by her tight-lipped expression. A few seconds of staring was enough to sustain him for a little while, at least.

Once everyone had settled into their chairs and finished coughing and clearing their throats for the third time, a high-ranking member of the Greater Council—the highest-ranking, if paper were to be believed, though Yarid knew Gorun held the most actual power—shuffled down the steps dividing the two banks of Council alcoves and leading down into the Pit, clutching both railings as if his life depended on it. And it very well may have. Councilor Mundt was one of the oldest people alive. His liver-spotted scalp was egg-like in its utter lack of hair. He made Gorun appear to have the vitality of an erupting volcano.

After Mundt's painfully long descent, there was another period of awful waiting as he shuffled to the center of the floor. A few of the functionaries and clerks stepped out of the way with a slight bow of respect and deference. Those who thought they understood where true influence lay in the Council stood their ground, almost making *Mundt* go around *them*. Yarid thought their brazenness foolish; they were, after all, looking up at *all* of the alcoves, even those of the lowest Councilor. He had no tolerance for those who caught a glimpse of the trunk and thought they could plot the entirety of the root system as a result.

By the time Yarid thought he, too, was at risk of dying of old age, Mundt finally made in the center of the Pit and turned to address those sitting in their alcoves. "This session," he wheezed, "of the Council," and then proceeded to blink once, "of the Wall," followed by a long pause, "is now …"

A dozen or so people shifted in their chairs. Gazes met other gazes. Someone even belched, stifling the noise poorly. Mundt's head had dipped. One bold clerk in a preposterously feathered hat reached toward him and gave the old man's sleeve a little tug.

Mundt then lifted his head. "Commenced."

There was an audible collective sigh, and then business began.

Thus began the seemingly endless stream of supplicants, whining about their problems. A man whose crops were mauled by his neighbor's pig, which had gotten loose. A father, whose dowry letter outlined different benefits than the one his new son-in-law had. Actually, two such fathers— perhaps word had spread that the Council was acting favorably in such circumstances. A troupe of players complaining about the use of a stage somewhere in Caney Forks, which Sherin Firnaleos chastised them about at length, Caney Forks being her hometown.

It was all very tedious. While Yarid had voted on a few of the measures—abstaining on a particularly important one just to keep his rivals on their toes—his heart wasn't really in it today. They were all such mundane matters. None of it interested him; none of it seemed to matter.

Usually when Yarid felt this way, recognizing it only made him feel worse, because he knew that this was what life had doled out for him. This was his fate, and though it had its perks, it ultimately amounted to nothing. Such a feeling could sometimes drag him to the brink of despair, and would appear from out of nowhere. He couldn't explain it, and he couldn't predict it. Worst of all, he couldn't stop it once it came.

This time, though, wasn't that bad. He chalked it up to impatience. A couple of slightly more interesting guests would be coming in once all of these silly farmers, tradesmen, and merchants were finally shoved out the door. It wasn't enough to make the dark feelings go away entirely, but it was enough to make Yarid reckon that they weren't fatal. Something would soon happen that would pique his interest.

Wonder of wonders, he didn't have to wait that long. The herald, wearing a crisp white long coat and matching skull cap, stood in front of the twin steel-reinforced oak doors that led into the Pit. He bowed smartly at the waist and, once straightened, cried out for all to hear:

"Please welcome Erianna Vondallor, proxy to the Governor of Twelve Towers."

The room stirred in a susurrus of movement. Yarid found himself leaning forward in his chair ever so slightly as the doors opened.

The sudden silence was broken by the clack of high-heeled boots as the woman entered. A thin silver circlet held up her auburn hair in a loose pile that, despite—or perhaps because of—its complete lack of order, Yarid found appealing. Her dress could only be called such by way of habit; it was more accurately a state of undress. Dark green fabric that glittered like emeralds as she walked covered only the most important bits, baring shoulders, stomach, and knees, though even that last meager nod to modesty was ruined by the twin slits on either side that reached nearly to her hips.

And that neckline. Yarid almost wished he were standing in the Pit to get a better view.

Not a male eye was pointed elsewhere, not even those that Yarid knew tended to stray away from women. Yarid couldn't stop himself from staring. Whatever boredom that had plagued him had been driven off like a kicked dog. He was now *thoroughly* amused.

Strange, though, was her expression. Her nose was lifted high, and the poise she affected made her seem to tower over everyone, though she was shorter than many of those in the Pit, even with her high heeled shoes. Yet despite everything, Yarid could see something in her eyes that was very subtle, very deep.

252

Fear.

Interesting. Yarid leaned back as he considered the implications. Twelve Towers held to a rather isolationist policy. The Governor was also technically a member of the Lesser Council, which was unusual, since Councilors tended to live in Garoshmir, and Governors led from within their home city. Whenever that had happened in the past, the Governor would still attend Council meetings occasionally, at least whenever their own interests were at stake. Shad Belgrith had never once set foot in Garoshmir and had only sent proxies to Council sessions a handful of times. Only the Greater Councilor Sherm sat in Twelve Towers' alcove, and he did little more than keep the seat warm.

Because of this, Yarid suspected that Belgrith preferred to rule over her people utterly, without interference. She likely also thought that the Council was weak, beset by bickering and self-crippling indecision, and didn't require much in the way of appeasement. Which wasn't true, of course; the Council had merely not cared to bother with her affairs. Should Twelve Towers catch the eyes of the Council in a bad way, it would learn that the Council was not to be trifled with.

There was no risk of that now, however, not with the fact that Twelve Towers' Patterners were the ones responsible for the Runeway—and the only ones who knew how to complete it. Greed was very predictable, and that *did* weaken the Council. Not only did Belgrith know this and exploit it, she also had the ability to build something no one else could. The Runeway itself.

He suspected she was very shrewd. And based on what he saw in her proxy, very, very cruel.

Yarid smiled. This might actually be fun.

Erianna Vondallor stood with a hand on her hip, scanning all the faces fixed upon her with arresting blue eyes. She looked up on them without respect, just as she seemed to face this task without relish; this was just a duty to her, and those gathered just people. The discomfort many of the Councilors felt radiated off them. Fools, all of them. Yarid's smile widened.

The woman's voice was loud and commanding. "My mistress," not her Governor, Yarid noticed, "has learned that construction of the Runeway has been discontinued. She had hoped that, with what benefits the Runeway is set to deliver to everyone, all objections would have long been dealt with."

It was as good a slap, and just as blunt. She was no diplomat, that was for sure.

But at least one person had not been stunned by it. Frandera, Greater Councilwoman from Siltwaters in the west, regarded her with a raised eyebrow. "We understand the Governor's concern, proxy." Two insults in one sentence, a reminder of low status and also a reminder of Belgrith's position with relation to the Council. Very economical. Yarid approved. "It is something that the Council would have liked to discuss with her personally. Since she mentioned she would be in Garoshmir, we had hoped now would prove to be such an opportunity." Frandera tilted her head. "So where is she?"

Well. They certainly spoke the same language.

"On business. As proxy, I have full authority to speak on behalf of my mistress." Erianna leveled her gaze on the Councilwoman. "One of my tasks, however, was given in no uncertain terms. To find out why the construction of the Runeway has stopped, and to ensure that it continues immediately."

"Well, you're in luck," said some insignificant fool on the Lesser Council. "That's what we're here to discuss today—"

"Tell us, if you please," Frandera said, cutting him off. "Why is your Governor so adamant that this continue so promptly?" Then, almost as if to herself, "What does she have to gain?"

"Wealth, of course," said Erianna. "The fraction of the tolls that my mistress would receive, an amount this very Council agreed upon, would nearly triple the amount of taxes that our district currently receives." She began pacing slowly, though her eyes never left Councilwoman Siltwaters. "Not to mention the benefits that her subjects—" not constituents, which was how any politically-minded Councilor would refer to them, "— would receive from increased mobility and trade. Furthermore." She spread her hands in attempt at a gesture of goodwill, and even faked a smile as she eyed everyone in the room. "She was ever interested in the well-being of those people of the Council, and everyone they represent. She is a friend of mankind in a time when mankind has very few friends."

That fake smile faltered briefly. "But perhaps that time is past." Then it disappeared completely.

No one seemed able to make sense of that last little statement. Even Frandera clamped her mouth shut, eyes narrowed.

"So," Erianna continued, "my mistress has received a basic summary of what has stopped construction, though it said little beyond that the Governor of Naruvieth has objected to increasing prosperity in his district."

"That," said the Lesser Councilman who had been interrupted earlier, "is one of the things we hope to resolve today." Pembo Sint. He looked like an underfed weasel, and had the charm of one, too. Yarid hated the man on a day when he spoke and hated him even more when he smiled. He was smiling now. And speaking.

"Good." Erianna nodded once. "My mistress will be pleased when you remove this obstruction to progress. She is, of course, willing to negotiate the means of removing it, should it be necessary."

It sounded much like a threat, but everyone knew what she really meant: money.

"Naruvieth isn't yet a district," said Frandera, frustration evident, "since no representative of theirs was able to sign the Accord, and thus they have no Governor or Councilors. Currently, they are merely a territory. That said, the man claiming to represent them further claims that it isn't merely the territorial government of Naruvieth that objects to further construction of the Runeway, but the *people themselves*. A number of Naruvieth's citizens privately own the land where the Runeway is intended to go, and none of them have accepted the terms of purchase, no matter the cost."

"So?" Erianna shrugged a shoulder. "Build it anyway."

Sherin Firnaleos stood then, dwarfed by her imposing husband at her side. "Though they are just territorial citizens, the people of Naruvieth do follow the very same laws outlined by Andrin's Council drafted before the building of the Wall. To the letter. In order to claim any legitimacy as his Council's heirs, we must abide by their right to sell or dispose of their land as they see fit." She sat back down and said in a clear yet softer voice, "Lest we become the very creatures that Andrin sought to save us from."

Yarid tsked silently. No one really thought that the sheggam were a threat. Aside from the odd Knight of the Eye turning, which itself hadn't been seen in over a hundred and fifty years, they *weren't* a threat. There weren't too many these days that held that bad behavior could turn one into a sheggam. Perhaps some of the more superstitious backwater folk, but even they didn't admit it publicly.

Sherin, though, didn't quite believe that either. Yarid had heard her speak many times, and she seemed to think that a violent human was no better than a sheggam. It was almost as preposterous as people actually turning into sheggam. Yarid was convinced the sole root of her influence lay in her ability to cause others to wonder what she could possibly say next.

That, and the nameless fear they felt whenever they remembered who her husband was. Rannald stared with his hands folded behind his back in the very image of a soldier, casting judgment on the Twelve Towers woman down below with his cold regard. His presence here was a mystery. Did it have something to do with how their marriage was going? Yarid suspected so. Something for him to check on later.

Erianna didn't seem to even notice Rannald. Her eyes were for his wife only. Erianna shook her head, almost sadly. "Foolish, foolish woman," she muttered, almost to herself, though the words carried to every ear in the Hall.

Muttering erupted, but Erianna cut it off. "As I said, my mistress has given me leave to attend on her behalf. Thus, I am within rights to hear Naruvieth's terms on her behalf and determine if they are acceptable." She stepped to the side, though everyone in the Pit seemed to think it wise to give her a wide berth.

"Well then," Gorun said in his gravelly voice at Yarid's side, "let us proceed. Bring in the Naruvian." Though he and Yarid often bickered and disagreed about nearly everything, right then he was somewhat proud of the old man for taking some measure of control over the situation.

From what Yarid already knew, the Naruvian had been staying in the city for the better part of a week already, so Yarid was not surprised when he was very easy to produce … unlike the Governor of Twelve Towers. They waited only a few moments before the double doors groaned open to admit the man.

Chapter 43: The Naruvian

I t was with minimal interest that those gathered in the Chambers of the Council watched the doors open to the man from beyond the Rift, the very same Rift that had closed Naruvieth off from Accord lands for over six hundred years. Someone down in the Pit even stifled a yawn. The Runeway had bridged the Rift for a year now; while few people in the Chambers had ever laid eyes on a Naruvian, most had deemed the prospect unworthy of the effort. A year was a long time to these people. Looking at Naruvians had become … passé.

So it was that Yarid himself affected a mostly disinterested pose. Though in truth his attention was fully fixed on what lay beyond those doors.

Surprise number two.

What to expect? Surely the proxy from Twelve Towers set the bar high with her garb and her demeanor. Yarid almost worried that he was expecting too much of the man from Naruvieth, as though nothing less than two heads sprouting from his shoulders could live up to the standard that Erianna had set. Even now, she stood off to the side among the rabble, arms folded in a position that drew the eye—though it wasn't precisely the arms themselves doing the drawing. Many were too busy staring at her to bother with a foreign man. Though she herself watched the door, gaze impassive and stern in an almost practiced fashion.

Once the doors had fully opened, the man stepped in and took in everything in the Chambers with a single calculating gaze. And what *power* in that gaze. Though the effect was palpably different, it was instantly apparent that this man was Erianna's equal, if not her superior, in terms of presence.

Yarid felt it like a punch in the chest. By the dead silence in the Chambers, he knew the others felt it, too. But why? The man was more poorly dressed than the lowest functionary in the Pit. His tunic was too long for fashion, and his sandals were laced halfway up his calf—*over* his leggings. Granted, Naruvians had no use for leggings in their bizarrely hot land and doubtless thought of them as a strange contrivance, but a little

257

common sense went a long way. This man clearly had none when it came to dressing to impress.

Yet impress he did.

He was darker of skin than most in the Chambers, as though he had worked in the fields his whole life. His straight brown hair, not quite long enough to put in a tail, was held out of his eyes by a leather headband with some sort of emblem in the center—Yarid couldn't quite make it out from this distance. The man was firmly built but not as large as the two Sentinels that admitted him, and certainly not compared to Firnaleos.

Yet none of that seemed to diminish him. Not the slightest bit.

While the Naruvian walked into the center of the Pit, only two other people moved. Rannald Firnaleos stepped to the edge of his wife's alcove and rested his gloved hands on the railing, and Erianna Vondallor unfolded her arms and let them hang at her sides.

The man stood in the center of the Pit as if it had been built so many centuries ago for the sole purpose of giving him a place to stand on this very day. He casually rested a hand on the hilt of the sword at his hip, which Yarid only now seemed to notice.

Though he wasn't sitting at an ideal angle to study it, Yarid could tell that the sword was finely crafted, if the scabbard and hilt were any indication. He didn't have time to gather much else about it. The man spoke.

"I am Tharadis, Warden of Naruvieth as appointed by the people there," he began. The herald at the door gave a start when he realized he had forgotten his duties. The Naruvian's voice wasn't raised, but carried firmly throughout the Chambers, each word echoing faintly.

"I stand before the Council of the Wall, heirs to Andrin's Council, the very council that helped him build the Wall that stands between mankind and the creatures that would destroy us. Know that I supplicate myself before their legacy as a debt of honor, and not before what you yourselves have accomplished."

It took most of Yarid's self-control to keep from laughing at the astounded expressions he spied on nearly a dozen faces around the Chambers. Even crusty old Gorun had a look of astonished, speechless indignation. As it was, Yarid couldn't stifle his grin, but he did put his fingers to his lips to cover it up.

Well. Today was shaping up to be very interesting indeed. He shifted in his seat ever so slightly to make himself more comfortable for the show to come.

"There is one consideration to make before we hear your plea, Tharadis of Naruvieth." Councilwoman Frandera stood and leveled her haughtiness at Erianna—to no visible effect, of course. "Proxy, do you wish to await the presence of your ... Governor, before this man presents his case?" She had almost said *mistress*.

"No," said Erianna. "As I said before, I have the full trust and authority of Shad Belgrith of Twelve Towers in this matter. If anything, she would like this obstacle to the Runeway's construction to be resolved before she personally addresses the Council."

"Very well." She gestured to the Naruvian. "If there are no further objections or concerns, the floor is yours to make your case."

Tharadis nodded. "You all know why I have come." He slowly turned his gaze, seeming to meet every pair of eyes in the Chambers, even those of the lowlies down in the Pit. "At least on a superficial level. Yet the fundamental cause of my being here has escaped you. From what I understand, most of you were in favor of the construction of the Runeway, and those that aren't only defied it due to some petty interest of their own or their constituents. None of you thought for a moment that what you were doing was *wrong*."

Just then, Yarid noticed something odd behind him: the two Sentinels, who typically stood utterly impassive and disinterested to all that went on in the Council Chambers, were no longer at attention, but were eyeing Rannald up in Sherin's alcove. Yarid quickly glanced at the Captain of the Sentinels. The man gave an almost imperceptible nod to the men at the door; they nodded in return.

Then left.

Never, *ever* have the Sentinels left their posts at the doors to the Chambers while the Council was in session. Not even for a change of guard. Not even to relieve themselves. They would rather piss their trousers, and had once in a notorious incident a couple decades before Yarid had begun his stint as Councilor. It was still talked about to this day.

However, these Sentinels had left with nary an eyebrow raised.

Save one particularly bushy, white eyebrow belonging to Gorun. "That's odd ..." The old man leaned forward in his chair as he watched the doors close behind them. "They've never done that before."

Yarid wasn't paying attention to the old man but was watching Rannald. His wife's eyes were wide with worry as Rannald left out the door at the back of her alcove. Yarid couldn't tell if they had exchanged words before

Rannald had left. Once the door shut behind him, Sherin leaned with her elbows on her knees, hands holding up her face. Her face was pale, her eyes getting wider by the moment, and she appeared on the verge of crying.

What in the Abyss had just happened?

Pembo Sint, apparently unaffected by these historic events happening in the background, stood and wiped his thinning black hair away from his beady little weasel eyes as he addressed Tharadis. "Why, pray you good fellow, should we think that the construction of the Runeway is wrong? It's a monument to all that mankind has achieved since Andrin's Wall was built, and done so in the same vein as *that* great monument. We have pushed back the darkness that was said to have lain behind that Wall," a very diplomatic—and skeptical—choice of words, if Yarid did say so himself, "and brought what was left of mankind into an era of peace unrivaled in the recounting of all history. And now we bring man to an era beyond even that, where the distances that have separated people from loved ones and from opportunities long thought out of reach are but a trifle."

"I am not here to dispute the value of the Runeway," Tharadis said. That was a surprise, considering his purpose in coming. "However, given the nature of how it came to be, I am skeptical that such value will remain unmolested by those whose sole legitimate purpose is to protect their people." He didn't give anyone a moment to digest that. "But you keep saying this word, 'we.' Exactly what was your personal role in the construction of Andrin's Wall, Councilor?"

Pembo's eyes darted from side to side, as if damning the rest of the Council for not coming to his aid, and sat back down.

Tharadis nodded and allowed himself a fierce half-smile. "I leave Andrin his due for what he has done. The very least you could do as the heirs of his Council is the same. I fear it is this very attitude, that because you wear the same mantels of the great men and women of that era, you somehow have the right to take what you want, as payment for accomplishments you have never accomplished."

Gorun's rising from his seat was like a hacked and burned tree stump suddenly growing roots and standing upright. "You imperious runt," the old man wheezed. "You call this supplication? If you wish to beg any favors from this great Council, you do so with the manner of a barking, snarling dog that still expects a treat."

Yarid gaped at his Greater Council counterpart. Even *he* seemed affected by this madness of blunt speaking. Maybe it was in the air. A silly thought of course, but Yarid covered his mouth just to be safe. He didn't want the same condition to afflict him as well.

"I ask for no treat, Councilor," said Tharadis, as calm as the surface of a frozen pond. "Nothing that is not due to myself and my fellow Naruvians as befits our humanity."

Sherin, obviously thinking this man was speaking her language, rose. "We of the Council of the Wall of course respect all of our citizens and want to do best by them. Rather than trade further insults, which gains us nothing, what would you have us do?"

"Very well." He spread his hands. "At this moment, all I ask is for you to listen to me as I provide my arguments for why the Runeway should not be finished. And then, of course, I ask you to heed my advice, but whether or not you do is up to you."

Mollified, Sherin Firnaleos sat back down.

Tharadis began to pace, but it seemed purposeful, not at all a nervous habit. Those in the Pit, including the proxy from Twelve Towers, had settled back to give him room, watching him with as much interest as everyone else. And with a much better view. For the first time in his life, Yarid felt a stab of envy for them.

Tharadis stopped his pacing and raised his hand, four fingers outstretched. "I have come prepared with four arguments. I will present the first one, and if it fails to sway you from your course, I will present the next, and so on, until I have exhausted all four arguments. Think of them as four chances to do what is right."

Sherin leaned forward in her chair. "What happens if we reject all four arguments?"

"If it comes to that, I will tell you."

She sat back, frowning. She clearly didn't like the sound of that, and judging by the concerned muttering, neither did anyone else. It didn't take long sitting in these seats that one became able to recognize a threat when he heard one.

Yarid thought he would need a hell of a lot more than four arguments to gain their favor. But perhaps he realized that dealing with most of those that comprised the Council wasn't worth more than four thoughts. They wouldn't budge, no matter what he had to say, and they would just get lost in the details anyway.

Tharadis dropped his hand back to the hilt of his sword. "The Runeway, while it doubtless brings value to those who built it, comes at a cost that is unacceptable to many of those south of the Rift. That cost is their private property. That cost is their homes."

"This concern has already been addressed," said Frandera with a poorly-concealed scoff. She stirred the air with her thick fingers dismissively. "These people have already been approached and offered fair, even generous, values for their homes. I certainly hope you are saving the best of your arguments for last, Tharadis of Naruvieth. Otherwise we have a very tedious afternoon ahead of us."

Tharadis was unfazed. "Fair?" he asked. "Generous? According to whom? And by what standard? Doubtless whatever you consider to be 'fair' and 'generous' is whatever happens to be cheaper than forcibly removing them from their homes."

Frandera narrowed her eyes. She likely had thought exactly that. "We judge what is fair and generous based on the average prices for such homes. And trust me," she added, "it was difficult to come up with more than a pittance for some of them."

Tharadis nodded. "That much I understand. But there's more to it, isn't there? You don't simply intend to walk away if these offers are not accepted. These offers you mentioned, *they* are not the price I am referring to."

"Then what is this price?"

"Simple. Their free will." He paused. No one filled the silence until he spoke again. "If they do not give you what you want, you will simply take it. Those that live nearer to the Rift, where you intend to finish building the Runeway, may lead a simpler lifestyle than you are used to. But do not think for a moment that they are stupid, that they can't see through your threats hidden within your promises. Naruvians tend to be a proud people, though it's not pride in their rulers or the dirt they live on. They are proud of what they themselves have built from nothing, and they are not keen to hand it over to a pack of bullies they have never even met, no matter *what* the offer."

Well. That didn't bode well for the rest of these discussions.

"So," said Tharadis before anyone else could squeeze in a protest, "I have presented my first argument, but let me summarize it for you in case I was being too opaque. Building your Runeway requires land you do not own and will not own unless it is taken by force. The use of force against these innocent people is unacceptable to me, as their sworn protector and representative, and as a human being."

He scanned the faces in the Chambers. His hard, unyielding gaze seemed to linger on Yarid longer than on anyone else, even though he hadn't said a word this whole time. Yarid stifled a shudder and silently berated himself for being intimidated by such a country bumpkin. *And a moralist, no less.* At Yarid's side, Gorun was having one of his rare fits of total awareness. When the old man put his mind to it, he could look downright frightening. *Cut from the same cloth as the Naruvian,* he thought. Perhaps that's what had Gorun so interested.

"You have heard what I have to say regarding the first of my arguments. I hope it is enough to sway you." His voice was neutral, not betraying any doubt as to the realism of that hope. "Will you now abandon the construction of the Runeway?"

Pembo Sint, ever the weasel, decided to speak up. "We have yet to hear what the Governor of Twelve Towers has to say. It is only fair that we give both sides—"

"Will you now abandon the construction of the Runeway?" At that moment the man drew his sword, its nearly silent loosing from its scabbard a stark counterpoint to his shouted words, which echoed sharply around Chambers. More than a few were discomfited by the outburst; some were even startled. Yet the moment they were over the shock, many stared in open awe at the blade.

Yarid found himself among them. That dual-edged sword was unlike anything he had ever seen. From what he could see in this light, it had a matte texture, like fired, unglazed clay … but it was a color unlike any he had ever seen in a sword. Blue as a clear afternoon sky. It was remarkable, so much so that Yarid had to force his mouth shut after a few seconds of gawking.

Briefly he wondered just how effective such a blade could be. Yarid's clumsy servants were always dropping his dishes, which shattered with the slightest mishandling. Now that he thought about it, he remembered hearing rumors about an indestructible sword—though of course there was no such thing. He doubted, however, that a man such as this would ever do anything merely for effect, inadvertent showman though he may be. Yarid knew from the short time he had been watching this man that the Naruvian was an immanently practical man. At least when it came to things like clothing and weapons.

In more abstract matters, he was turning out to be much more foolish and idealistic.

The Naruvian's stance, while clearly martial in its intent, was something

Yarid had never quite seen before. His feet were planted shoulder-width apart and he held his sword above his head, such that the blade was parallel to his shoulders. His hand gripped the hilt so tightly Yarid felt his own knuckles burn just watching it. The flat of the blade faced the same direction as the man's drilling eyes. It seemed as if the fact that his sword had a flat texture was all that kept you from seeing your own doom reflected in it.

Sherin Firnaleos was the first to recover herself. "Enough of this!" She stood and slammed the palms of her hands down on the railing. "You say you will not deal with those who bully you. But what are you doing now? Waving your sword around in a room filled with unarmed people with no one to protect them?"

The fact that the Sentinels had all left the Chambers suddenly revealed itself in a new light. A few here and there shifted uncomfortably in their seats, evidently not wanting to be in the same room as this mad, blade-wielding Naruvian without any Sentinels.

Sherin didn't seem frightened at all. Merely scandalized. "How *dare* you?" she continued. A trickle of sweat trickled down the curve of her cheek. Whatever feelings she had felt when Rannald made his exit were obviously quashed by the moral raving she exhibited now that there was a scent of violence in the air.

Much to everyone's surprise, Tharadis sheathed his side and bowed to her deeply. "I apologize." He sounded genuinely contrite. When he stood back up, he was staring at her expectantly.

She got the hint. "As of this time, we have not decided to discontinue the construction of the Runeway."

Tharadis nodded. *Of course*, Yarid mused. *A direct answer to his question was all he wanted.*

How often is such a thing sought in these Chambers?

Gorun leaned over to him, whispered hoarsely, "You're letting your Lesser brethren seize control of this situation."

"Hasty fools," Yarid said. "And if you think they have control of this situation, you haven't been paying attention."

Gorun sat back with a huff, but he had no retort. He likely felt as out of his depth as many of the others. That was what happened when the ability to comprehend frank speech atrophied from years of neglect.

Yarid was amused, to be sure. But that wasn't the only reason he wasn't taking the reins. Something here wasn't exactly as it appeared, and the disappearance of the Sentinels was a variable that upset most of Yarid's predictions. Even Erianna, the proxy, seemed somewhat subdued, as if uncertain how to react.

Everyone seemed to be wondering what the man with the sky blue sword would do next.

Yarid settled deeper into his seat with a slight smile.

They didn't have long to wait. "All right," said Tharadis, calmer than his sword-waving a moment ago should warrant. "I have tried to dissuade you from continuing construction on the Runeway by appealing to your sense of justice. That, apparently, has failed. I will now attempt to sway your decision by presenting my second argument." He raised two fingers, as if his audience were naturally disinclined to count that far without help.

"And what," said Councilwoman Frandera, "might that be?"

Chapter 44: Appeal to Reason

T he Naruvian drew a small roll of parchment from a pouch on his sword belt. "I have here," he said, voice carrying throughout the hall, "a sealed document from a Patterner from Naruvieth named Larril. Now, I am no Patterner myself, so I can't vouch for the basis of his claims. He has explained to me somewhat the grave danger that the Runeway presents, but he said the bulk of his findings would only be comprehensible to someone who was an expert on the subject."

"Danger?" Pembo Sint, recovered from the last thrashing of his ego, sneered. "Whatever danger are you going on about?"

Gorun made a gesture with his skeletal, liver-spotted arm, and a thin young man standing in the Pit—one of Gorun's personal staff, judging by the slashes of green in his garb—rushed forward to retrieve the scroll. Gorun moved his arm again and the man rushed up the stairs. It wasn't long before he had been admitted to the balcony Yarid shared with Gorun, panting and sweating. Yarid shot the young man a withering look. It wasn't as if he had run a very long way—not that Yarid could comport himself much better, but he wasn't a courier. He had people for that.

Gorun cracked the seal on the scroll and stared at the paper with only a finger's length between it and his face. Yarid was amazed the old man could still read at all.

"Patterner Gherao," said Gorun without looking up from the paper. "Are there any Larrils in your ledger book at the Academy?"

A portly, balding man with a trim beard, wearing the brown of the Academy Patterners, stepped out of the crowd in the Pit. "No, Greater Councilman Gorun," he said. "I looked into it earlier in the week when I learned Warden Tharadis would be presenting his case. I can confirm that Larril of Naruvieth is no Academy-trained Patterner."

"Thank you, Patterner." Gorun handed the paper back to his man. Each word he spoke was slow and measured. "We the Council have endowed the Academy of the Higher Sciences with a certain degree of trust—trust that is not easily won. There are certain things that most of us simply can never know, and in regard to those things we must put our faith in those that do."

He shrugged fatalistically. "We are, after all, only human. But tell me," he said, now solely addressing the Naruvian, "why should we trust this Larril when he has not demonstrated to us the depth of his understanding?"

"A valid point," said Tharadis. "Which is why I am not asking you to trust his character. He has told me that all the evidence of this danger is in what you already know about the Runeway and Andrin's Wall, and all the Patterns surrounding them. He merely spells it out in that letter." He lifted a hand in Gherao's direction. "Give it to your man and see what he thinks of it."

Gorun seemed to weigh this—though Yarid knew his show of concern hid a search for something to exploit. Gorun sent his man down to Gherao, who read the scroll after fishing a monocle out of his pocket and affixing it to his face.

He read it several times, frowning more deeply with each passing moment. He looked up at Gorun, holding the paper aloft. "I cannot substantiate these claims."

"Is there sufficient reason to hold construction until they *can* be substantiated?" asked Councilor Jacobs. A hungry light had entered his deep-set eyes. With his investments in the Rafters' Guild, he was one of the few who wanted the Runeway to fail.

Gherao frowned briefly at the paper again. "What he claims is certainly … unorthodox. Some of his ideas are a bit outlandish, I would say. But if they are true …" He withdrew into himself, staring intently at nothing in that way that scholars did. Finally, he seemed to remember that all the most powerful people alive in the world today were staring at him. "Yes, well. He used untested methods to come up with his determination. Even before we could attempt to verify what he *says* could happen, it would take years of study just to confirm his methods." The man looked worried.

"Well," said Jacobs, "what does he say? And keep in mind your audience."

Gherao nodded and wiped his face with a kerchief. "Well, to put it simply, he, ah, believes that the Runeway's completion will create certain … stresses. He does know quite a bit about certain aspects of the Runeway."

"Is that all that difficult?" asked Pembo Sint. "After all, it's no secret."

Gherao cleared his throat. "The existence of the structure itself is no secret. But most of its Pattern is, and that is what he was able to ascertain purely from extrapolation of data available to him in Naruvieth." What was clear on his face was that it was something he himself could not have done.

267

"But what does this mean?" asked Sherin Firnaleos. "Does this show that the Runeway is a threat?"

"It's certainly irregular—"

"Allow me to preempt your question, Tharadis," said Gorun. "I am not swayed by your second argument." And if Gorun wasn't swayed, it was unlikely that anyone else in the Greater Council would be either.

Tharadis glanced around the Hall to see if there was anyone else who had something to say. Yarid could feel the eyes of several other members of the Lesser Council upon him.

Looking to him.

For guidance.

He stifled a smile, sent it inward. Outward, he opted for a mask of compassionate resolve, and stood.

"You have given us much to think about," Yarid said. "However, you yourself have indicated that these are pieces of a greater whole. How are we to make any decision at all in the face of incomplete knowledge?"

"You don't need complete knowledge, nor will you ever have it," Tharadis replied. "If you wait until you know everything there is to know about even the most mundane topic, you will never reach a decision again in your life. Which," he added, "in my view, is preferable to the current circumstances. However, all I intend to do is provide you with *sufficient* justification to cease construction. If anything I say achieves this, my job here is done."

"Very well." Yarid kept the bitterness out of his voice; sophistry was a strength of his, and he didn't like it very much when he was beaten in a verbal spar. *Not such a bumpkin after all.* "Sufficient justification has not been met. Please proceed."

Tharadis nodded in acknowledgment without a ripple of anger or frustration on his face. *Where does he get his patience?* Shores knew that the Council tested Yarid's often enough.

"I find this whole matter of four arguments very tedious," said Sint, not quite under his breath.

Gorun leaned forward. "I assure you, Pembo Sint, that I would not stop you if you wanted to quit the Council."

"Of course not," Sint said in his most amicable tone, much like a snake hissing in a friendly fashion.

Tharadis addressed the Council. "I have tried to dissuade you from continuing construction on the Runeway by appealing to your reason. I have presented to you an argument that shows there is reasonable suspicion that continuing on this path is dangerous. You have chosen not to heed my warnings or the evidence presented by a Patterner. Appealing to your reason and sense of self-preservation has failed. I will now attempt to sway your decision with my third argument."

Chapter 45: Third and Fourth Arguments

I admit," the Naruvian said, "that my third argument isn't a very good one."

Pembo Sint leapt to his feet like the avatar of some long-forgotten god of exasperation and cried, "Then why are you wasting our time with it?"

"In the hope that it isn't a waste of time. I don't believe it will convince you, but if there is a chance that it will, no matter how small, I will take it."

"You understand," said Yarid, "that this little preamble doesn't inspire much confidence." Despite his words—and the still-sharp humiliation he'd suffered at the hands of this Naruvian—Yarid found himself eager to hear what madness the man had in mind for his next argument.

"Yes." Tharadis folded his hands and looked down at them. Silence stretched. All his forcefulness, his strength, seemed leached out of him. He raised his eyes.

"Deep in the lowlands outside our city is the Wishing Well. It is a place that is important to the history and culture of Naruvieth and explains how Wardens have since governed it."

What followed was a story of a small family, sent out into the desert to die by a cruel and vicious Warden who felt threatened by the father's defiant words. The family prayed to the World Pattern, but instead of saving them, it created a useless oasis around them right before they died. Of course, the way Tharadis told it, the Wishing Well was some great boon to the dying family, but Yarid couldn't help but see the story for what it was— one of a spiteful world, spitting on the faces of weaklings as they drew their last breath.

As he told his story, Tharadis appeared ... *sentimental* was the only word Yarid could think of to describe it. Under any normal circumstances, it would have rung false—even more so than the usual lies in the Council Chambers. However, this Naruvian seemed as naive, and perhaps as innocent, as a child.

Yarid had been a child once. He did not trust the little bastards.

He could see others going through the same dilemma, rarely-felt compassion and oft-felt skepticism warring on their faces. The Council sessions were typically as regular as ticking of a clock or the workings of some obscure Crafter-made mechanism. Even supplicants like Erianna, bold and strange as she was, did not upset the workings of the machinery; she was merely another piece of it for a time, and her inclusion was an expectation and did not interfere with the course set. This man, though …

Machines, in order to properly function, could not suffer dilemmas.

It was time for action. Yarid couldn't allow this to fall the wrong way. It was time to get the machine working again.

Once the tale was done, Yarid stood. "I—no, *we*, all appreciate what you have shared with us today." He spread his hands to encompass the Council. "We sympathize with the people in your story. It is a hard thing to lose what you hold dear. It is a fate that many of the less fortunate in Accord lands have suffered. Business opportunities dry up; homes are lost. Families displaced because of hard times in their area. Many people go without food, a situation that we of the Council of the Wall are desperate to counter.

"That is why we have come together with the Governor of Twelve Towers to build the Runeway. Time has shown that the public works projects that the Council has undertaken, including the roads," he didn't mention how much in the way of taxes it took to build those roads, of course, "have improved the lives of all of our citizens.

"You ask us," Yarid continued, "at what cost? I now ask you the same. You come here with the pain of your people. What of the pain of ours? Whose pain is the greatest? And what is the best course to relieve such pain? We are convinced that the Runeway is the way, and we are sure that once it has been built and the benefits made clear, our brothers and sisters in Naruvieth will be convinced as well."

Yarid had been waiting for this moment. When the other Councilors were closest to recanting was also the time when they were weakest. They are looking for an excuse to return to the familiar, the comfortable. Yarid had made a science of determining when these moments occur, and he had made a name for himself by turning them into moments of strength. Before now, Tharadis had made an interesting, if flawed, case. Now everyone could see the nature of those flaws. Now they could see that all the man was after was pity, but it was a pity that he was unwilling to return to others.

Yarid settled back in his seat, feeling more than a little satisfied with his performance.

Tharadis sighed. "As I said, this was my weakest argument."

There were a few chuckles. Yarid felt a sudden surge of anger, though none of it showed on his face. Instead, he wore a knowing smile, as if he had been in on the joke the whole time.

"I take it this means you haven't decided to end construction."

Yarid merely shook his head.

"So," said Councilor Frandera, "is it finally time for the main course of the evening?"

"Indeed." Tharadis's demeanor suddenly became grave. "I had truly hoped it wouldn't come to this. I have tried to dissuade you from continuing construction on the Runeway by appealing to your compassion. As you rightly asserted, anyone can claim that an action hurts their feelings, but that doesn't mean that the action was unwarranted. That is why we have justice, to determine the rightness of an action. This rests on your reason, because that is how we determine the facts upon which justice depends.

"But you have abandoned all of these things. You treat the people of Naruvieth as dogs to be trampled and beaten when they have something you want. You regard them as less than men and women, incapable of taking care of themselves and doing what is right. You regard them as beasts. As sheggam."

Protests sprang up instantly at the word *sheggam*, but Tharadis wasn't finished. He raised his arm to regain their attention and projected his voice. "I appeared here before in the hopes that we could work together, peacefully and freely, to achieve goals that were in our common interests. No one from Naruvieth, no representatives of its government or private citizens, were present when the Accord was signed. Nevertheless, you treat us as a territory, subordinate to the whims of those who were present. This meeting could have changed our relationship for the better, had you been willing to respect the rights of our people. Since you did not, the government of Naruvieth will cease to recognize any claim to authority over it given by the Council of the Wall and the members of the Accord."

If there was protest before, there was outrage now. Yarid flinched from the wall of noise that swept over him. He was too shocked to scream and spray spit and shake his fist. Was this man declaring his territory's *sovereignty?*

Tharadis crossed his arms and studied the shouting faces, jaw clenched. He was a pillar of stone amidst a boiling sea. The only person in the room who was not thrashing about was Erianna, the proxy. She, too, had her arms crossed and was watching Tharadis intently.

It would have been an exaggeration to say that Gorun leapt to his feet, but he was standing before Yarid had even noticed him moving. "Order!" he cried. "Order!"

The tumult finally settled, though there was still the occasional outburst. "Let us make sure there is no confusion on this matter, Tharadis of Naruvieth." Gorun's voice was quivering with more than just age. "Are you claiming secession from the Accord?"

"No," he answered. "I am claiming there is nothing for us to secede from. We never signed the Accord; we have no reason to now. We have gone over six hundred years without your help ... or your interference. And we have done quite well. We *are* a sovereign nation. I am merely making it official before the Council of the Wall."

"He's justified," said Sherin Firnaleos, choosing then to jump in. "Legally, anyway. There's no provision prohibiting the secession of a territory."

Pembo Sint leaned so far over the railing he nearly fell out of his balcony. "Just because it isn't prohibited doesn't mean it's allowed!"

"We are not and never were a territory of the Accord," said Tharadis.

"But there *is* a provision!" Councilor Jacobs had even taken to defending the Council against this line of argument. It seemed he had *some* loyalty.

"Yes," Tharadis said, "but only for local governments that are part of the Accord. Naruvieth is neither local, nor part of the Accord."

"This is madness!" cried someone else, Yarid didn't see who. "Madness! This must be stopped!"

And so it went for a handful of minutes. After Gorun had apparently had his fill, he pounded the railing with the palm of his hand, though the act brought him some obvious discomfort. Once he had the attention of the Hall, he stared daggers—rusty, weathered daggers, but daggers nonetheless—at Tharadis. "Is this the fourth argument? A renunciation of the Accord?"

"I won't argue the meaning of 'renunciation' as I believe I've made myself clear on this point, but no, it is not the fourth argument. It only lays the groundwork for it." He scanned the room, and his gaze was just as hard as Gorun's, with ten times the sharpness. "My fourth argument is the argument of blood and steel. As a sovereign nation, Naruvieth will not tolerate invaders on our lands. If you continue building the Runeway, it will be seen as an act of aggression, and we will put forth the full military strength of our nation to repel you."

No protest. No outrage. Just shocked silence.

Somewhere in the direction of Sherin Firnaleos's alcove, a sob was heard.

The twin doors to the Council Hall were thrown open. Soldiers marched into the Pit, side-by-side in lockstep. Each footfall was a chorus of thunder. Polished breastplates and helms reflected the light from the Patterned lamps.

The Sentinels.

And not just a pair, as was the most that one normally saw in the Council Hall. First a dozen, then two dozen pushed their way in, though they didn't need to do much pushing. The lowlies in the Pit did their best to get out of the way, some even climbing up the stairs that divided the alcove wings and taking a seat there.

The Sentinels made a circle around Tharadis, and as more poured into the Hall, a second and a third circle. Though the whole of their order wouldn't fit in the Pit, Yarid reckoned a sizable fraction were crowded in here.

As one, the Sentinels drew their swords and held them high. In the span of a breath, the Pit had turned into the toothy maw of some massive monster.

The circles of Sentinels parted as another figure made his way to their center. The helm this one wore was plumed with a spray of violet.

Captain Rannald Firnaleos.

All of the Sentinels were imposing, but Rannald most of all. With his faceguard lifted, he circled Tharadis, eyeing him up and down. Tharadis returned the study impassively.

Rannald halted and looked up at his wife's alcove. She leaned against the railing, staring down. Something silently passed between them. Sherin's face was cold and getting colder.

Rannald nodded as if he had been expecting the reaction. He turned and addressed the Council, voice booming. "War with these people is not the only answer." It seemed that Rannald had been standing outside the doors, listening. Yarid didn't have time to wonder why.

"Of course," said Frandera. "They *could* respect the rule of law."

"The Naruvians do not recognize our laws," Rannald countered. "That much has been established. I assume that as Warden," he said, turning back to Tharadis, "you have total authority over military matters."

Tharadis seemed to ponder this for a moment. Military matters had never risen their head for Naruvieth, since they had been cut off from the Accord for nearly the entirety of its existence. Until now, there had been no one for them to go to war with. "Yes, I suppose I do."

Rannald turned back to the Council. "If things progress on their current course, we will be killing the very people we were hoping to trade with. I wish to put a stop to that before it even begins. I want to prevent this war."

Jacobs opened his hands in pleading. "We're open to suggestions, Captain."

Seeing that there were no objections, Rannald continued. "All right. One of the original Articles of the Accord stated that any method of dispute resolution agreed upon by all affected parties could stand in place of governmental action, insofar as it does not violate any of the other Articles of the Accord or the described Rights of Man."

There were a few moments of furious paper shuffling down in the Pit, and the head of one of the clerks popped up from behind the circles of Sentinels. "Confirmed."

"Further," said Rannald, "that the affected parties could delegate the means of the resolution to willing participants, even if they were not involved in the original dispute."

"Confirmed."

"Also, that the government *itself* could qualify as one of the affected parties in such a situation."

"Con … confirmed." The little clerk who had been so eager to help suddenly looked like a mouse watching a trap slowly descend upon him yet was somehow unable to flee.

Rannald smiled. He turned back to Tharadis. "If you were to make a military decision, here and now before witnesses, would your people abide by it?"

The answer was long in coming. "Yes. It would be enforced, but only if written down and signed by me. And they have ways of telling if it was written under duress."

"If you told your people to stand down and not defend against the invaders as they completed the Runeway, they would do it?"

"They would adhere to the law," said Tharadis, somewhat cautiously. His expression was a more subdued version of the clerk's. "Anyone who violated the law would be treated as a criminal, just as under any normal circumstances."

"This war you've promised could end a lot of lives, and ruin many more.

Worse, your people would lose. Naruvieth is a small land compared to the Accord, has no standing army, and has no experience in combat. Peaceful though the times may be, those north of the Rift have had some practice killing each other at times."

"You underestimate the willpower of those fighting for their homes."

"No," said Rannald, meeting his eyes, "I don't. I know very well the strength of that force." He scratched his chin briefly. "And I would hate to see it crushed by the ranks of those who have no such care."

"Captain Firnaleos," boomed Jacobs, "is any of this leading anywhere?"

"Yes, Councilor." Rannald began to raise his arm and froze mid-motion. After a moment's hesitation, he beckoned to one of his men. The other Sentinel dropped to a knee, bowed his head, and in a single deft move, offered the hilt of his sword to his captain.

Rannald's head tilted slightly, as if he were about to look up at his wife's alcove again. He didn't, though. Instead, he reached out and wrapped his fingers around the sword's hilt, lifting it from his man's hands.

He stared at his own face, reflected in naked steel.

Yarid knew that sword. The amethyst in the pommel was unmistakable. Guiding Light.

Rannald lowered the sword to his side. "If the Council of the Wall and the acting representative of the Naruvian nation consent, I wish the decision to continue construction to rest upon the outcome of a trial by combat. Between myself, and Tharadis of Naruvieth."

Chapter 46: A Presentation of Swords

I think," said Yarid, stifling the outcries that erupted at Rannald Firnaleos's suggestion, "that decorum has been sacrificed to emotion." *That* shut people up.

"We are the Council of the Wall, after all," he said. "Not some traders' guild." There was some muttering down in the Pit, doubtless from representatives of one of the traders' guilds. He pressed on. "It is important that we fairly weigh the propositions given to us, especially when the stakes are high. I think that we should give proper, reasoned consideration to Rannald's proposal. After all," he added with a smile, "when have the Sentinels involved themselves in politics? Never, as far as I am aware. I think that, in and of itself, should warrant our careful deliberation."

Puzzled expressions spread throughout the room, then quickly turned into calculating gazes. What *did* the Sentinels have to gain from such a proposal? Why now, here? What interest did they have in the Naruvian? The truth was, Yarid only wanted to buy himself some time to think it out. He thrived in chaos; that was his true element. But that was only because he usually was the most unpredictable force in play. He didn't like that both Tharadis and Rannald had chosen to trump Yarid in that regard. It also didn't hurt to remind Rannald that the key players in this little drama were the Council. It was their decision, after all.

Rannald Firnaleos was studying Yarid with interest.

Yarid ignored him. While the discussion resumed at a more civilized level, Sherin walked out. Yarid watched her go, wondering if Rannald's decision to take up the sword again would have any effect on their marriage. While they tended to be rather private—and secure against any breaches of privacy, much to Yarid's chagrin—everyone knew that Sherin's rigid pacifism and Rannald's captaincy were a source of conflict within their marriage, and it was always assumed that his unwillingness to hold a sword was some sort of compromise for the sake of their relationship. If it was, then perhaps certain opportunities, previously hanging from the tree, were ripe enough to bear fruit for one watching the ground. *And what delicious fruit it would be.*

However, it was just as possible that this could have cemented their relationship by the very fact that Rannald was doing this to stop a war. It could make her feel like a fool, perhaps even change her mind about things. Probably not, though. Pacifists were stubborn, unreasonable creatures by nature, and Sherin more so than most.

More urgent, however, was the current situation. Before joining the Sentinels and eventually becoming their Captain, Rannald had led a rebellion in Caney Forks, a swampland which had been the last holdout of slavery in the Accord. He hadn't been a slave himself, but he had convinced them to take up arms and fight their way to freedom. The rebel forces were crushed of course—slaves had no chance against trained soldiers—but the Council had stepped in to ensure Caney Forks ended their practice. It was one of the few times Yarid had failed to sway the Council, and that failure still stung.

Rannald had survived the war, and for good reason: he had killed every man in his path. He had developed a reputation as an absolute monster on the battlefield—but he was only one man, and couldn't fight every battle himself. But those where he did fight, he won.

Of course, Rannald hadn't touched a sword in years, so his skills could have suffered from neglect. And no one really knew anything about Tharadis. Stories had trickled up from Naruvieth about how he had killed his way into the position of Warden, slaughtering all the men in his way. Some say it was only a dozen deaths between Tharadis and his office, while more preposterous estimates claim it was an army he had butchered. Rumors like that always had the stink of exaggeration about them, but these were rather consistent in that the spilling of blood was involved.

And there was that strange blue sword. Would that be enough to hand the advantage to even an average swordsman? Even if it wasn't enough to help him defeat Rannald, it should make the odds a little more interesting.

After an admonition by Frandera that this sort of decision would be final, a vote was called. Yarid made it clear, with a few subtle gestures and glances, that he would be calling in favors for some of those who seemed to vote opposite the way he wanted. Some of those favors would be wasted, he knew. It was likely for some of them, their show of indecision was simply that—a show, and their "favor" of voting the way Yarid wanted was what they were planning to do anyway. But it was important enough that he would rather waste favors than see anything but an interesting outcome.

The tally was counted.

The Council was in favor of Rannald's solution, trial by combat.

That meant it was all up to Tharadis.

Rannald turned to the man and whispered something to him. Councilors leaned forward, but Yarid could tell that they, like he, were unable to hear what was said. None of the functionaries bothered to lean forward; they presumably didn't want to push their faces through a wall of Sentinels that had their swords drawn.

Tharadis's eyes widened briefly, then he nodded.

Aloud, he said, "I accept the terms." His eyes met Rannald's. "Trial by combat for the fate of the Runeway, and of Naruvieth."

If tension were a taste in the air, Yarid would be gagging. The two of them squared off. Rannald stood as though the sword in his hand were an unnatural thing one moment, though the next it seemed as if he had reattached a long-lost limb. Tharadis took a deep breath, unsheathed his own sword, and lifted it over his head in that same strange stance as before.

Rannald saw that and started, as if slapped. Of all the things that could possibly happen next, he begun to chuckle low in his throat, as if something had been confirmed for him.

This would be the first time that blood would ever have been spilled in the Council Chambers. Many of the Councilors seemed hungry for it.

Rannald was the first to move.

It wasn't a move Yarid—or anyone else, for that matter—could have expected. In much the same way as Rannald's man had first presented his sword, Rannald dropped to a knee, bowed his head, and offered Tharadis the hilt.

Tharadis, for his part, tapped the edge of his own sword against Rannald's shoulder. A muffled clang rose up from his cloaked breastplate and Rannald staggered, as if the weight of such a gentle tap were a burden with the weight of the world.

Tharadis sheathed his sword and took the one offered. "I declare you vanquished." He raised the sword. "And the matter of the continued construction of the Runeway, as witnessed and agreed to by all involved parties, is now resolved. You are legally prohibited by the very law upon which your authority rests from resuming construction. Should you choose to continue, you would thus be choosing to violate the Accord, and all claims to office or authority would be henceforth forfeit."

Sint stabbed an accusing finger in Tharadis's direction. "Even though you cheated!"

Rannald's jaw tightened as he stood. "There was no cheating here, Councilor. Every aspect of this trial by combat was lawful and binding." He turned to the crowd of lessers. "Isn't that correct?"

That same clerk, sounding much-harassed, said, "Confirmed."

"Besides," Rannald continued, more calmly, "the Council often declares that it is the citizen's responsibility to know the law, and that ignorance of the law is no excuse for breaking it." He cocked his head and blinked innocently. "Does the Council regard itself as above such limitations?"

"Point taken, Captain," said Frandera, "though we could all do without the sarcasm." She sighed as she turned to Erianna, who was still leaning against wall with her arms folded, face empty of expression. "I believe you now have much to tell your mistress, proxy."

Erianna straightened and strode to the center of the Pit. "She will not be happy." For her part, the proxy sounded like she couldn't care less how her mistress felt about the situation.

Frandera faked a smile. "Well, once she appears, we will be happy to discuss it with her further. Until then, I believe we may call this session of the Council of the Wall to recess."

Yarid made himself scarce by ducking into the hallway before anyone else could. He didn't want anyone to ask him why he made them vote in favor of the trial by combat if it were only to end with Tharadis winning— even if it was by default. He knew that's what they would think. As if it was Yarid's fault! Besides, if they were so concerned about it, they should have never gotten themselves indebted to him.

But honestly, he was less concerned with the other Councilors than he would if they were a cloud of gnats. He was more interested in the outcome. The Runeway, once it was supposed to have been built, would have been a constant, something those of weaker mind and constitution would be able to count on. A man like Yarid, who thrived on constant change, had little to gain from such a thing, despite all of its supposed advantages.

This new alliance between the Sentinels and the Naruvian, however … What did it *mean?*

The Dome and Spire had several small rooms that could be reserved by Councilors for a variety of different functions, such as entertaining, making discreet deals, or making discreet, ahem, *alliances*, the kind where one tamps down the lights. One could also use the rooms to hide, which was exactly what Yarid intended to do. He sent one of his three servants scurrying, and within a handful of minutes, he had a private sitting room where he could be alone with his thoughts.

He didn't like it. Those thoughts rattled around in his head, raising a clamor. Distracted, he gestured at one of his servants. "Send for Tirfaun." There was just too much for him to take in all on his own. Tirfaun's presence would let him think at his own pace.

He sat down on the divan, floral in design, and waited while one of his servants poured him a goblet of light red wine and set it on the short bronze table in front of him. The other servant fluffed the cushions, changed the flowers, and turned down the wicks on the smoky oil lamps on either side of the small room to keep Yarid from getting a headache. Though he suspected it was already too late for that.

Yarid closed his eyes and pinched the bridge of his nose. Yes, definitely too late. *Damn you, Tirfaun, for making me wait.*

A knocking on the door. Doubtless his third servant, back from his errand. But why knock? Before Yarid could summon a threat, the door swung inward. The other two servants looked up. Their eyes widened briefly, and they scurried out.

Yarid's back straightened as they fled the room. "Where do you think you are going?" One of them glanced back briefly, but neither slowed. They left him alone. What in the Abyss were they thinking? He would flay them!

It wasn't Tirfaun who stepped into the room and shut the door behind himself. It was his manservant, Jordin. "I don't remember calling for you," Yarid said, irritated. "Where is Tirfaun?"

The balding older man didn't respond, but rather made his way to the far corner and tugged up the knees of his gray trousers to crouch down. Apparently, he hadn't taken himself shopping for new clothes yet. Jordin studied the wall intently for a moment, running his fingers across the intricately-scrolled molding where the wall met the floor. He walked his hand up with his fingers until he had measured two handwidths up and knocked gently.

"Abyss take you," Yarid snarled, "answer me! And what the hell are you doing?"

Jordin finally looked over. There was darkness in his eyes, and none of the subservience Yarid had seen every time their gazes crossed. He almost couldn't believe that this was the same man. Yarid wanted to leap up and scold him but ended up inching back on his couch.

With grave purpose, Jordin crossed to the couch, but turned to the side at the last moment. He grabbed one of the cushions and held it up in front of Yarid. "Put this over your face," he said improbably.

"Are you mad, Jordin? Just what—" The next moment, he was eating cushion.

Before he could even make sense of that, Jordin's fist slammed into his stomach, blasting all the air out of him. The pain was at once sharp and dull, as if someone had dropped on axe on his gut while he had been sleeping.

"Just so we're clear on the true nature of our relationship," said Jordin calmly, as if he did this every day. "And don't bother calling for help. The men outside are mine and always have been." He pulled the cushion away.

Yarid lay on his side, wheezing. Every breath was agony. He glared up at Jordin, who was blurry in the dim light. And, Yarid was ashamed to realize, through his tears.

Jordin's gaze sharpened, like a hawk's. "What, no questions? I was at least expecting a, 'Why are you doing this?' Or at least a, 'What do you want?'"

Yarid forced a grin. "You obviously haven't been doing this very long. Or have you only heard about it in the stories?"

"Yes, you are the master of intimidation. An amateur like me has no chance, does he?" Though Jordin himself didn't look the least bit intimidated. "But that's about all you're good for, isn't it? Certainly not for ensuring the gears of fate don't grind to a halt."

Ah, Yarid thought. *The Runeway.* "Here's a question for you," he said. Each word was agony, but he forced himself back up into a sitting position. "Who are you working for?" Yarid cocked his head. "Come to think of it, you've never mentioned your family. Is there a reason for that? Does someone have them?"

"I've never mentioned my family because you never asked." The words were nearly spat out, clearly a sticking point. So Yarid had guessed right.

"Well," he said, leaning back now that he felt he had some control of the situation. "I see that we are both at the mercy of this mysterious party. Clearly, they have a message they want you to deliver, or else you wouldn't have revealed yourself. What is it?"

Jordin sighed. All of his years seemed to pile back up on him. "Salvage the Runeway situation. They know you called in your favors just to see what would happen with that duel. They're not stupid, and it's dangerous to assume you know half as much as they do. You're as much to blame for this as either the Naruvian or that damned Sentinel."

"Shores, Jordin. You almost sound as if you *care*."

A knife appeared in Jordin's hand. Its short curved edged glimmered in the lamplight. He held it steadily, not at all like a man who was afraid. Yarid knew then that perhaps the man really *had* been doing this kind of thing for some time.

"All they said was that you had to remain alive."

Fear clenched in Yarid's belly, but he strove to keep it from showing. He raised his hand in a gesture of peace. "All right," he said, dropping his hand. His voice was steadier than it had any right to be. He shrugged. "But what do they expect me to do? It's *law* now, as agreed upon by all the members of the Council."

Jordin narrowed his eyes. "The law has never stopped you before."

"Breaking the law is one thing. Forcing the entire *Accord* to break it is something else entirely."

Jordin grunted. "You'll think of something, won't you?" He lifted his blade and waggled it. "Or you die."

"And what happens to you if I die?"

Jordin shrugged. "I don't care what happens to me. And neither should you." He put his knife away. "Think of something."

"How long do I have?"

"The Governor is petitioning the Council later today, correct?"

Yarid had a feeling the Governor wouldn't be *petitioning* so much as *demanding*, but, "Yes. We reconvene in three hours."

Jordin nodded. "You have until then."

Chapter 47: A Flash of Yellow

There." From the small grassy hill where they stood, Chad pointed at the tall walls and the sprawling city beyond. "That's the city. Garoshmir."

Nina nodded, though her head didn't move as fast as she'd expected, making her feel dizzy. Truth was, she'd barely understood what Chad was talking about, she was so tired. But she trusted him, and simply decided to agree with whatever he was saying.

Though it was getting to be late in the afternoon, the wall to the north shone like a bone under the high noon sun, dwarfing the walls surrounding the city. Andrin's Wall, Nina knew. It was impossible to mistake it. Everyone knew Andrin's Wall, even the people who'd never seen it before. Nina smiled, thinking how jealous Esta would be, but the muscles in her mouth felt ... *heavy*. As if they, too, were too tired to move. Her eyelids fluttered.

"Hey, Nina. Nina!"

Chad caught her elbow as she fell to her knees. Why was she on her knees?

Nina swiveled her head to inspect Chad as he lifted the edge of the bandage on her wrist. It was all soaked through with red. Her fingers were wet with red, too. Chad's face paled.

"This looks deep. Deeper than I thought." He released the edge of the bandage and met her eyes. "We need to find a healer."

"But, my mother—"

"Can wait," Chad said, cutting her off. He helped her to her feet.

"I'm steady," she said. "I can walk."

He nodded skeptically but let her be. "There's guards at the gate," he said, turning towards the city. "They don't look to be letting just anybody in there. We can get in faster and with less trouble my way."

Without waiting for a reply, he led her down the less inclined part of the hill, circling around to the hill's shadowed side. When Chad pressed his fingers into the grass, the shadows darkened to pure blackness. He crawled in. Nina followed.

They didn't have to walk very far in the shadow world until they found an image that satisfied Chad, though to Nina it just looked a confused jumble of shifting shapes. They slipped out into a wide, crowded street, filled with more people and horses and carts than Naruvieth surely had. Each side of the street had stalls hawking everything, from woven rugs to glass bottles to grilled meat that made Nina remember just how hungry she was.

Chad hooked Nina's arm in his own and dragged her to the nearest stall. A short fat man with a black beard called out for passersby to sample his wares, which happened to be the most delicious-looking pink apples Nina had ever seen. The apple merchant pretended that the two of them didn't exist when it was obvious to Nina he could see them. They were standing right in front of his stall when everyone else was ignoring him, after all.

"Pardon me," Nina said in her most polite voice. The man continued to ignore them.

"Hey, mister!" Chad lifted Nina's bloody hand up high. "We're looking for a healer! Hate to bleed all over these fine-looking apples."

The man's thick eyebrows bunched together in a menacing V as he finally regarded them. "The city guard will make you bleed a lot more if you ruin any of my goods."

Nina bowed her head. "Sorry for the bother." She started to pull a protesting Chad away from the stall when the man sighed.

"All right, all right. You look a mess, girl." The man's expression softened. "Head to the north end of the avenue and take a right. Healer's at the top of the steps."

She bowed again, smiling this time. "Thank you."

The man shooed them away, not unkindly, after Chad awkwardly tried to mimic Nina's bow. Once at the top of the stairs, Nina spotted a shop with a sign hanging near the door of a woman knitting, but what she was knitting was not a sock or a scarf but a person lying down. Chad nodded when he saw it too.

"Wait here," he said, leaving her leaning against the corner of the shop. She watched him glance both ways before disappearing into the alley right next to the healer's shop. What in the world was he doing in there?

When he finally came back, he gently shook her until she opened her eyes again and helped her in.

Books, dried herbs, and various bottles and measuring instruments lined the shelves tucked in the back of the shop behind a counter. A plump gray-haired woman with a peaked white cap and an apron that had likely also been white once sat behind the counter, tapping the side of a spoon over a bowl. Little bits of yellow powder fell off the edge of the spoon with each tap. The woman paused, her face frozen in intense concentration, when the small bell hanging from the door rang, announcing Nina and Chad's entrance. The woman took one look at Nina's hand and waved them in.

"Come on, then, into the back." She ushered them through a narrow passageway that led into a room at the back of the building and sat Nina down on a low table, curtly gesturing Chad to a stool. Once he sat down, pulling his knees up against his chest, the woman studied the two of them. "You have any money?"

Nina certainly didn't, but much to her surprise, Chad pulled a silver coin out of his vest pocket. "It's all I have, missus." His eyes were wide, tears gathering at their edges. "Is this going to be enough?"

Nina was shocked out of her stupor. What a liar he was! Those tears weren't real at all! And where did he get that coin? As the woman reached to take it from him, he gave Nina a quick little wink.

"That'll do, boy. Now," she said, pocketing the coin and turning to Nina with a smile that dimpled her round cheeks. Apparently, she had been fooled by Chad's little act. "Let's get you stitched up."

After it was all over, the healer made Nina lie down. The leather strap around her arm was really tight, making her fingers tingle, but at least they weren't bloody anymore. "I want you to stay here for now. And drink this water," the healer said, holding Nina's head with one hand and tipping the cup up with the other. "All of it. There you go."

"Nina," Chad said, standing next to the healer, "your mother said your family's here, didn't she? Who did she mean?"

Nina wiped her mouth and frowned. "Well, she wasn't really making sense. She said my father was here, but that can't be right. I know Uncle Tharadis is here, talking to the council about the big road." The healer started and gave Nina an appraising stare, but Nina ignored it. "He's the only one that would've come."

"Hmm." Chad folded his arms. "You aren't going anywhere anytime soon, but someone needs to tell him you're here. If he finds out you're here at all, he might think you're still in Falconkeep." The healer's head spun to face Chad, eyes so wide they nearly bugged out of her head. "We really don't want him to go there looking for you, right?" Chad asked.

Nina shook her head vehemently, though in truth, she thought Lora Bale ought to be the one afraid of *him*.

"All right, then." Chad's mouth spread wide in that grin of his. "While you're healing up, I'll find your uncle and bring him back here."

"You know what he looks like?" Nina asked.

Chad gasped in mock betrayal. "Of course I do. He's only the most famous man in Naruvieth. After me, that is."

Nina turned to the healer, whose mouth was gaping like a fish's. "Can I sit out front near the window? I want to watch for my uncle."

"Of—of course, little one." The woman smiled, though her face was so pale, Nina thought she might need a tourniquet, too. Nina followed her out to a narrow bench next to the window and sat down while the healer went back behind the counter. The window was fairly small, with little bubbles in the glass, but it was better than sitting in that back room with no way to watch the street.

"Chad," Nina said when the boy was halfway out the door. "Make sure you ask my uncle for some money. So you can pay back whoever you *borrowed* that coin from."

Chad grinned sheepishly, face reddening as he purposefully avoided looking in the healer's direction, and dipped low in an extravagant bow that shamed the bow he had given the merchant. He ducked out the door and disappeared into the crowd, though Nina knew he would be looking for someplace secluded and full of shadows.

Nina looked through the window, clutching the Raccoon Family. She wondered how Rogert, Noil, and Wenny were. Nina hoped they were all right. Thinking about them, how Nina had to leave them behind, made her want to cry, but at least Vidden and Alicie wouldn't bother them anymore. At least she had done that much for them.

In her mind Nina called out for her mother, but her mother didn't answer. Maybe she was out looking for Uncle Tharadis, too. She sighed, about to give up and just lie down when she caught a fleeting glimpse of a familiar flash of yellow cloth in the crowd outside.

She frowned. Was that Esta? And who was that bearded man she was with?

At first, Nina thought it was impossible that Aunt Esta was here. But then she remembered what her mother had said: her *family* was waiting here. That meant Esta could be here, too.

Ignoring the stern glance from the healer, Nina took off the tourniquet, leapt off her bench, and rushed outside to find her aunt.

Chapter 48: The Search Ends

L et's take a right at the bottom of the stairs."

Esta nodded at Ander's instructions as he pointed. The foot traffic in Garoshmir was still heavy at this hour, even though many of the stalls packed along the market streets were beginning to pack up their wares for the day. Already, Esta could see candles lit through the windows of some shops. She supposed it was the rush of shopping that happened at the last moment before things closed down for the day. People often did the same thing in Naruvieth.

With the tips of his fingers of his left hand, Ander kept a gentle pressure on the small of her back. It wasn't a possessive touch, like Nedrick would've used, but rather a simple necessity due to the crowds. In truth, Esta didn't mind the man's touch. The whole episode with Meedith had made her realize just how vulnerable—and stupid—she'd been. Ander was no Shoresman, of course, but she was still glad for his reassuring presence as he guided her through the winding streets of Garoshmir.

"Follow the curve and go left," Ander said. "There'll be a foot bridge. Keep sharp after that; it's a bit of a rough neighborhood. But I know some people there. We should be able to find out where your brother is staying." Under his breath, almost too quiet for Esta to hear, he added, "Damn fool for not staying at the Dome and Spire, if you ask me."

Esta smiled. The guards at the city gate had been just as flummoxed when they'd told her and Ander that Tharadis had asked directions for an inn, even though his written summons clearly stated an apartment was available for him in the same building as the Council Hall. It was just like Tharadis to refuse extravagance and insist on paying for his own lodging. Thinking of his mulish pride only made her realize how much she missed home, how much she wished she could just grab Tharadis and Nina by the hand and drag them back whether they liked it or not. Shores, she even found herself missing that fool Nedrick. She was glad Ander was walking behind her, unable to see the tears forming in the corners of her eyes. *Foolish girl.* She never should've let that woman take Nina.

A few streets back, Esta had caught a glimpse of a girl through a shop window that reminded her so much of Nina. If only it were that easy. If only Nina weren't trapped in that awful Falconkeep. If only she could just walk right into that shop, wrap Nina up in a hug, and take her home right now.

But of course, it wouldn't be so easy. Nothing, Esta was beginning to realize, was ever that easy.

After they crossed the arched wooden foot bridge Ander mentioned, the street narrowed into an alley. There weren't nearly as many stone buildings here. Most of them were daub-and-wattle, and some were made entirely of wood, leaning slightly and looking as if the tiniest spark would set them ablaze. The smell on this side of the river turned Esta's stomach, and it wasn't hard to see why—refuse littered the uneven paving stones, forcing Esta to watch her step. She even had to walk around two dead cats, drowned by the look of them. Covering her nose and mouth with her hand, she decided it was best not to look so hard at what she was stepping around.

She couldn't fathom what kind of person would live in such a place, but clearly people did. Clothes hung from lines strung across the narrow width of the alley, blocking out parts of the twilit sky. She wished she hadn't needed to leave her spear and knife in the stables outside the city walls, but Ander had convinced her she couldn't enter armed. He could, because he was part of the Way Patrol, which was sanctioned by the Council.

Again, she was glad Ander was behind her. The alley was rather narrow, though. If trouble arose ahead, Esta could only hope that she wouldn't get stuck between it and Ander's axe.

To Esta's relief, they didn't have to go far. Ander stopped her when they came to a rickety wooden door, barely tall enough for Esta to step through; Ander would have to duck, even though he had left his helmet out in the stables, too. He knocked.

Moments later, the door opened inward, expelling a cloud of perfumed air so pungent it stung Esta's eyes. A short, stocky woman stood half-hidden behind the door, peering out at them suspiciously. Her pale, blocky face was heavily made up, rouge so thick that it flaked. A maroon satin wrap trimmed with tiny brass bells covered her hair. Cheap, gaudy rings adorned her fingers. The woman's gaze lingered on Esta a little longer than she would've liked before turning to Ander. "You."

"Me," Ander replied.

"That all you're carrying?" she asked as she glanced at the axe on his belt.

"It's all I've ever needed."

The woman grunted. "Leave it with Mick and we can talk. Come in, come in, girl. Don't gawk at me like that." The woman shuffled into the building, impatiently gesturing Esta to follow.

"In you go." Ander's fingers felt stiff against her back as he guided her through the door.

Esta turned her head and dropped her voice to a whisper. "What is this place?"

"A brothel," he answered.

A towering man with his heavily-scarred chest bare save for a worn leather vest, presumably Mick, took Ander's axe from him as he continued guiding Esta in. The short woman gestured for them to enter a richly-appointed parlor.

Or at least that was how it looked at first. Esta noticed that everything only appeared to be of high quality—a bureau topped with painted plaster instead of real marble, furniture studded with colored glass beads instead of gems. Another woman, this one tall and in a shocking state of undress, stood next to the parlor's sole sofa, hands folded in front of her, eyes lowered. Esta quickly averted her gaze, but the woman just stood there, wearing almost nothing at all. Feeling her cheeks flush in embarrassment for the poor woman, Esta forced herself to calm down; it was a brothel, after all. She supposed such garments, if they could even be called that, were normal here.

Esta whirled to face the short woman, while Ander leaned against the door jamb, arms folded and eyes fixed on Esta.

"I'm looking for my brother. He's here to talk to the Council about the Runeway, but we're not sure where he's staying." The words spilled out of her in a rush. Esta didn't want to stay in this place a moment longer than she had to.

"The Council, you say?" Smiling, the woman stepped forward and reached up to touch Esta's cheek. "Such lovely coloring, girl. My, it even looks natural. Where did you say you were from?"

"Naruvieth. My brother's the Warden there; he's the one I'm looking for. If you help me find him, both of us—my brother and I, that is—we would be very grateful."

The woman's smile faded, and she turned to Ander. "The Warden's sister."

His eyes never left Esta as he spoke. "You have my assurance." Esta's head swiveled between the two, but she couldn't make any sense of the exchange.

The woman sighed and turned back to Esta. "Some tea?" She picked up a small, empty ceramic cup from the end table next to the sofa, handing it to Esta. But before Esta had a grip on it, the woman let go. The cup barely brushed Esta's fingers before shattering on the hardwood floor.

Tsk-ing, the short woman put her hands on her hips and shook her head as she surveyed the damage. "An expensive mistake, girl. It'll cost you. In order to cover the costs, we'll have to put you to work for a long, long time." She looked up and met Esta's gaze. There was a flash of genuine pity in her eyes.

"What do you mean?" Esta asked in a tiny voice. Though the room hadn't changed, she felt as if the floor had dropped out from under her. "No, I'm not … I'm looking for my—"

"Hush, now dear." The woman turned to Ander. "You're sure this brother of hers won't come looking for her?"

"Wait," Esta said, but the woman was no longer listening to her. She hadn't even touched the cup, not really. It wasn't her fault. She knew that; everyone did. Esta knew then that none of that mattered. The truth didn't matter to these people. Not even Esta mattered.

She looked at Ander's face. His eyes were cold. Unfeeling.

Everything had been a lie. She was worth less to him than the shattered cup on the floor.

She bolted for the door. Ander's fist in her stomach stopped her.

The room *did* change then—it spun until Esta was flat on her back. The impact of the hardwood floor jarred her teeth and sent a wave of nauseating pain through her head. Each breath felt like fire. It was a struggle to keep her eyes open. *No*, she thought. *This isn't real. None of this is real.*

All she could see was the parlor's ceiling, dark green paint flaking in places to reveal the white plaster underneath. Everything here was so shoddy, so fake. She heard voices, but they seemed disembodied, disconnected to everything she thought she knew. *This isn't real.*

"I said I give you my assurance, and I meant it. He won't come looking. Officially, she's already dead. I filed the report at the Waystation. A real tragedy, it was."

"Oh? And who was the killer in this sad little story?"

"Meedith, of course."

"Meedith? Won't she … talk?"

"You and I have nothing to worry about. Meedith won't be telling anyone anything."

"I see. And who did the deed?"

"Lannod."

"Owly? But Meedith was his own—"

"Yes. But who better? He's been wanting to put a knife in her for years. Ever since she burned his tongue out."

"Mm. I suppose I shouldn't be worried about him. But you're sure no one else can cause us trouble? I'd hate to have to put an end to our arrangements."

"Now that you mention it, I might need to put the screws on our stablehand, but I'm sure he'll come around. Otherwise, we're clear."

"Good." A pause. "Beth, don't just stand there. Get her onto the sofa."

"Yes, mistress," said a new, feminine voice.

Strong but gentle hands pulled Esta up onto the sofa. Once Esta was seated, head resting on the hard armrest smelling faintly of mildew, the voices continued.

"I suppose you'll want some sort of finder's fee, Ander."

"Free rein."

"Ha! You must be barking mad!"

"Not for all of your girls. Just this one."

"Oh, grown a soft spot for her, have you? Three times a month, no more. No cuts, no bruises. No *more* bruises, I should say."

"Four."

A sigh. "You'll put me in the poorhouse yet, Ander."

"Hardly. I should ask for more, for all the coin she'll bring in."

"Well, I know men, and I know you. You'll want to have your first go right away, yes? She could use a bath first."

"No need. I'll take her as she is."

"Fine, it's up to you. Beth?"

Those same strong but gentle hands lifted Esta up again, this time leading her up a flight of stairs.

"Help me," Esta whispered.

"Shh. None of that," came the feminine voice from earlier, speaking softly now from just behind her. "Just don't think about what's coming, okay? You'll get used to it eventually. Everyone does."

Esta heard the words but didn't understand. They made no sense. Such words couldn't possibly be meant for her.

Chapter 49: The Visitor

Yarid wasn't eager to return to the Council Hall. The three hours that had passed since his meeting with Jordin had left him on edge. Which interfered with his ability to think of a way out. Which left him more on edge, swirling him deeper into a vortex of panic and doubt. By the time he had sat back down in his alcove a quarter hour before the Council reconvened, he felt as bedraggled as if he had spent the last several nights drinking instead of sleeping. And still with no solution in sight.

He realized, with sudden stark clarity, just how unfair the whole situation was. Why did *he* have to be responsible for the construction of the Runeway? It wasn't merely his vote that sent them on this course—though most of the other votes were things he had engineered. Still, he knew just how unfair the world was—just ask Councilor Nangrove—so it didn't help to sit around, pining after better days. That would only lead to one of his blacker moods. No, all he could do was try to straighten the kinks as much as the rest of the world allowed.

The lamps had begun to brighten. Gorun had yet to show, which was fine by Yarid; he didn't need the old man distracting him with his complaints about aching joints and the youths of today. There were two related problems here that Yarid could see. The first was the Naruvian. Even if he were dealt with and tossed in a ditch somewhere, there's no telling what the rest of Naruvieth would do. If that man was an accurate sample of the whole, they would become maddened with irrational revenge and become even more of a problem than they are now. As much as Yarid preferred a messy solution, he didn't like causing problems that he himself would end up dealing with.

The second problem, of course, was the people threatening him. Though the Naruvian was nearly as pompous as Gorun, Yarid didn't want him dead. His moralism was a predictability; and in the world of the Council of the Wall, predictability was its own sort of chaos, as evinced by the improbable series of events just that morning. If nothing else, Tharadis kept Yarid sharp.

Those threatening him, however, were an irritant. Bribed servants, knife-wielding bullies … Yarid was not impressed. He preferred a more

293

subtle game. And as often as he found himself waking in the morning and regretting opening his eyes, Yarid was now genuinely terrified of the serious prospect of death. Especially when dealt by someone as lowly as Jordin.

How embarrassing that would be.

Could Tirfaun be of use here? Snooping was his specialty, but then it wasn't exactly a secret that he consorted with Yarid. It was likely that whoever was threatening Yarid had made what they considered to be adequate protections against Patterners before coming out in the open with their threats.

The Council Hall begin to fill, but Yarid barely noticed. He smiled. His enemies likely had adequate protections against *most* Patterners. But Tirfaun was extraordinary. Yes, using him might be the best option. Yarid couldn't simply let such threats stand unanswered.

"Please welcome Shad Belgrith, Governor and Lesser Councilor of Twelve Towers."

After her proxy's remarkable presentation, many of the Councilors—and most of the men in the Pit—watched the twin doors to the Hall open with keen interest. Yarid paid little attention; his mind was filled with plots. How best to use Tirfaun? The man could sniff out the culprit quicker than a bloodhound … but that wasn't all he was good for. He could wreak retaliation so subtle that his victims would never be able to gather evidence that Yarid had anything to do with it. Except, of course, his knowing smile when he first witnessed their devastation.

A number of pleasant and violent fantasies paraded before his mind's eye, and it wasn't until the Pit was filled with soldiers wearing burnished bronze armor and holding gleaming pikes—much like it been filled with Sentinels earlier in the day—did he remember the real world around him.

"What in the unholy Abyss is happening, Gorun?" he said quietly but sharply.

"Hush, you fool. Belgrith's men are filling the Hall." The old man looked troubled. "Or did you not see the procession earlier? I thought even someone as oblivious as you would have seen *that* coming."

"Of course I knew about the procession. The only person who knew about it before me was Shad herself. I just … what are they doing in *here?*"

"Threatening us, no doubt. It seems the only way people think they can get our attention is through intimidation." Gorun shook his head, which made Yarid sick to watch. He was surprised it remained attached to Gorun's skinny little neck. It seemed like memory and willpower were all the kept the man from falling apart. "Things used to be different. When I was on the Lesser Council, we garnered *respect*, from everyone. No one ever—"

"Drown it, old man. Your reminiscences annoy me."

The door to their personal alcove opened. Both Yarid and Gorun spun around in their chairs in surprise. Two of Shad's soldiers stepped into the alcove, shoving aside the servants, and shut the door behind themselves. They stood at attention on either side of the door, eyes forward and focused on nothing in particular in the manner disciplined guards had. Like the others, these two had pikes in hand—leaning at an angle to fit under the alcove's curved ceiling—and swords at their hips. Yarid could smell the oil of their polished plate breastplates and chain skirts.

He shared a glance with Gorun and noticed that all the other alcoves were equally occupied.

At least there is no confusion about where Shad stands with the Council, Yarid thought wryly. He tried to remember what it was like to be bored again and wondered why he ever complained.

A woman walked into the Pit, and even Yarid gawked. Shad Belgrith made Erianna Vondallor look a prudish old woman. Little more than strips of gauzy green fabric covered her feminine bits. Her choice of "clothing" would be scandalous in the bedroom. And here she was, in the Hall of the Council of the Wall. It didn't help that she had a figure that most women would sell their souls to have and most men would sell their wives to ... do things to.

Yarid realized right away, though, that her choice of clothing was more a matter of practicality than of fashion.

Nearly every inch of exposed flesh had been pierced.

Fear seized Yarid, and he struggled to tamp it down. *No*, he reminded himself. *That is just a superstition. Piercings cause sheggam transformation as much as dancing causes the rain to fall*. Still, he shifted uncomfortably in his seat as he watched her make her way to the center of the Hall.

Body piercings had never been banned outright anywhere in the Accord, but the effect had been the same. Everyone had been told as a child: *make sure to wash the wound if you scrape your knee! Never take off a poultice until the healer tells you to! Expose your blood to the air too long and evil will find its way inside you!*

Growing up, Yarid had always thought it was nonsense, but later, he had read the histories from Andrin's time and before. And everyone knew the tale of the Battle of Skullslide, where the sheggam had only wounded the soldiers of Green regiment. The shegasti power set into their wounds, and the wounded turned. The regiment tore itself apart within a few days. It was a more gruesome defeat than if the sheggam had slaughtered them outright.

Of course, that was a long time ago. The histories had been oral for decades after Andrin's Wall had been built was civilization was allowed to resume. Most of the accounts of what happened before then were second-hand.

There were some who doubted the stories. Some even doubted the existence of the sheggam. They were fools, of course; sheggam had been seen south of the Wall twice since the creation of the Accord. Both times were when Knights of the Eye had taken their powers too far. Those idiots claimed to protect the lands of man from the sheggam threat, when they themselves were the only source of such a threat. Yarid hated few people, but he had a special torture chamber in his heart for the blatant stupidity of the Knights of the Eye.

If there was any proof to the claim that shegasti could worm its way into wounds, it was found in the Knights. That was how they gained their peculiar advantages: a piercing, which was somehow infected with shegasti. The Knights were always the first on the scene whenever the corpse of one of their brothers washed up somewhere, but a few had been examined by outsiders.

Without fail, there had always been a piercing in their flesh. Sometimes metal, but more than a few bone piercings had been found as well. Yarid shuddered to consider where those bones had come from.

It was true that the Knights could be prey to the same superstitions as everyone else, and that the piercings were merely the manifestation of that. But both cases of turning had been Knights, and no one else since the beginning of modern written history had turned.

Likely it had something to do with the fact that they were the only ones to pierce their skin.

That is, until Shad Belgrith came along.

Whatever appeal she'd had before Yarid noticed the piercings shriveled up into a ball of nausea and tucked itself into his stomach. Not even the sight of Erianna, standing with her head bowed deferentially behind her mistress, intrigued him. She was guilty by association. Even Shad's skin seemed to have a sickly, gray pallor to it. *No,* Yarid thought adamantly. *Just a trick of the light.*

His reaction must have been obvious. "Oh, Yarid," said Gorun with a hard grin, "what is this? Dare you *judge* someone? How quaintly moralistic."

"Sarcasm hardly suits you, old man." Odd. Gorun seemed to be the indifferent one. They had switched roles. *The bastard.*

Shad Belgrith scanned those assembled. When her eyes met Yarid's, he almost felt violated. Unsmiling, she stared him down, apparently reveling in his discomfort. *The bitch.*

"Councilors." Her clear, firm voice rang throughout the Hall, quelling the quiet muttering. "You disappoint me."

No one responded.

She began to pace around the small bit of clear space in the Pit. "I thought we had an agreement. One that benefited us all." She paused, as if to remind them how much she had invested in the project they had halted. "I gave you resources. I gave you techniques that eluded your most gifted builders. And I gave you my most skilled Patterners ... all so you could betray me."

"Governor Belgrith," said Frandera, "I am sorry to say that the law regarding this—"

"*You betrayed me!*" Tears welled in Belgrith's eyes; her fists were clenched. In that moment, she looked so much like a poor, maligned child that Yarid's heart briefly went out to her—until he remembered this child with a temper had a pike for every Councilor's neck in this room.

"You betrayed me," she said again in a quieter voice. "That was a mistake. One that you can still rectify."

Pembo Sint, apparently unaware of the danger all around him, leaned forward with a wicked grin. "We could have another duel—"

"Shut up, you twit." Frandera turned back to Shad. "I must admit that we were outmaneuvered, and now our hands are tied. Whatever authority granted to us by the Accord would become null and void were we to betray the law each of us swore to uphold." She opened her hands. "We have worked for years, just as you have, to see the Runeway become a reality. We have just as much incentive as you do to see it finished. Unfortunately, as a political institution, we just don't have the means to do so anymore. We have bridged the Rift and met our long-long brothers and sisters of Naruvieth, and though our relationship is currently not ideal, we are glad to have them back among us." She left out that they had declared their sovereignty and were no longer 'among us'. "We consider what we have been able to accomplish up until this point a victory, and we hope that you will join us in celebration of the advances we have made."

Sherin Firnaleos, recovered from whatever troubles her husband had caused her with his earlier antics, spoke up. "I believe you have some explaining of your own to do, Governor." She gestured at the pair of heavily-armed men standing behind her. "Such as why you deemed it necessary to bring soldiers here with you. The Council of the Wall has always stood for *peace*. Such displays of brute force have never accomplished anything but hardship and suffering." She, too, was just as oblivious as Sint to the danger these soldiers represented, it seemed.

"You stand for peace," Shad said, "until you don't." She gestured to Erianna behind her. "My proxy has told me all about your husband and how you approved his request to shed blood in this very Hall to solve your problems."

Sherin froze. She didn't rise to the bait.

Shad Belgrith smiled coldly. "But you misunderstand my intentions. These soldiers are not here to threaten. They are here to make you feel safe and comfortable."

"How do you reckon that?" Pembo Sint asked.

"I want to ensure that you are not disturbed by what you are about to see. The Council, I've learned today, is governed by fear. I would hate for such fears to lead to rash action." She gestured to one of her men in the Pit and stepped to the side with her hands folded behind her with Erianna, who suddenly looked shaken, at her heel. The man took off out the door.

Steel-shod boots clicked loudly out in the tile-floored hallway beyond the doors. Each footfall crunched; the weight behind them must have been immense. Were it not for the fact that the slow, measured pace were made by two feet, Yarid would have guessed it made by a draft horse.

A massive form, cloaked from head to toe, filled the doorway nearly to its full eight-foot height. The improbable man that stood there did not look fat at all, but what few details his dark, roughly woven cloak betrayed indicated a dense bulk of muscle. His back was arched slightly, a shadow-obscured face jutting forward like a horse's—though for some reason, Yarid's mind seemed unable to make out any other details of that face. Huge gloved hands hung at his side, lower than a normal man's would hang. Yarid had seen pictures of apes in a children's illustrated reader when he was very young; those pictures came to mind now. There was more animal than human in the cloaked figure before them.

"Governor Belgrith," Gorun said, his voice quivering more than usual. "Who is your guest?"

"A friend, Councilor. I give you Orthkalu." Her smile widened. "From north of Andrin's Wall."

Before the full meaning of those words could sink in, the cloaked form lifted its hood.

Its skin was the color of a drowned corpse. Crimson eyes, with only flecks of yellow for pupils, stared at the Councilors intently. Lips twitched, briefly revealing rows of narrow fangs lining its long muzzle. The hood fell away to reveal a thick, greasy mane of black hair, hanging limply around its massive shoulders.

A single word reverberated through Yarid's mind, crowding out all other thought: *sheggam.*

He must have stood because he felt himself slammed back into his seat by a firm, gauntleted hand on his shoulder. "Easy there, friend," said the soldier standing next to him. Where had he come from? The man's grip tightened.

Yarid got the hint. *That's no way to treat a friend.* But he took a deep breath, leaned back in his seat, and pretended at nonchalance. He didn't know if he succeeded by any measure, but the soldier seemed mollified enough to release his grip. Yarid rolled his shoulder to loosen it up and froze when he again caught sight of the beast standing in the center of the Pit.

A sheggam.

Here.

How? The Wall is impossible to breach.

He noticed more than a few of the soldiers were providing "safety and comfort" to various other Councilors who had reacted in much the same way as Yarid. One woman—Yarid couldn't think of her name at the moment—screamed and thrashed as two of Shad's men carried her out the back door of her alcove. Sherin Firnaleos was aghast. Councilor Mundt was slumped in his chair, passed out. Maybe even dead. Neither of the soldiers standing behind him seemed all that worried. Or interested.

"Abyss take me," muttered Gorun. He buried his face in his hands. "Abyss take me *right now.*"

In a daze, Yarid turned back to the Pit. Shad stood next to the monster, casual as can be, and spoke. "Orthkalu has come to speak to us in his official capacity as the ambassador of Sheggamur. I can personally vouch for his intentions. He wishes us no harm. He merely wants to repair the relationship between our peoples, which was so damaged by the misunderstandings of the past."

"Misunderstandings?" Sherin Firnaleos nearly launched out of her seat. "You call the intended destruction of the entire human race a *misunderstanding?*"

There were similar outbursts, but Shad waved them down. "Those are precisely the sort of misconceptions this meeting is meant to correct. After all, what can we really know about the past? The written histories of that time were lost, and stories were told and retold for many years before anyone thought to write them down. And can we really trust them? All we have is one side of the story. We have never even heard the *voices* of the victims of our centuries-long prejudice and superstitious ignorance, much less their side of the story." She nodded at the sheggam. "I think you should hear what he has to say before dismissing him outright."

Protestations arose from all corners. "Are you mad?"

"I can't believe this! This is preposterous! This is—"

"Get this woman out of here! And that … thing! Get them—"

"Traitor!"

In all the hubbub, the door to Yarid's alcove crashed open and Tirfaun was crouching at Yarid's side before the two soldiers could molest him.

"I'm going to kill him," he said without preamble. His face was fierce.

"Him?" Yarid stared at Tirfaun, then at the sheggam, then turned back to Tirfaun. "You can kill one of them?" he asked quietly and glanced over his shoulder at the soldiers, who were now watching them keenly.

"One of who? What are you talking about?" Tirfaun rose slightly to peer over the railing. He paled visibly. "Apoth's blood! Is that a …" He trailed off and shook his head. "That … changes things. Maybe it …" He frowned in concentration.

"Who do you want to kill?" Yarid asked.

Tirfaun noticed him again. "The Naruvian, of course. He's the one I told you about."

Yarid searched his memory and remembered a cryptic warning the day they had gone to visit Councilor Nangrove. Tirfaun was often full of cryptic warnings, though, and Yarid didn't think he'd need to remember every single one. "I don't think that killing the Naruvian will change the outcome of today. Rannald Firnaleos saw to that."

"Drown me, but talking to you is like speaking to a child. The Naruvian changes *everything*. Even a blind man could at least feel the ripples that man's footsteps sends throughout the world. You can't tell me you believe everything that happened today was an accident, can you?"

"Of course not. Rannald Firnaleos engineered it for some reason."

"Yes. And what reason is that?"

Tirfaun had a point. "So, what are you suggesting he is?" Yarid asked.

Tirfaun ran his fingers through his thin gray hair. "I honestly don't know. He's set off alarms with all the other Patterners in the city, though, and even a few outside."

"They told you this?" Yarid was skeptical anyone besides himself talked to Tirfaun of their own volition.

"They don't need to. I can feel their anxiety like it's my own."

"Have you ever considered that's all it is? Your own anxiety?"

Tirfaun met his gaze. "Have I ever given you reason to doubt me?"

Yarid raised his hands. "No, you're right. If there's anything I trust, it's your Patterning. But merely knowing he's a problem doesn't tell us how to fix it. Especially if we don't even know what kind of problem he is."

While Tirfaun squatted and leaned back against the wall to ponder this, Shad Belgrith raised her hands. "Please," she said. "I beg of you, *listen.* That is all I ask."

All it took for the rest of the Councilors to quiet down was a little more forcible restraint by Shad's soldiers.

"Thank you," she said. She took a deep breath to compose herself. "It's easy, when you are sitting in such comfort, to look upon others with disdain and judgment. We of the Accord have become fat with wealth and peace, so much so that we have forgotten what it means to suffer. We need for very little. Especially those of us in positions of power, who can merely take what we need when we need it from those who have it. Yet where does that leave the ones deprived by our greed and excesses?

"To think that we are so much better than everyone else, just because we took what they themselves made, is an injustice so great it sickens me. How many are starving in the streets of this city? A thousand? Two thousand? And what have any of you done but make them worse off?" She was accusing them of the same crimes that Tharadis did. Interesting, though, that they used the same justification to achieve contradictory goals. With the Council of the Wall caught in the middle.

Belgrith shook her head and looked up at Sherin Firnaleos. "Hypocrites, all of you. You say you are for peace. But what gesture of peace have you *ever* made to our neighbors to the north? Have you ever spoken to one, tried to understand his thoughts, his dreams, and desires? You act as if you know them so well, when most of you probably didn't believe the sheggam even existed before today."

She shrugged, ignoring the grumbling coming from the alcoves. "How long has it been since two cities of the Accord have fought each other? Five, six years? How long before that? Not long at all. Our history of 'peace,' as you called it, is a lie. We are a warfaring species. We kill each other as best as our weapons allow, and then abandon all real progress to develop better weapons. That's all we've ever been good at. Killing each other, and killing ourselves. We are the true monsters here." She stabbed a finger at the beast. "*Not* them."

"You seem to forget one important detail, Governor," said Councilor Frandera, voice heating. "We are all that's left of humanity because *they killed all the rest.*"

"Really? Can you be so sure? You sit here behind your gleaming white wall that protects you from the rest of the world. How can you claim to know anything about it when you don't even have the ability to look? Andrin didn't want to face the truth, so he walled it off for the rest of us and called the truth threatening. All we have are the stories he told our great, great-grandparents, doubtless enforced with an iron fist." Shad gestured at Erianna, who mysteriously produced a sheet of paper from somewhere on her person.

Shad held the paper high. "This is a letter from an emissary from a region of Sheggamur called Eleankuron." Mutters rose up at this. "Yes, you've heard of it. It's an old place, and grand I'm told. Grander than even Andrin's Wall. The emissary who wrote this is human."

"You expect us to believe that?" Frandera asked. "You just told us how ignorant we were for simply believing in our histories because we weren't there, and you expect us to trust you now? To place our faith in you, rather than the man that saved our civilization?"

"The man who *claimed* to save our civilization." Belgrith shrugged. "What really can we claim to know? All we have heard are the stories of one side. I personally don't know anything about Eleankuron. I've never been there—and I never will know anything about it unless we learn to broaden our horizons."

"You come," Sherin said, eyes burning, "bearing the standard of knowledge. Yet it is our knowledge that you ask us to betray."

Belgrith looked genuinely puzzled at this. "How can you ever claim to gain knowledge without an open mind? That is all I really ask of you. To keep an open mind."

"A reasonable request," said Pembo Sint with a smug expression on his weaselly face. Then he seemed to remember that a sheggam was in the room with him. His expression faltered and he looked to regret his outburst but realize he was committed. "We are the Council of the Wall, and if nothing else we are committed to fairness. We can't really be fair until we hear both sides, can we? Merely listening can't hurt us. It is the fact that we listen to both sides that makes us what we are." Almost as an afterthought, he added, "And listening doesn't mean that we have committed to any course of action."

"True," said Frandera. "It can't hurt anything just to listen to what … he … wants to say. If nothing else, we can become a little wiser about the world." Yarid recognized the tone of her voice. She wanted to know what she could about the beasts on the other side of the Wall. She could be shrewd, but her shrewdness was no secret to Yarid. She might as well have announced her suspicion for all the good her attempt at circumspection was.

And her words made sense. What harm could listening possibly do? If the beast asked something of them, they could always say no. And one could never have too much information.

Still, something about the situation left him uneasy, and it wasn't merely the guards. He could see a similar sentiment mirrored on the faces throughout the Hall.

"All right," said Gorun. "Unless anyone has any further objections to listening to a supplicant, which would be unprecedented, I say we allow the emissary to speak."

Yarid blinked at Gorun. He leaned forward and whispered, "You're throwing in with them?"

"No, of course not. Just because he looks different doesn't mean we can simply judge him."

Yarid eyed him warily then sat back in his chair. Such a sentiment wasn't exactly in keeping with Gorun's stodgy conservatism. He doubtless wanted to hear what such a creature could possibly say, just like Yarid and Frandera. It was odd, though, that he should speak such a desire openly. Gorun was usually subtler than that.

But then subtlety was apparently on its way out the door, to sit in a midden with all of yesterday's fashions. Yarid wondered where that left him. Unfashionable, or better than the rest of them? He wasn't quite sure what to make of that. Being unfashionable certainly didn't appeal to him, as fashion was a sort of power in its own right.

"Thank you," said Shad. "For your generosity. I was honestly worried that you wouldn't be open to discussions. I'm glad you've proved me wrong." She turned to the sheggam, who had since pulled his hood back up over his head to obscure it. Still, the creature's ghastly face was burned into Yarid's vision as surely as if he had stared at the sun.

Shad and the sheggam spoke to each other quietly. Yarid leaned in to see if he could hear what was said, but he was even more interested just to hear what the voice of such a creature would even sound like.

The sheggam turned to address them. "Our world is wounded." The words were thick, wet, and harsh, but intelligible. Yarid found himself wondering just how intelligent these creatures were. He didn't remember any accounts that indicated they were even capable of speech. Only brutality.

It spread its arms. "Our world is wounded," it said again. "Torn apart by strife and division. Our peoples were once one, with great things in our future. It is a cruel thing to see such potential wasted.

"The Wall built by Andrin, the betrayer of your people and ours, is the great symbol of this failure. It has kept our people apart for time beyond measure. And it still stands, as a mark of our collective shame for the crimes of the past and the legacy of hate that we share." It shook its hooded head. "With its ancient spell of confusion, created by the blood of Andrin's own Crafters, it has created an impassable barrier between us, and has even destroyed the seas around you. It is a *prison*."

Yarid was shocked to realize that it *was* a prison. He had never thought of it that way. Yet the fact that he could change his mind so suddenly set all the alarms in his head clanging. New truths, obvious in retrospect, can sometimes be very appealing. Yarid knew when he was being manipulated.

But to what end? He hoped his comrades were as wise to it as he was.

The sheggam continued. "Your Governor and fellow Councilor is correct. War is a way of life for you. One that you yourselves may not have chosen, but it is one that you have also left unchallenged. How many border disputes have you officiated today? Three, four? And the southern land, Naruvieth. They are open in their hatred for the unification of all peoples. They seek to weaken and divide you, using your integrity and sense of justice against you.

"That is how the enemy works. They take what is best about you and turn it against you. You trust in your fellow man, believe him to be righteous and good unless he proves himself otherwise. Yet it is this very trust that has betrayed you. You believe that mankind is all but extinct, that you are the only ones that are left? That is a *lie*. Humans are more numerous north of Andrin's Wall than here in the Accord. And there, in the land of Sheggamur, they have found peace. There is no conflict and no war. They live in coexistence with my people and with each other."

"Let's assume," said Frandera, "that we believed you. We could either be correct in doing so, and gain a friendly relation with you. Or we could be wrong, and you destroy us. You see, the risks greatly outweigh any potential gain."

"I assure you," said the monster, "that there is no risk. We aren't asking you to tear down the Wall. We don't even begin to know how."

"So? What do you want then?"

"We haven't earned your trust. We understand that." Again, it spread its arms wide, though it was about as comforting as a bear on its hind legs. "All we would like is the opportunity to earn it. We had hoped that some measure of trust had already been made with all that we have shared."

"Shared?" asked Sherin Firnaleos. "Governor, what have you not told us?"

The sheggam turned to Shad briefly, who suddenly looked somewhat modest. As much as someone dressed like that could. "I confess," she said, "that I have not been entirely honest. I assure you, however, that no lies have been told. I said that Twelve Towers would provide the techniques necessary to build the Runeway. What I did not mention, was that they did not originate there." She took a step back as a storm of protest erupted through the Hall, bowing her head humbly to weather it.

Even Pembo Sint was aghast. "You mean one of the greatest monuments mankind has ever built is a *sheggam* invention?"

"I, for one," said Sherin, "am glad that the Runeway's construction has been halted. And if hadn't been, I would have made sure of it myself, knowing what I know now."

Sint, ever quick on his feet, shot a slimy grin at her. "You and what army?"

Gorun, in the grandfatherly manner he adopted when it suited him, calmed the Council down. "Patterner Gherao."

The man's bald head popped up. "Yes?"

"How extensively has the Academy studied the Runeway?"

Gherao tapped his chin as he pondered the question. "It's impossible to know everything about it, especially in its unfinished state. But we have good reason to suspect that it is totally benign, and that it will only do what it was intended to do."

"So you do not believe that is, in some way, a weapon? Even knowing its source?"

"Well, ah …" He pulled on his collar. "I admit to some suspicion. But I believe that to be rooted in my own personal prejudice. No one has seen any indication that the Runeway would act differently to how we expect."

"You're sure?" asked Sherin. "What about what the Naruvian said, the danger he mentioned?"

"No. At least not intentionally. The very same power that prevents the sheggam from crossing Andrin's Wall prevents their Patterners from seeing beyond it."

"Which raises an interesting question." Councilor Frandera cocked her head as she regarded the sheggam. "How is it you are standing here before us?"

Utter silence, broken only by the sound of Yarid blinking. It was incredible to him that no one had thought to ask this until now. Though he thought he understood why; when a near-mythical beast, one of a breed that slaughtered nearly all of mankind, steps up to greet you, you don't think about introductions.

You run like the Abyss is snapping at your heels.

That instinct was alive and well in Yarid.

The sheggam didn't answer right away. "The Restless Ocean."

"Impossible!" someone shouted. "No one has crossed the Restless Ocean since Andrin's Wall was built!"

"Not impossible," Shad Belgrith said. She gestured to her companion. "Obviously. He's here, isn't he? Unless somehow the Wall's power has somehow been defeated. And we would know it if it had." True, as far as Yarid had heard the Patterners describe it in the past. The Wall had been built to show, in rather dramatic fashion, if its Pattern had been compromised. Its brilliant white color would fade to yellow, and the whole thing would come crumbling down, leaving all of the Accord and Naruvieth naked to the sheggam horde doubtless waiting beyond. No one could mistake it if they tried.

"What the Councilor says is true," said the sheggam. "None have crossed the Restless Ocean since Andrin's Wall, another way in which Andrin sought to trap you on this tiny peninsula. But it was not from a lack of trying. Every five years for the past two hundred, Sheggamur has sent an emissary skilled in Patterning to offer a gift to set right any past misunderstandings. I am the first to survive, it seems."

"And not without great personal cost," said Shad. "When Orthkalu washed up near the docks of Twelve Towers, his craft was broken in half and he was half-drowned. Both of his feet were swollen and needed to be bled. It was weeks before he could walk or eat on his own."

"And your first thought was to see a sheggam walking and eating in the halls of Twelve Towers," said Councilor Jacobs, his tone thick with skepticism.

"Yes, of course. Twelve Towers is a civilized place. We don't simply go about slaughtering every stranger we see."

No one thought it worth pointing out that most strangers weren't sheggam.

Yarid turned to Tirfaun and said softly, "I don't suppose you can corroborate any of this."

Tirfaun shook his head. "No easier than you can."

Yarid nodded. He didn't believe in Shad's magnanimity any more than he did the sheggam's. But more important than any of that was the fact that Shad's soldiers were still at every door. And with the Sentinels up and leaving, the Council of the Wall was completely at her mercy.

The Sentinels. Though they recognized no such official role, they had always kept some semblance of order in Garoshmir, acting in particular to protect the members of the Council. Everyone, Yarid included, had thought this would never change. All it took was one man from Naruvieth to take them away, making the Council of the Wall vulnerable … right when they needed protection the most.

The Naruvian.

Yarid clenched his fist, flexed his knuckles. "All right," he said. "You can kill Tharadis. So long as you make it discreet." There was no telling if Tirfaun was right, but it was better to be safe than sorry. The matter of getting revenge on those who threatened Yarid would have to wait. And when it came down to it, he might just do what they wanted him to anyway.

Tirfaun owl-eyed him. "I wasn't asking your *permission,* you buffoon. I was merely giving you the courtesy of a warning."

Yarid chuckled softly. "Good old Tirfaun."

Tirfaun grumbled at this and, without so much as a simple farewell, snuck out between the two guards.

That still left the problem of Shad Belgrith. There was no doubt in Yarid's mind that, if provoked, she would use the force of her troops against the Council of the Wall to get her wishes. And weren't they ultimately the same wishes as those of the Council anyway? While he suspected there were enough on the Council who would continue to quash the Runeway's further construction, now that the "legalists" were on board with those who merely have a selfish interest in seeing it stopped, there might still be a way to finish the Runeway without compromising the Council's claims to legitimacy.

Only one question remained.

Yarid tucked his arms against his chest and rubbed his cheek as he studied the monster down in the Pit.

Would granting this creature what it wanted be worse than death by Shad's soldiers?

Yarid thought. And considered. And smiled. And stood.

"Ladies and gentlemen of the Council," he said, projecting his voice, "and our esteemed guests from near and far. We have been hard at work this day trying to resolve the differences that have come between us. But I think that the emissary spoke true; we should continue striving to work together, no matter how impossible it may seem."

All eyes were on him. "As it just so happens, I believe there is a solution that will satisfy all of us gathered here."

Chapter 50: To Conquer Fear

T ell me," Tharadis asked as he walked down the curving hallway outside the Council Chambers, "why you just made enemies with the whole Accord."

The man at his side, Rannald Firnaleos, was large, nearly half a head taller than Tharadis. He wore no expression that Tharadis could discern, but there was a certain world-weariness that shaped his features. He walked in silent consideration before answering.

"We didn't. We aren't enemies with the people of the Accord. I don't even think we are enemies of the Council." He frowned slightly. "We might at least be instrumental to what saves them. And if we are enemies now, we were always enemies. The mission of the Sentinels hasn't changed; the Council simply never cared to figure out what our mission is."

Pairs of Sentinels flanked the two of them as they walked, and more of them were in front and back. He was completely surrounded by Sentinels. Yet Tharadis got the distinct impression that he wasn't a captive. They were acting more like his honor guard, their attention focused on the people walking past them rather than on Tharadis.

"And what is the Sentinels' mission?"

"Ah." A small smile broke on Rannald's face. "Already you prove yourself to be wiser than them."

"I'd hoped you'd have figured that out earlier."

Rannald chuckled, shaking his head. "Everything you say only makes me realize I made the right decision. A man without unearned guilt or shame is hard to find." The smile fell from his face. "We who lead can't afford humility. It makes us look indecisive before our followers, who depend upon our strength. It makes us look weak before our enemies, who thrive on such weakness."

"True," said Tharadis, "but a false show of weakness can lead your enemies to make a fatal mistake."

Rannald nodded. "As we just proved back there, in the duel. They had believed you capable of failure when I had ensured your success."

"Yes. But why did you do it?"

They walked down a short flight of steps and out of the Dome and Spire. The sun shone through a break in the clouds, but it did little to dispel the constant chill in the air. Tharadis was glad to finally be done with all this.

Home was waiting for him.

They walked along the edge of the roundabout, where a number of carriages waited, as well as a massive wagon. Tharadis guessed it belonged to Shad Belgrith, though what such a huge wagon could possibly contain, he couldn't imagine.

"Our mission," Rannald said, eyes fixed on the ground a few paces ahead of him, "is to conquer fear. Not to destroy it or ignore it or any other such stupidity. But to truly *master* it. In the Ritual of Joining, the Sentinel rite of initiation, we face our worst fear. That is it. We merely face it, like looking into a mirror. But how we act from that point on determines the kind of life that we lead. If we choose to lead one at all."

Tharadis turned to look at him. "You don't fear the fear."

Rannald briefly met his eyes, that slight smile returning. "If fear is a river, one must learn to swim. One must accept the river for what it is before one can cross it."

"If fear is a river, then what am I?"

"A rope," Rannald said, "thrown to a drowning man." He pulled Tharadis to a stop. "Perhaps you don't even see it in yourself. But the mere *existence* of a man possessing the slightest shred of honor can be enough to sustain another man. Just knowing that he is alive, that he breathes and is real. That salute. You know the name of it?"

Salute? But then Tharadis remembered: holding the sword above his head, the same way he had when he faced Owan all those years ago. "My brother called it the Fool's Salute."

"It was Andrin's own salute. They say he charged into a horde of sheggam holding this salute, screaming with the wrath of a hundred apoth. The sheggam broke ranks and fled, and Andrin and the people he led were able to ride to safety." Anger flashed across Rannald's face. "Your brother is no man if he thinks Andrin was ever a fool."

"You don't need to worry about my brother." He didn't want to think about Owan anymore. But of course, the harder he tried not to, the more vibrantly Owan's spilled blood bloomed in his mind's eye. Tharadis shook his head to clear it of the memory. "Listen, Rannald. I'm not sure what you think I can do for you. I appreciate that you think I'm a good man." He meant that; Tharadis imagined not many people in the Accord would right now. "But I just don't see how our interests align."

Rannald shrugged. "What is just for one is just for all."

Tharadis scrubbed a hand over his jaw in exasperation. *I wonder if I sound like that,* Tharadis thought, remembering his speech to the Council. "Fair enough, but I meant that on a more practical level."

"And I've told you our mission. The *entirety* of it. Our aim is simply to conquer fear. We have no other charge than that, and it is up to the Captain of the Sentinels to determine how best to fulfill our mission." Rannald tapped his breastplate, as if Tharadis could have possibly forgotten who the Captain was. "For years, we have merely been the de facto protectors of the Council of the Wall, though in truth we were adrift. Waiting for a flag to rally behind, a flag *worthy* of the effort. We are not a religious order, but even we have our beliefs. We believe that one day someone would come charging into the midst of monsters, a sword held high in defense of what he believed was good and true, ready to face the forces that would destroy him."

Tharadis felt the bare skin of his arms prickle. "It almost sounds like a prophecy."

Rannald shook his head. "I've been told it's nothing of the sort. Merely a hope, a dream passed down from Sentinel to Sentinel. Much like a person knowing that the Pattern of the World guarantees no soul mate, but still he dreams of finding her." He smiled somewhat sadly, his gaze briefly abstracted before returning to the here and now. "And while the monsters we face are different these days, the fear remains the same."

Tharadis sighed. "Since the way to fulfill the Sentinels' mission is determined solely by the Captain, I suppose I have no say in the matter."

Rannald grinned. "How could you? You aren't even a Sentinel."

"All right." Tharadis gripped the hilt of Shoreseeker tightly, stared dead into Rannald's face until all mirth had fled. "Then consider my advice. If I believe you or any of your men are getting in my way, I will remove you by any means necessary."

Rannald locked eyes with him and nodded sharply. "I knew that before you said it."

"Good." Tharadis let go of Shoreseeker, relieved. He hoped he was done threatening people for a while.

"What will you do now?" Rannald asked.

"Head home. This trip has taken longer than I'd planned. I'm sure my second is pulling his hair out right now. He always tells me he's not fit for command."

"The Sentinels keep a few horses. You can take one. I can send a detachment with you." Rannald nodded to the west. "Just outside the city is the caravan heading down to Naruvieth. They were supposed to leave today, but the arrival of Shad's army put a kink in their plans, so they'll be heading out tomorrow. It might add a few days to the trip, but the rest of the Sentinels and I will leave with the caravan."

Tharadis frowned. "You … plan on coming to Naruvieth? You would just pack up and leave Garoshmir behind?"

That same faintly sad smile returned to Rannald's lips. "My wife might take some convincing, but perhaps the Council could use an ambassador in Naruvieth interested in keeping the peace."

Tharadis nodded. Truth be told, he would like an ally like Sherin Firnaleos. After a long moment, Tharadis extended his hand. "Then I hope you're able to convince her."

Grinning, Rannald seized his hand and shook it. "As do I."

Chapter 51: Minister of Relief

Minister Aelor, in charge of the Ministry of Disaster Relief, which was arguably the most important branch of the Accord government, waited patiently as the doormen pushed open the dual doors to the Council Hall. Or at least as patiently as could be expected. He was a *very* busy man, after all. The doormen made a very big show of their task, and Aelor had to forcibly will his fingers not to comb through his beard. Yes, it was impatience that made him want to do that. Not nerves. Definitely not nerves.

It wasn't every day that the Council sought his wisdom in affairs of state. In fact, they hadn't called on him much at all. It was likely a testament to his ability to run his Ministry so well that they gave him full autonomy. It was his job to save the Accord lands from *disasters*, not mundane things like the Council dealt with on a daily level, like shop licenses and missing chickens. Aelor's job was essentially the savior of mankind. He was as important as Andrin's Wall, if not so long lived.

So he had been a bit surprised when Councilor Yarid's manservant came to him, requesting his audience at the Hall of the Council regarding the matter of "a small debt." In truth, it was a rather large debt; Aelor doubted Yarid would be able to even the scales, no matter what he was willing to give. As if Aelor appearing before the Council were some great privilege, and not a bother. Most definitely a bother, he thought with a snort that briefly drew the attention of one of the doormen.

His foot started fidgeting. He had to slap his leg to calm it. *Traitorous leg. I'm not nervous. Not one bit.*

Once the doors were opened wide enough, he squeezed through them, sucking in his stomach. And before the herald could announce him, Aelor raised his hand and said in his clearest voice, "I am the Minister of Disaster Relief, Aelor. I believe you need me."

Everyone in the room stared at him in shocked amazement. *Of course,* he thought with a smile. Instantly his impatience seemed to wash away. *They're amazed because they know I'm their savior.*

Someone in one of the alcoves stood. Aelor, with his somewhat poor eyesight, had to squint to see it was the long-haired fop in silk robes that summoned him. Yarid. "That's right, Minister," said the Councilor in his most supplicating wheedle. "We do need you and your expertise."

"Well, I should hope this isn't a mere social call. I'm a very busy man, you see." Aelor looked around the room. It was nearly overflowing with bodies, even more so than the last time he had been here. And there were an awful lot of soldiers.

He turned back towards Yarid's alcove. "So what is it that you want, anyway?"

"It's not a matter of want, but need." Yarid spread his arms. "And what we need is your help. With an event that could cause hundreds, possibly thousands, of people to lose their jobs and their homes. An event that could devastate trade routes and upset the delicate balance of our fragile Accord."

Aelor combed his beard again but stopped himself once he realized what he was doing. "That sounds like something I can help with."

Another Councilor, the one named Gorun, stood. He looked like a bundle of flesh-colored sticks dressed in a sack at this distance, and his voice was withered with age. "It's a disaster, good Minister, of a sort that has no precedent in the Accord. It is an economic disaster. One that will ruin us if not dealt with swiftly and decisively."

"Swift and decisive action is the policy of the Ministry of Disaster Relief," said Aelor with a confident voice, though he was beginning to have doubts. It wasn't like the Council to sound so desperate. It made them sound weak. He knew they would never beg unless they were manipulating someone, or unless they were forced to.

A massive cloaked figure, standing nearby, caught Aelor's eye so suddenly he started with a small, undignified yelp. The figure's regard turned to Aelor, and he felt such a massive chill that he forgot where he was. His attention was drawn towards the figure's face like a physical object drawn towards the ground—only it kept on falling, falling, falling. The face could not be seen, as if it were shrouded not in shadows but Aelor's own uncertainty, his own refusal to see what he knew should be obvious. Aelor wanted to look away but forgot how—he could no longer feel the muscles in his neck, or had forgotten how they worked or even what they were, and even his name was running away from him, as if sand between fingers, but what were fingers? Even the ideas of physical reality and bodies were but bits of dust, blown away by the squall of that unseen, unseeable face.

With a crash, the mystery vanished, and Aelor knew everything, *saw* everything, as if some supernatural veil had been lifted from his eyes. Primal fear overwhelmed him, and once his mind could form a word, only one came: *sheggam.*

Aelor fell to his hands and knees. Vomited. Smelled piss, saw it puddle around him.

No. Not merely a sheggam. Something worse.

A sheggam Patterner.

No one or nothing else could have twisted his mind like that. He had heard tales of human Patterners, like that vile Tirfaun, warping the minds of men with their magic.

This monster had done this to terrify him.

And it had worked.

Aelor's voice was hoarse when he could speak. "Whatever you want, I'll do it."

"Just so we're clear," Yarid said as if Aelor hadn't collapsed to the floor and messed himself badly, "that you're willing to declare the cessation of the Runeway's construction a disaster, which grants you authority to usurp the Council's authority in such matters?"

"Yes."

"And that you will use your authority to overrule the previous judgment of the Council and continue construction."

"Yes, whatever you want. Just … just let me leave."

Aelor didn't see what happened next, but a few more words were exchanged, and a pair of the soldiers lifted him to his feet and half-carried him out the door. Once he was able to walk on his own, he hurried down the hall, eager to be away from Councilors and debts and power and all the things that came with them.

Chapter 52: A Distant Chime

The humans bickered amongst themselves, as humans were wont to do. One group wanted to dispatch a cadre of Patterners immediately; another group tried to stall for time, as their economic and political interests clearly didn't benefit from the Runeway. Orthkalu, patiently weathering their pointless exchanges, didn't care how they finished the job. Only that they did.

Foolish humans. Orthkalu was surprised how easily they were manipulated. Instill a little guilt, and they will tie the noose around their own necks. Of course, threats and intimidation had their place as well, and were, in many ways, far more satisfying. But Orthkalu found it delightful when an entire civilization decides to march to the gallows on its own, as this one was doing now.

Amidst the shouting and fist-shaking, Orthkalu stood completely motionless, hood draping forward to block distractions. He focused his mind on more important things—things unseen to the others in the room. Scents and flows of air washed over him, flooding his senses with the shape of things, and most importantly, with the shape of his web of Patterns. Or at least, the Patterns he had designed—the Accord's own Patterners had done the hard work of putting them in place. So far they had done an admittedly fine job in implementing his ideas. Once finished, the Runeway would be a monument without equal. A monument solely to Orthkalu and all the power it would afford him.

As the Accord Patterners had determined, travel over the Runeway would speed up tremendously. But Orthkalu had gambled on their ignorance and won: what they didn't know was that it wouldn't move things like carts and horses. It would only aid in moving bodies imbued with shegasti.

They were, in effect, constructing a road whose sole purpose would be the invasion, conquest, and ultimately destruction of their lands by Orthkalu's sheggam forces.

Orthkalu afforded himself a small smile at the thought, baring his fangs under the shroud of his hood. While even this wasn't his endgame, it was a consequence that was delicious in its own right.

No, even if he didn't have an army of sheggam at his back, Orthkalu would still have the Accord build his Runeway. Without it, his ultimate plan, involving the Rift, would not come to fruition.

The coarse hairs on the back of his neck stiffened and saliva flooded his mouth as he considered the Rift.

It was the counterpoint to Andrin's Wall, created at the same moment, in a pendulum swing reaction to the Patterns inherent to the Wall. Orthkalu couldn't imagine the raw power found in the Rift. It would be like tapping into the Godhall of Shegasti itself.

With the Runeway's own Patterns bending the Rift to Orthkalu's purpose, its power could make him a god.

Getting here had been a delicate act. A simple invasion had been out of the question from the beginning. It was simply too risky, and the ferals Orthkalu commanded could never be counted on to execute a plan. They were only able to interfere with the plans of others. Usually by killing them. No, Orthkalu had needed something to give to the humans. Something that would earn their trust. And ideally, something that would ultimately help him get to where he needed to be. The solution he found, elegantly enough, was the very thing required to tame the forces of the Rift: the Runeway.

Orthkalu turned his head slightly, listening to the sounds between sounds, carried through hallways and the cracks between doors and their frames, the tiniest hints of change that only a master Patterner could sense. Something had caught his awareness, something he had hoped he would never hear.

The alarm.

The invasion was beginning. Far, far earlier than Orthkalu had hoped.

He cursed inwardly. Damn that Marinack. She was too weak to keep the ferals in line. Orthkalu had feared as much, but had had little choice. She was the one amongst the invasion party most in command of her wits, but apparently that hadn't been enough.

Orthkalu straightened and headed for the door, much to the squawked surprise of the humans in the Hall. Shad Belgrith stared in shock, then began blubbering questions at him, but he ignored her, effortlessly shouldering open the double doors that led to the outer hallway. Shad's soldiers stared at him passively, not making any move to seize him in spite of his sudden change in behavior. *One can always count on the obedience of fools,* Orthkalu mused as he made his way out of the building, heedless of the shocked gazes of the human passersby.

Beyond the coach Shad had come in on was his wagon, sitting at the outer edge of the great roundabout with blocks under its wheels. The oxen yoked to it watched Orthkalu, the whites of their eyes showing. As he approached, the wagon jolted heavily to the side. The handful of attendants assigned to the wagon scrambled away, startled.

Orthkalu unhooked his Pattern-inscribed staff from the side of the wagon and swiveled one of the metal rings at the bottom, which changed the alignment of the etchings. The small lantern at the top of the staff flared to life, casting a wavering orange light.

Satisfied, Orthkalu threw open the wagon's rear doors, which themselves were nearly twice as tall as a human man. *I've kept you waiting, my Abyssal beast.*

The inside of the wagon was dark, but the darkness was pushed away by two glowing orange eyes from within, burning like embers, filled with menace.

Orthkalu threw back his hood and smiled grimly. *I hope you're ready to ride.*

As if in answer, the beast in the wagon stamped its six hooves and let loose a scream that chilled even Orthkalu.

"Yes," he whispered, still smiling. "You're ready."

Chapter 53: Escape

Only about half of the people filling the Council Chambers seemed to care that Orthkalu had left and was now free in the city, but Erianna, still leaning against the wall with her arms folded, noticed that one person took particular note. Her mistress gawked at the open doors through which Orthkalu had just wordlessly passed. Shad Belgrith actually looked on the verge of tears, if only for a moment, before tightening the set of her jaw and turning to the commander of her guard, standing at attention at her side.

"Our business here is concluded. Ready the men for departure, and … and find out where Orthkalu went." Her voice was commanding as always, but there was a forced air of casualness to it, as if she were pretending not to be worried about Orthkalu's unexpected departure.

The commander saluted and barked some orders. Men formed up around Shad in a protective ring as she walked out. Much to the apparent relief of the Councilors, Shad's men left the alcoves, too, filing out of the Council Chambers.

No one said a word to Erianna.

It wasn't long before she found herself the lone remaining member of the Twelve Towers retinue, drawing the silent gazes of several Councilors while the others continued to bicker. She wore a placid expression, though in truth, she didn't want to be left alone with any of these people after what her mistress had just put them through. Stifling the urge to hurry, she sauntered through the doors and into the hallway. She hoped the act was more convincing than her mistress's.

A few dozen people were going about their business in the high-ceilinged hallway, giving little more than a passing glance to Erianna. She knew none of them. Shad's soldiers were already gone, making good time like the disciplined, obedient, unquestioning soldiers they were.

Erianna knew she should turn left and follow them, make her way back to the carriage where Shad would be waiting for her. She knew it, yet she couldn't make herself lift her foot.

She forgot about me. She forgot, but she will soon remember.

Erianna was shocked to realize she had a choice here. She could go left and follow the soldiers, returning to her mistress, possibly receiving a beating for tarrying as long as she did.

Or she could turn right.

What lay down that path? Erianna didn't know. Her fantasy of escape had been precisely that: a fantasy. But her breathing and pulse quickened as the truth of the situation began to sink in: *I could go right.*

She could go right. But only if her will allowed it. Only if she freed herself from Shad right now.

The choice is only real when I make it real.

She took a deep breath and turned.

And as she walked down the hall, Erianna smiled as only a free woman could.

Chapter 54: Unwelcome News

"Captain!"

Rannald turned to see Arrion Metsfurth approach with his helmet tucked under his arm, his short orange-red hair darkened with sweat. His eyes glowered over his jutting cheeks. He shoved his way into the narrow alley, past the rear guard, stepping over the mounds of unidentifiable trash prevalent in the maze-like streets of the Common District. He gripped a mustached, panicked man in commoner clothing tightly by the arm. The rough treatment was nothing personal, Rannald was sure; Arrion trusted almost no one outside of the Sentinels. "He says he has a message for you."

Rannald raised a hand. "It's all right, Major. I know this man. You can let him go."

Arrion did so with obvious reluctance and a parting glare, stepping back under the cover of an old broken-down fruit stand that had been dumped and abandoned here. Tharadis stopped at Rannald's side, looking distracted.

"What is it, Macks?" Rannald asked. Macks was a merchant of middling success that Rannald had known since his days back in Caney Forks, before he had joined the Sentinels. He wasn't what Rannald would consider a close friend—the man simpered, bowed, and scraped far too much—but aside from Sherin, Macks was one of the few people here Rannald had known from before coming to Garoshmir.

The man dusted off his plain woolen trousers as he goggled the company of Sentinels surrounding him. He scratched at his mustache nervously as he spoke, nearly muffling his words. "Just got word about the Council. Thought you should know, since you just came from there."

Rannald frowned. "Something happened after we left?" Standing at Rannald's side, Tharadis perked up at this, focusing all his attention on the merchant.

Macks only then seemed to notice Tharadis and nearly staggered back under his gaze. After a moment, he regained his composure, turning back to Rannald. "Yes. Some minister or some such declared the Council's decision no good and decided himself to restart construction."

"Does he have the authority to do that?" Rannald asked. At his side, Tharadis turned away, cursing under his breath.

"Seems that way. At least no one on the Council is giving him much trouble." Macks gave Tharadis a wary glance. "Just thought you should know."

Rannald sighed. "I guess this means war."

Tharadis was silent for a moment, then said, "It's what you were hoping for, wasn't it? A horde of monsters, me riding at the front, screaming my lungs out with my sword raised high?" Bitterness tinged his voice.

"One doesn't need to hope for monsters. They will always be with us. But the rest of it … yes."

Tharadis chuckled softly, shaking his head. "You know what I want? What I've always wanted?"

Rannald said nothing.

Tharadis put his hands on his hips and looked up to the sky. "To be left alone. For the people I care about to be left alone. That's it. That's all I've ever wanted."

"It's what any decent person wants. But every indecent person out there is working to make sure that never happens. They want to hurt you, take what is rightfully yours. Someone has to stop them. That is why the world needs us, Tharadis."

Rannald turned to Macks. "Thank you for coming to us with this," he said with a gesture of dismissal, but the merchant looked as if he had more to say. Judging by the way he was shifting from side to side on his feet, dry-washing his hands, he didn't want to come out and say it. Rannald would have to drag it out him. "What else is there, Macks?"

The merchant bobbed his head and leaned in, his voice quiet and conspiratorial. "There's something more important—*much* more. You aren't going to believe it if I say it."

Rannald rested a fist on his hip. "And we aren't going to hear it unless you do."

Macks bobbed his head and leaned in even closer. "They say the governor of Twelve Towers brought herself a real sheggam."

"What do you mean?" Rannald asked. "Another Knight of the Eye finally turned?" He hadn't heard of such a thing happening in his lifetime. It didn't seem likely, but the notion made his arm hairs stand on end.

"No. From across Andrin's Shores-damn *Wall*." Macks grinned but his eyes were filled with terror. "Wouldn't've believed the tale myself, but I saw the thing leave the Dome and Spire, mount some beast straight out of nightmares with a staff in its hand, and ride south."

"That beast," Tharadis said, his interest now intently focused on what Macks was saying. "Was it in a giant wagon?"

Macks nodded vigorously. "Like a horse, I guess, but ... all *wrong*. Too many legs, for one thing."

Tharadis took the man's hand and shook it firmly. "Thank you telling us this. I know you must have feared for your life. If I find a way to repay you for it someday, I will. I promise."

"I'll ... hold you to that," Macks said, bewildered, before dipping his head and ducking out between the other Sentinels with a final glance back at Tharadis.

Rannald frowned once the merchant was out of earshot. "What was that about?"

Tharadis had one hand tucked under an elbow, his other hand stroking his chin thoughtfully. "This changes things," he said, not really answering Rannald's question. "Shad brought the sheggam. She—no, the sheggam— built the Runeway. The sheggam is heading south. For Naruvieth." His hand dropped from his chin, limp. "No. For the Rift." He turned, continued walking west at a brisk pace.

"Wait, Tharadis! How do you figure that?"

"It doesn't matter. We ride for the Rift."

Rannald jogged to keep pace. "To do what, exactly?"

"Hey!" cried a boy's voice.

A dozen swords whispered free of their sheaths in a heartbeat, Tharadis's stunning blue blade among them. All of them were pointed at a small boy. Likely Naruvian, as he was a little darker than most Accord people, but he wore a tattered vest and short trousers like a Garoshmiri street boy. He was crouched on top of a large earthenware jar tucked away in a dark nook in the alley. The nook's shadow was dark, but ... there was no *way* he could have been sitting there without them noticing. He wasn't a dozen steps from where Macks had talked to them, and not two steps from the Sentinels in the lead. Yet, judging by their wide-eyed expressions, they were just as surprised at his appearance as Rannald.

Rannald had reached for his hilt, too, but grabbed only air. He had forgotten that he had relinquished his sword after his brief duel. He growled in annoyance at himself. "What are you doing here, boy?"

The boy was grinning ear to ear, perched like a bird, and took a bite of an apple he was holding. He couldn't have been more than twelve years old. With his mouth full, he said, "You're the Warden, aren't you? Tharadis, right?" He didn't wait for an answer. "The name's Chad. We've been looking all over for you."

Tharadis sheathed his sword. "We?"

Chad nodded, taking another bite. He slid off the jar and stood. "Me and Nina."

Tharadis stared at him wide-eyed. "Nina's here? In Garoshmir?"

"Yeah." Chad grinned. "Thanks to me, we got out of Falconkeep."

Rannald snorted in disbelief. Chad raised an eyebrow at him in reply. "You don't believe me? It was almost as easy as slipping in the middle of a bunch of stiff-as-sticks soldiers." His grin was unnerving.

Tharadis grabbed the boy by the shoulders. "Chad, look at me. Is she okay? Where is she now? Is she nearby?"

The boy looked somewhat ashamed. "Told her to stay put, that I would find you. She was hurt—not bad, just a cut, but she needed help. I tried looking for a little while, but when I went back, she'd taken off on her own. I figured if I kept looking for you, I'd have a better chance of finding her."

"Can you help me find her, Chad?"

The boy looked ready to object, as if stubbornness were in an inborn trait. But then something changed in his gaze. It was an emotion Rannald knew intimately. *He's afraid.*

"Okay," Chad said, dropping his eyes. "But only if you promise I won't have to go back to that place."

"Chad, look at me." The boy met Tharadis's gaze. "I don't know what kind of place Falconkeep is. But I promise that you will never have to go back. I don't care if someone tries to take you. I will stop them. I swear on my life."

Chad nodded. Tears looked ready to fall, but admirably, the boy kept them in check. "I'll show you where I left her." He pointed in the direction they were already headed.

Tharadis nodded and turned to Rannald, but Rannald raised a hand to forestall him. "You don't even need to ask, Tharadis. I'll send out men to help widen the search. Where should we look for you if we find her?"

"Once I find Nina, I'll head to the caravan. If I don't find her right away, I'll check there in an hour or so. The … the sheggam," apparently the word was as hard for Tharadis to say as it was for Rannald to hear, "has a good lead on us already. Finding Nina is my first priority, but we need to do that as fast as possible."

"Understood." Rannald turned his men and gave the orders. They dispersed immediately, fanning out in different directions. When they were gone, he turned back to Tharadis. "Who is she?"

"Nina?" Tharadis hesitated. "My sister-in-law's daughter."

An odd way of putting it, Rannald thought, but didn't press him. "If we find her first, we'll make sure she gets to you." Rannald felt a sudden need to find Sherin. Just knowing that a sheggam was here, in the Accord … It was foolish to worry, but he knew he'd feel better if he could see she was safe. Once they found Nina, he would look for his wife, if for no other reason than to put himself at ease. And then he would join Tharadis in putting a stop to this sheggam. *Monsters, indeed.*

Tharadis nodded in thanks, grabbed the boy—who squawked in surprise—and jogged out of the alley.

Chapter 55: Attack

Corporal Roren Hocker simply loved days like this one.

A handful of fluffy clouds drifted across the sky, occasionally blanketing the setting sun, which otherwise shone along Garoshmir's skyline between the battered wooden posts supporting the guard tower's roof. A large warning bell dominated the center of the tower, though now its main purpose was to collect as much dust as possible. Hocker was on guard duty, which meant he was leaning against one of the posts with his arms folded, chewing on the old pipe he had bought back in Ahlin, before he had come to Garoshmir to join the Guard. He had been chewing on this same pipe for years, such that it couldn't rightly draw smoke anymore, but it was better than chewing on some twig he had found in the dirt. Besides, he and that pipe had been through some tough times and bad weather out here on this old guard tower. Chewing on that old pipe was almost like chewing on an old friend … or something. Well, not really like that at all, but that pipe was as good a friend as he had.

Hocker didn't bother to stifle his yawn—he was alone up here, like most days—and nearly dropped his pipe over the edge. But he caught it before it fell too far out of his mouth. The stone wall atop which he stood—fortified in places with wooden planks where wide cracks had developed— was a good three times as tall as him, and he didn't want to have to go down all those stairs to fetch his pipe out of the trampled mud around the gate nearby. Someone would likely see him. There were men guarding the gate, too, weren't there? He had heard about Private Shain getting a good dressing down for that once, something about dereliction of duty or some such. What a bother.

Hocker tapped out a neat rhythm on the wood post with his knuckles as he half-stared, half-studied the tree line to the east. He had heard the song for the first time just the other night, at the Iron Saddle. He couldn't remember the words to the song to save his life, but oh could he remember that tune! It was the kind of tune you'd remember till you rotted in your deathbed. Hocker reckoned he'd be humming it still when his soul washed up on Farshores.

The branches in the trees normally stirred whenever a breeze breathed through them, so Hocker had taken to ignoring any movement he saw there. Now there was movement, and it barely registered in his eyes. But after a few moments he noticed something was different this time. Colors he didn't usually see, pale gray and tiny flashes of purple, leapt out of the shadows between the trunks of the trees. What in the world looked like that? Nothing, as far as he knew, so Hocker took a deep, hard look at what was rushing out of those trees.

What he saw there froze him with terror. The pipe slid out of his mouth, unnoticed, bounced once on the edge of the wall, spun through the air, and landed stem-first in the mud, forgotten.

Years of dust shook from the bell as its deep, hollow peal rang out across the city, signaling an attack.

Sherin had to leave.

Emotions battled within her. So much had happened, and it was difficult to put it all in perspective with all the noise. She stepped outside of her alcove into the long, curved hallway outside the Council Chambers. A pair of her aides stood there in their high-hemmed robes, looking at her anxiously.

"Is there anything we can do for you?" one asked.

Sherin cradled her head in her hand, closing her eyes for a moment, before looking up. "Yes. Some water please."

The servant bowed her head and disappeared.

The Accord lands had stood on the precipice of war. Sherin wanted to blame the Naruvian and his thick-headed willfulness entirely, but he was only partly to blame. Shad and her … *guest*—it was hard to give name to such an impossible creature, even to herself—shared much of it as well. And the Council was not without fault, considering that some, if not all, of Tharadis's arguments were valid. It wasn't right for the Council to simply take people's homes, even if it were for the greater good of all—even the greater good of those whose homes were lost. The Council wasn't some conquering army, seizing land like it was the spoils of war. Down that path lay darkness, a darkness that Sherin fought against daily. She had lived in such dark times before, back when she was in Caney Forks during the slave rebellion.

Back when she had first met Rannald. *Oh, Rannald.* Sherin sagged against the wall, holding her face in an effort to hold back the tears.

She knew his vow to never touch a sword was merely symbolic of his vow to leave violence behind him. She wasn't stupid. But that didn't matter. He had gone back on his word. He had held his sword, even if for only a few moments. If he couldn't stay true to such a simple vow, how could he hold true to the greater, more important one?

It felt as if, in that one moment, he was turning his back on himself, on the man he had become since he and Sherin had married. Back when they had met, he was a violent brute. His notoriety was without equal, and he became a legend to those fighting in the rebellion. And he hadn't done it for his sake; Rannald had never been a slave. Yet he struggled just the same to put the plight of slaves to an end.

With a sword in hand.

It had been so hard for Sherin to reconcile those two contradictory aspects of Rannald's character: the glorious servant of good, and the violent murdering warrior. He was at once the most beautiful and repugnant man she had ever known. It was only once he had sworn off holding a sword forever did she even think of marrying him.

Could she still remain married to him? Could she even *love* him anymore? It wasn't so simple. She knew *why* he had done it—his action may have averted a much greater tragedy. In a way, he had done it to preserve Sherin's values, to prevent a war that, at the time, looked inevitable. But at what cost? Perhaps Sherin had been a fool in two ways: thinking she could prevent the world from falling back into its barbaric ways, and thinking Rannald could keep from falling back into *his* ways.

She knew she was confused, and it was still too soon to come to any conclusions about how she was supposed to live with this. She had to think.

The aide returned with a mug of water. Sherin downed it in a single swallow and handed the mug back. "I'm going outside to get some fresh air." The aides nodded and followed her down the hallway and up the winding stairs to the rooftop garden on the eastern wing. Sherin loved this garden; it was spacious, open, and filled with life. Small, leafy trees, some with flowers blooming, grew out of vases sitting on short pedestals. This high up, the wind kept the garden's natural fragrance subtle but ever-present. Beyond an iron railing encircling the garden, Garoshmir sprawled before her. The clarity of sight and smell up here gave her a clarity of mind. This was her favorite place to think.

A distant sound caught her attention. Was that … a bell? Another bell, and then another, joined the first. Soon the sound of bells filled the air, drowning out whatever peace Sherin thought the garden could give her. She knew what the bells meant. She simply couldn't understand why anyone would ring them now.

Frowning, she turned to the pale, wide-eyed faces of her aides. "Let's find out what's going on."

Chapter 56: Lost

Mom," Nina whispered, holding the Raccoon Family close to her face as she walked amidst the press of people. She could faintly hear the burble of water nearby. A river, maybe? "Did you see which way Esta went?" It hadn't taken Nina long to get lost in the crowded street, even with her mother's ghost trying to help her. It turned out that ghosts could only be in one place at a time, just like living people, and her mother couldn't go up above the rooftops and tell Nina where to go at the same time. If only Nina were taller.

... turn ... go there ... Her mother's voice was faint, so Nina lifted the Raccoon Family closer to her ear. Sometimes that worked when she couldn't hear so well; she didn't know why.

"What?" People brushed by, frowning down at Nina like she was crazy.

Turn back, came her mother's voice. *That place isn't safe for you.*

"But what about Aunt Esta?" Nina asked.

It isn't safe for her either.

That made Nina's stomach do a flip. "But that's where she went! What are—"

The sight of a man suddenly squatting down in her path startled her. "Hello, little girl. Are you lost?" The man had expensive-looking clothes, made of embroidered silk. There were shiny rings on his fingers. At first, Nina thought he was a nice-looking man, smiling at her like that, but his eyes didn't look so nice.

"Not really. I have the Raccoon Family." She lifted it to show him.

"Oh?" He glanced left and right. "Are your parents around?" He shuffled a bit closer. "Maybe if they are, I could help you find them."

"I don't know." Nina scrunched up her nose at the smell of his breath. It smelled like old wine. "I killed my mom, so she's a ghost now. My dad is dead, too, but I don't know how to talk to him. My uncle is the one who murdered him—he's the one I'm looking for. My uncle, that is. I think my aunt is here, too. She's not dead." Nina jerked her thumb over her shoulder in the direction she just came from. "My friend and me, we just came from Falconkeep—"

As Nina spoke, the man's smile slowly started drooping into a frown, but at this last bit of her story, he abruptly stood and stepped into the crowd, disappearing into it.

Nina sighed. Oh well. He didn't look like he wanted to help her much anyway. Continuing towards the burbling sound, Nina lifted the Raccoon Family back up to her ear. "Hey, mom. Are you there?"

Silence. Nina was alone again. She was starting to wonder if leaving the healer's shop was such a good idea after all.

"Did you see which way she went?"

Tharadis leaned forward, hands gripping the edge of the counter tightly with Chad just behind him. Tharadis still didn't know how Nina ended up here in Garoshmir, even though Chad had tried explaining on the way here to the healer's shop. Tharadis knew of Chad, even if he'd never met the boy before, and he didn't think that Chad was lying. But just because Chad was telling the truth didn't mean it made any sense. The little he had told Tharadis—something about a white-haired woman and a chase through the woods and a disappearing gate—was easily the craziest story Tharadis had ever heard.

Yet Chad was adamant that Nina was here, in the city, and that he had left her here, in this shop. Tharadis understood that much at least.

The healer standing on the other side of the counter twisted her fingers in her stained apron. Her eyes were fixed on Shoreseeker, sheathed at his hip. Tharadis realized he was probably frightening the poor woman. He straightened, taking his hands off the counter, and awaited her answer as patiently as he could.

"I told her to stay put," the healer said with a defensive tilt of her chin. "She was looking out the window one moment and gone the next."

"Which way was she looking?"

The woman paused a moment, frowning in consideration. "Left, I suppose."

Tharadis nodded. "Thank you, and sorry for the trouble." But as he turned to go, Chad tugged on his hand.

"We still owe her a silver," Chad whispered, though it was obvious that by the healer's deepening frown she could still hear.

Tharadis fished two silvers out of his coin pouch and set them on the counter. "Thank you for taking care of my daughter." Chad gaped at him like a fish, silently mouthing the word *daughter*.

The healer's gaze flicked from the coins to Shoreseeker back to Tharadis's face. No, to the Warden's emblem centered on his headband. He'd forgotten he was still wearing it. She didn't say anything further, so he nodded his thanks and pushed open the door, Chad quick on his heels.

Tharadis broke into a jog as soon as he was outside. He almost forgot Chad was there with him, trying to keep up. He slowed, but only a bit. He was so focused on finding Nina that he hardly noticed all the shoulders he bumped into and all the cursing that followed. Nina was alone in this enormous city with dark fast approaching and he had no idea even where to begin looking. His heart felt like it would beat right out of his chest, and it was getting worse with each passing moment.

Nina. Where are you?

Chapter 57: Run

With her aides hurrying to keep up with her, Sherin strode down the narrow street, frowning at the odd feeling in the air. A few people had stopped in their tracks, glancing all around in worry as the bells continued to ring throughout the city. Just as many others pretended not to hear them, shouting to cry their wares to passersby just as uninterested in the bells. Yet no one could truly ignore the bells; Sherin could see rising concern in their faces just as she knew it was in her own.

The first bell to be rung was at the east gate, she was sure, so that was where she was headed now. It was common practice that when one bell was rung, those manning the other bells throughout the city rang their own to ensure that everyone heard the alarm. This had the unfortunate effect of causing panic when there was nothing to worry about. This wouldn't be the first time that had happened. If that was all it was—and Sherin desperately hoped it was—she would give the prankster an upbraiding he wouldn't forget.

But if it was something else …

Sherin picked up the pace, breaking into a slow jog, which was all her dress would allow. She didn't know how she knew, but she felt that something really was wrong. Too many strange things had happened recently. But perhaps that was all it was. She was on edge because of Rannald, the Naruvian, and the … the *sheggam*. No, she couldn't blame the bell ringer for her being on edge. Just having one of those creatures in the city would have made her ring that bell like a madwoman if it had been her charge.

A gently arched stone bridge stood over the small river cutting through this part of the city as it continued its way west. Sherin continued her quick pace over the bridge but froze just on the other side.

Up ahead people were running toward her. Screaming.

Her frown deepened as she glanced over her shoulder at her aides, but they looked just as confused. The people didn't seem to be running towards anything. Rather, running away.

A small troop of Garoshmir Guard, armed with long, gleaming halberds, rushed past Sherin in tight formation, headed in the same direction as her. Sherin immediately began to feel that her initial instinct, to investigate the ringing bell, had been foolish. Dangerous, even. With an ever-tightening knot of anxiety forming in her stomach, Sherin turned around to head back towards the Dome and Spire. If this was something that a Councilor of the Wall could fix, she could fix it later.

The eastern bell went silent. Then the southeastern, only moments behind the first. The screams, now to Sherin's back, rose in intensity.

Skin prickling, she broke into a jog.

A thick crowd of people had formed up ahead, eyeing the commotion behind her with rapt interest. Her rising fear overcame any sense of propriety. She ran straight into the knot of people, shoving them out of her way, shouting, "Move! Get out of here!" She heard her aides behind her doing the same.

The expression on one of the gawkers on her left, a tall, graying man whose height allowed him to see over the heads of everyone else, suddenly changed to sheer terror. He pointed, screaming, "*Run!*"

Chaos erupted. The people, standing calmly just a moment before, transformed into a screaming, running, trampling, elbowing mob.

Sherin scrambled to get through them, too afraid to look over her shoulder at what had caused the pandemonium. Someone punched her in the shoulder; an elbow clipped her wrist. She didn't care. Sherin was throwing her own limbs about in her mad dash to escape.

She heard steel clash behind her, a scream cut short. Something small sailed over her shoulder into the crowd, but her mind couldn't make sense of it at first. *Wouldn't* make sense of it. Had that been … a severed hand?

Tears filled her eyes, made it hard to see. It was so hard to breathe. Sherin paused only a moment to wipe her eyes—the prospect of getting lost was as terrifying as staying in this place. Someone fell to his face at Sherin's side, then was yanked out of sight—fast. Whatever had taken him was immensely powerful.

Sherin didn't see it. She ran.

Someone—or some*thing*—shouldered into her, throwing her against the wall of a shop. Her head smacked against a window, cracking the glass, but not breaking it. She slid down the wall until she was sitting, finally seeing the horror unfold before her.

Beasts ran through the crowd, ripping people apart with claws and teeth. They were sheggam, she was certain, but different from the one she had seen. That one had seemed more … *human*.

These were frenzied animals.

She had to hide. Ignoring the throbbing in the side of her head, she glanced around for cover.

A grain cart, parked against a wall up ahead. The bed was low and wide. She could hide there for now.

She crawled towards it quickly, shoving aside anyone who came too close to trampling her. Panic closed her throat as she heard more people dying all around her; many of the buildings around here had been built snugly, with few alleys. There weren't many ways to escape. The best she could hope for was to hide and wait for them to pass her by.

But she knew they wouldn't. They would find her and they would kill her.

Just as Sherin reached the back end of the cart, a woman rolled under it and, seeing Sherin, kicked her in the face.

Blood sprayed from Sherin's nose. Beyond terror, Sherin grabbed the woman's foot and began half-pulling herself under the cart, half-pulling the woman out.

The woman began to thrash. Something reached under the cart—a long, gray arm, fingers tipped in black claws. The claws gripped the woman's hair, pulling her screaming out from under the cart and yanking her free from Sherin's grasp.

Sherin hesitated; she knew that would be her fate soon enough. The cart was no place to hide, but she had no choice. She crawled under it and tucked herself against the wall, pulling her shaking legs up against her chest to create the smallest profile possible.

She tried not breathing—she didn't want her breathing to give her away—but it was impossible. Each breath only came faster and faster as bodies dropped all over the street in sprays of blood and gore.

More people were left injured than dead, she realized. Severed limbs, hair ripped from scalps, broken limbs. The screams were overwhelming her, swallowing her. The world was awash with agony, and Sherin was drowning in it.

Some of the beasts carried weapons. Some were little more than clubs, others were roughly forged swords, too large for a man. Sherin watched as a man scrambled backward right next to the cart. The blade of one of the swords, as wide as her leg, crashed down. Shards of paving stone shot everywhere. The man's arm rolled under the cart and came to a rest right next to Sherin.

The man turned to Sherin and met her eyes. His screams were muffled as sheggam claws slowly reached down to rake across his face, drawing runnels of blood.

Something landed heavily on the cart, shaking it. The cart lurched as if that something had leapt off. Several more sheggam jumped up and then off the cart, landing in front of it before engaging in more slaughter. Other sheggam took a less-roundabout path, rushing through the crowd directly. When the next sheggam landed on the cart, Sherin heard the axle down past her feet groan.

Then it snapped.

The cart collapsed.

Sherin squeezed her eyes shut, expecting it to crush her, but amazingly, she was still alive. When she opened her eyes, the bottom of the cart was inches closer, now tilted at a wild angle.

She shifted her feet and noticed they weren't moving. The broken axle had stabbed into the ground, pinning a loose fold of her dress.

Her heart raced. She knew she had to stay here for now, but that she had to be able to get away when it was safe. She would have to rip her dress if she wanted to get—

She looked over.

Crouched down and staring at her was a sheggam. Snarling, it reached for her.

Chapter 58: Stronghold

The sheggam's claw snagged a hold of Sherin's sleeve. Sherin jerked her arm away as it tried to pull her out from under the grain cart. Hot breath, reeking of blood, washed over her face as the sheggam's long muzzle snapped at her.

Sherin couldn't hold it in anymore. She screamed. She screamed until her throat was raw.

Something sharp jabbed into her head. She craned her head up towards the front of the cart only to see another set of claws only an inch from her eyes. Sherin flinched, wriggling towards the back of the cart, where there was no room for them to reach under thanks to the broken axle. She wedged herself there, pulling her knees up against her chest to make herself as small as possible. Another sheggam joined the first two, then another. Sherin lost count of the claws reaching for her, scraping the stone near her head and her arms. They were only inches from her. If that axle hadn't broken and the bottom of the cart dropped a bit, they would've gotten to her easily. Now it was too tight.

But how long could she last like this? How long before they finally got her?

How long until she threw herself at them just to get it over with? *Shores ... help me.*

Someone, help me.

Please.

Something heavy landed on the top of the cart. Then another. And another.

The front axle groaned.

If the sheggam couldn't reach her, they were going to crush her.

"No!" Sherin started pounding her fists against the bottom of the cart. "No! Get me out of here! Get me out of here!" Her screams became wordless. Words had no meaning anymore. There was only fear. Pure, animal fear. Everything wanted to kill her—the sheggam, the cart, the world. Everything was a threat.

More sheggam jumped onto the cart. The front axle splintered but held.

Some of the sheggam reaching for her wriggled out from under the cart, not wanting to get crushed. Some were too busy trying to tear her apart to sense the danger.

Sherin squeezed her eyes shut, shaking all over.

The jumping had stopped. When, she didn't know. How long had she been under there? She had no idea. But she looked around her.

The sheggam were gone, though she could still hear them nearby. There were other strange sounds—a man grunting? Steel?

Was it a trick? Sherin didn't care; if it was one, she would just fall into it and that was that. With a frantic urgency, she yanked on her dress, ripping it free, and crawled out from under the cart so fast she split one of her fingernails down the middle. She barely felt it.

When she was halfway out, she looked up. A man towered over her, armored in steel, cloak flapping. The sword in his hand slashed left and right, sheggam blood in its wake, a constant crimson arc. The sheggam scrambled over each other, jaws snapping frantically, in their haste to kill him. His feet remained planted, unmoving, as he cut them down. He was a stone in the storming ocean; waves and waves of sheggam crashed against him, but could not shake him.

He was terrible.

He was magnificent.

He was, some dim part of her mind realized, her husband.

The last of the sheggam fell at his feet, cleft from the tip of its snout nearly to its neck. Rannald's sword had split its head nearly in two, hacking between its eyes through skull and brain alike, its muzzle, top and bottom split in half, looking like the mouth of some grotesque worm in its ruined state. There were dozens of such corpses scattered in an arc around him— lopped off limbs strewn upon pools of reeking innards, clumps of flesh, chunks of armor. A moat of sheggam blood surrounded him as if he were a one-man stronghold.

He stood there panting. The sword in his hand was so dinged and nicked it was a wonder it hadn't snapped, not to mention how it cut so cleanly. Pulse pounding in her ears, Sherin followed the edge of that horrible blade with her eyes up to the face of its owner. Rannald turned to her, and when his eyes fell upon hers, tears began to mingle with the blood spattered on his cheeks as he smiled.

Sherin had never been so happy to see his face.

Yet the horror of the scene before her, not only the blood and violence but that ... *thing* in her husband's hand, forced a scream from her throat as her eyes rolled back into her head. She slumped to the ground, unconscious.

Chapter 59: Encounter

E xcuse me, I'm looking for a little girl. She—"

Without even glancing at him, the man shrugged free of Tharadis's gentle grip on his arm, not even giving him the time to ask his question. Everyone Tharadis had asked was like that, most people heading the same direction—west, he thought—while some people milled about in confusion. He thought it had something to do with the bells that had just started ringing. They didn't sound like the typical bells that marked daylight hours. They rang more frantically, and a few of them had stopped ringing. It didn't take a Warden to figure out that the bells meant trouble, but no one seemed to know what kind of trouble. Did it have something to do with Shad Belgrith's soldiers? He couldn't say exactly why, but he didn't think that likely, though he didn't know what else it could be.

"Uh, Mister Warden." Chad was tugging on his arm again. Tharadis felt bad that he kept forgetting the boy was following him. He silently reprimanded himself and vowed to keep better track of his charges.

"What is it, Chad?"

"I'm pretty good at finding people. I think I should go ahead and look for Nina on my own."

Tharadis shook his head firmly. "No, you're staying with me. I don't want to have to go looking for you, too." He crouched down and took the boy by the shoulder. "Chad. I know how much you've done for Nina. You've been very brave in helping her escape that place. But Nina's lost now because you two got separated. I'm not blaming you, but I need you to understand that our best chance is to stay together for now."

Tharadis tried softening his words, but Chad looked wounded all the same. To his credit, though, he nodded. Tharadis didn't want to spend so much time telling the boy what they had to do—even a moment not searching for Nina was too much—but neither could he afford the boy getting any heroic ideas.

Exhaling heavily, Tharadis stood and continued on. But before he took another three steps, he felt a palpable change of tension in the air, rippling through the crowd from some unseen point up ahead. Frowns began to crease foreheads and heads swiveled towards the source of the disturbance.

Then people scrambled out of the way as a man staggered into view. Tharadis couldn't see where he'd come from; maybe one of the narrow alleys that crisscrossed Garoshmir. At a glance, it was easy to tell the man was wounded. Blood soaked his untucked shirt. He clutched something to his stomach with one arm, his eyes wild and pained.

"She ... gam ..." Fingers clawed, he lunged desperately for support from the nearest onlooker, but she stepped aside in horrified disgust. With nothing to hold onto, the man collapsed, spilling the contents of his arm. His intestines. He went still.

Everyone gaped at the man in disbelief—not at his death, Tharadis knew, but at his final word. *Sheggam.*

Tharadis pulled Shoreseeker free, which seemed to shock people more than the dead man, and turned to tell Chad to stay behind him. But Chad was gone. Where in Farshores had he gone?

Like a dam breaking, the street erupted in chaos. People ran in every direction, screaming and flailing, tripping and crashing and trampling. Shoreseeker clenched tightly in both hands, Tharadis shoved his way forward like a fish dashing upstream. Around the corner, two hulking figures, flesh gray as rot and dressed in worn leathers and heavy mail, hacked away with massive swords blunted nearly to clubs, crushing as much as cutting. There was nothing human about the creatures' long muzzles, no recognizable emotion in those crimson eyes.

Sheggam. He'd never seen a sheggam before—no one alive had—but he knew without a doubt that's what he was seeing.

Their eyes met his. He rushed towards them.

Someone fell, sprawling right in front of Tharadis, tripping him and sending him flying forward. A sword whistled past him, cleaving the air where he'd stood a moment before. His shoulder smashed into a sheggam's knee. The leg folded under Tharadis with a sickening crunch. Tharadis rolled away from the roaring beast, swinging Shoreseeker where he thought the other one would be. Thick links of mail split under Shoreseeker's blade, but he couldn't tell if it struck flesh. He sensed another strike coming and spun to the side at the last moment. The powerful thrust barely missed him, and without Tharadis there to slow its momentum, it punched right into the wounded sheggam's chest, goring it. Tharadis finished his spin with a flick of his wrist. Shoreseeker clove up through the unwounded sheggam's jaw, splintering jawbone and skull before completely removing its face from its head. It fell dead on its unmoving companion.

Breath coming in ragged gasps, Tharadis scanned the street as he rose to his feet. He was the only one left standing; everyone living had already fled. Eight dead bodies—not including the two sheggam—lay on the street. That had taken mere moments. Far more would have fallen had Tharadis not been there. His stomach twisted with worry. Worry for everyone in danger, but overwhelmingly worry for Nina.

"Chad?" he called.

No answer.

Tharadis quickly checked the faces of the dead. None were children. But that didn't mean Chad was safe.

Sheggam. No one was safe if sheggam were here.

Tharadis whirled when he heard shuffling behind him. It was Chad. Where had he been hiding? No matter; he gripped the boy's shoulder. "Are you hurt?"

Chad was rather pale for a Naruvian, but he was even paler now. His eyes were wide as he stared at the carnage and his whole body trembled. Tharadis wondered if the boy was too shocked to think, but then to Tharadis's immense relief, he shook his head.

"Okay. I need you to stay by my side. No more running off." He gave Chad's shoulder a squeeze. "I've heard you're good at hiding." Uncanny at it, if the rumors from back in Naruvieth were to be believed. "If you see any danger, no heroics. Just hide. Okay?"

Chad finally lifted his eyes to meet Tharadis's. His jaw tightened. "I'm the best hider there ever was." Fierce. Despite the tears now running down his cheeks.

"Good." Tharadis released his shoulder. "Then let's go find Nina."

Chapter 60: Trappings Discarded

In dim light of a single tallow candle, Ander's bearded face stared down at Esta from where he stood at the foot of the bed. His face was still as he unbuckled his axe belt, tossing it across the room next to where his boots lay.

The room was small, unfurnished save for the lumpy straw-filled mattress and a small footstool near the unshuttered window. Just enough for men like Ander to do what they came to do.

Over the past few minutes, ever since she'd stopped crying uncontrollably, a realization slowly seeped into her. Men like Ander were the only kind of men she would know from now on.

"Pull your dress up around your waist."

Esta didn't comply, instead looking over his shoulder at the open window behind him. A faint breeze stirred the limp linen curtains, revealing the wood shingle rooftop of the next building over, as well the fast-fading twilight. The breeze carried with it the sounds of the city, growing as night began to settle in. Beneath it all was faint ringing of bells. Esta didn't know what the bells meant, but she focused on them. Better to focus on what happened outside this room than in.

A sharp pain exploded in her big toe as Ander twisted it. "I said pull up your dress." His voice was calm, completely devoid of anger. It would've been better if there was anger in it. Or any sort of feeling at all.

Esta complied, and he let go of her toe. The breeze tickled the bare skin of her thighs. Ander grunted in satisfaction, as if he were inspecting breed animals and not a woman. But maybe there was less difference between them than Esta had thought. Tears filled her eyes again.

Ander pulled off his tunic and tossed it aside before working on the mail shirt beneath. Nighttime revelry was in full swing now. Esta could hear a bottle shatter on the street below, laughter, the constant of susurrus of distant voices. The bells. And was that … shouting?

"You told me Meedith was going to sell me to a brothel." Esta's voice was weak. It was the first time she'd spoken to him since the whore—the *other* whore—carried Esta up here.

343

"She would've. It was a good idea." Ander stood there, fully naked now. Scars crisscrossed his lean, well-muscled body. With his wild beard and all the trappings of civilization discarded on the floor in a heap, he looked more beast than man. His eyes were feral and hungry. The eyes of a hunter. A predator.

The rooftop. She would look at the rooftop. Much better than meeting those eyes.

As he clambered onto the bed, she caught a glimpse of something silently moving on the rooftop. Something pale and naked, like Ander, but nearly twice as large. Lank black hair hung around its strange, elongated face as it crouched there, crimson eyes watching her.

Esta closed her eyes. The rooftop was no better than here. Her ears registered the sounds of night gradually changing; all she could hear now was a chorus of shouts. Or were they screams? *They're not real. That thing on the roof isn't real. Nothing is.*

Ander was nearly atop her, his breath panting and frantic, when the window exploded.

Wood and plaster sprayed throughout the room. A massive, snarling weight slammed into Ander's back, crushing him into Esta, pinning her down. The weight didn't relent, only getting heavier and heavier, even when Ander began thrashing and roaring. Esta could taste the sour sweat of Ander's chest as he struggled against her. The scent of him smothered her.

Esta couldn't move. She couldn't even breathe. She had no idea what was happening. She didn't *want* to know. She lay there, the other whore's words ringing like bells in her head.

You'll get used to it eventually.

The heavy weight shifted and Esta filled her lungs involuntarily. Ander's roar of rage suddenly sharpened into a hysterical shriek. Warm wetness spilled over Ander's hips, soaking the bunched-up fabric of Esta's dress, and down the back of him until it dripped onto her bare thighs. The sound of ripping followed a moment later, but Ander wasn't wearing any fabric. He screamed even more frantically.

More sounds. Crunching sounds. Wet sounds. Esta had heard such sounds before, a long time ago. The image of dogs eating filled her head, but she didn't really know why. Maybe that's what was making the sounds. A giant dog. Yes, that had to be it.

Ander stopped screaming. Then he stopped struggling. He even stopped twitching.

Breathing became easier. For some reason, Ander was a lot lighter now. Esta could still hear the dog eating. She could even feel it tongue through the skin of Ander's chest. But that didn't make sense—wouldn't Ander's heart and lungs get in the way? Esta didn't feel like puzzling it out. The world was beyond making sense. She wasn't even afraid anymore.

She felt nothing. Nothing at all.

The enormous dog—or whatever it was—stopped eating and sniffed the air. Then, with a sudden lurch, the heavy weight leapt off the bed. Its feet thudded onto the floor before it smashed open the door, cracking the frame. The floorboards out in the hall creaked with each step. A succession of screams followed, but some of them cut off quickly while others lingered on.

Esta lay there a while, hearing them but not really listening, then pushed Ander off her with little effort and stood up next to the bed, the sticky folds of her dress falling back around her legs. Blood was everywhere, on the floor, on the walls, even on the ceiling. What remained of Ander was enough for a throw rug. Barefoot, Esta turned and went out into the hall, stepping over the splinters of wood and plaster.

The bodies in the hall, many of them without clothes, were people she didn't recognize. Some of them mewed softly; others were silent. The one on the stairs, though, triggered something in her memory—a name? Beth perhaps—but the memory fled as suddenly as it arrived. Esta stepped over the broken form and went outside through the rickety wooden door.

Absently, she glanced up as she shuffled down the streets, only one thought penetrating the fog of her mind.

Night had finally fallen.

Chapter 61: Eye to Eye

errin Fayel, Commander of the Knights of the Eye, had been camped in the heart of the thicket for days, along with the other forty-two Knights of his order that remained. Waiting, for a man whom he was sure would not come. That man had forsaken everything the Knights believed in, and wouldn't heed his former commander's call. That man was beyond redemption, yet still, Herrin had to try.

The familiar sensation tickled his neck as he was kneeling on the wet, loamy bank of a stream that meandered through the woods, washing out the cook pots. He glanced to the north-east, towards the source of the sensation. Herrin had been mistaken. The man was coming after all. Herrin could feel his approach almost as clearly as if a sheggam stalked his camp. And for good reason.

He stood, drying off the pot with a rag, and turned to the camp. There were only a few torches among the tents; it wasn't yet full dark, and the Knights of the Eye could see better at night than other people. Some were napping, and some playing dice and drinking strong tea, laughing and speaking quietly. A few stood guard around the camp. One of these, a man named Rigg, walked up to him, staff in hand. Even with his face silhouetted as it was, the camp's light behind him, the tightness in Rigg's expression was obvious.

"I know," said the Commander as he whipped the rag over his shoulder. He tucked the pot into the crook of his arm and stepped up the steeply inclined slope of the stream's bank, snapping twigs and rustling ferns. "Dransig comes. Let us gather the men."

Preparation took only moments. Torches were doused, cloaks fastened, helmets donned. Herrin ordered everyone to leave their staves behind. Their short swords—only used for dispatching sheggam—stayed at their hips.

From this deep in the woods, he couldn't see the lights of Garoshmir in the distance, but Herrin knew it was from that direction that Dransig came. He kept his hands hanging free at his sides, but several others gripped the hilts of their swords. Knights of the Eye feared very few things—the sheggam, and those who danced dangerously close to the line that separated humans from the monsters. After what Dransig had done, it wasn't clear just how close to the line he was. If he hadn't crossed it already.

The thought made Herrin nervous. In spite of himself, he checked to make sure his sword was clear in its scabbard. He hated showing fear to his subordinates, but he hated being unprepared even more.

As Dransig neared their position, his presence nearly glowed in Herrin's awareness, almost as strongly as a sheggam would have—and certainly more strongly than those of his loyal Knights. Behind him, Herrin heard the word *abomination* muttered, but he didn't turn to address the speaker's indiscretion. Now was not the time.

Dransig stepped into view silently, eyeing them warily. The embroidered mark of the Eye had been removed from his tabard, picked clean of every thread. Almost as if the man had declared his unwillingness to see. The sight of it removed infuriated Herrin.

Dransig's staff rested on his shoulder, one wrist hooked over it. He was not close, but he didn't need to be for them to have a conversation. If that was indeed what he had come for.

Herrin spoke first. "I'm surprised you came." Indeed, Herrin had been surprised when his messenger came back yesterday, reporting that his message to Dransig had been successfully delivered. Dransig wouldn't have been found unless he wanted to be.

For all that Dransig had done to himself, he still very much looked burdened with age. His shoulders were slumped, his eyelids heavy. "And I'm surprised to stand here unmolested. Considering what your men have been trying to do."

"You mean, considering what *you* had done. If you came all this way to protest your innocence, you've come a long way for nothing."

Dransig shook his head. "My guilt is earned, and felt keenly. But I didn't come because of that."

"Then why?"

"To see if you had finally come to grips with reality."

Herrin smiled, though he didn't feel a shred of pleasure. His smile was fueled by anger. "Insults are just as welcome as protestations."

"I intend no insult. Only to present facts." Dransig briefly glanced over his shoulder. "The Runeway is keyed to shegasti. For humans—well, humans with no trace of shegasti in their blood—it will do nothing. Except pave a way for monsters to sweep across all the Sutherlands unimpeded. I think you know this now, but you've done nothing."

"You forget one thing. Andrin's Wall still stands. Threats to the Sutherlands can only come from *within*." He made it clear with his gaze and his tone who among them could count as a threat. He paced, never taking his eyes off Dransig. "You claim to bring facts, yet you forget the facts of our mission. The Knights of the Eye are the *protectors* of mankind. Not its slayers. We cannot allow an assassination of any human to be performed in our name. No matter the supposed cost. Or have you forgotten the oath you swore on that very staff?"

Dransig dropped his gaze and seemed to grow even more weary than before. He had likely hoped Herrin Fayel, Commander of the Knights of the Eye himself, had turned traitor to his cause, as Dransig had. The old man proved himself a greater fool than Herrin could ever have imagined.

Dransig seemed deep in thought for a moment. Then he tossed the staff to the ground halfway between himself and Herrin. "Forgotten? No. But I would gladly forsake it if it would save lives." He rested his hand on the hilt of his sword.

"Ending lives to save them." Herrin shook his head. "I hope that's not all you came here for."

He could feel a couple of his men change their stance ever so slightly. It was subtle, but clear even to Dransig, by the way his eyes shifted, that they were assuming a more offensive position. Herrin turned his head a fraction; it was all the signal they needed to drop back to their original positions. By leaving their staves behind, they were granting Dransig sanctuary—insofar as he remained human. If not, well, that was what the swords were for.

"All? That isn't the half of it. In fact, that part of it doesn't even matter anymore." Dransig took a deep breath and released it slowly. "I've become more ... sensitive. I can sense things with more precision than the average Knight of the Eye."

Herrin cocked his head. "And?"

"Something's coming. Something I've never felt before."

Very little frightened Herrin Fayel, but the tone of Dransig's voice chilled him to the bone. "You think—"

"No. I *know* what it was. If you won't help me carry out my charge, then at least you should know it's time to carry out yours." He turned to leave.

"Dransig." Herrin's voice carried its own warning. "Stay here, stop what you're going to do. I will grant you sanctuary for as long as you remain. You will be safe. But if you leave these woods, I won't protect you anymore."

Dransig paused. His laugh was as much a cough. "Protect me? I'm doomed in any event, and your chance to protect anyone has long since passed." He continued to walk, then stopped again. "Unless you finally heed my warnings. I fear this may be the last of them."

When it was clear that Herrin wouldn't respond, Dransig snorted and silently stalked away, leaving his staff behind.

Once back in camp, Herrin turned to Jerem, his second. "Send out scouts. Have them report back if they sense anything … unusual."

Rigg paused. "You trust him?"

"His words? I've never once doubted them. It was his choices and his commitment to our cause that were in doubt." *And the blood in his veins,* Herrin thought. *My poor, twisted old friend. What have you done to yourself?* "Jerem, you'll have command while I'm away. You know what to do if the scouts find anything worthy of our attention."

Jerem picked at the scar under his eye like he always did when he was worried. Doubtless he didn't relish the prospect of facing a real sheggam, if indeed there was one. "And if I need to send for you?"

Tossing back his cloak, Herrin grabbed his staff and tucked it under his arm. "Follow the scent of treachery. I will be there, with the Eye on my chest watching on in judgment." Herrin left the camp, heading toward Garoshmir. He knew, from the depths of his soul, that his sword would taste sheggam blood before the night was out. And that blood would belong to a sheggam who once called himself a Knight of the Eye.

Dransig staggered at the edge of the woods, catching a tree to support himself. The trunk of tree, as healthy as any other, splintered under his inhumanly strong grip as easily as if rotted. He fell to his knees. His breathing sounded like choking, but he could barely hear it over the fierce pulsing in his ears.

And the infernal Song, ever on the distant edges of his consciousness. The Song of Pain, which yearned to be sung aloud in blood and the rending of flesh.

No no no! I will not turn! The pounding in Dransig's head was almost too much to take, yet he got to his feet and loped on, out onto the grassy knolls, Garoshmir not far beyond. Joints popped as his limbs began to elongate. Frantic energy surged through him like insects swarming beneath his skin, demanding release.

Dransig strangled it with all his might. *I will not turn!*

At least ... at least not yet. He forced down the Song of Pain, and with that, his body slowly, painfully returned to a fully human state. Still, he knew he didn't have much longer. Perhaps not even the night. He would resist as long as he could, but it was futile to pretend that his resistance could last forever. The shegasti now leaking from his body overwhelmed even *his* senses; he was sure all the nearby Knights could feel him as clearly as seeing a beacon in the night. No doubt Herrin had sent someone to kill him before he got too close to turning, if the man didn't follow Dransig himself.

As well he should, Dransig thought grimly as he limped down the grassy slope, struggling to stay on his feet. *I deserve and accept such a fate. Just give me a little more time.*

A little more time to find my daughter. Find her, and kill her.

Chapter 62: First Taste of Freedom

Aylia, the red moon, slowly shifted across the sky like a star that had forgotten its place in the firmament. It was much larger than a star, however, if not as big as her grayish-white brother Foth. And though Foth remained the same size no matter when it was spotted, Aylia grew and shrank in cycles. It had long been said that Aylia was a harbinger of suffering, especially when it was larger in the sky.

Tonight, it was the largest Erianna had ever seen it.

Long ago, she had dismissed such superstitions as a misguided attempt to make sense of the world. Now, crouched amidst a stack of discarded baskets as she listened to a world gone mad, she wondered if perhaps there was some dark purpose to the moon, guiding events to ensure more darkness and pain. Perhaps it was there to punish her, a mere slave daring to live free. Why else would such horrors be unleashed upon them mere hours after declaring her freedom?

Screams. The night was filled with them. No, what was happening to these people had nothing to do with her. And as frightening as the prospect of freedom was, she refused to believe that seizing it, much less wanting it, could be a crime. She was a slave no more and would no longer think like one.

The thought, as empowering as it was, did little to keep Erianna's hands from shaking.

Slowly, as quietly as she could, she raised herself up out of her crouch until she could see beyond the stack of baskets. The street curved up a slope, turning into wide stone steps. She couldn't see very far. Behind her were shop fronts surrounding a dead end with no alleys between them. The doors were locked; she had already tested them before hiding among the baskets. She'd considered busting out a window and crawling into one of the shops, but she didn't want to make any noise and draw the sheggam to her. So she had hidden herself among the baskets left out in front of one of the shops.

Erianna knew, though, that she couldn't stay here forever. The sheggam would come. And though running might not help her for very long, she decided that running would be better than simply accepting her fate, the same bloody fate that so many others had found tonight.

As soon as she stepped out from behind the baskets, the sound of something behind her shattering startled her into a headlong sprint around the curving street and up the steps.

She didn't stop until she was three blocks away, panting as her thigh muscles burned with exertion, at the corner of a main intersection. A few of the streetlamps were dark, but the others cast flickering light on the scene. Bodies littered the streets here. At the corner was a shop, where it seemed people had broken through the front door. Those who weren't fast enough lay dead, crammed between its jambs. More people had died climbing *out* of the shop's broken windows, backs ripped to shreds. Apparently, they thought they could escape danger and found out—the hard way—that there was no escape. Not tonight.

Part of Erianna wanted to throw up everything in her stomach, but she forced herself to steadiness. An odd mist clung to the ground in patches, mist almost as thick as cotton. She had seen this mist once before, back in Twelve Towers. Erianna was certain it was what began Shad Belgrith's transformation into something … less than human. Erianna made sure to keep her distance.

Amidst the twisted forms of the dead she could make out weapons—swords, arrows, an axe with a broken shaft—as well as the remains of a shield. Some of the bodies, she noticed, belonged to sheggam.

Good. At least someone had put up a fight.

She calmed the roiling in her gut before walking over to where some of the fallen lay. For a moment, she decided to forget her newfound freedom, and put herself back in the mindset of Shad's slave—killing all emotion while forced to do something unpleasant. It was a skill she had honed over the years. She pulled apart two bodies that had been dismembered, and then a group of four that appeared to be more intact. The horrid smell of death, of viscera and even fouler things, threatened to overwhelm her composure, but soon she found what she was looking for: a shirt of chain mail.

The soldier who had worn it had died from having his groin split open until all of his guts had spilled out of the bottom of him. She cleared her mind of the details and simply went about undressing him, ignoring the cold, clammy feel of his pale skin.

Her own garments, such as they were, didn't do much to keep out the night's cold. As soon as she'd tugged free the dead man's linen undershirt, Erianna quickly removed all of her own clothes before pulling on the shirt.

Luckily it didn't smell as bad as the man she'd taken it from. Then she stripped him of his heavy quilted shirt. On another body nearby she found trousers, though they were almost too baggy to be useful on her, and tucked their bottoms into her boots. She pulled on the mail shirt, tying up her hair in a bun to keep it from getting snagged in the links. The mail was much heavier that she had expected, but it was a comforting weight. Obviously, it hadn't helped the dead man, but it felt good to know she was at least trying to ensure her survival.

It was something, but it didn't seem like quite enough. Careful to stay clear of the mist, she rooted around until she found a sheathed knife. She pulled it free, inspecting its narrow, double-edged blade. It would do. She slid it home and found a belt and began to strap the knife to her waist.

The sound of a blade sliding free of its sheath from behind halted her.

"You."

A human voice. Not a sheggam. She almost wept in relief. Slowly, she raised her hands and turned around to face the man who had spoken.

She found herself looking down the length of a sword that she had seen once before, earlier in the day, the tip of its remarkable sky-blue blade only inches from her face. Gripping the sword was Tharadis, the Warden of Naruvieth. Not far behind him squatted a boy, no more than ten or eleven years old, who smiled up at her like a mischievous little monkey. The smile was forced, however, and it didn't reach the boy's eyes.

Erianna met the Warden's eyes. They burned with rage. "This," he said. "This is what you helped to bring about." With his free hand, he gestured towards the dead.

Erianna didn't flinch at the accusation, as much as part of her wanted to. "You want to blame me. Fine. I won't stop you. Kill me if you want. Kill me if you think it will bring any of these people back."

The Warden stepped closer until the edge of his blade rested against her neck. She didn't know what kind of material it was made of, but she felt certain that if she moved at all, it would open up her throat.

"Give me a reason why I shouldn't."

Erianna swallowed. She felt the scrape of the blade against her skin as she did. "I can't say I don't deserve it for what I did. No, for what I *failed* to do. I should have defied her sooner." Erianna closed her eyes. "I was a slave in all but name. If I had defied her, she would have whipped me and put me in the dungeons. If I had tried getting a message out, she would have thrown me from one of the Towers. If I had tried to escape, she would have cut off my toes. But ... knowing what she is capable of ..."

Perhaps it *would* be better if this man killed her now. She had her freedom, and that was all she ever wanted from life. If that's all she had when her life ended, that was better than anything she had ever expected to have. And at least this way she wouldn't end up with her belly clawed open, dying in a pile of her own innards. She lifted her chin, giving him an easier target. She felt a tiny trickle of blood roll down her throat, even though she couldn't feel the cut that caused it.

"Answer a question first," he said. "If I had been one of Shad's men come to take you back, would you let me?"

Her eyes shot open and she lowered her head to face him. "I would have cut you open or died trying."

She could feel his eyes weighing her, as if they alone could sense the sincerity of her words. Finally, he dropped his sword, but didn't sheathe it. "We're looking for someone. A little girl, eight years old. Black hair, skin like mine. Her name is Nina."

Erianna rubbed her throat, fingering the tiny cut there. It was almost too small to feel. That sword must have been sharper than any blade she had seen before. "I haven't seen many people. Living ones, anyway. And I haven't been looking too closely at the dead." She dropped her hand. Her voice softened. "Especially not the children."

The Warden nodded, as if he'd expected as much. He turned to the boy, who had taken an interest in the paving stones beneath his feet. "Chad." The boy looked up. "I want you to take Erianna out of the city. There's a caravan just west of the city. It'll be safer than here. I want you two to stay there. Help anyone you see along the way get there too."

The boy, Chad, frowned as he stood. "What about Nina? I can help you find her."

The Warden tousled the boy's scruffy hair. "I know, and if she shows up there before I find her, I want you to wait with her for me. I imagine quite a few people are going to get the idea to go to the caravan, so she might head there too."

Chad's frown didn't go away, but he nodded anyway. Reluctantly. It was obvious to Erianna that he thought he would be more help here, but she knew he was putting on a brave front. "Do you really think this caravan is going to be safer than anywhere in the city?" she asked.

Tharadis turned to her. "It can't be any more dangerous. Garoshmir wasn't built for defense. Not even the Dome and Spire would keep the sheggam out. After all, who would attack it? Many people didn't even believe the sheggam were real until today."

Erianna's eyes drifted back towards the shop front, where people had died trying to get in and died trying to get out. No, there were no safe places to hide in the city. But would a caravan be any better? *As he said, it certainly can't be any worse than this*, she thought.

Erianna nodded. "All right." She looked to the boy and tried her best to smile. "I don't know my way out of the city. Do you think you can—"

The boy jerked upright, eyes widening as they focused on something behind Erianna. Then she heard the heavy booted footfalls, too heavy for humans. Sword in hand, Tharadis rushed past, calling, "Go, now!" Without looking behind her, Erianna grabbed Chad by the hand and dragged him in the opposite direction of the erupting sounds of combat.

Chapter 63: Words and Flame

The Archivist's Room in the Academy Library was tiny, by far the smallest room in the library. It was tucked away in the corner, hidden under a staircase and protected with a massive steel door disguised as a wooden pantry door. The hallway leading to the mostly-useless staircase was kept purposefully dusty to discourage people from thinking it contained anything of value. But the second-most valuable object in the library, or even in the whole of the Academy, was housed in that small room.

It was a small device consisting of strange red metal, unlike anything else seen in the Accord, roughly shaped like a ring standing upright on a stand, much like the globes that were occasionally seen in certain departments within the Academy. But this ring held no spherical map of the world.

Three spikes, made from the same metal, were attached to the ring, their sharp tips pointed inward. Patterns were etched all over the Crafted device, combining the two forms of magic in ways developed centuries ago, before Andrin's Wall and the sheggam scourge which precipitated it, now lost to the oft-destructive path of history. In fact, this device was created to counteract such destructive tendencies. It served to preserve human knowledge from the inevitable ravages of time.

Yet the device was only a tool, a means for such a task. The device itself could hold no knowledge. Which was why it was second in value to the green Memory Orb which hung on a chain around Alyssa's neck.

She sat down on the well-cushioned but backless stool in front of the bench upon which the red metal device sat. After unlatching the frame hanging from her neck, she took the Orb out of it and hefted it. Though she felt its weight all the time, it was so much heavier when she held it. As if she were feeling the weight of its importance settle onto her hand.

This Memory Orb was the true reason why the library existed. The books, though by any other measure priceless, were expendable. Because even if the books were gone, the knowledge they contained were safe. All of them had been copied, by Alyssa and the archivists before her, onto the Memory

Orb, using the metal device in front of her.

She placed the Orb between the spikes, which, at an unseen cue, slid inward to trap the Orb in place. Using magic that Alyssa could manipulate if not fully understand, the device, simply called the Etcher, would then inscribe tiny irregularities deep within the substance of the Orb. What shape the irregularities took depended entirely on Alyssa.

She hooked a string of red hair behind her ear and took a deep breath to calm herself. Then she gently gripped the Orb with the tips of three fingers from each hand. Each motion she made would change the Orb, writing to it. It was up to her to make sure that the correct Patterns, correlating to the text in the book she was transcribing, were etched into the Orb. All of her training in the Academy was focused on this one task.

The Orb stored nine thousand seven hundred and twenty-two scrolls. Six hundred and one clay tablets. Nineteen thousand seven hundred and fifty-nine letters. Official documents beyond counting. And three thousand and eighteen books.

Yet one more remained. One of the most important books, called *First Night, Last Night*, sat on the bench next to the Etcher, open to its final two pages. Ostensibly, it was about the formation and arcane rituals of the Knights of the Eye. But hidden within was information about the greatest tragedy known to man: the sheggam scourge.

Suppressing a shudder at the thought of sheggam, Alyssa studied the words on the final page, committing them not only to memory but converting them to the Pattern she would etch into the Orb. Once that was done, she turned the Orb slightly.

A tiny filament of off-green, appearing like a slight flaw, came into being near the center of the Orb.

She shifted it again, slightly, committing more of the words to the Orb, then again. She had transcribed almost the entire page already when she began to smell the smoke.

The skin on the back of her neck prickled as she turned from her task. Fire was a librarian's greatest fear, and though the task she was engaged in was the counter to such problems, the thought of fire in the library still made Alyssa very nervous. After all, she could burn just as easily as a book.

Finishing the transcription could wait. She put the Orb back in the frame hanging from her neck and stood, looking at the door. Thin gray trailers of smoke rose from the top seam in the door frame. She hadn't been here long—less than an hour—and this room was far away from the normal stacks of books. If that much smoke was already coming into the room …

Cursing herself for nearly forgetting it, Alyssa snatched the Etcher and stuffed it into the pack hanging at her hip. Sweat sprang from her brow, though if it was caused by either the sudden rise in heat or her own anxiety, she didn't know. She knelt down and touched the door lever.

It was warm, but not hot.

She pulled the lever down, and the catch holding the door in place slid back. The door opened a crack. Smoke spilled in all around the door and the room became considerably hotter. Alyssa crouched lower and threw the door open.

It was worse than Alyssa could have ever expected. The hallway was filled with smoke. If Alyssa had been standing, it would have been down to her shoulders. Even so, her eyes burned. Murky orange light flooded the end of the hallway, at the intersection. The sound of burning was not at all like the pleasant crackle of a fire in the hearth, but the roar of some hellish beast.

Alyssa placed the Memory Orb back in the fixture hanging around her neck and crawled halfway down the hallway before she noticed the body.

It lay in the orange light, unmoving and silhouetted so she couldn't see its eyes. She thought perhaps it was a man but she couldn't say for certain. His arms were splayed in front of him, head cocked to the side.

Perhaps he had breathed too much smoke. Alyssa would have to take him with her when she escaped. She couldn't just leave someone to burn, even if it slowed her down and made her own escape that much more difficult. She couldn't live with herself if she had the opportunity to save someone and didn't.

She crawled over to the man faster, determined to get him out of there if it was the last she ever did.

The body moved. Though by the way its arms were still splayed in front of it, it didn't move on its own. Someone or something dragged it back.

Alyssa froze. Was someone else there?

The man stirred slightly, then groaned.

Then he screamed.

Alyssa's heartbeat pounded in her ears as she scrambled back the way she had come. She barked her knees climbing up the stairs. Hot smoke blinded her and filled her lungs. She coughed.

The man's screams were cut short with a violent ripping sound.

A window. She had to find a window. She had to get out of there. Why wasn't there a window somewhere? If only she could see!

She coughed again. Her lungs burned painfully as she collapsed to her side. A window. Where was she? She had climbed the steps, but she couldn't remember how many. She was on a carpeted floor now. Was she on the landing?

Alyssa searched her mind. She knew the library front and back; she hardly ever left it. She knew where all the windows were. But it was so hard to think.

The man was dead. Someone or something had killed him. Alyssa coughed again.

It would hear her. Panic filled her. She tried crawling again, but even her muscles were beginning to burn.

She was on the landing. She was sure of it. But was there a window there? She wanted to find out, but it was so hard to move.

The bottom step creaked. The bottom step never creaked when Alyssa stepped on it. Something much heavier than her was standing on it.

The next step creaked.

Alyssa struggled to her hands and knees, began crawling towards what she hoped was the opposite wall. The window would be there. It *had* to be.

Her fingers painfully hit the molding at the base of the wall. Her hand spidered up the wall, searching.

No window.

She coughed again. No. There had to be a window! She knew there was! She swept her hand left and right across the wall.

Then she felt it. Cold glass.

Without a second thought, she punched through it. The glass sliced her hand along the bones of her wrist. She punched again, ignoring the pain in her eyes, her lungs, her hand. She heard a roar behind, though she couldn't tell if it was the fire, trying to escape with her, or the beast on the steps.

She had no time.

With the last reserves of her strength, Alyssa threw herself through the window.

The impact jarred her shoulder, but the glass exploded outward. And as she fell through the air, she caught a glimpse of something through her watery eyes—a massive, pale hand, each of its fingers tipped with a talon. Snatching at the air where she had just been.

Then the window erupted in a sudden gout of flame, outlining the horrible creature for the briefest moment in an infernal blaze that then consumed it. The creature screamed in agony and then in death.

The next moment, the ground rose up and slapped Alyssa in the back. She blacked out.

Chapter 64: Swords Drawn

J erem, acting Commander of the Knights of the Eye, stepped onto the Runeway, short sword drawn and gripped tightly. The scar under his eye itched worse than ever, but he resisted the impulse to scratch it. Now was not the time to be self-indulgent and weak. A stiff wind tugged at his cloak, snapping it behind him, but the force of the wind cowered before the surge of dark energy pulsing through him.

The Runeway.

About this, Dransig had been right. There was no denying it, yet Herrin Fayel had told Jerem and the others that he had always believed what Dransig had told them. Shortly after Dransig had betrayed his oaths to the Knights of the Eye and fled, Fayel had sent men—Jerem included—to discover the true nature of the Runeway.

It had been just as Dransig had warned. Purest evil.

Yet even so, Fayel had said it didn't matter to the Knights. Andrin's Wall still stood; therefore, the only sheggam threats could come from the Knights themselves. That, Herrin had told them all after Dransig had betrayed them, was the true calling of the Knights of the Eye. Protecting the world from themselves.

Now, though, all of that changed. Two scouts had stumbled back into camp in the woods, nearly sick with fear, yet, at the same time, feverish with the desire to spill sheggam blood. Something was coming, they had said. Something so rife with shegasti that it was a tower of flame, and that made Dransig look like the ember of a blown-out candle wick.

Jerem felt it now. It was impossible not to. He couldn't see it with his mortal eyes, but the Eye, the one that could see beings infected with shegasti, sensed it more clearly than anything before.

And, just as Dransig predicted, it was using the Runeway. Coming straight for them.

All the Knights of the Eye stood arrayed behind Jerem, swords drawn and ready to fulfill their primary mission—to be the barrier between the world of men and the world of the sheggam.

Like Andrin's Wall. *But hopefully, we'll do a better job of it,* Jerem

thought, gritting his teeth. *Nothing will get past us.*
Nothing.

The land around them was featureless, save for the forest where they had camped a mere ten-minute walk away. Otherwise, the coarse, rocky grasses were flat for miles around. And of course, the Runeway itself was as flat as a knife blade. There would be no surprises here. Whatever was coming—Jerem wasn't yet ready to admit it was a sheggam—would be in clear view before it came upon them.

The first thing he saw was a wavering orange flame, hovering above the Runeway in relative darkness. Or at least that's how it seemed. It was still far too distant to see clearly, but it seemed to be closing the distance at a remarkable speed. *How is it moving so fast?*

Jerem suddenly realized just how little about the sheggam he, and the rest of the Knights, really knew.

He kept his eyes pinned on that flame but turned his head slightly to address the Knights. "Anyone who breaks ranks is a traitor, no different from Dransig. And will get a sword in his back." It was as much a reminder to himself as to the others.

Of course, no one broke ranks. The Knights of the Eye weren't cowards, and whatever fear they now felt would be overwhelmed by their willingness to kill. Such was the nature of their training and their lives as Knights—learning how to hate the sheggam, learning how to kill the sheggam.

At the edges of his enhanced hearing, Jerem heard something strange—a rhythmic metallic clanging, punctuated by silence. It almost sounded like a horse galloping along the Runeway, but that was impossible. Horses steered clear of Knights; they would flee like mad at the merest scent of a sheggam. Besides, the number of hoof strikes was wrong.

"Ready … steady …" Rigg murmured behind Jerem. "Here it comes."

Then a form resolved in the darkness: a six-legged monster, horse-like but twisted almost beyond recognition. Eyes burned like coals, and Jerem caught the glint of row upon row of fangs in its strange, circular mouth. Glossy black skin—or was it covered in scales?—rippled with each thunderous stride, metal clanging upon metal in a hypnotic rhythm.

Even with his enhanced senses, he could see little of the massive, cloaked rider, as if shadows had deliberately gathered around its face. The staff it held was nearly the width of a streetlamp—and indeed, the orange flame Jerem had seen first came from what appeared to be a lamp at the end of the staff. When the horrid mount and its rider were but seconds away, it lifted its staff.

The world went silent then, as if the creature before them had stolen all sound.

The lamp erupted in light. Ropes of flame exploded from the lamp, lancing toward the Knights as fast as a snake strikes.

Jerem threw himself to the side, rolling towards the edge of the Runeway, but it was more luck than anything else that saved him. One of the ropes of fire singed his cloak, and apoth only knew where his sword ended up, but he came to his feet as the screams of his men and the sounds of sizzling flesh filled his ears.

It was over in an instant. A dozen corpses made, and the sheggam was already riding on. It had treated the Knights of the Eye with as much regard as a cloud of gnats.

In a few moments, it was well beyond their reach, riding much faster than a man could run. Jerem hadn't even had time to raise his sword against the sheggam. He doubted any of them had. They had barely even slowed it.

He looked at the bodies around him, scorched and severed by sheggam magic. Emotion threatened to buckle his knees. Nearly a dozen dead, and for what?

"Sir." Rigg trotted up. He looked worried, but unharmed.

Jerem breathed a sigh of relief that the man still lived. "What is …" He didn't finish his question, but his attention was seized and dragged north. With the Eye, he sensed them.

Hundreds, maybe thousands, of those towers of flames. A sheggam army.

"Shores take me," he whispered. A single sheggam had nearly wiped them out. What chance did they have against so many?

"Sir," Rigg asked, "what should we do?"

He sighed as his gaze swept over the carnage. "The only thing we can," he replied. "One defeat doesn't change who we are. Gather the living, but leave the wounded behind. We will head north to make good on our oath. Or we'll die trying."

Chapter 65: Piled High

A soldier's body lay twisted at the base of the wall separating the districts of the city, not three paces from where Erianna crouched. A thin strip of skin was all that connected the head to the neck. Its eyes stared at her. Erianna did her best to ignore that damning stare as she peered around the corner of the gray stone building, but it wormed its way into her and made her shudder. It wasn't as if she could've saved him. She'd be lucky to save herself, and extremely lucky to save Chad, too.

Not true, the soldier's eyes seemed to say. *You could've prevented all this. You could've warned them.*

Gripping her knife tightly in her fist, she took a deep breath. Yesterday was gone. She had to think about now. Regret couldn't change the past, but it could make you lose the future. *Focus on what's important,* she thought, scolding herself. *Focus, Erianna!*

Chad squatted behind her, the fingers of one of his hands hooked into her belt, heedless of her mail shirt, which she was sure was rubbing his knuckles raw. Still, he didn't complain, and neither did she, not as long as she knew he was close. She glanced back at him. He, too, was taken in by the soldier's eyes.

"Hey," she whispered. He glanced at her as if she'd startled him from a dream. "Are you ready to move?"

Wide as his eyes were, he nodded without hesitation. She could sense a certain unexpected confidence in his expression. Young though he was, he had a look that said he was no stranger to death and blood. The thought almost broke Erianna's heart. But perhaps it would be enough to save him.

If anything can.

Slowly they crept along the building's edge, keeping to the shadows, with the high gray wall on their right. Erianna didn't know Garoshmir enough to tell exactly what district lay on the other side of that wall, or even which one was on this side. Nearly a dozen columns of smoke rose into the sky, blotting out stars. Both moons still sat in the sky, but Erianna didn't know enough about them either to gauge her position. Was she even heading west? She thought—no, *hoped*—she was, but it was so hard to tell in all the chaos and confusion.

She gestured for Chad to stay behind her when they reached the edge of the building. Just beyond it, the road opened up into a vast square, surrounded by three- and four-story buildings. In the center was a large fountain, though it was cracked, water spraying out of it in uncertain spurts. But it was what surrounded the fountain that caught Erianna's breath in her throat.

Piles of bodies.

She had no idea how many there were, thrown atop each other like trash. Two hundred, maybe more. Countless streaks of blood led to each pile. Within the piles, she caught sight of movement. Soft groans filled the air. These people were alive. Gravely wounded, dragged here, but alive.

And there was nothing she could do about it.

Over a dozen sheggam roamed between the piles, all of them clutching weapons. They were waiting for something—for what, Erianna had no idea. She didn't intend to wait around to find out. She hated that these people had to suffer, that they were so helpless, but she could tell by how much blood painted the cobbles that none of them were getting out of here alive.

She spotted another street that fed into the square, just past one of the nearest piles. A single sheggam prowled there, carrying a long, heavy spear. Iron plate and boiled leather, spattered in blood, covered its broad chest and shoulders. A heavy bow and quiver hung over its back. Its eyes scanned the square, passing over where Erianna and Chad hid, but luckily, its gaze swept right past them. These sheggam weren't like the others she had seen, those naked, frenzied beasts. These were still monsters, to be sure, but they had some measure of self-control. They even seemed to be in some loose formation.

A pair of sheggam stepped out of that street, each dragging two or three limp forms in each hand. Some of the bodies were missing limbs, leaving heavy red trails. Those ones wouldn't last long. The sheggam tossed the bodies one by one on the piles, eliciting pained moans. Then they turned back to the mouth of the street and waited.

There was no point in waiting around here. There was no way to get through all these sheggam. Erianna and Chad would simply have to find another way around. She was about to turn and go when something else caught her eye—a flash of yellow. Erianna squinted to see it more clearly. Between the two of the farther piles stood a girl—no, a young woman. The flash of yellow Erianna had seen was the young woman's dress, though the whole front of it was crusted in blood. She didn't seem to be moving, at least not very fast, but it didn't seem that she was injured either. That wouldn't last long, not with so many sheggam nearby. Once they caught sight of her …

At her side, Erianna heard Chad breathe in sharply. She hadn't heard him move up next to her. Frowning, she turned to him. "What is it?"

He pointed at the woman in the square. "I think that's Nina's aunt."

Chapter 66: The Smoker

I can save her," Chad said. "I know I can."

Erianna was amazed at the boy's sudden transformation. It was almost as if he believed he could do it. Which was, of course, utter madness.

"No," she whispered sharply. "You and I both know that's not possible. I know you want to save her. *I* want to save her—save all of them." Careful not to alert the sheggam, she made a small gesture at the piles of wounded people in the square. "But I'm too worried about getting ourselves out alive."

The boy broke his gaze away, huffing through his nose, tight-lipped. Moments before, he looked ready to pass out from fear, but now, he was *certain* he could do this. Erianna shook her head; she couldn't understand what came over him all of a sudden. She firmly took his hand, and looked back around the corner.

Three more sheggam had entered the square in the few moments she'd looked away. Her stomach sank. There may have been a chance to sneak through them all before—a tiny speck of a chance, but a chance, nonetheless. Now, it was hopeless. Every shadow was being watched by at least one pair of sheggam eyes. But for what? She still hadn't figured that out.

No. There was no way out. They would have to backtrack. They'd lose precious time, with no guarantees of finding a better way, but this way was lost beyond all doubt.

She glanced to the young woman in the blood-smeared yellow dress—Nina's aunt, which would make her Tharadis's sister, or maybe sister-in-law. Strange; he hadn't mentioned her. Had he not known she was in the city? The woman continued shuffling along aimlessly. She wouldn't last moments; the way she was walking, she might run straight into one of the sheggam. Transfixed, Erianna watched. What was wrong with her? How was she so oblivious?

One of the sheggam turned, sniffing the air. Its eyes fell on the woman. Instantly, the sheggam's body tensed, lowering into a fighting crouch, the long-handled spiked mace drawn back, ready to strike. Yet it didn't rush forward. It stepped nearer, slowly. The woman didn't seem to notice at all, not even when its muzzle was mere inches away from her. She just continued her aimless shuffle.

Erianna waited for the inevitable strike, heart pounding in her chest. Yet that strike never came. The sheggam's eyes slid right off the woman, as if he no longer found her interesting. Then he turned back to watching one of the other streets.

She was alive. Somehow, the woman was still alive.

It seemed such a shame that even after all that, Erianna would have to leave her behind. Perhaps she would be fine on her own. Perhaps better off than anyone else. "Let's get out of here, Chad," she said, pulling him along.

"No, I mean it. I really can save—"

Erianna jerked to a halt as soon she had taken three steps back the way they had come.

Up ahead, a wave of white mist rolled across the ground like surf on a beach. Unlike surf, Erianna quickly realized, it didn't fall back. It just kept rolling toward them, its massive bulk spanning the width of the street. Slowly, yet relentlessly. Deeper back it was thicker—*much* thicker. Enough to swallow her where she stood.

Not a surf at all. No, it was an avalanche.

Erianna's mind went back to the first time she had seen this mist—back in Twelve Towers, when the sheggam ambassador had given her mistress the gift of it. How it changed Shad, made her less human. Erianna's stomach lurched as she realized why the sheggam hadn't killed all those people—they had been waiting for *this*.

They were going to grow their army.

Instinctively, she took a step back as the leading edge of the mist spilled over the toes of her boots. Chad's hand tightened in hers.

Shrouded by the mists lumbered a massive wagon, covered in canvas, by the color of it. Strangely no axles creaked, no wheels clattered against the cobbles. And there were no horses in front of it. With each sway of its bulk, a heavy thud echoed against the walls.

Soon its bulk parted the mist. Erianna saw that the canvas was not canvas, but flesh, loose, sagging flesh, the color of boiled meat. Two eyes the color of blood clots stared straight at her. Black hair, like the mane of a horse's corpse, arced over the thing's body. Flaps of skin flanked its spine like the gills of a fish. Mist vented out from under these flaps, adding to the avalanche.

Erianna stared in horror. This thing—whatever it was—it was coming for them. There was no place to go. This was no mere sheggam. This was … It was …

Chad stepped in front of her and pressed his fingers against the shadowed outer wall of the building. The shadow's darkness somehow seemed to deepen, and then, as if the wall weren't made of brick, his fingers *sunk in*. Then his arm, then the rest of him went into that shadow. Erianna glanced up to see that huge, bulky creature, so close now—how had it gotten so close?—as it opened its wide maw, exposing dozens of fangs, its twisting, blackened tongue. Something yanked her towards that inky shadow on the wall, and then she was submerged in darkness.

Before she could pull another breath into her lungs, she fell to her knees, completely disoriented. The ground felt soft, almost spongy. Chad stood before her, still holding her hand. He was reaching over her shoulder, doing something to the wall she had just stepped through. "Where are we?" she asked, glancing about. This place was dark. Strange. The air tasted wrong. Her own voice sounded wrong.

Chad stepped back. He hesitated before answering. "Underground." He helped Erianna to her feet. "Come on. We can get Nina's aunt from down here."

Chapter 67: Raining Bodies

Despite all the madness Erianna had seen that made this day seem like an impossible nightmare, she still couldn't swallow the notion that Chad had led her into some twisting network of tunnels beneath the streets of Garoshmir. It was all too strange, though some hopeful part of her thought maybe they really were underground and Erianna had just gone mad. With so much panic coursing through her, she wasn't in a position to judge if she was mad or not. Maybe once they were out of there. Wherever *there* was.

Chad led her by the hand as if this place were normal and the world Erianna knew was the strange one. He seemed confident, at ease—yet alert. He scanned each of the strange windows they passed, glancing into each smoky image. Erianna looked at one, a scene of carnage in the main room of someone's home. She felt detached from the scene, as if she were viewing a painting of some past event. Yet she knew it was real, and that it was how the room looked now. She hated that feeling of detachment, even though she knew it was all that was keeping her from losing her mind completely.

Chad stopped. "She's not here. Where is she?" He looked up. "Can you … lift me up?" By the discomfort in his voice, it was like he was asking her to burp him and sing him a lullaby.

After switching her knife to her left hand, she crouched down and helped him to her shoulder. He couldn't have weighed less if he were made of sticks. At that height, his shaggy mop of hair nearly brushed the ceiling. He tilted his head back and studied the ceiling. Erianna couldn't get a good look at it, holding him that way, but she could see something faintly in the ceiling as well. Almost like the images in the walls, though none of the details were clear.

"Huh," Chad said. He reached up and did something to the ceiling, touching it perhaps, but Erianna couldn't see clearly from where she was.

The ceiling darkened to pitch black, and then it started raining bodies.

The first one crashed into Erianna's shoulder, throwing her against the opposite wall. Her head and left shoulder slammed into it, jarring her teeth.

She felt more than saw Chad slip off her and heard a brief cry that cut off when he smacked into the floor. Nearly a dozen bodies had fallen through the ceiling—Erianna's mind was still struggling to process how—and now lay about in a loose pile, pitiful moans drifting up from between twisted limbs. One had clearly died, pulped head lying in a pool of dark blood. Others stirred.

One was Nina's aunt, lying limp with her eyes open and unfocused.

Another was a sheggam.

It was already on its hands and knees when she noticed it, blinking blearily as it tried to get to its feet. Erianna didn't waste any time. Ignoring the grinding pain in her head and shoulder, she pushed herself off the wall and threw herself on the sheggam's huge, leather-armored back.

How she'd managed to hold on to her knife, she had no idea, but she made use of the advantage. Yet blinding pain erupted from her shoulder as she tried to raise the knife. The sheggam swung its elbow back, connecting with her arm and throwing her off its back. She fell to the ground with a thump, spots of light filling her vision. Her hands were empty. She'd dropped her knife.

The sheggam slowly turned as it rose to its full height, clumps of its hair curtaining its eyes as it leveled its gaze at her. Lips peeled back to reveal teeth. Erianna could tell she hadn't injured it at all with her pathetic attack. Merely annoyed it.

Now it loomed over her, taloned hands reaching back. Erianna knew what would happen next. She could see it all play out in her mind. Those hands would swing down, clap both sides of her jaw, breaking it. She would choke on broken bits of teeth, feel them rip through her throat. Her lungs would fill with blood, but she wouldn't die. Not before the sheggam mist came down here, worked its way into every little cut, and changed her into one of *them*. She knew that would happen, because that's what happened to slaves who dared to live free, a lesson she'd always known and heeded—until today. She flinched, waiting for that inevitable fate.

It never came. The sheggam roared as it fell to a knee. Blood sprayed from a deep cut on the back of its leg. A figure rose behind the sheggam, gripping Erianna's bloodied knife—not Chad, not Nina's aunt, but one of the wounded that had fallen through the ceiling. An old woman, wearing a simple brown woolen dress. She had the look of a farmer. Strands of her iron-gray hair clung to the mix of blood and sweat that streaked her pale, lined face. Without any hesitation, the old woman seized the sheggam's mane in a tight grip, yanked back its head, and plunged the knife into its eye.

The sheggam's cry faded to a gurgle, then a soft wheeze. Its arms went slack at its sides and it fell forward, yanking the knife out of the woman's grasp.

"Thank you," Erianna whispered.

The old woman smiled in answer before an arrow took her in the neck and threw her to the ground.

More arrows fell out of the blackness of the ceiling, some bouncing harmlessly off the strange, spongy ground while others found targets. The sheggam remaining in the square likely saw their companion and their quarry vanish into a hole and decided to investigate with a storm of arrows. Shafts as thick as her thumb whistled past Erianna as she scrambled towards the wounded. One arrow left a slash along her left thigh, just below the protection of her mail shirt—not that mail would do much good against *these* arrows. Sprawled atop two others was Nina's aunt, alive and unharmed. Though her eyes were open, she didn't so much as flinch when an arrow plunged into the stomach of a man she lay on, mere inches from her face. Erianna seized her by the wrists and yanked her out from under the hole. She half-led, half-carried her to where Chad huddled against the wall. Eyes wide, the boy was hugging his knees tight against his chest and shaking uncontrollably. Erianna sat the young woman down next to him.

"Chad." Erianna rubbed his arm. "Chad. You did it. You saved Nina's aunt. Look, here she is."

When he didn't respond, Erianna worried he'd fallen into the same mindless state of shock as the young woman. But as she continued to rub his arm, his shaking lessened and he spoke. "Not the others." Without looking at them, he tilted his chin at the wounded—though none of them could be called that anymore. The arrows had stopped falling, yet some of the bodies sprouted nearly a dozen. More sheggam must have filled the square. How long until they came down here to investigate?

"Chad, where are we really?" Erianna shook her head; wrong question. "How can we close that hole?"

He exhaled deeply. "Only I can do it."

Erianna nodded; she'd thought so. She had no idea what this place was, but she knew that it was as good as Chad's realm. She stood and helped him up. "Then let's get it closed."

Yet when she turned, white mist was already spilling out of the ceiling, stark against its blackness as if materializing out of nothingness.

Erianna's blood turned to ice. She knew with her wounds she wouldn't last long in the mist. Even a scratch could spell the end of her. Instinctively, her hand went to her throat, where the Warden's sword had nicked her. It was closed, but the wound on her leg was fresh.

She snatched Chad by the waist and hurriedly lifted him to the hole, submerging him fully in the mist. "Do it now! Close it!" She could feel the mist's wet touch curling about her wrists.

"I can't see!"

"Just do it, Chad!" The strain of holding him like this was making her arms shake. "*Do it now!*"

The mist was all she could see now, like a blanket draped in front of her eyes. It wouldn't be much longer before it found the blood dripping down her thigh. Chad's weight shifted.

"Okay," he said.

Erianna staggered back, clutching him tight against her chest. The mist cut off, yet what remained continued to drift down and cover the dead. At least none of them would turn. A sickening high note, but at this point, Erianna would take what she could get.

She lowered Chad, coughing and sputtering, to the ground a good distance away from the mist before slumping against the wall next to Nina's aunt. Exhaustion overwhelmed her. But they couldn't rest for more than a few moments. The mist didn't look to be dissipating. With a groan, Erianna stood, helping up the young woman too.

"Chad," Erianna said.

He looked up at her.

Erianna gestured to the ceiling. "Don't you *ever* do that again."

Chad stared at her, tears welling in his eyes. For a moment, Erianna thought she had gone too far, but then Chad erupted in laughter.

"Yeah," he said, standing and dusting off the seat of his trousers. "I don't reckon I will."

Erianna smiled. "Let's go find that caravan." She took one of Nina's aunt's hands as Chad took the other. "Who knows? Maybe Nina will already be there waiting for us."

Chapter 68: Harmony

A single guttering lamp sat in the corner of the wood shop's back room. Half-finished chairs, bowls, and tables lay on the three benches that stretched across the room, casting wavering, skeletal shadows. An assortment of tools—planes, files, mallets, chisels, squares, hand saws—lay on the benches, abandoned next to the unfinished projects. A single worker lay mauled in the shop's front room, his back torn out, his blood sprayed on the many finished works that served as the shop's displays.

Even here in the back room, where Tharadis crouched to catch his breath, he could smell the blood. The wood shavings that covered the floor didn't mask the scent, instead merely adding a sweet, tangy undertone. Tharadis was disturbed to find he was getting used to the smell of blood.

He had killed both sheggam after Erianna and Chad fled but had run into more during his search. Sometimes running away was easier than killing them, sometimes not. His lungs burned and his thigh muscles ached. He didn't want to rest any more than he had to, but he knew that if he didn't, he wouldn't be much use out there. He couldn't find Nina if he was dead.

Four sturdy support posts stretched up to the ceiling, bracketing the work bench in the center of the room. The only window was in the front room of the shop, now shuttered, but thin bars of dim light filtered through the slats and ran across the floor. From where Tharadis crouched, he could see through the door leading to the front room and watch the second door, leading out to the street. He didn't like being cornered like this. But he didn't plan to stay long. Just long enough to catch his breath.

Tharadis scratched an itch on his neck. In the lamp light, he saw blood on his fingers. Not his own, he realized as he checked his neck again. He wiped his hand on the floorboards, leaving a red smear.

Something passed in front of the shutters just outside the shop, blocking the light. Tharadis gripped Shoreseeker in one sweaty hand and pushed himself to his feet, heart thumping wildly. He didn't know how much more fighting he could take. His hands ached; his muscles burned. He didn't know how many sheggam he'd fought, nor how many brushes with death he'd had. Fighting a sheggam wasn't anything like fighting a man. They were far less interested in self-preservation than causing harm. Tharadis had had to adapt to their ferocity, and he'd had to do it fast.

Those who hadn't adapted fast enough littered the streets of Garoshmir with their corpses.

The shadowy form outside the window was far too large to be human. It stood frozen in place, as if scenting the air. Tharadis hoped it would just keep on moving, but he knew such hope was fruitless. It would have moved on already. Somehow it knew he was here.

Gripping Shoreseeker before him, Tharadis lowered himself into a defensive crouch.

The curved edge of a giant axe exploded through the window, spraying glass and wood in the shop. The pale, clawed fist holding the axe punched out the remaining glass and bits of shutter, revealing the monster's snarling face. Its crimson eyes found Tharadis.

With a roar, the mail-clad sheggam launched itself through the window before landing on clawed feet and rushing toward him.

Up the stairs, Nina. Quickly!
With the sound of her heartbeat loud in her ears, Nina scrambled up the dark, narrow steps as fast as she could.
Quietly!
Nina did as her mother commanded, creeping up the steps so the bent wooden steps didn't creak so loudly. It was hard not to run with those monsters so close behind her.

Outside, a few moments ago, her mother's voice had suddenly urged her to run down a side street and into a large apartment building with lots of little windows, saying monsters were coming after her. Nina hadn't questioned her. Walking through the city, she'd already heard the screams and seen the smoke—she'd even seen all the hurt people, lying down in the street and not moving, as much as she wished she hadn't. She'd even felt the faint touch of their ghosts as she had passed them.

She had run, and even now in the still darkness of the stairwell with only the sound of her heart and her heavy breathing, she could feel the monsters just as easily as if they were here in the stairwell with her, staring at her.

At the top of the stairs, Nina came to a long hallway with a bunch of doors. A window at the end of the hall looked out on the wooden siding of the next building over. She couldn't see anything out that way, not unless she wanted to poke her head out like a fool. A few feet to the right of the staircase, one of the doors was open. Four long scratch marks were carved into the wood. Seeing those only made her more terrified. But all the other doors were closed, and she didn't want to risk opening a door with squeaky hinges.

Yes, that room is empty. It's safe to go in. On your belly, dear. It will make you quieter.

Nina nodded at the wisdom of that, slowly creeping along the bare wooden floor toward the open door as her mother instructed. The Raccoon Family, still clutched in one hand, dragged loudly against the floor. Nina wrapped them around her neck, twisting the last two Raccoons into a loose knot. Crawling was easier and quieter after that.

Smart girl. Your father must be proud.

Nina smiled at the thought of her father as she entered the room, feeling a little less scared—but only a little. Lucky for her, a long carpet stretched across the floor of the tiny apartment. There was little else in the room—a low bed made of wood planks, a small stove with no fire in it, a few shelves with a bunch of things Nina couldn't make out in the darkness. Across from the door was a large opening big enough to be another door, its curtains pulled back to reveal a balcony.

She crept forward along the carpet to get a look. She didn't like the moonlight spilling in. It made her feel like anything could see her—which was silly, of course. The monsters were down on the streets, not running around on the rooftops.

She hoped.

Nina stopped when she could just see the street down below over the balcony's edge.

Her breath caught in her throat.

Sheggam, came her mother's voice.

Nina wouldn't have believed it until she saw the hulking, pale creatures with her own eyes. Two of them padded forward on all fours, sniffing the air like dogs. The third one stood on just his back legs, like a person—but not quite. As if it were only pretending to be human. All three of them were naked, but the one walking on two feet carried a long chain in one hand, dragging it along the paving stones.

Nina, I'm sorry, her mother said, *but we're not safe here. I'm going to look for a way out. I want you to stay here and whatever you do, don't move a muscle.*

Nina wanted to cry and tell her mother not to go, but she was too afraid to even open her mouth. She desperately wanted to back away from the balcony's edge—she knew they would spot her up here, she just knew it!—but she feared to move in case the floorboards happened to creak under her. All she could do was wait and trust in her mother.

The monsters would leave eventually. They had to.

Sudden shouting from down below startled her.

The three monsters spun as ten or so soldiers rushed out of a pair of dark alleys feeding into the side street, swords flashing as they ran at the monsters. Nina looked away and started shaking when the first soldier was … when he lost the fight. Nina didn't like the sounds the soldiers made when they lost. But a bunch of them did right away. Nina had never heard such horrible sounds, and certainly never so many all at once.

She lifted the Raccoon family close to her lips and whispered, so afraid she was barely daring to breathe. "Mom, are you there? Mom, get me out of here. Please."

When the sounds finally died out moments later, Nina looked up. Five soldiers still stood, wiping their swords.

"I say we get out of the city while we still can," a burly soldier said, his low voice carrying up to the balcony.

"You afraid?" asked a tall, thin man with red smeared on his armor. He stood lopsided, like his leg was hurt.

The burly man looked away. Even Nina could see the shame in his face, but she didn't understand it. Only stupid people would be brave right now.

"We're Sentinels," said the tall man, tapping his fist to his chest. "And we have our orders. Until we get word that she's been found, we keep looking."

The burly man snorted. "A fool's errand. The Warden and his niece are likely already dead."

The Warden … and his niece? Nina's breath caught in her throat.

They were looking for *her?*

She didn't move. She didn't even blink. She'd seen what they did to those monsters.

That's what they would do to her if they caught her. She was a monster, too, after all.

The soldiers didn't stay, and once they were out of sight, Nina collapsed on her side, sucking breath after breath between racking sobs. She buried her face in the crook of her arm to stop the sounds, but it did little to muffle them. Someone—or something—would find here her, and then they would come to get her.

Why did everyone want to hurt her? It wasn't her fault that she was a fensoria. It wasn't her fault that she was a monster.

Nina.

With a yelp, Nina leapt to her feet, searching for the source of the voice. Relief filled her when she realized whose it was. "Mom!"

Shh, darling. Keep your voice down.

Nina nodded, holding the Raccoons close. "Can we leave now?"

Yes, it's safe to leave. But before we do, I need to see where we can go. I'm afraid I must ask you to wait a little longer.

Nina didn't like waiting, but she nodded, slowly creeping back into the relative darkness of the apartment and sitting on the bed. There she waited with her knees tucked up tight against her chest, counting her breaths until her mother returned.

She was relieved when she heard her mother's voice again. *All right, my love. Head back down the stairs.*

Even knowing the monsters were dead and the soldiers were gone, Nina padded down the stairs softly. "Where's Aunt Esta?"

I'm sorry, but I couldn't find her.

"What about Uncle Tharadis?"

Uncle. There was something very sad about the way her mother said the word. *Tharadis is your ...* Her mother paused. *He's close by. But it's not safe where he is.*

Maybe it wasn't. But Nina knew that it would be safer with him than anywhere else in the whole world. "Take me to him, mom. Please."

Points of light flared in Tharadis's vision as his head smacked against the wall. He tried to lift Shoreseeker, but his hands were empty. He wasn't even sure when he'd dropped it. The fight had only lasted moments, but in that time, the sheggam's axe had become firmly lodged in one of the support posts, its handle snapped off. Tharadis had managed to get a cut on the sheggam's thigh, what would've been a crippling blow on a man, but the sheggam barely limped after.

Tharadis tried to steady himself and failed, sliding to the ground in the corner of the room. The sheggam shoved aside a cart, toppling it and spilling tools across the floor, to stand before Tharadis. It stared down at him with its lips peeled back, large chest heaving beneath its grease-blackened mail shirt.

Tharadis dropped his gaze to the sheggam's claws. He knew the next time those claws moved, he would die. A gnat could defeat him now. He'd lost Shoreseeker somewhere, but the sheggam had only lost its axe; its claws and teeth could kill Tharadis just as easily.

The sheggam's image split in two. Tharadis squinted, trying to keep it in focus. He'd hit his head harder than he had realized.

But the sheggam didn't rip him apart. Instead it crouched down to where the tools had scattered, pushing them aside as it inspected them. It paused, and then picked up a long, coarse wood file.

The sheggam slowly turned back to Tharadis.

Before he even saw the sheggam move toward him, he felt its wide, bony fist hammer into his face, again smacking his head against the wall. The blow brought pain washing through his entire body, so excruciating it made him want to retch.

The sheggam grabbed Tharadis by the left wrist, dragged him across the floor, and then pressed Tharadis up against one of the support posts with his arm extended up. At first, Tharadis had no idea what was happening and was too dazed to do anything about it.

The sheggam reversed its grip on the wood file, drew its arm back, and stabbed hard.

Pain erupted in Tharadis's left hand.

This was worse than his head smacking the wall, worse than any physical pain he had ever experienced. He screamed so loud his throat burned. Through his blurred vision, he looked up to see the file buried deep into the meat of his palm, the flat of its rasping surface running up and down, grinding against the bones of his hand. Blood pumped out of the wound and down his wrist. Half of the file's length was buried into the support post, pinning his hand to it. There was no way it was coming out.

Tharadis felt the sheggam's breath as it leaned closer. "Don't worry," it said, its voice guttural yet calm. "As long as you stay standing, you won't rip your hand in half." Tharadis knew it was telling the truth. A wound like this couldn't handle his body weight. The agony threatened to buckle his knees. He had to lock them to keep the file from ruining his hand further.

The sheggam picked up Shoreseeker and stepped in front of Tharadis, gingerly holding the sword in front of itself like an offering, though it was clear it wouldn't give the sword back to Tharadis. The sheggam stood just outside of Tharadis's reach, the light from the front room framing its bulk.

"Now you know the truth," it said, lips peeling back from its teeth. "Now you know pain. Let it pierce the veil of lies. Describe it to me." The sheggam's crimson eyes were hungry. "Describe your pain, your *truth*, to me."

After the savagery he'd seen, Tharadis wasn't expecting such eloquence from a sheggam. He had thought of them as little more than beasts, even the ones that carried weapons. Perhaps many of them were.

This one was clearly much more than that.

Still, even as the sweat dripping down his forehead stung his eyes, Tharadis matched the beast glare for glare. "It … hurts."

The sheggam squeezed its fists around Shoreseeker. The hand holding the blade began to drip blood, but the sheggam only had eyes for Tharadis. "You won't be able to stand if I sever the tendons in your heel."

"Why?" Tharadis could barely get the word out through the agony ripping through him. He didn't care about the answer, but the longer they talked, the longer he lived. And the longer he lived, the better his chances of getting out of this—he hoped. "Why come here? Why kill all these people?"

"Because the song demands it." The sheggam tested Shoreseeker's edge with a claw. It grunted as if impressed.

"What song? What are you talking about?" More fiery pain shot through his arm as Tharadis shifted slightly to glance up at his hand. The sight of it was almost as horrifying as the pain itself. It was all Tharadis could do to keep from vomiting. Still, he forced himself to look. If the handle were gone, he might have been able to slide his hand off the file. If the sheggam didn't get bored of their conversation and cut him down first. Or if Tharadis didn't pass out first. But there was no way to remove the handle quickly and without attracting the sheggam's notice. *Think*, he told himself, as if the command could push back the encroaching shroud of unconsciousness. *Think!*

"The song of pain." The sheggam's breath hissed between its bared teeth. "Pain is the loneliest thing in the world. Every hurt, every agonizing sensation, seeks—no, *demands*—companionship.

"The song of pain is a single screeching noise that blisters your ears with no end," the sheggam continued. "The pain of others is like … harmony. Without that harmony, the song can drive you mad. The ferals you've no doubt seen," the sheggam added, gesturing to the door, "running around without thought, are doing everything they can to create that harmony. The need of it boils their blood. Even in the act of killing, those brief moments of pain felt by their victims before death are sweet relief from the song of pain. With enough blood on their teeth, perhaps the ferals will become more civilized." The tone of its voice held no hint of irony.

Tharadis watched as it approached, racking his brain for another question, anything to buy himself more time. But he could barely focus beyond the pain in his hand. It was all he could do to keep his knees from buckling and destroying his hand completely. Blackness encroached at the edges of his vision.

The sheggam's face moved close to Tharadis's, until there were only a few inches between them. He could feel its hot breath on his face. Beyond the sheggam, Tharadis though he caught a flicker of movement—was that the shop's front door opening? The sheggam didn't seem to notice it.

"Healing yourself is possible." The sheggam tapped the flat of Shoreseeker's blade against Tharadis's chest. Eyelids drooping, Tharadis glanced down at the sword. With its tip, the sheggam lifted his chin until he was looking into those crimson eyes again. "I can change you. Make you better. Stronger. You won't die from old age or disease. Predators will cower before you because *you* will be the predator."

Tharadis struggled to remain conscious. He now knew that if he passed out, death would be the best thing that could happen to him. "I won't ..."

Again, something behind the sheggam caught Tharadis's eye—someone standing in the doorway.

A wide-eyed girl, black hair falling over her shoulders and a string of wooden eggs painted like raccoons clutched to her chest.

Involuntarily, Tharadis sucked in a lungful of air.

Nina. No.

The sheggam saw something in his eyes and spun towards the door. Nina stepped back until she bumped into the door jamb as tears suddenly rolled down her cheeks.

In his final moments, Tharadis was going to watch his daughter die.

The World Pattern had taken so much from him already—it had fractured his family, forcing Tharadis to kill his own brother. But worst of all, it had taken the one person he loved more than anything.

The World Pattern's only redemption was giving him Nina. She was more than just a reminder of Serena; she was Nina. His daughter. Though he dearly loved the rest of his family, they weren't a part of him like Nina was. She was the whole world to him.

A hand was such a small cost to save the world.

Sudden clarity of purpose cut through the haze of pain, sharpening his senses. Time seemed to slow to a crawl. Tharadis felt the bones in his hand slide apart and splinter as he yanked his hand down. The teeth of the wood file ripped through his flesh. Tharadis noticed this with detachment, as if it were merely some grotesque painting he were viewing and not the ruination of his own hand. The sheggam started to turn, Shoreseeker gripped tightly in its fist. Tharadis could see alarm registering in its eyes.

Speed and surprise were paramount. Tharadis braced himself against the post, coiling himself like a spring. With all the strength in his body, he launched forward. To Tharadis's heightened awareness, the sheggam moved so slowly it seemed nearly frozen. It was almost laughable how easily Tharadis spun under the sheggam's sword arm and pressed his back against the sheggam's side. In that same fluid motion, Tharadis hooked his hands over the sheggam's wrist. Fresh pain roared through his ruined hand, but it was a distant sensation, as if it were happening to some phantom limb.

Then he jerked his hands down as hard as he could.

The sounds of breaking bones and ripping tendons filled the air, but only a moment before the sheggam's roar of pain drowned them out.

Elbow bent at a horrifying angle, the sheggam's fingers spasmed and went limp. Shoreseeker slid from their grasp.

Before it touched the floor, Tharadis snatched Shoreseeker out of the air, sweeping it around in a wide arc. The blade met chain mail, then flesh, muscle, bone, and organs, before exploding out of the sheggam's back in an eruption of gore.

The sheggam's top half fell to the floor a moment before the bottom half.

Nina stared at him, mouth agape.

Tharadis smiled faintly at her, then fell to his knees, dropping Shoreseeker to the floor. He put his hands out to brace himself, but when his ruined left hand hit the floorboards, whatever surge of energy that had helped him save his daughter vanished, replaced by screaming agony. He gritted his teeth, panting, sweat dripping from his hair as he watched the sheggam's blood pool around his hands.

He didn't notice the white mist flowing out of the sheggam's wound until it started pouring into his own.

Chapter 69: Deception's End

Tharadis yanked his hand back, head swimming as he staggered to his feet. The white mist coming out of the sheggam's wound drifted around its body, yet a moment before it almost seemed as if it had been alive. He hoped that he had imagined the mist rushing into his mangled hand, but he knew what he had seen.

Tharadis tried to step away from the mist and staggered, catching himself on a workbench and scattering tools. His head pounded. Bile rose in his throat.

"Daddy?"

He turned toward the voice, blinking blearily. Nina stood there, eyes as wide as saucers.

Nina. She was safe. He smiled again, and as well as he could without collapsing, beckoned her closer. "Come here, Neensy. Stay away from the thing on the floor."

By the look of horror on her face as she stared at the dead sheggam, the warning was unnecessary. Swallowing audibly, she edged towards Tharadis. When she was close, Tharadis eased himself to a squat and reached out with his good hand to brush a strand of hair from her face. He could see the fear in her eyes as she looked down at his hand.

"I'm okay, Neensy," he said. "I'll be okay." He wasn't so sure about that, now that he thought about it. The room felt like it was floating on the ocean during a storm. It was all he could do to keep from vomiting. "Can you bring me Shoreseeker, Neensy? Be careful. It's sharp. And don't touch the mist." Nina nodded. Tharadis closed his eyes and felt himself slipping off before she came back and prodded him with a finger.

He opened his eyes again and smiled his gratitude as she handed him Shoreseeker. With her help, he cut a strip of cloth from his tunic and wrapped it tightly around his left hand. Just as he was about to tie off the makeshift bandage, he froze. "Neensy," he said, voice dropping to a whisper. "What did you call me just now?" He kept his eyes fixed on the bandage.

Her reply was longer in coming, her voice as quiet as his own. "Daddy."

"Why?" The word choked him. "Why don't you call me Uncle Tharadis, like you always do?"

"Daddies shouldn't lie to their daughters."

Tharadis finally met her gaze then. Tears fell from her eyes, and he found his own eyes filling with them.

Without wasting another moment, he gathered her up in his arms, squeezing her tight, stroking her hair. Her skinny arms squeezed him back. That moment was theirs and theirs alone. The world around them fell away, and it was just the two of them together. *My daughter.*

Our daughter.

With her in his arms, he wept as the weight of those lies he had carried fell away, shed like the terrible burdens they were. He hadn't realized just how much the lies had crushed him. In that moment, he realized that bearing them had been almost as hard as bearing the loss of Serena.

No longer.

"I'm sorry, Neensy." He could feel each of her tiny sobs as she pressed herself hard against his chest. "I wanted so much to tell you for so long. I wouldn't have done it if it weren't to protect you. I hope you forgive me."

She nodded against him, unspeaking.

"How did you know?" he asked.

Nina stepped back and wiped at her face, moving back only far enough to hold her raccoon family between them. "I don't think she meant to," Nina said, "but mommy told me."

Tharadis felt the hairs on the back of neck stand up. When Nina saw the look on his face, she quickly lifted one of the raccoons to show him. "See? Here. This is the daddy raccoon. She painted it to look like you."

Tharadis made a show of studying the raccoon, but it didn't look any different from the others, except for being a bit larger than the ones he assumed were the raccoon children. "So, I look like a raccoon, do I?" She grinned and he mussed her hair. "Well, you must be smarter than me. I don't think I could've figured it out." He didn't think Nina was telling him the whole story, but it didn't matter. She was here, she was safe, and he wouldn't have to lie to her anymore.

Tharadis was reluctant to release her, but they couldn't stay here any longer. In the back of this shop it was almost possible to forget what was going on outside—but simply hiding and hoping wasn't going to save them. The sheggam's corpse across the room was reminder enough of that. Tharadis stood and flexed his wounded hand experimentally. A line of dark red running down his palm stained the bandage, but the bleeding had stopped, and the pain was a fraction of what it was moments ago.

That alarmed him.

The he noticed a feeling lurking in the pit of his stomach—a promise of healing. Of strength.

Of pain.

He had read *First Night, Last Night*; he knew what that promise meant. He was infested with shegasti.

The Knights of the Eye used small pieces of sheggam bone, usually pierced through their skin and hidden under their clothes, to invest themselves with shegasti power, giving them the ability that gave them their name—the capacity to sense nearby sheggam, as if with a unseen eye. Now, though, these bones were ancient, most dating back to the time when sheggam bones were harvested in battle, and Tharadis suspected that much of their power was already spent. And compared to the white mist, the raw, distilled essence of shegasti, even the freshest of sheggam bones were dilute in their power.

He had seen how drawing on that power had changed Dransig. And Dransig had been sipping from a pinhole; if Tharadis were to try the same, it would be like standing under a waterfall.

He knew he could heal his hand with his power. And he also knew that Nina's life depended on him resisting the temptation.

"Nina, listen to me." Tharadis crouched down and took her by the shoulders. "We can't stay here. I think we'll be safer with the caravan outside the city. That's where Chad will be waiting for us."

Nina nodded and he continued.

"I'm not going to lie to you." *Anymore*, he added silently. "It's going to be very dangerous."

He could tell she was scared, but also doing her best to be brave. "Okay," she said.

"We'll have to go very fast, and I don't want to lose you ever again. So I'm going to carry you on my back. When I do, I want you to hang on tight, but not too tight. Can you do that?"

She nodded and he brushed her hair out of her eyes. He smiled, hoping that this wasn't the last chance he got to see her face. Escaping the city was going to be harder than he let on. "One more thing, Neensy."

"Yeah?"

"Whatever happens, don't open your eyes."

Chapter 70: Flight

U ncle Tharadis—no, her *father*, she reminded herself—crouched down so Nina could climb onto his back. After checking to make sure the Raccoon Family was securely tied around her neck, she stepped on his thigh and climbed up. As he stood, she squeezed her knees tight against his side to keep them from shaking too much.

He turned his head until their noses were almost touching, a small grin on his face. "You okay back there?" She nodded and he gave her a reassuring pat on her arm. "Remember what I told you?"

"Yeah," Nina said. "Don't open my eyes."

Not that she had needed the warning. She'd already seen much more than she'd ever wanted to.

"Okay, then," her father said. "Let's go."

Nina buried her face between his neck and her own arm, squeezing her eyes shut.

Her world was darkness now.

She heard her father step through the sticky puddle in the middle of the room. Nina shuddered. With her eyes closed, sounds seemed so much louder. She felt as much as heard Tharadis wipe his sword on something— the monster's body, she supposed. Just like the sounds, she was much more aware of his movements as she felt the flex of his muscles. It was a comforting feeling, knowing that even as she closed her eyes to everything around her, her daddy was doing everything he could to protect her. She felt much less alone than she had before, with only her mother's voice for company. Her father was here and he was real. He would keep her safe.

"I love you, daddy," she said, voice choked.

He paused to squeeze both of her hands in his bandaged one and rubbed his thumb along her wrist. "I love you too, Neensy." He hooked his free hand under her leg. Floorboards creaked as he started forward. He halted as Nina sensed a change in the light. They were outside.

Tharadis turned his head, first left, then right. Even with her face pressed against her arm, she could still smell the foul stench of the street, something between a privy and a butcher shop. Even squeezing her face tighter against her arm didn't stifle all the smells.

She hoped they didn't have far to go.

Tharadis turned left and started jogging.

His were the only footsteps Nina heard, but other noises filled the air. Distant shouts, mostly, and crackling fire. No matter how she positioned her face, her ear was still exposed. She could hear everything as if it were happening right next to her. Even though the smoke stung Nina's nose whenever they passed through it, she was glad for it. It overpowered all the other smells and made her forget about them, if only for a few moments.

It was strange. The streets, which had been so crowded just hours before, filled with talking and laughter and merchants arguing with customers, were empty now. Abandoned. Nina could almost imagine that everyone was in bed, sleeping peacefully. She wished she *could* imagine it.

But then she heard something straight ahead of them: a man weeping. It wasn't the sound a man made when he was hurt. Nina had heard that before, and that was more like angry shouts than this. No, this man felt something worse than injury.

An image flashed in Nina's mind of the man, whom she couldn't see, holding a small, unmoving body in his arms. In that brief imagining, the face of the man belonged to her father, and the face of the child …

She almost opened her eyes then. The imagining, she thought, couldn't be any worse than the reality. But she merely clung tighter to her father and remembered what he told her to do. *We're still okay,* she told herself, squeezing her eyes even tighter shut. *We're still okay.*

Tharadis had slowed to a walk when the man's crying could be heard, and now stopped to peer left and right. Nina could feel his heart thumping through his chest. Every one of his muscles was tight, ready to spring. He took another step forward. The sounds all around them changed somehow. Nina realized why: they had stepped into an intersection.

The man's weeping was even clearer. But there was another sound coming from the same direction. It almost sounded like the slow *drip, drip, drip* of water falling on the paving stones. But Nina knew that wasn't quite right.

With a sudden, sharp gasp, she realized it wasn't *drip, drip, drip*.

It was *click, click, click*.

Tharadis quickly stepped to the side, pressing himself and Nina against a brick wall, hard. They paused there, Tharadis's breaths coming quick and deep. The clicking had stopped, and so, too, had the man's cries. Her father tugged her hands down a little away from his throat; she hadn't realized she was squeezing him so hard.

Two more breaths, and he was running.

He stopped so suddenly Nina's knees slipped. Before she could fall, she tightened her grip with a yelp. Tharadis coughed and then he was running back the way they came.

Behind them, where he had stopped just a moment before, the sounds of chaos erupted. People screamed, something roared, something hard hit something soft. The screaming stopped, and the roars faded behind them as Tharadis ran.

Without warning, Tharadis fell to his stomach. Nina thought something bad had happened to him, but then he started crawling over the ground. Wood scraped against Nina's head and then her back. Everything grew darker. They were under something. A cart?

No. Stairs. Fast and heavy footsteps—human footsteps, it seemed—accompanied by panicked breathing, shuddered the planks above their heads. Nina wanted to brush away the dust and dirt that fell in her hair, but she didn't dare let go of her father's neck. Five, six people ran down the steps.

There were more footsteps out on the street, but these sounded wrong. Not like people. Each step was accompanied by little clicks, like … the clicking of a old dog's overgrown toenails. The people on the steps paused, then tried to scramble back the way they had come, kicking and screaming and pulling each other out of the way. Someone fell, hit the stairs hard, cried out as someone else stomped on them. The inhuman steps came fast. A whoosh, like something cutting the air. A wet sound. More whooshing, more wetness. Things dropped onto the steps—Nina didn't want to think about what they were. A line of warm liquid dripped between the planks onto Nina's neck.

She began to shake.

With his bandaged hand, the hand not holding Shoreseeker, her father reached up and held her hands, entwining his sweaty fingers with hers.

With a frighteningly loud snarl, the monster loped away from the stairs, its retreat punctuated by barks and growls. Tharadis's breathing was calm and slow, almost as if he were trying to be quiet. But why? The monster was gone.

Then she knew: there was another still there. She could hear the steps creaking beneath it. It snuffled the air as loud as a horse. Then it started feeding on the pieces of people lying on the steps. Hot breath, reeking of rotten meat, washed over Nina.

Someone groaned above her. No, the beast wasn't feeding on the dead people. It was feeding on the *living* one.

Tharadis's muscles tensed as he drew back his sword arm.

He stabbed upward. Wood splintered. The feeding, and the moaning, stopped.

Roars in the distance. Tharadis wriggled his sword free and yanked it back. Liquid spilled onto the ground. More roars, getting closer. Tharadis frantically scrambled out from under the steps, stumbled to his feet and bumping Nina's shoulder hard, and ran like death was on their heels.

Nina heard the loping steps behind them, getting closer. Death *was* on their heels.

Her father pivoted to the right into a narrow passageway, sweeping his arm, knocking things over. Baskets, shovels or rakes, pottery. Two or three of the monsters were behind, crashing through the obstacles, jaws snapping and snarling. They weren't far behind. Nina could hear them as clearly as if they were only inches away.

They left the passageway. Smoke filled the air. Fire off to the right, crackling and warming Nina's arm and leg, but only briefly. Tharadis ran forward. People nearby, running. Some whimpering on the ground, in pain. Shrieks as the beasts fell upon them and ripped at them, shrieks that quickly ended.

Tharadis turned to look over his shoulder, his pace slowing. He was getting tired. Too tired.

And it was her fault. "I'm sorry, daddy," Nina whispered to the back of his neck, but he didn't say anything. He hadn't heard her.

They came to a stop, Tharadis panting as he leaned against something. A wall, made out of timber. Dogs barked in the distance, their yelps more panicked than Nina had ever heard in a dog. Tharadis gave Nina's arm a reassuring squeeze with his injured free hand, then twisted his torso, as if peering around a corner.

His breath audibly caught in his throat.

From the direction he was looking came the sound of metal dragging heavily against rock, like an iron rod dragged across the paving stones. The sound slowly came closer. Nina also heard hoarse, low laughter and heavy, limping footsteps. The laughter was not made by a human throat, Nina knew. The metal thing was dragged through something wet. The laughter kept coming, louder with each passing moment.

Tharadis backed away, slowly at first, then sprinted with all his might in the opposite direction, his legs and arms pumping furiously, his exhaustion apparently forgotten.

He ran, taking various turns, until thin, stiff branches snagged at Nina's shoulder and hair, and the air smelled noticeably fresher. Like a garden. She could still hear the noises, but they sounded distant. As if it were happening on some other world.

Tharadis slowed to a walk, then stopped, using his arm to prop himself up against another wall, this one covered in vines that tickled Nina's shoulder. His head drooped, but still Nina clung to him.

He straightened and patted her hands. "It's okay, Neensy. We can rest."

She slid down his back to her feet. "Can I open my eyes?"

"Sure."

She did, blinking to clear them. Moonlight from both moons shone through the sparse cloud cover, enough to clearly see where they had stopped. They were in a garden, just as she had thought. A very maze-like one. They stood on a small, round terrace encircled by stone benches. Between them, tall hedges curved in different directions, creating twisting passages.

Tharadis took Nina's hand in his own. The strip of cloth covering his wound was sticky. "Come on," he said, leading her down one of the paths. "Let's find some place to rest a moment."

He was holding her hand gently. Still, she didn't let go, even if she were causing him pain. She couldn't. Not yet.

She noticed he still gripped his sword tightly in his other hand. "Is it safe here, daddy?"

The path forked. They went right. "We'll be safe once we're outside the city."

They weren't outside the city, so that meant they weren't safe yet. Still, the gardens calmed her. Here, she *felt* safe. Her father was here. He would protect her.

Further in, he sat down against the wall and crossed his arms over his knees. Only a handful of moments passed before his eyes were shut tight and his head bobbed forward. Shoreseeker's tip drooped and finally rested against the bricks.

Nina snuggled up beside him, slipping inside the protection of his arm, but he was so deep asleep that he didn't even stir when she touched him.

Exhaustion pulled at her, too. She didn't want to stay awake anymore; she wanted to dream of being somewhere, anywhere, else.

Sleep had almost claimed her when she saw the crimson glint of eyes down the path, shrouded in streamers of white mist.

Chapter 71: Flight II

For the briefest moment, Nina hoped that she really had fallen asleep, and that this was just a nightmare. But she knew by the wild beating of her heart that she was awake.

"Daddy," she whispered as she shook him. She didn't want the monster to hear her—even though its eyes were already fixed on her. "Daddy, wake up."

The sheggam was wounded. White smoke poured from the cuts arcing over its blood-smeared skin. It dragged itself forward. Nina noticed both of its feet were missing, the legs beneath its knees now little more than ravaged stumps. It left red streaks on the stones as it pulled its body toward her. It didn't even seem to know it was wounded; all she could see in its eyes was a hunger. A hunger for her.

"Daddy, please." Tears fell from Nina's eyes. She shook her father harder, and he even stirred a little. But he still didn't wake up.

Nina. The small voice seemed to come from all around her. Nina realized it was coming from the Raccoon Family still around her neck.

"Mom!" Her father stirred at the word.

Shh, dearest. I'm here, came her mother's voice. *Listen to me. Wake your father, but whatever you do, do not scream.*

Nina glanced up. The sheggam was only ten steps away now. Its lips peeled back as it came for her, baring dagger-like teeth.

Nina's breath came in gasps. She didn't know if she could keep herself from screaming. Why couldn't she scream? Were there more nearby?

She eyed Shoreseeker, still held loosely in her father's hand. She didn't know the first thing about fighting. And every instinct within her warned to run and hide, not fight.

With a burst of speed that seemed impossible for something so ravaged, the sheggam raced forward, breath hissing.

There was nothing for it. She slapped her father's face.

Tharadis's eyes popped open.

With its massive, powerful arms, the snarling sheggam threw itself at Nina.

392

Gripped tight in Tharadis's fist, Shoreseeker cleaved into the sheggam's elbow first, then connected with its jaw as the sword continued its upward arc. A normal blade wouldn't have done nearly the damage that Shoreseeker did, not with a reverse upward cut like this. But Shoreseeker shattered the sheggam's jawbone and ruined its pale flesh with equal ease, carving its way through its skull.

As if a ball had been tossed to her, Nina caught the sheggam's severed face. She stared down at the horror she held, blood and mist oozing between her fingers, before she dropped it.

Nina screamed.

Roars sounded from all around them.

Tharadis leapt to his feet. Without a word, he threw Nina on his back. She wrapped her arms around his neck, gripping one blood-slicked wrist with her other hand as he ran.

A massive form burst out of the hedges just ahead of them. Howling, the sheggam thrust its spear towards her father's middle, but Shoreseeker turned it aside and gored the beast all in one motion. Tharadis hadn't slowed during the brief battle. He continued running down the twisting garden passageways, sometimes going left at a fork, sometimes right. He never stopped to consider which way to go; it was as if he had already made the choice before he even knew he had to.

Nina heard snarls and heavy clicking footsteps all around them, but was amazed when they finally burst onto the street without encountering any other monsters. There had to have been dozens of them in the gardens; Nina had heard them. How had her father known which paths would help them avoid the sheggam? It was almost as if he had memorized the garden's twisting pattern of passageways. But how could he have done such a thing? It just didn't make any sense.

She didn't have time to ponder it. Once down the street, they squeezed through a narrow archway, past wooden shelves that had collapsed, the clay jars that had once stood upon them in ruins on the ground. Beyond that, they found themselves in an area three times as wide as the archway had been, its paving stones sloping downward. Small wooden stalls, covered by multi-colored cloth awnings, flanked the area. A market at one time. But now the stalls were as ruined as the shelves in the archway, the awnings shredded, scattered, and befouled by mud and other things. While the stalls on the left were damaged, the ones on the right had been completely smashed and dragged away from the wall, to make way for the nightmare that Nina now saw.

A dozen people had been stripped and flayed. Each hung from a single, thick spike of rough metal, hammered through the meat of their arms just below their wrists into the stone wall. Their toes barely touched the ground, giving them just enough purchase to offer hope but no escape. For those that still lived, anyway. The skin had been peeled from several of them, thin strips still clinging to their bodies, dangling like gory streamers. Others had been bled dry, various bladed metal objects stabbed into pale limbs. A few still drew breath. One of them, moaning—

"Nina." Her father gathered her close in an embrace, pressing her face against his stomach. "Nina," he said again, pointing to the other end of the market with Shoreseeker. Reluctantly, she turned to look. Another archway, like the one they had just come through. It was clear of rubble, a sight which calmed her suddenly uncontrollable breathing. "We just need to get over there. Beyond that is a thoroughfare, and a couple of side streets. Then we'll be at the gate, free of the city. It's not much farther."

Nina nodded without thinking. But she couldn't shut out the moaning she heard. "What about the man on the wall?"

Tharadis crouched, cradling her cheek and rubbing a thumb across it, and looked into her eyes. "Do you want me to help him?"

She hesitated, then nodded again. She was afraid—more afraid than when she was at Falconkeep. But seeing her father fight and do whatever it took—she couldn't explain it, but it made her feel stronger somehow. Like she *had* to be stronger.

"Okay, I'll help him. Go hide in one of those stalls. I'll be back shortly."

Without looking back, she ran over and crouched behind a low wooden wall, focusing her attention on the exit. A small trickle of gray smoke rose up against the night sky, growing larger. The building next to the far archway was on fire.

A sound like raw meat dragged across a dull knife greeted her ears. The man yelped, but only for the briefest moment. Nina hugged her arms, rubbed her hands up and down them. Her teeth started chattering.

A short time later, Tharadis crouched in front of her.

"Did you save him?" she asked.

His answering smile was all wrong. Not a smile at all. "I did the best I could." He helped her up when they heard the sound of someone stepping on broken pots.

Tharadis yanked her back down. "Stay hidden," he whispered. "Don't come out until you see me. Don't make any noise." He looked over her head, cursed quietly. "Get ready to run, Neensy."

He took her hand, but she yanked hard on it and pointed to their intended exit.

Tharadis turned to see the roof of the building abutting the archway suddenly fall inward with the sound of heavy beams groaning and finally snapping. Smoke and ash erupted upwards, the force of the explosion spraying bricks and flames into the archway. The arch itself bent and cracked, then finally crumbled in a heap of burning wood and stone, blocking their path.

The only way out was the way they had come.

Tharadis turned around, peering over the wall of the stall towards the first archway. He motioned for Nina to stay put, then stood, Shoreseeker held in front of him. He slowly advanced.

Moving as quietly as she could, Nina lifted her head to look over the edge of the wall. Two monstrous armored shapes, both holding crude but massive swords, stood at the market's mouth, bathed in the orange light of the fire. They paused a moment, studying Tharadis.

Then they sped forward, closing the distance in moments.

The one in front swung its sword, faster than Nina thought such a heavy thing could go. Her stomach clenched in a knot as she watched it speed toward her father's head.

But Tharadis bowed under it. His shoulder took the beast in the stomach, staggering it, and Tharadis spun off it, Shoreseeker lancing into the second sheggam. Its eyes popped open in surprise as the blade pierced its chest.

The first sheggam recovered quickly. It swept its blade around—and yet again Tharadis flowed beneath its swing. Tharadis dragged his own sword across the beast's belly, spilling entrails. The sheggam fell to its knees, stunned at its own death. A moment later, the sheggam collapsed in a twitching heap.

Tharadis grabbed for Nina, but four more sheggam burst into the market, one wielding an axe and another with a sword. Muzzles frothing and snarling, the two armed ones ran forward. Both swung their weapons in the same arc. Tharadis brought Shoreseeker up in time—if only barely—yet even so, the combined force of their swings crushed him back against one of the broken stalls. Wood groaned beneath him as both sheggam leaned forward, putting more weight on their weapons. The muscles in Tharadis's arms strained as he fought to hold them off. Sweat sprang from his brow.

He gripped Shoreseeker's hilt with both hands, which Nina imagined was stabbing brutal pain into the wounded one. Tharadis's eyes flicked to one of the unarmed sheggam, running on all fours behind the others—straight towards where Nina hid, a few paces from Tharadis.

She crouched, helpless and gripped in terror, as the sheggam opened its mouth wide, baring fangs and a tongue mottled black and pink, rancid breath spilling out as it lunged for her throat. She wanted to scream again, but the sound never reached her lips.

With a furious roar, Tharadis shoved both sword and axe away—right into the face of the approaching sheggam.

It didn't die as Nina hoped. The blow from the axe stunned it, and the sword's edge left a nasty gash under its eye. But it shook its head like a wet dog, flipping its greasy black hair about, and snarled at Nina, even more incensed than before.

None of that mattered, though.

Her father had broken free.

What he did next was like a dance. Each motion was so fluid, it seemed like something he had rehearsed a thousand times—or something that came to him by instinct. It was a flurry of motion, yet not hasty, no stroke wasted. Every time his blade moved, flesh parted, spilling blood and guts and severing limbs. It was as elegant as it was horrifying.

In the space of a heartbeat, all four sheggam were in twitching pieces on the ground.

With a single twist of his wrist, Tharadis shook the blood free of Shoreseeker's blade, then sheathed it.

Both of them turned at the sound of snarls nearby. Without a word, he gathered Nina onto his back and jogged out of the market, back the way they had come. Again, Nina squeezed her eyes shut.

For some time—how long, Nina had no way of telling—all she heard was the sound of her father's quick yet heavy footsteps as he carried her through the city. She didn't think they were going the way he'd told her they should, but if they weren't, she trusted he knew what he was doing. His breath was coming heavily. Small as she was, Nina knew carrying her for so long couldn't be easy, especially when you had to fight for your life. Occasionally she felt him jump over obstacles; every time he did, she felt as if she were floating. Any other day, she would have smiled at the sensation. Now, it just turned her stomach.

Tharadis turned sharply. The sound of his footsteps flattened; they were no longer in a narrow, echoing alley. The gentle lapping of water came from the left.

Then there were more footsteps. Nina didn't need to open her eyes to know they belonged to sheggam.

Tharadis broke into a full sprint. "Nina!" he shouted. "Take a big breath and hold it!"

Before she could make sense of this command, Tharadis leapt, and they were in the air again. Only this time her father's foot didn't meet the ground right away.

They were falling.

As they did, Nina felt them twisting in the air. Her father's right arm, the one holding Shoreseeker, jerked hard. Shoreseeker's edge bit into something.

A monstrous shriek split the air. It came from only inches away. Hot, horrid breath washed over Nina's face.

She opened her eyes and looked straight into the gaping maw of the beast falling alongside her. Terrified, she let go of her father's neck.

The surface of the river slammed into her back.

The impact forced all the air from her lungs. Water rushed up her nose. It stung like mad. She fought the instinct to breathe, but even in the brief moment since she was submerged, it was getting harder and harder to fight it.

She couldn't tell up from down and thrashed madly, desperate for air. The water stung her eyes, and it was too dark to see anything anyway. She knew she didn't have much longer.

Something under the water bumped her leg. She jerked away, expelling what little air she had left.

When her head broke the water's surface, Nina sucked air into her lungs. She coughed and sputtered, but she could breathe. She'd thought she would never breathe again.

She treaded water, rubbing her eyes so she could see. Again, something floating in the water brushed against her arm. Even though her vision had cleared, it still took her a moment to realize what it was.

A human arm, gnawed off at the elbow.

Nina whimpered. Other things, *lots* of other things, floated in the river. She wanted out of the river. She didn't care what lay in waiting for her on land. She only knew that she had to get out of the water.

Where was her father?

Something else was wrong. Her hands went to her neck.

The Raccoon Family was gone.

Tears stung her eyes as she scanned the water. It was so hard to see anything. Everything was wrong. Her father was gone, her mother was gone, and she was all alone in this horrifying water.

A huge white corpse floated face-down beside her. She realized it must have been the sheggam her father had fought while they fell. White mist bubbled up around it. It was dead now; Nina was sure of it. It was a small comfort, though. She didn't want to be alone with that thing.

Something in the water moved toward her. Nina felt her heartbeat surge.

It was her father's head, partly submerged. His eyes fixed on hers as he held a finger to his lips.

Nina almost wept with relief when she realized he was okay. But she kept silent, as he asked. She let the current pull her to him. He grabbed a hold of her wrist and pulled her closer.

"Stay still and be silent," he whispered into her ear. Nina nodded as the river slowly pulled them west, under a footbridge, and out of the city.

Chapter 72: Pattern's Victory

A gust of wind streaming over the ramparts tugged loose a few strands of her white hair as Lora Bale surveyed the battlefield below.

For that was what the grounds outside Falconkeep had become. Dozens of sheggam already lay dead among streaks of blackened earth, laid to waste by Lora Bale's small army of fensoria.

Sheggam. She snorted, a corner of her mouth lifting in amusement. Lora Bale had long known that the World Pattern wanted to be rid of her. It hadn't taken any skill to discern this; it was a truth she could feel in her bones. Falconkeep, and by extension Lora Bale, had simply become too powerful for the World Pattern to let live. However, mere human armies wouldn't be enough to uproot her. The World Pattern had had to summon the sheggam from beyond the Wall to deal with her.

But she knew something that the World Pattern didn't. She was invincible.

She shifted her head a few inches to the side. A breath later, a thick-shafted arrow zipped past her ear, passing through the space her head had just occupied. She didn't even flinch. She had seen the arrow's path before it had even been loosed.

To any other Patterner, the winds were a dear friend, whispering secrets that the World Pattern often tried to obscure.

To Lora Bale, the winds were a slave. No arrows would touch her.

Another line of flame erupted along the ground near the stables, throwing dozens of screaming sheggam in every direction. These ones had been carrying a ladder. Where had they gotten that? A flutter of concern rose in her chest, but she shoved it down. The ladder was smoldering splinters now. It was nothing to worry about. Still. The sheggam were more resourceful than the stories suggested.

She walked over to Zeho, standing a few paces away. He gripped the edges of the merlon tightly in his gloved hands, brown hair stirring in the wind. Soot streaked his Falconkeep uniform, as it always did whenever he called his flames. His eyes were locked on the rushing sheggam, but his mouth was split in a wild grin. Though the night was cold, sweat ran down his face. At sixteen, he didn't have long to live, even if he did survive this battle. He had no reason to hold back, but more than that, Lora Bale knew that he would give his life to protect Falconkeep. He might even *hope* to die for the sake of Falconkeep.

Lora Bale would not get in the way of his ambition. She touched his shoulder, gently at first, like a mother might. Then she squeezed it tightly. "Keep going," she whispered in his ear. His smile widened.

As she stepped past him, she scanned the ramparts. Several more of her young soldiers were positioned at various intervals, waging war with their powers on the hundreds of sheggam down below. But Lora wasn't interested in them right now.

Where were her war tables?

She felt them before she saw them. She turned and saw two of the littler Falconkeepers struggling to drag one of the heavy wooden tables up the stone steps to the ramparts. Lora frowned. Those weren't part of the group she had sent to fetch her tables. And why were they bringing only one?

Again, that flutter of panic. This time, it was harder to smother.

Three more arrows flew past as she strode to where they had set the table, pale-faced and panting. Lora frowned at them. "Where are Char and Storn? Why aren't they with you?"

The fat, freckled boy named Noil wiped his hand across his forehead. "They said they had to do something else. Said there was a breach in the east wall."

A breach? No, that was impossible. "Set it up over here and get the other two. And don't waste any more time. Understood?"

Both nodded as they shoved the square table to where she'd indicated and scrambled off. Lora sighed through gritted teeth, telling herself she was more frustrated than afraid. There could be no breach. Just flights of fancy from frightened children. *You'll not have me yet, World Pattern.*

She swiveled several of the handles protruding from the table's sides, adjusting the positions of the various lodestones beneath the war table's surface. In moments, she was satisfied with the configuration. Using her body to block the brunt of the wind, she unhooked her pouch of iron filings from her belt and dumped its contents on the table. Within the space of a heartbeat, the filings danced their way over the table's surface, drawn by the lodestones into a perfect Pattern.

First one, and then over a dozen lightning bolts rained down upon the sheggam army, accompanied by cracks of thunder that shook the air. Once the Pattern was spent, Lora began twisting the handles again, changing the rippling shape the filings made.

But something broke her concentration. Screams from behind her, from within the walls of Falconkeep.

She spun, her eyes wide. "No!" she whispered fiercely. She worked faster—too fast. She jostled the table with her hip, throwing one of the lodestones out of place. Quickly she reached over to twist the corresponding handle.

An arrow clipped her shoulder.

Lora Bale stopped and stared down at the welling blood, feeling more betrayed than injured. *Damn you, winds!*

Wait. Why had Zeho stopped calling fire?

She glanced at where he stood—or at least where he had been standing. Now he lay there, his legs hanging over the rampart's edge, dangling above the courtyard. His head was gone.

Behind Zeho's body loomed a massive, pale-skinned beast, naked save for the clumps of black hair draped over its shoulder. It gripped a heavy wooden club. Lora could see bone flecked among the gore smeared over its surface.

Lora Bale's eyes met the sheggam's, her jaw slack. "But I was invincible," she said. The wind carried her words away as the sheggam sped toward her.

In the moment just before the sheggam's club met her skull, Lora Bale conceded that the World Pattern had finally won.

Chapter 73: Reunion

A dim, unwavering gray light glowed in the various alcoves in the Council Chambers in the heart of the Dome and Spire. Not enough light for a normal man to walk about in complete confidence of his footing. But Dransig was hardly a normal man. *Hardly a man at all anymore,* he thought grimly. The figure standing in the middle of the cavernous room, back to Dransig, was as clear to him as if it had been standing in sunlight. A figure that was too tall, too muscular, too angular to be human. But a figure that, despite all its changes, was recognizable to him.

"Shad."

At the sound of her name, she twitched slightly. But she didn't turn to face him yet. "Father. I was wondering when you would come to find me."

Her voice was recognizable, but ... *wrong* somehow. Had the years changed her so much? Or was it the shegasti that infected her, as it did him? Little clothing covered her; it would have merely been an obstruction for her piercings—as well as the changes her body would undergo as a result of the turning. Seeing her like this stole something from Dransig, nearly staggered him. All those piercings, to let the shegasti in ... But had he any right to judge and condemn her?

He drew his short sword and held it in front of him. *I have that much humanity in me,* he thought. *Enough to kill my own daughter.* The irony of it made him want to laugh or vomit. He didn't know which.

She turned to face him then, but stopped partway. From this angle, Dransig could see that the transformation had already changed her face. Her mouth and nose were more muzzle than not, the tips of fangs poking up over bloodless lips. Her spine was curved, hunching her shoulders as she held her overlong arms, tipped with claws held in front of her. After a moment she met his eyes. He wondered what she saw there. Her face betrayed nothing. At least, nothing more than the ultimate betrayal. *My daughter ... sold the Accord to monsters to become a monster herself.*

"There's nothing you can do to stop it, father. It's already begun."

"I know." He had seen the mayhem destroying the city, saw horrors

402

beyond imagination. It was everything he had feared would happen, and worse. He had failed to prevent it. All he could do now was put things to rights. At least some of them. "That's not why I've come."

The edges of Shad's mouth curled up in a slight smile. Dransig saw a hint of the girl she had once been, back before her mother died. Back before Dransig fell into a deep well of grief, abandoning his true name and thus the governorship of Twelve Towers to find solace in the austere purpose of the Knights of the Eye. But that girl was gone now, consumed by the monster he saw before him. Just as Dransig was gone, consumed by the monster he had become.

"You never replied to the letter I sent you," she said. "I waited. Waited for *years*. I told you all the things I had done since you left Twelve Towers to me." She turned away. "I know you received it. I spoke to the man who personally saw it to your hands. And you never once wrote to me. You never came home."

"Your mother was the only home I knew," Dransig whispered.

"You've been adrift, then," Shad said, voice flat. "Homeless."

Dransig nodded, though she couldn't see him. "Yes."

"You never loved me, did you, father?"

The breath he took shuddered his lungs. He had tried to steel his nerve for this meeting, a meeting he had been dreading for years. *If I am to die,* he thought, *I will do it without regret.* "There is a difference between never loving, and never forgiving."

She cocked her head slightly and nodded, as if she heard the wisdom in his words. She turned. He expected tears in her eyes, but they were dry. Dransig wondered if she—or he—were now beyond the capacity for tears.

"I learned all I could about the Order, father. If you're going to use that sword on me, you'll have to wait until I've completely turned."

Dransig tapped his chest where his sigil once was. "I'm no longer a Knight of the Eye."

"No? Just a murderer then." Shad smiled again, but this time it was a smile of bitterness. "All this time, I sought redemption. I thought if only I could be like my father, maybe he would forgive me for what I'd done. Or at least come to love me again." The smile withered. "Yet here you are, sinking to the level of your unworthy daughter."

"You must pay for what you've done!" Dransig shouted. "You *murdered* your mother!"

Shad staggered back, clutching her chest as if Dransig had already stabbed her. "She was a horrible woman! I saw what she did to you. I *felt* what she did to me." She quivered. "It was worse than anything I've done to myself since … or anything you could possibly do to me. I was a little girl. I was your *daughter*."

"Don't." It was the only word Dransig could summon.

"I only wanted to help you, to show you I was worthy of carrying on your name. Dransig Belgrith, the uncompromising statesman." Shad shook her head. "The only man I've ever loved."

Dransig lowered the tip of his blade. "Repent. Tell me you sincerely regret murdering her, and I will spare your life."

Shad shook her head. "I was a little girl, driven mad by an abusive mother. What is there to regret?"

"You can change. You can start right here."

She laughed softly. "No one can change what they are. You and I, both of us. We're beasts. Killers. As much as we may aspire to be better, that's what we are."

"Two strokes, then," he said. "One for you. One for me."

Shad paused. Nodded. "That's how it must be, it seems."

Dransig took a deep breath. He lunged, blade flashing in the dim artificial light.

But before he took a step, he collapsed to the ground, blade clattering to the floor.

Shad fell to her knees and gathered him up in her arms. "Father," she whispered. "You're hurt."

"No. Just old." How long had he been fighting the shegasti, keeping it from taking him over? It felt like more than a lifetime. It took all he had to keep it at bay, stall it long enough to do what he needed to. Two strokes of the sword were all he needed.

But perhaps more than he could handle. He coughed, spattering flecks of blood against his daughter's neck. The cough loosened his control slightly. He heard as much as felt the joints in his left hand pop and spread. He shuddered as he tried to rein it in, but all he could do keep it from spreading.

Dransig felt another presence at the doorway behind him. Not a full sheggam—the feeling was too weak. "Herrin?" he rasped.

"Yes." Dransig heard the steel-capped staff drop to the floor and Herrin Fayel's sword whisper free of its scabbard. "It looks like I'm here to do what I tried to stop you from doing."

Shad suddenly flared so bright that Dransig couldn't see anything at all. He heard her roar, felt the overwhelming river of shegasti pouring out of every one of her pores. She dropped him carelessly to the ground, jarring his shoulder, and leapt over him. The clash of steel and claw echoed throughout the Council Chambers as the sheggam, who had been his daughter only moments before, engaged the Commander of the Knights of the Eye.

The stone floor felt cold beneath Dransig's head as the sounds of battle erupted behind him. "Goodbye, Shad." And he found that he still bore the capacity for tears.

Chapter 74: End of the Road

Herrin Fayel gripped the sheggam—which, until moments earlier, had been the human Shad Belgrith—by the hair. Or at least, he held part of the sheggam. During their battle, he had managed to pry the beast's jaws apart and, in a single jerk powered by the shegasti running through Herrin's own blood, rip the sheggam's head from its body. He tossed the head away, which landed wetly, and picked up the edge of his cloak before stepping over the corpse.

Killing the sheggam had taken less time that Herrin had expected. But then it had been a new sheggam, still getting used to its changed body. Herrin had trained his own body for many years for just such an occasion. He had to remind himself that this time, he had been lucky to face one so inexperienced.

He clucked disapprovingly as he knelt down next to Dransig. "You don't look well, old friend," Herrin said. Dransig was alive but barely, looking as if in the throes of a seizure, he was shaking so hard. Sweat darkened his gray hair, yet the old traitor had the gall to open his eyes and fix Herrin with a hard glare.

"That … was my daughter you killed," he said through chattering teeth.

"Your daughter killed herself," Herrin said. "Just as you had. It just took a little longer for you."

The fire went out of Dransig's eyes. In its place was the look of defeat. "The … others?"

Herrin shook his head. "I fear they'll be gone before the night is out. There are just too many sheggam for them to deal with."

Dransig bared his teeth in a snarl. "Vin …dication." The snarl turned to a grimace as the pain overtook him. "We're … the last … of our damned order."

"No, old friend." Herrin unbuckled Dransig's belt and gently lifted the tabard and mail shirt over the old man's head. "I'm the last." He continued to remove Dransig's armor and clothes until he was wearing nothing but his loin wrapping.

Herrin stood and studied the older man. There were scars crisscrossing his body—or at least they would have been scars, but the wounds looked as if they had never healed. Like the skin was just … held there, stitched together by something far more ephemeral than gut.

Of course, that was exactly the case. Shegasti, far more than a normal man could take into himself, bound his body together.

Many of the wounds Dransig had suffered over the years—some of them delivered by Herrin himself, when Dransig turned traitor—would have been fatal, even to a normal Knight of the Eye. But a normal Knight of the Eye tapped into only a trickle of shegasti, through a single piercing of sheggam bone.

Dransig had twenty-two piercings. Stolen from the Knights the night of his betrayal, heaping injustice upon injustice.

Yet that betrayal was finally catching up with him.

Herrin crouched down, removed a glove, and brushed his fingers along the thin curved bone hooked into the skin beneath Dransig's nipple. "You are worse than a traitor to your oath," he said quietly. "You are an abomination. You are the very thing our Order was created to destroy."

Dransig squeezed his eyes shut. "Then may it destroy you, too."

Herrin clucked again and yanked the thin bone out of Dransig's skin. Dransig's eyes shot open. His back arched as if he had been struck by lightning. He groaned between tightly clenched teeth as a narrow line of blood blossomed across his shoulder, slowly sheeting his collarbone in glistening crimson.

When the next piercing was pulled out, a chunk of flesh from Dransig's back flopped to the ground as if it had been severed free by a phantom sword. Dransig's eyes rolled back into his head.

By the time Herrin had pulled out the sixth piercing, Dransig finally stopped thrashing. By the time the twenty-second piercing had been pulled out, Dransig was in pieces.

His duty complete, Herrin stood and looked down at the mess at his feet. "Goodbye, old friend." There was the faintest tremor in his voice. His cloak flapped about him as he spun on his heels and walked away from the two corpses who were once father and daughter.

Chapter 75: Making the Best of It

Yarid stepped over the remnants of a dish cabinet. The contents—polished white bowls and cups of the finest quality seen in the Accord—crunched under the soft leather sole of his boot like brittle bleached bones. To his right, the window to his pantry had been broken in. A body hung over the sill, arms draped over the counter. Not all of the glass had been broken out; a single, thin shard stabbed up through the woman's chin. She wore the servants' garb of his house; he should know her face. But as he stared at her, he could recall nothing about her. As if his mind refused to acknowledge she had ever existed.

Perhaps it was always that way, he thought, more disturbed by this thought than by the scene of violence surrounding him. He shuddered and stepped into the hallway.

More bodies. Yarid had no idea why he was here. He had never felt truly at home on his estate; the Council Chambers brought him far more comfort than this place ever had, as odd as that was. Shouldn't he have felt at home in his home? Perhaps that question, more than anything else, was what had driven him here when the chaos began.

Or maybe the fact that a sheggam emissary had been standing in the Council Chambers earlier that day, tainting his true home with its presence. Where else could Yarid have gone?

A moot point, he thought as he quickened his pace. The sheggam invaders had clearly been here already. He had been searching his manse for someplace he could hide, somewhere where he could wait for this disaster to pass him over. So far, he had found nothing. Perhaps there was nothing. Anywhere.

He tried not to look at the man with his chest split open. He tried not to look at the severed head whose body was nowhere to be seen. He tried not to look at the faces he should have known. If he looked, he might not be able to keep choking down the mad scream that was stuck in his throat, clawing its way up to his lips.

Yarid's eyes blurred with tears and he ran as fast his soot- and mud-stained robes would allow.

Shores take me. What have I done? Never mind that nothing he did had had any effect. This would've been the result no matter what, thanks to what he had done in helping that sheggam emissary. He had been ready and willing to help the monsters that had brought this destruction.

When they found his body, would anyone recognize his face?

Would anyone care?

He staggered into his sitting room and leaned against the doorjamb to catch his breath. Much to his surprise, the room seemed to be relatively untouched. A single lamp hung from the center support post, casting deep shadows around the room.

Two figures sat in the near-darkness.

Yarid gasped in horror. *They're here! Waiting for me!*

"Yarid," said one of the figures. It was certainly human. And old.

Yarid let out a shaking sigh. "Don't scare me again like that, old man. What are you doing here?"

Gorun rose with a groan and took the lamp from the post. The light shifted, revealing Jordin on the hard sofa, the one that Tirfaun always sat on.

Yarid looked at him. Then back at Gorun. "Ah." Of course. Someone had used Jordin to threaten Yarid, someone with the wit to keep Yarid in the dark. Who better than Gorun? "Well played, old man. So, you've come to finish the job, have you?" Yarid crossed the room and slumped into a chair near Jordin. Yarid's old servant, sitting stiffly, did not meet his eye. "Make it quick. I'm sure you've got more important things to fuss over."

"I'm not here to kill you, Yarid." Gorun stood over him. "You did what I asked."

Yarid couldn't help himself. He laughed. "You mean the Runeway? A lot of good that did anyone. It will never be completed, and if it were, so what? Everyone will be too dead to use it."

"Not everyone." With his thin, spotted hand, Gorun lifted a silver chain out of the neck of his robe. Hanging from the necklace was a pendant of a sort Yarid had never seen before. It looked ancient, like a tooth, or a bone, but not quite as solid. Strands of light gray fiber looked ready to peel off. The length of it, no longer than a man's finger, was capped at both ends by poorly hammered iron. Yarid could just make out tiny etchings all over its surface.

"It's hideous," Yarid said. "Don't tell me you've been getting fashion advice from Jordin."

Gorun smiled. "It's what is keeping me alive. It can keep you alive too, if you stay near enough to it."

Yarid didn't like the look of absolute calm, of absolute certainty, in Gorun's eyes. "I suppose you're not going to stay in my house, are you?"

"No, Yarid. My loyal servant," Gorun nodded at Jordin, "and I are headed somewhere else."

"And where might that be?"

"Sheggamur."

"You're mad, old man, for two reasons. One. You think you can just hop over Andrin's Wall. Two. You think I'm going to put myself in a worse situation than this."

Gorun sat down. "You're smarter than this. The Wall is nothing now; the sheggam have proved that. And Sheggamur, for all its problems, is now a safer place than here."

Yarid narrowed his eyes. "What are you talking about?"

"Orthkalu, the sheggam emissary, wasn't lying. At least, not about that. Sheggam and humans coexist up there. There are even opportunities for enterprising humans to rise within the ranks of sheggam society. Of course, we wouldn't have the same level of luxury that we had as Councilors of the Wall. But sometimes sacrifices must be made for the sake of survival."

Yarid's mind reeled as he worked through Gorun's words. He leaned forward, eyes wide as the pieces of the puzzle all fell together. "Shad Belgrith was not the one who made all this possible. *You* were."

Gorun set the lamp down on the table between them and shrugged. "Her father was my protégé before he abandoned his old life. So she came to me for help when Orthkalu approached her. I'm the one who actually negotiated the deal." His gaze sharpened. "You seem to think any of this was avoidable. It wasn't. The sheggam were coming one way or another. It's one thing to sit back and let it happen. It's quite another to make the best of it."

Yarid leapt to his feet. "Make the best of it?" He swung his arm in the direction of the hallway and the horrors it held. "How do you intend to *make the best of that?*"

Jordin quickly—and easily—wrestled him back down to his seat.

Gorun shook his head. "I understand you're upset. I would be lying if I said I wasn't too, by the things I have seen."

Yarid scoffed and looked away.

Gorun continued. "But we can't change this. It was inevitable. The

410

sheggam were always going to come. There's a reason the sheggam hunted mankind down until Andrin built the Wall. Because the Wall was all that *could* keep them out. Once that was no longer true, we were lambs for the slaughter." He seized Yarid's hands in his own. *"Think*, son. Not on what should have been. But on what is."

Yarid wanted to shake his hands free of Gorun's cold, wrinkled ones. But he didn't. "That pendant," he said after a moment. "What does it do?"

Gorun smiled. "It keeps the three of us from becoming sheggam food." He stood, pulling Yarid up with him. "Come. Let's put this awful mess behind us and start fresh."

Start fresh, Yarid thought uneasily as Gorun tugged him out of the house with Jordin quick on their heels, *in a land full of sheggam.*

Chapter 76: The Dangers of the Night

Tharadis's eyes snapped open.

He inhaled sharply, struggling to make sense of his surroundings, then relaxed. The scent of the crackling fire in front of him and the weight of his sleeping daughter in his lap reminded him where he was. The caravan.

Countless people, now maybe several thousand, huddled on this hill around fires just like his, seeking protection in the circle of wagons and the handfuls of weary soldiers standing guard at its edges. They hadn't stopped him at the line of wagons. They had taken one look at his face, carrying a soaking-wet Nina in his arms, and admitted him without question.

All it had taken to get here: the constant fighting in the city, finding Nina, escaping through the river until the two of them washed up at the caravan's edge ... it was all a blur, like a nightmare he wanted to forget. A nightmare he knew he would never wake up from.

Four more familiar forms slept around the fire, huddled under filthy scraps of blankets—forms he had believed he'd never see again. He was happy to see that Chad and Erianna had made it out alive. So had the red-haired librarian, Alyssa, though she suffered worse injuries than the rest. She flitted in and out of consciousness, but at least the gash in her head wasn't bleeding so much now.

But what Esta was doing in Garoshmir was utterly beyond Tharadis. She hadn't spoken when he and Nina first arrived. She hadn't even noticed them standing there. Erianna said something about the night being too much for her, that she needed time. Tharadis had simply nodded, sat down, and slept, letting all his troubles wait for when he could deal with them again.

He was so exhausted he doubted if a sheggam gnawing on his hand would have stirred him. He wondered what, then, *had* woken him.

A sharp throbbing in his wounded hand answered him.

He lifted the hand to inspect it. Blood was crusted on both the front and back of the bandage, but fresh blood no longer soaked through. Still that promise of healing and pain pulsed within the wound. Tharadis felt a moment of panic, wondering if in his exhaustion he had let his guard down, letting the shegasti take him over. He wondered how he would know if it had already begun.

He forced the panic down. He hadn't turned into a sheggam. Not yet, at least. But how much time did he have? How long before he was a threat to everyone he loved?

Tears burned his eyes as he brushed a strand of damp black hair from his daughter's sleeping face with his uninjured hand. Would he have to leave her so soon after becoming her father in truth?

If that's what it takes, he thought. *If that's what it takes to keep her safe.*

Another throb came, but this time, something was different. The promise was still there, buried within. But something else was there: a call.

A call to come south.

His eyelids fluttered. Whatever it was, it could wait. He was simply too tired to comply.

The call came again. *South.*

Come south to me.

Tharadis's chin lowered until it rested against his chest.

Come south to me. Protect your master.

South. The Rift.

Tharadis lifted his head. The fog of sleep cleared. His eyes widened as he remembered.

The sheggam from the Council session. He had built the Runeway.

He was going to the Rift.

Tharadis had to go. Now. He moved to wake Nina and say goodbye. To tell her he loved her. But his hand froze an inch from her shoulder.

Goodbye. He knew it might be the last time. He knew it was mad, but some part of thought that if he didn't say goodbye, it wouldn't have to be. He slipped out from under Nina and nearly broke into a sprint. But he stopped to stare down at her face. *Beauty once more*, he thought, wiping at his cheeks before breaking his gaze and running for the caravan's edge.

"Warden?"

Tharadis stopped at the familiar voice and turned. A trio of soldiers jogged over to him. Sentinels, Tharadis realized when they were close enough. The man in the lead removed his helmet, revealing close-cropped red hair and an angular face. As one, the three of them saluted him.

"Lieutenant Metsfurth," Tharadis said, returning the salute. "I'm glad to see you and your men are alive."

"You, as well, Warden." Dim firelight flickered over the planes of

Metsfurth's face, revealing a troubled expression. "Warden, sir. Captain Firnaleos hasn't arrived yet. And given the situation, we … don't know if we should expect him."

Tharadis knew better than to mutter some meaningless words of encouragement. He knew how hollow they would sound. Besides, he could see what the man was really trying to ask him: *tell us what to do.* "I don't know what you expect of me, Lieutenant. I know very little about the Sentinels."

"I understand that. But you are the Warden of Naruvieth. And our captain … thought highly of you."

Tharadis sighed. He wanted to help, but he knew the situation in the south, whatever was going on down there, was far more critical than whatever the Sentinels would face. He simply didn't have time to stay here and order them around.

But perhaps he didn't have to. "Lieutenant, you are the ranking Sentinel officer here. That means it's up to you to keep this caravan safe. Until all of this gets sorted out, that's going to be your primary task."

Metsfurth studied him with his brow furrowed, but after a moment, he nodded. "You're right. Of course you are." He exhaled as if a great burden were lifted off his shoulders. Sometimes a few simple words were all a person needed to get their head straight. "But what about you?"

"I … have to head south." Tharadis shook his head. "I think this invasion was just a distraction, for whatever's happening down there."

Metsfurth lifted an eyebrow. "The invasion is a distraction, you say."

"I don't really know. Possibly. All I know is that I need to go south to stop something that might be even worse than this."

Metsfurth stared at him as if he had just said the moons were falling. The two Sentinels behind him shared a glance. Tharadis had to admit it sounded crazy even to himself, but he didn't know how better to explain it.

"Well," the lieutenant finally said, "I can't imagine what that might be, but I wish you all the luck. You're going to need it if it truly is as dire as you say." Again, they saluted.

Tharadis returned it. "Thank you." He seized the man by the arm before he could leave. "If it's not too much to ask, my daughter and my sister are over there." He nodded in the direction of their fire. "Along with some friends. If you could—"

"Say no more, Warden. They will be safe and awaiting your return."

If I ever do *return,* Tharadis thought, releasing the man's arm. He knew he shouldn't expect special favors, but he couldn't just leave them vulnerable either. "Thank you, lieutenant. I hope Rannald comes back, but if he doesn't, I'll know the Sentinels are in good hands." He turned and threaded his way between the wagons and the soldiers standing guard, who only stared as he left the protection of the caravan for the dangers of the night.

Chapter 77: The Caravan

The sheggam bounded up the hill with breathtaking speed, leaping over the broken branches and shattered stump with ease. Rannald hadn't heard it coming, only caught a glimpse of it a moment ago as he briefly lost his footing in the loose soil. Sherin, struggling in his arms, finally broke free. She half-ran, half-stumbled away from him into the brush, her panting interspersed with panicked cries.

The sheggam, sensing weaker prey, veered in her direction.

Rannald cursed as he got to his feet. He ran after her as quickly as he could, but the sheggam was just so damn *fast*. It held no weapons—and clothes that were more like rotted strips of cloth—but its teeth and claws were enough to tear her to pieces.

Her sleeve caught on something in the darkness, throwing her to her knees. Eyes wide with terror, she yanked on her sleeve. It ripped, but held her fast.

The sheggam sped forward, jaws gaping with lips pulled back.

A pit formed in Rannald's stomach as he realized he couldn't get to her in time. The beast would have her.

Let others fear. Rannald roared, swinging his sword, yet knowing it was too late. He might get the kill, but not fast enough to save Sherin.

Then the beast turned, as if it heard a sound. But it wasn't looking at Rannald, didn't hear his battle cry.

It looked south.

The sheggam didn't even have the time to register surprise. The blade crunched into its snout, ripping through flesh, cartilage, bones, and brain, exploding out the eye socket with a spray of red. A third of the sheggam's face went spinning off into the trees as the beast collapsed and slid down the slope, wispy tendrils of that strange smoke rising from the bloody remains of the head.

Rannald glanced around briefly and, satisfied there were no other pursuers, rushed to Sherin's side. "Shhh, it's okay now. It's just me. Rannald."

She was on her back, breath coming heavy and fast, staring at him with

416

no recognition. Ever since he had found her, it was as if she had no idea who he was, or even who she herself was. Her sleeve was still caught, pinched between a couple of roots poking up out of the ground.

With a quick chop of his blade, he cut the fabric free. Sherin yelped at the sudden motion and began scrambling away from him again on her hands and knees.

He jogged around her and crouched down. "Sherin, it's me." He held out his hand.

She paused, still breathing quickly, but stared at his other hand. The one holding his sword. She was terrified, not of the sheggam that had nearly killed her, but of *him*.

He considered dropping it, but only for a moment. It didn't matter if she feared him or hated him. She would live; he would make sure of it. But he couldn't do it empty-handed.

He needed his sword. She needed his sword. Whether she saw that or not.

"Come on. Let's go." He took her tightly by the hand. She no longer resisted, but he had to drag her as often as not over the hill.

Rannald glanced over his shoulder. They were far enough away from Garoshmir that he could no longer hear the hundred fires roaring, or the screams. The sounds of nature—the rustle of leaves, the chirping of crickets, the crunch of leaves underfoot—seemed like a lie, a betrayal of all those he had left behind in the city.

But his wife was alive. He did it for her, and he would do it a hundred times more. He would leave everything and everyone behind if it could buy her but one more day of life.

Rannald just hoped he had bought her at least that much.

They burst through a line of shrubs and stopped. A hundred or so wagons were clustered not far ahead of them in apparent disarray, silhouetted by a series of controlled fires. Forms ran toward the caravan—human, by the look of them, some limping, others crying out for help. Soldiers stood in wary groups, holding torches in front of every face before admitting any of the refugees. Checking to see if they were human.

It looked safe. At least as safe as he could hope for.

As he approached, he called out, "I have a Councilor of the Wall." It was all they needed to hear; he guessed his voice was known to even these men. They moved aside quickly. "And bring me whoever's in charge."

Most of the people in the caravan were wounded; the rest ran around frantically, administering aid, barking orders, moving wooden planks, crates, or whatever else they could find to build up the makeshift barricade at the caravan's edge. Rannald guided Sherin over the deep wagon ruts crisscrossing the soft ground to a crate to sit, then quickly wiped his blade on his leg before sheathing it. Sherin's breathing had calmed. Now she gripped his hand tightly. Firelight reflected in the tears on her cheeks.

"Rannald," she whispered. *"Rannald."*

He pulled her close and squeezed his eyes shut against the tears that threatened.

"Captain," came a man's voice from behind.

Reluctantly Rannald let go of her and turned. Four Sentinels stood at attention next to an overweight man in a leather jerkin tightly gripping a blood-spattered mace. "Major Metsfurth," Rannald said, nodding to Arrion, at the Sentinels' lead.

"Glad to see you're alive, Captain." No hint of gladness could be seen on the major's face. Rannald couldn't blame him.

"Likewise. All of you." Rannald turned to the other man, the one he didn't know. "You're in charge here?"

The man shrugged. "I'm the caravan chief, so I suppose so."

"What have you heard?"

"Just got word that a bunch of the buggers just turned south of a sudden. All at once, like a flock of birds."

South. "How long ago?"

He shrugged again. "Couldn't have been a quarter hour, half hour."

"How many? All of them?"

A haunted glaze came over the caravan chief's eyes. "Most. But not enough."

"Captain." Major Metsfurth's left eye was swollen and he had suffered a shallow gash on his arm, but otherwise looked unharmed. His uniform, however, looked and smelled like it had been dragged through a sewer. The other Sentinels fared little better. "Tharadis was here. He brought his daughter with him."

"Daughter? I thought he was …" *Looking for his sister-in-law's daughter.*

Ah.

Metsfurth nodded as he followed Rannald's thought process, apparently written on his face. "He left her here. The girl's aunt is here too, but … she's not well."

418

"She's hurt?"

"Not physically, but …" He didn't need to explain further. "Tharadis said he had to go south immediately. You just missed him. He left right after all the sheggam headed off. I think he thought something worse was going to happen, but he didn't say what."

Rannald chuckled wryly. "Worse than a sheggam invasion, eh?"

"He said the most important job the Sentinels could do now is help make the caravan safe. So that's what we've been doing."

Rannald nodded his approval. For now, the Sentinels would do what they could here. Whatever the Naruvian was doing, it was beyond the likes of Rannald Firnaleos. Tharadis was on his own. "Light some arrows and loose them towards the city. It will signal to anyone who gets free of the city that we're here. And it will make it a little easier to see if anything approaches."

The chief frowned. "But that will also signal the sheggam that we're here."

"If there's a lesson in any of this," Rannald said, "it's that the sheggam are always coming." He turned to his men. "See it done."

The Sentinels saluted and left. Rannald helped Sherin up and turned back to the caravan chief. "Take us to the Naruvian's daughter."

Chapter 78: Bones

Hundreds of bodies were laid out on the ground. Some of them moved; many did not. Clouds of flies and bloodsuckers circled the barely-living and the dead. Few moved in attempt to disperse them; most were too weak to do so. The scent of death flooded the air, forcing Rannald to cover his nose and mouth with his forearm as he followed the caravan chief along the narrow, winding path between the bodies packed together tightly. Sherin clung to Rannald's arm like a frightened child. Soldiers, nurses, and anyone else able enough to help wove between those on the ground, administering what aid they could. Those needing help greatly outnumbered those giving it.

"The smoke or fog, whatever it is," the chief said. "Some of the wounded got infected. Started changing, right before our very eyes, in ways a man can't unsee. Brothers turning to beasts." His pace slowed as he stared at the bodies. He shook his head. "Killing a man you know to save yourself ..."

Rannald guessed by his tone that the chief had done the deed himself at least once. He had seen it back in the city—the wall of fog rolling over those crying for help, those same cries changing to something altogether alien, frightening. The stories all told of such things, the shegasti power infecting open cuts and sores, but many dismissed them as mere fables used to frighten children into avoiding dangerous play. *Today*, thought Rannald, *myth becomes indisputable fact.*

He followed the chief's gaze to a particular soldier making his way through the wounded. That man had no poultices, no needles or gut. Only a well-used dagger. The man's motions were mechanical as he checked for signs of infection and turning, pulling back eyelids and prodding wounds with the hilt. Rannald turned away before he had to see the man find someone infected and use that dagger of his.

They put the wounded behind them, making their way through several spear racks, most empty, scattered about as haphazardly as everything else in the caravan. Beyond this, a large ring of soldiers surrounded an open area filled with cook fires and tents, with women and children gathered around the fires in frightened clumps. The soldiers were of different loyalties—

some Sentinels, some city guards, others the personal guards of various Councilors—but all of them stood armed and at attention, vigilant in their charge. Rannald realized the caravan chief must have been a far better leader than he seemed at first glance.

The sight stirred a shred of hope in Rannald's heart, but he knew that if but two sheggam made their way to this line of soldiers, it would falter and buckle. Then the slaughter would begin. Mere vigilance would not be enough to save them.

The chief led them to a group of three women and a small black-haired girl, sitting around a fire. All of them looked like they were just waking up. He was surprised to see Chad there as well, curled up and sleeping fitfully near the fire. One of the women Rannald recognized from the library; her dark red ringlets and spectacles were hard to mistake, as was the fist-sized green orb hanging from a heavy chain around her neck, marking her as the library's archivist. She clutched it tight against her chest. *Everyone seems to be clutching something,* Rannald noted, loosening the grip on his sword as Sherin tightened her grip on him.

The girl sat on the lap of a young woman who couldn't be much older than twenty, lounging against a broken wagon wheel propped up against a crate, staring off at nothing. Her yellow dress was soaked in blood, but her skin appeared to have been mostly wiped free of it, revealing the same deep tan as Tharadis. The sister.

The third woman crouched by the fire Rannald didn't recognize immediately, because she wore different clothing now—or rather *more* clothing, likely scrounged from the dead, judging by the fact that she wore men's trousers with a bloody hole in the thigh, and the gambeson and mail she wore were far too large. She stared directly into Rannald's eyes, unbowed and unrepentant.

Erianna Vondallor.

Rannald shoved Sherin behind him as he drew his sword.

No one moved, though they weren't frozen by fear. They were simply numb to danger.

Erianna spoke. "I understand you think me an enemy, Rannald Firnaleos. But I am Shad's slave no longer. Her will no longer defines mine."

Rannald gritted his teeth, lowered the point of his blade so that it was inches from her chest. "You … helped her bring these things here."

Erianna stood, Rannald's blade following her up. "I am no more to blame than your wife. Less, since I was a slave with no choice in the matter.

If you're going to seek your vengeance, take it up with the Council of the Wall." Erianna looked down at the fire, closed her eyes, and sighed. "No, even they aren't to blame. They didn't know what sort of threat they faced. Only Shad did."

"You could have stopped her."

Erianna faced him, firelight reflecting in her eyes. "You're a fool if you think this could've been avoided. If there was a way for the sheggam to come here, they would have, no matter what any one of us did, no matter who among us died along the way." She squatted back down and began to idly stir the coals with a stick.

Rannald felt the sting of painful truth in her words. He sheathed his sword and turned to the little girl. She was watching him, wide-eyed. "Your fath … You must be Tharadis's …"

"I'm Nina. Tharadis is my daddy." She seemed very proud of this fact.

"Nina." Rannald tried to smile but doubted himself successful. "Your father is a very important man, and he loves you very much."

The girl nodded and stared down at her hands resting in her lap.

Erianna stood and pushed her hair out of her eyes. "This place isn't safe. These men are doing what they can, but they aren't organized enough. We're too close to the treeline. The sheggam could come at us with barely a minute's notice."

Rannald sighed. "I was thinking the same thing." He turned to the chief. "Has any word come from the other cities?" It was a stretch to hope for; it would take a few hours for a man on horseback to reach them from even the nearest town.

The chief shook his head. "Sheggam've been spotted running every which way since the beginning. Wouldn't be surprised if they've run down that Runeway and knocked on a few doors by now. Hordes of them. Thousands."

"It couldn't be much worse than here," Erianna said. "Garoshmir is done. We have to go somewhere fortified. Ahlin, perhaps."

Sherin stepped around Rannald and spoke, her voice hoarse and low. Her eyes never lifted from the ground. "Ahlin will never take us in, even if they aren't yet overrun. They won't take any chances with the sheggam about. They won't trust anyone." She chuckled mirthlessly. "And who could blame them? If they had any sense, they'd put arrows in anyone who ventures close. Especially if they learn that the Council of the Wall invited this disaster upon them."

Rannald seized her by the shoulders. "Don't you dare believe that you are responsible for what happened here. Like she said, you had no idea."

"No," Sherin's voice lowered further. "I really didn't."

Rannald released her. He felt the gazes of Erianna and the caravan chief fixed upon him. "Tharadis went south to stop something worse from happening. I don't know what could be worse than this, but that's why I'm not the man for the job. Like he believed, my place is here. Making everyone here safe is something I can help with."

"Orthkalu came up through the vents in Twelve Towers," Erianna said. "It's likely that the rest of them came from there, too. As far as I know there's nothing stopping more of them from coming. What happens if they do?"

Rannald looked north. He could see the white line of Andrin's Wall softly reflecting the moonlight, stretching from horizon to horizon where not obscured by trees and hills. *Andrin's Wall can no longer protect us,* he realized. The wall may as well have been torn down, turned to rubble, for all the good it would do them now.

They could no longer rely on it. There was only one thing left to protect them.

The strength of their steel.

"If more sheggam come," he said between gritted teeth as he freed his sword and raised it high in Andrin's Salute, "we will build a new wall. From their bones."

Chapter 79: The Red Moon

I t was a ridiculous plan. Tharadis was only half-convinced it would work. But he had to try *something*.

With Shoreseeker gripped tightly in one hand, he pressed himself against the outer wall surrounding Garoshmir and crept forward. The southern gate leading into the city lay ahead. Though it had only been a few days, it seemed like an age since he had first passed through that gate.

Although the stone was cold against his back, smoke and heat rose into the night sky. It seemed like the whole city was burning. Right now, that was something that Tharadis could use to his advantage.

His breath caught in his throat and he froze as a hulking, pale form loped out of the gate on all fours, not ten feet from where Tharadis stood. It passed through the knee-high grass before its claws clacked against the surface of the Runeway. Once there, the sheggam broke into a full sprint. Heading south.

Tharadis released the breath. It ignored him—if it had even noticed him at all. It had seemed totally focused on heading south. Which meant that the call throbbing in Tharadis's left hand wasn't his imagination at all.

What kind of sheggam could call him like that? Except a sheggam who was also a Patterner?

The thought chilled him. Still, it changed nothing. That only made it all the more important for him to stop whatever was going on down at the Rift.

Tharadis crept forward and peered around the corner of the gate. The guards, of course, were nowhere to be seen. The outer portcullis was still raised. The inner one was down but smashed to pieces. Beyond it, bodies littered the street curving away. The only movement came from the low flames lapping up the wall of a small shed next to the inn. It would do.

Tharadis picked up one of the narrow splinters, about as long as his forearm, from the wreckage of the portcullis and crossed to the where the shed burned. He cast his gaze to the gaps between the buildings, the broken windows, the rooftops. He saw nothing. He was alone—for now, at least.

He held the splinter in the fire until it caught, then, careful not to let the flame go out, headed back out the gate and towards the Runeway.

Halfway there, the small flame went out as if smothered.

Tharadis frowned at it. The stick was dry and there was no breeze. The grasses hadn't stirred at all. What had blown it out?

He jogged back to the portcullis, sheathed Shoreseeker, and picked up another stick that looked like it would catch flame. At least if one went out, he would have the other. He lit both sticks on the fire, which had spread to the inn, and walked back towards the Runeway, even more carefully this time.

First one stick, then the other, went out.

Something was wrong.

He dropped both sticks and drew Shoreseeker.

Amid the grasses grew a single short, gnarled tree, not twenty steps from where he was. Tharadis blinked. Had that tree always been there? He could have sworn it hadn't been there a few moments ago. But how could a tree be invisible and then suddenly appear?

A man leaned against the tree, a man Tharadis didn't know. He was older, gray streaked at his temples, and dressed like a beggar. But there was an arrogance in his posture that set the alarm bells in Tharadis's head off. The man lifted his gaze and met Tharadis's eyes. A venomous smile spread across the man's lips.

"So you're the Warden." He gave a slight bow of the head. "My name is Tirfaun." He held a long stick in his hand, likely a branch from the tree he leaned against. There was a wide patch of dirt at his feet. It was almost too dark to tell, but Tharadis thought he could see small ridges in the dirt, as if this man, this Tirfaun, had been drawing in it.

He did so again now, lowering the tip of his stick until it touched the dirt. Then he gave it a little sweep to the side.

Something seized Tharadis's ankles, then yanked one of them forward. Tharadis spun, then landed flat on his back. The wind burst out of his lungs. He tried to climb to his feet, but he couldn't move his hands.

Blades of grass wrapped around his wrists like manacles, slowly squeezing tighter.

Then, as if before their master, the blades of glass between Tharadis and Tirfaun bowed out of the way, providing Tharadis a clear view of Tirfaun as he etched in the dirt. More and more of the grass bent over Tharadis's arms and legs, wrapping around them, binding them.

Tirfaun smiled. "Finding it hard to move, are you?"

Tharadis fought against the grass, but he may as well have struggled against steel chains. He couldn't imagine how mere grass was holding him so tightly.

Tirfaun stood with one foot on the bent trunk of the tree, seemingly idle as he drew designs in the dirt near the base of the tree with the stick. Only his eyes seemed intent; the rest of him was utterly at ease. He kept his gaze trained on whatever design he was drawing in the dirt even as he spoke.

"I never thought of myself as a hero." A corner of Tirfaun's mouth rose in a half-smile as he worked. "I doubt anyone has. Yet here I am, putting an end to a threat greater than the world has ever known. Greater," he said, pausing in his etching to wave the stick around in an encompassing gesture, "than the sheggam are now or have ever been."

Seemingly of their own accord, the grasses near his neck and head began to twine together, as if some unseen weaver were braiding them. As they started to drape themselves over Tharadis's neck, he panicked and began thrashing, but it was no more effective than the flopping of a fish caught in a net. He felt them tightening around his neck and then his forehead, pinning him so tightly that the most he could do was clench his fists.

"Stop that," said Tirfaun. "The more you struggle, the tighter they get." He chuckled. "Though I suppose you need to die sometime. Perhaps sooner is better, eh?" He paused a moment, staring down at his handiwork, before continuing again, his voice softer. "The others are all fools. They stopped listening to me years ago. Lora Bale and her lust for control, Penellia with her silly obsession—she's dead now, you know. Perhaps they both are. I'm sure your Larril could have stopped you, but even he couldn't see the menace that you are, the horrors that you leave in your wake. Which leaves only me."

A slow smile spread across Tirfaun's face. "A hero deserves rewards, wouldn't you say?" He turned to meet Tharadis's eyes. "You have a niece—no, she's your *daughter*, isn't she?" The smile widened as he focused on his Patterning again. "Yes, the Warden's daughter. A prize like none other."

Tharadis could barely make sense of the other man's words. It was getting harder and harder to breathe. He felt more than saw his belt unbuckled by blades of grass like a hundred tiny hands working in concert. Shoreseeker was then passed along them. Tirfaun bent down to pick it up without ceasing his slow etching of the dirt or breaking his attention from it. "Let's not give you any further reason to hope, shall we?" He hefted Shoreseeker in his hand and smiled.

Tears stung Tharadis's eyes. Despair flooded through him. Taking away his sword hadn't changed his situation at all; Tharadis wouldn't have been able to reach it anyway. There was nothing he could do now. He would die and no one would stop the sheggam. Ashes drifted from the night sky like flakes of snow. He could hear the crackling of the fires burning across Garoshmir, and visions of those who had died flickered across his vision. The sheggam had finally come to the Accord, and now they were headed for the Rift. The last pocket of human civilization left in the world was coming to an end, and this madman was smiling and drawing in the dirt while it burned.

Tharadis finally relaxed his muscles and quit struggling. What difference would it make if he lived a few moments or a few minutes, tied up like this? He would still be dead, and nothing would change. The throbbing in his hand was worse than before, and he could feel an echo of its pain in his head. Tharadis could feel the tips of his toes and fingers beginning to tingle.

A parade of faces marched through his mind. They were the faces of the dead. His father, his brother, and even—*Shores take me, Serena*—all the faces of those he had loved and lost. Then he saw the faces of the men he had killed, starting with Forrigan and Trandsull. Even more faces flashed in his mind, belonging to people he didn't know. Faces belonging to the corpses in the streets of Garoshmir.

He had failed them all. He had lost them all.

And now I go to the land of the dead. To find what was lost.

The faces continued to cycle in his mind, though one he didn't recognize at all drew his focus. This face wasn't like the others, which were frozen in memory. This one, a man's face framed by long wavy hair, was getting closer.

Then it smiled.

"Don't look so surprised," this face said, though its lips didn't move. "I'm not dead yet."

The face vanished.

A strange sound, like the cracking of a massive boulder, split the air, louder than anything Tharadis had ever heard, making him wince in pain. It forced the very earth beneath him to shudder. Yet when the echoes of that sound faded, it took with it all the other sounds of the world: the crackling fires of the burning city, the subtle breath of wind over the grasses, even the sound of Tharadis's own breathing. What little he could see from where he lay looked different. All was still, frozen in time. All the color had washed out, too, as if the world were drained of hue.

Yet one hue remained: red, bleeding out of Aylia, the red moon that now dominated the sky, as if begging for Tharadis's attention. It was massive, larger than should have been possible. It was now more than double its normal size, and it grew, grew, *grew*, until it filled half the sky. Details resolved, dark patches becoming canyons, lighter spots becoming mountains. Tharadis had no idea what he was seeing, or how it was possible. Perhaps death had finally come for him, and this was the vision it took.

"No," said the voice from before. "You're not dead yet, either."

The face faded back into view. Tharadis couldn't quite tell the color, ghostly as this face was, but there was a hint of amber in the shoulder-length locks that framed it. Tharadis realized that it wasn't merely a face—he could see shoulders and arms, clothed in fine fabrics so white they glowed. The tall man—or hallucination, Tharadis couldn't quite tell—stood next to where he lay, smiling down at him.

Tharadis tried to pull air into his lungs but found that even *he* was completely immobile. He tried to struggle but had no more luck with that than breathing. All he could move were his eyes.

He could faintly see through the man. Behind him, Tirfaun was frozen in the act of drawing his Pattern, his stick pinched between his fingers.

The apparition turned to briefly regard Tirfaun and looked back down into Tharadis's eyes. "Do not worry," he said. "Our conversation will be private." His smile widened, flashing teeth. "We do not have much time. I have come to offer you two things, each dependent on the other. You may refuse them, but I doubt you will. You see, I know what you want, and I know you have wanted it for a very, very long time."

Tharadis stared up at him, but he didn't say anything. He didn't know what was going on, but he imagined that whatever he was seeing and hearing had something to do with the lack of air and the pain in his head.

The man shook his head. "Tsk, tsk. I am *real*, my friend, not imaginary. Just like my offer. Many people do not trust me, but that is because I am one of the few people in this world who is actually *honest*. I am a man of my word. I do not make many promises, but those I do, I keep."

The man bent down, close to Tharadis's face, his voice dropping to a whisper even though no one could possibly hear him. "First, I will give you the means to save yourself. I know what you were trying to do with the fires. That was brilliant, something I would have done myself. But you

428

cannot really pull off that trick now, can you? At least, not unless you have the power to summon a light with nothing more than the effort of your mind."

Tharadis struggled to make sense of the words. Was the man offering him ... magic?

"Yes, *true* magic. Not that silly Patterning business that requires your hands."

Tharadis matched the man's intent gaze. *What else?*

The man chuckled softly and hooked a loose lock of his hair behind his ear. He took a knee and crouched down even lower. "Do you remember what you asked for in the place you called the Wishing Well? Do you remember your wish, the one wish you have kept with you all this time, even though no one in all of time and space had the power to grant it?"

Tharadis's eyes widened.

"That is right, Tharadis. You can see her again. And there is only one place in the world where you can do so. You know where that place is, do you not?"

The name of that place came to his mind as clearly as the memory of his wish: *Farshores.*

"That is right. Farshores is real, my friend. Here, in this world. Head north, through the lands now called Sheggamur, and you will find the Astral Sea. If you can cross it, you may make it to Farshores. Do this, and you will find her waiting."

No. That's impossible. She's dead. The World Pattern took her from me.

The man stood. "Do your people not believe that the spirits of the dead go to Farshores? While that place is no afterlife, there is more truth to your belief than you realize. The spirits of the dead *can* go to Farshores—and so can the living," he said. "You can see her again. You can bring her back."

Impossible.

True, Tharadis had kept that wish in the back of his mind, constantly hoping that someday, somehow it would be granted—but he knew the truth. It was beyond the ability of anyone short of an apoth to grant.

The man sighed. "Why does everyone feel so inclined to compare me to gods? I have something the apoth do not." He tapped his temple and smiled. "Free will. A power they will never have. You have that power, too, Tharadis. Though if you do not accept my offer, you will not have it for long. It is a privilege reserved only for the living."

I don't trust you.

The man shrugged. "I am not asking you to. Whether or not you believe me is irrelevant. But you *will* go there, because there is a shadow of a hope that I am right. I felt the wish that you made. It nearly shattered my bones with its power." He smiled, briefly glanced up at the sky, where the red moon hung. "That was quite a feat, considering where I currently reside."

What do I have to do?

A faint smile spread across his ghostly lips. "It is easy. Accept my first gift, and search for my second. That is all I want from you. And I promise that I will not take anything from you, either."

What's to stop me from taking your gift and staying put?

"Then you are not really accepting my gifts, are you? I will know if you are lying. Besides, I am certain you will accept."

There's a catch. There has to be.

He shrugged again. "Maybe. But whatever it is would be worth enduring just to find out if I am right, would it not?"

Tharadis closed his eyes. The hope that he might see Serena alive again was tantalizing. He feared that he was walking into some trap, but there was one thing the man was right about: if there was a trap with Serena in the middle, Tharadis would walk into it without hesitation.

What do I need to do?

"I will do the hard part. All you need to do to accept my terms is speak my name aloud, and then everything you want will be yours."

Your name?

The man bent down and whispered it into Tharadis's ear, then stood. He waved farewell and his form began to fade like smoke pulled away by a gently blowing wind.

Time and color and sound returned with a crash, and the moon, so large just a moment before, was back to its normal size. Out of reflex, Tharadis shifted his body to see if he could move again. As he did, the grasses tightened sharply.

Panic returned as he struggled to breathe.

Tirfaun abruptly stood. "What was that? I felt … Something is wrong. Something *happened*."

Tharadis struggled to suck in air, anything to salve the agony in his lungs. Soon the darkness at the edges of his vision swallowed even the sight of Tirfaun. There was only the red moon above him. Tharadis felt parts of him go numb as other parts of him screamed in pain. His lungs felt like they would burst.

But then he noticed through the haze that Tirfaun stood over him, a frown creasing his forehead. "You know, don't you? Tell me what you saw. Now."

The pressure on Tharadis's throat eased slightly, just enough to let him pull in breath. He coughed as tears ran down his cheeks "I ... saw ..." Another fit of coughing seized him.

"Well?"

The man's name echoed in Tharadis's mind before it crossed his lips: *"Noredren."*

Tirfaun stared down at him with eyes full of terror. "Where did you hear that name?"

Tharadis didn't respond. He felt something growing deep within him, like a new muscle in his mind. He didn't know what to do with it at first, but then he suddenly *flexed* it. And he knew, without a doubt, the tiny point of light that appeared in his vision was his to control.

Tharadis stared at the tiny point of light he had created, and he moved it.

Chapter 80: Light

The tiny point of light floating above Tharadis's head danced to the rhythm of his need.

He needed to escape.

He needed to keep his daughter safe.

He needed to see Serena again.

Serena. Her name was the trigger, bringing to mind exactly what he needed to create: a hearthsflame. Or rather, the essence of a hearthsflame. Its Pattern.

The point of light spun and twirled, racing about to first create the encapsulating oval, then the leaves opening up from the stem. It was a hearthsflame as he'd never drawn it, in full-bloom. The same, yet different in small ways. The old design wouldn't work here. This was what he needed now.

It hurt to keep his eyes open as the point of light traced the Pattern, but that, too, was what he needed now. The image burned itself into his eyes. It wasn't enough for a Pattern to be held in the mind, he'd once heard. A Pattern needed a physical medium to affect the physical world.

His eyes would have to do.

Once the light finished its final stroke, completing the Pattern, Tharadis extinguished it. The afterimage hung there in front of him, something only he could see. Something triumphant. Something that was a part of him. *Serena.*

The grasses relaxed, freeing Tharadis from his bonds. He sucked in breath and rolled to the side just as the edge of a blade flashed above him. The knife nicked his shoulder before plunging into the ground.

Tharadis scrambled to his feet, still partially blinded by the image of the hearthsflame. He tried to blink it away, but it didn't help.

He heard Tirfaun yank the knife out of the ground. "How did you do it?" the man growled. "How did you summon that light? How did you untangle my Pattern?"

The rustle of cloth alerted Tharadis. He jumped back, feeling the blade cut through the air just in front of him. He continued backing away. He

432

could see Tirfaun now, but he was little more than a vague shadow. He couldn't see the knife at all.

"Answer me! Where did you hear that name?"

When the knife came this time, Tharadis sidestepped—straight into the gnarled tree. Startled, he didn't have time to defend himself. A line of fiery pain erupted across his chest as the blade slashed into him.

Tharadis gritted his teeth, clutching the wound and taking another step back.

His heel bumped into something.

"*Answer me!*"

Tharadis dropped to a crouch, the blade passing over his head in a thrust that would have plunged into his heart. He grabbed the object he'd bumped into. Relief washed through him as he realized it was exactly what he had hoped. Gripping it tightly, he swung it forward and up in one furious motion.

Shoreseeker's blade sliced Tirfaun open from groin to chin.

Guts slopped out of him. Tirfaun teetered back on his heels and collapsed, his entrails draped over his legs like a blanket.

Tharadis waited until his vision cleared. He wanted to see Tirfaun's ruined corpse. He stared at it until satisfied, then wiped Shoreseeker on the grasses and sheathed it. As if to remind him why he'd come this way in the first place, his left hand throbbed. *South*. He'd wasted enough time already.

He jogged to the Runeway where it ended—or rather, where it began—and called upon his newfound power. A point of light, like a tiny star, flared into existence a few inches above the Runeway's surface.

Tharadis willed it to move again. It created another hearthsflame, and again, it was different from any other he'd made. Like the harsh environment of the Face where the flowers normally flourished, this hearthsflame needed to adapt to its environment—that of the Runeway.

Another afterimage burned itself into Tharadis's eyes. But unlike the last time, when he moved, so too did the image, rather than staying fixed in the center of his vision. This was no mere afterimage, he realized. He had imprinted the Pattern onto his eyes—which had then imprinted *the Pattern itself* onto physical reality. He'd created a glowing object, a disk that floated a few inches above the Runeway, shaped like the hearthsflame's Pattern.

He stared at the disk a moment, amazed that he had created something out of mere *light*, and that he had somehow known how to do it. He reached out to touch it and found that it was solid—just as some part of him knew it would be. Then, wondering if he were truly sane, he threw his left leg up

433

onto the glowing disk, testing it with his weight, before grabbing hold of one of the curved lines of light comprising the petal with his bandaged hand. Wincing, he pulled himself up onto the disk until he was kneeling on it, both hands gripping some part of the Pattern.

Light, he thought. *I'm kneeling on a bunch of floating light.*

With a shake of his head, he carefully leaned forward, putting more of his weight on his hands.

The disk tilted forward and began to move south down the Runeway, picking up speed.

Chapter 81: The Highest Volume

O rthkalu's mount collapsed without warning. Sensing its imminent death, he slid from its back just before its legs buckled. He nearly lost his balance when he landed, but once he regained it, he wasted no time looking back at the dead thing. It had served its purpose getting him this far, even if he had to jog the rest of the way, a mere two hundred paces. His heavy steps clanged against the Runeway's surface. If all went according to plan, then Orthkalu would have no more need of the mount. And if it didn't go according to plan, then he would be too dead to care.

Only two paths were open to Orthkalu: absolute power or utter destruction. He would soon find out which path he now stood upon.

With staff in hand, he rushed toward the Rift, as the humans so quaintly called it. But it was more than just a simple vent in the earth—more, even, than the strange barrier most thought it was. Incomprehensible amounts of concentrated shegasti poured out of it. Even at this distance, its power roared over Orthkalu like a storm wind. The agony of it was exquisite, unlike any pain Orthkalu had ever experienced. The Song deafened him, threatening to obliterate any remaining sense of self he had. He could barely fathom the staggering level of power he felt, and he hadn't even reached the Rift yet. Here, the shegasti was so diffuse it would be invisible to human eyes.

Up ahead, the roiling orange light of the Rift, threaded with the blazing white that only sheggam eyes could see, beckoned to him.

The section of Runeway spanning the Rift looked so frail and thin in comparison to the Rift's ferocity. Though Orthkalu himself had designed the Runeway, he'd almost expected it to sway and rock in the face of such power—but of course normal objects weren't sensitive to shegasti and wouldn't react to it in the same way a sheggam or a human would. When Orthkalu came within ten paces of the Rift, he had to sling his staff's thong over his shoulder and crawl forward, clutching desperately at the folds and ridges in the Runeway, using them as fingerholds and footholds. Though he lay flat on the ground as he crawled, it soon began to feel as if he were climbing up a sheer cliff. Yet, strangely, instead of gravity threatening to pull him down, it simultaneously dragged him left and right, feeling as if it wanted to rip him in half and through both chunks of him to either side of the Runeway and into the maw of the Rift.

Into the Rift, Orthkalu mused, though his thoughts were but tatters flailing in the winds of the Song of Pain. Slowly, he put one hand in front of the other, his progress slow but careful. *Too soon for that.*

The Rift wasn't ready for to accept him yet, but it would be soon.

Chapter 82: Race

Wind roared over and around Tharadis as he shot south down the Runeway, clothes ruffling and snapping. The air threatened to rip him off his disk of light. He had no idea how fast he was going, but it had to be three, four, maybe five times as fast as a horse could gallop. He learned that by tilting the disk forward, it would go faster. Now, the front edge of the disk hovered a mere three inches above the Runeway. He was worried that if he tilted it any further, the edge of the disk might catch on something. He didn't know what would happen if it did, but he wagered it would end with him as a quarter mile-long smear of red on the Runeway.

Objects whipped past him at lightning speed, more distinct in the distance, yet appearing as little more than blurs as they shot by. Yet even the distant objects—trees, hills, houses, fences—were difficult to see with so much air hammering his watering eyes, even under the combined light of the stars and both moons. He dared not open his mouth; even breathing through his nose was like drinking from a waterfall.

Rather than hanging on to the outer edges of the disk, he clutched the inner whorls and sweeps of the Pattern—though his fingers weren't actually touching the disk. A sharp pressure kept them from meeting its surface—if it could even be called a surface—like two lodestones repelling each other. Already his fingers were cramped, especially in his left hand, yet he dared not flex them or loosen his grip. It took everything he had to hang on as it was.

With sudden alarm, Tharadis considered what would happen if something hit him in the face. A bird, or even a fly for all he knew, could be like getting hit with an arrow. But he couldn't slow down too much. That sheggam headed south for a reason, and now all the others were doing the same. Something was about to happen down there, and he knew that it had to be related to the Rift. He had no idea what the sheggam could want with it, but he knew that anything they wanted could only cause more death.

Still, he couldn't afford to be reckless. He shifted his weight back, lifting the front edge of the disk a little. It was a good thing he did.

Up ahead, two pale forms raced ahead of him on the Runeway.

They could only be sheggam.

Had he still been going fast, he would have been spotted before he could do anything about it. Now, though, he slowed further, until his clothes didn't ruffle at all, as he considered what to do. Silently he slid Shoreseeker from its sheath. Thankfully the disk itself made no noise as it sliced through the air.

The sheggam's massive, naked forms were hunched over, running more like wolves than men. They, too, were traveling fast, though powered only by their own muscle and nowhere near as fast as he'd been going.

He heard the sheggam's heavy, pounding strides as they ran—but something was *off*. Their footfalls were muted, as if they were running on soft earth rather than the metal surface of the Runeway. And they were coming from the wrong direction.

Tharadis turned to the right just as a third sheggam leapt with its claws stretched forward, jaws opening to emit an ear-splitting roar.

Tharadis swung Shoreseeker as he slammed the front of the disk down. The sudden jolt nearly threw him off and threatened to yank Shoreseeker free from his grasp as the blade hacked through flesh and ribcage—but both hands held firm. His wounded left hand, gripping the disk, screamed with agony. His right hand ached with the impact of the blow.

More loping forms emerged from the shadowy landscape, veering towards him. Three, four—then a dozen, then even more. All appeared to be the beastly sheggam; none carried arms. Quick as they were, many of them would fail to reach the Runeway in time to intercept him. But a few were already on it up ahead, joining the pair he had first noticed. They were charging straight for him. He glanced over his shoulder. More had fallen in behind him. To the front, to the back, to both sides—sheggam swarmed towards him.

One running alongside the Runeway turned its head just in time to see Shoreseeker cleave through it. The sheggam instantly collapsed, nearly wrenching Tharadis's shoulder out of its socket. The pain didn't slow him. He hacked left and right, cutting down more and more sheggam as they closed, smashing muzzles with Shoreseeker's pommel when their snapping jaws got too close.

Motion up ahead snagged his attention. He glanced forward just in time to see the sheggam in front of him, now numbering five, leap for him.

Tharadis kicked his feet down at the same time he yanked the front of the disk up, throwing all his weight back. His chest crashed into the disk painfully as it jerked to a halt.

Three of the sheggam went down in a tangle of limbs and snapping jaws. The other two danced to either side, paying their fallen comrades no heed at all. Tharadis sensed more than saw all the others rushing in.

He leaned forward. The disk sped ahead towards the two.

He swung Shoreseeker at the one on his right, earning a trio of slashes on his left thigh as the other sheggam raked at him with claws. Tharadis only felt a tugging in his skin; he knew the pain would come later—if he lived that long.

The three sheggam ahead were still struggling to get to their feet.

Tharadis had no choice. He quickly sheathed Shoreseeker, gritted his teeth, and with all of his fingers threaded through the disk's Pattern, he threw all of his weight down on the front edge.

The disk shot forward. The three sheggam looked up.

At the last moment, Tharadis pulled up on the front edge. Sheggam blood and flesh exploded as the disk ripped through them. Shards of gore-smeared bone sprayed up, pelting Tharadis so hard they would doubtless leave bruises. The angle had been just right; any lower, and the sheggam would have simply crashed into Tharadis. The disk cleaved through them like a giant axe, its momentum slowed only by its own angle, and not at all the several hundred pounds of flesh it had just destroyed. Whatever this disk was, it seemed to only follow its own rules.

Something, an errant limb perhaps, bounced up underneath the disk, smashing into the tips of Tharadis's fingers where they protruded. The pain made him gasp. At least one of his fingers was broken, though he knew it could be more. Still, he didn't slow, not until he was several minutes ahead of the leading edge of the pack. Only then did he allow himself to catch a proper breath.

After a few moments of resting, he pulled Shoreseeker free from its sheath again, eyes tearing at the pain caused by such a simple action, and sped ahead. He had a long way to go, and he expected to confront more sheggam along the way. He just hoped that he would make it in time, that it wouldn't all be for nothing.

To the east, dawn began to brighten the sky.

Chapter 83: Intoxication

O nce across, Orthkalu staggered to his feet. Through the mindless act of putting one hand in front of the other, he had finally made it to the other side of the Rift. As the Song of Pain waned, his mind cleared and he could begin to hear his own thoughts again. The heat on this side of the Rift was sweltering—an effect of the Rift's influence that any true Patterner would expect. Orthkalu, of course, was not surprised.

As he blinked, Orthkalu saw five human soldiers forming an arc around him, spears leveled warily at him as they kept their distance. Judging by their terrified expressions, they were certainly not expecting to encounter a sheggam on this day.

Smiling at their misfortune, Orthkalu swung his staff into his hands and swiveled its rings into position.

No flash of lightning, no beam of light. No visible effect of his staff's Pattern, save for the five ashen smears where men once stood.

Orthkalu sensed before he saw a sixth soldier charge over the nearby rise, shouting blearily as if he'd just woken up. Orthkalu didn't even bother with a Pattern. He turned aside the man's first thrust with his staff, tripped him, and brought the staff's iron-shod tip down on his head, crumpling helmet and skull alike with a satisfying crunch.

Because of how attuned his senses were to the Patterns comprising his environment, Orthkalu knew no other humans lurked by. All that remained was a small guardhouse and a simple wooden sign staked into the ground. The sign declared construction halted. It was no wonder the sheggam nearly wiped out the humans all those centuries ago—these pathetic creatures were stopped by mere *words*. He swatted the sign away and, gripping his staff firmly in front of him with one hand poised on its rings, began to craft a new Pattern.

The tip of the staff dipped and danced in the dirt as Orthkalu swiveled the Pattern-etched rings into the proper configurations. It was difficult doing both at the same time, even for someone of Orthkalu's talent, but he'd practiced for this moment for many, many years. He was ready.

In response to his new Pattern, the Runeway began to flex, bits of it grinding into new positions, twisting and buckling and folding as if a hundred invisible hands were reshaping it. There wasn't enough metal to complete the original design, but he wasn't limited to that. He was no longer dependent on the intellect of human Patterners. Orthkalu was here now, and he could do much more than they ever could.

As the final pieces bent themselves into the proper alignment, the edges of the Runeway began to glow a soft white. The shegasti pouring out of the Rift shifted in hue from orange to a deep red. Like wine, but far more intoxicating.

Finally. The Runeway was complete and serving its true purpose.

The Rift was his to claim.

From now until he was finished, Orthkalu would be vulnerable. No matter; he'd called his feral army. They would protect him from whatever threat might come this way. He snatched one of the human spears and thrust it into the middle of his palm. The pain of that small wound was a tickle compared to what the Rift could—and would—do to him. He pulled the spear free with a grunt and tossed it away. Blood and mist pouring from his wound, he walked to the edge of the Rift, knelt, and plunged his hand into the boiling red light.

Orthkalu screamed.

Chapter 84: Growth

Red lightning cracked through the Rift.

Power surged into Orthkalu through the wound in his hand. Woven through that power was pain. Orthkalu felt as if the two forces in opposition were ripping him in half.

But instead of obliterating his consciousness, the pain merely ... loosened it. He felt the tethers of his mind, normally so tightly intertwined with his corporeal form, drift away from it. He could no longer see, hear, smell, or taste the world ... but he could still *feel* it. Eddies of primal energy jostled his floating consciousness. He could feel connections upon connections, as if he were a spider sensing each tiny tremor from its ensnared prey through the threads of its web. But for Orthkalu, the Pattern of the World was his web, and man and sheggam alike were his squirming prey.

As his mind sailed high above his body, he was inundated with information. So much that it overwhelmed him at first, but soon, he was getting a clearer picture of things than his eyes could ever provide. Only now was he coming to realize just how limited his Patterning skills had been. Even though he was the greatest in all of Sheggamur, he now knew he had been but a worm crawling through mud, thinking it had been a giant.

Now, though, he truly *was* a giant.

His body, he was amused to discover as he turned his awareness back toward it, was following suit.

As if drawing physical mass from the shegasti filling the Rift, enormous masses of muscle, skin, and bone burst out of his body. Some appeared as boneless, whipping tendrils, others as nearly-formed limbs, flecked with patches of black hair. Bones, claws, and even teeth protruded at random from the growing mass that was Orthkalu's body. He had never cared for physical beauty or appearance, but even he could tell that he had become something truly monstrous. His body, if it could even be called such anymore, throbbed and spread like a pale stain across the ground. It was not how Orthkalu imagined a god would look, but he was not displeased.

All would look upon him and tremble.

442

Once the full power of the Rift was drawn into Orthkalu, even the apoth would fear him. And since the Rift was the balance to Andrin's hated Wall, once the Rift was drained, so too would be the power sustaining the Wall. It would crumble as dust before him. These human lands, these Sutherlands, would fall under his rule, and Sheggamur would quickly follow.

Something snagged his attention.

Orthkalu cast himself north, far ahead of the Rift. He couldn't quite tell what had drawn him, but it was small and fast—and coming straight towards him.

It was almost here.

Tharadis was almost to the Rift when his disk of light began to unravel. Luckily, it slowed as its whorls started to fray, giving Tharadis enough time to slip off the back. He watched as the remains of the disk tumbled onto the Runeway and vanished. He wasn't sure why it chose that moment to fall apart, though he suspected that the Rift was the primary cause.

Up ahead, the Rift glowed a deep red, threaded through crackling red thunder, intermittently splitting the air with peals of thunder. How that happened or what it meant, Tharadis didn't know, but he was certain nothing good could come of such a change.

He glanced behind him. Tiny pale forms loped in the distance, to his eyes getting larger as they approached. The sheggam. In the burgeoning light of dawn, their skin was stark white. They were still far off, but much closer than Tharadis had hoped. Whatever advantage he'd gained because of his disk was disappearing with each passing moment. He didn't think they'd reach him before he crossed over the Rift, but he wasn't going to take any chances. Tenderly avoiding the broken tip of his middle finger, Tharadis adjusted his grip on Shoreseeker and ran for the Rift.

A large black shape lay still in the middle of the Runeway, an unnatural number of legs sprawled out beside it. It had to be the mount that the sheggam ambassador rode out of Garoshmir on. Flies buzzed around its unmoving form. Tharadis ignored it as he passed, focusing on the task ahead.

Whatever that might be.

His bandaged left hand throbbed the nearer Tharadis came to the Rift, and once he reached the section of Runeway spanning the Rift, the pain brought tears to his eyes. A quick backward glance showed the sheggam much closer. Closer than he'd expected. Already he could make out the shape of their limbs, even through his pain-blurred vision.

He turned forward to stare down the length of the Runeway. What would he find on the other side? What would he do once he was there? He had no idea. But an uncertain fate was better than certain death, which was all he would find if he waited around for the sheggam to catch up to him.

Taking a deep breath, he ran across the Rift.

Chapter 85: Glimmer

What Tharadis saw on the other side of the Rift took his breath away.

At first, his mind couldn't make sense of it. Sprawling in every direction was a thick blanket of pale, fleshy material, hugging the ground in places, built up in thick, hill-like mounds in others. Before his eyes, it grew and spread, its surface twitching all over. Once he got over the shock of seeing it, Tharadis realized that this thing was alive.

The increased throbbing in his left hand confirmed what his instincts told him: this was the thing that had called to him, telling him to go south. This was what the sheggam Patterner had become.

The light of the Rift bathed it. In fact, much of whatever this thing was had already spilled over the edge. Yet instead of the destruction that was usually the fate resulting from touching the Rift, this creature seemed empowered by it. The parts nearest the Rift expanded, pushing the rest of its mass outward in slow-moving waves.

A chill swept through Tharadis. How could he hope to stop something like this, something he couldn't even comprehend? How could he kill something as strange and vast as this? Shoreseeker, as remarkable as it was, was still only a sword. Tharadis thought merely cutting this monstrosity would only serve to make it angry. There was simply too much of it.

As horrible a vision as this was, Tharadis felt his gaze drawn to the end of the Runeway, not twenty feet from where he stood.

It looked … different. Somehow, he knew that it was finished. He didn't know how that could be; he had seen the original plans, and they looked nothing like it did now. Yet he couldn't pull his eyes away, and there was something in the air, like a humming, but one he couldn't hear with ears, only feel in his skin. And in that humming there was a sense of completion, like the final notes at the end of a song.

A roar from behind made Tharadis spin. He ducked as a sheggam's claws swept through the air where his head had been. Shoreseeker's edge hacked through the sheggam's rib cage. Tharadis shoved it away as it died, spraying bloody foam from its lips. A dozen more sheggam were past the

Rift already, shaking their heads as if just waking up. Two groups of three broke off from the main group, stepping out onto that fleshy mass covering the ground and heading out to either side, their eyes fixed on Tharadis. They were flanking him.

Such a thing seemed impossible. These weren't the more intelligent sheggam; these were little more than animals. Ferals, he remembered them being called. Yet they didn't seem feral now. Their actions were far too coordinated.

Almost as if they were following orders.

He knew he couldn't fight them all, not like this. His only chance was to kill the one giving the orders. It wasn't much of a chance, but he knew that he was doomed unless he could find a way to destroy what the Patterner had become.

As if on cue, the main group rushed forward. Tharadis leapt off the Runeway and onto the sheggam Patterner's back. It shifted under his feet as if he were standing on a vast waterskin. Without hesitation, he stabbed down.

Blood, pus, and other fluids he couldn't name spilled out of the quivering flesh. The twelve sheggam roared at once, as if in agony. With Shoreseeker's tip plunged down, Tharadis ran farther out, opening up a long gash.

The ground—or whatever it was—twitched violently beneath him, throwing him on his back. He scrambled to his feet with just enough time to raise his sword and plunge it into another sheggam's face, lodging it into its skull. Yanking Shoreseeker free made Tharadis lose his footing. He collapsed to his knees. The remaining sheggam encircled him now, watching him. He noticed more had crossed the Rift and joined their ranks.

One lunged forward, jaws wide, before ducking back out of Shoreseeker's reach. Tharadis staggered to his feet, and another one came in. Again, his blade cut only air as the beast sprang backward. So, they were planning to tire him out. At least that meant they still thought he was dangerous.

Yet Tharadis knew their strategy would work. His lungs burned. Blood dripped from countless wounds. Broken bones screamed in agony. He had been fighting for his life the entire night with barely a moment to rest. He would die here.

But he'd be damned if he died on the back of this monster.

Tharadis rose to his feet, every muscle protesting the action, telling him instead to just collapse and be done with it. The sheggam seemed content to let him stagger over to the hard, unyielding surface of the Runeway. It wasn't as if he were a threat anymore. All they had to do was wait for Shoreseeker to slip from his numb fingers and they would rush in all at once. At least it would be over quickly.

Killing the Patterner was impossible. So was killing the crowd of sheggam that surrounded him. He was no closer to stopping this, whatever it was, than if he had never come at all.

As dark despair threatened to swallow him, one thing glimmered in his mind.

At least he wouldn't have to live without Serena anymore.

Chapter 86: A Delicate System

Though his eyes were closed, Tharadis could feel the gazes of the sheggam surrounding him. There had to be more than thirty by now, encircling where he knelt on the Runeway. Watching him.

He wondered what they were waiting for. He knew he was at his end; he knew he couldn't fight anymore. And if he knew it, so would they.

Perhaps it wasn't his time to die after all.

Off to the side, one of the sheggam spoke. "You are no mere warrior."

The words were clearly articulated. Completely at odds with the demeanor of any of the sheggam he had seen at the Rift. He had been right. That ... thing, whatever it was that the sheggam Patterner had become, was controlling them now.

Tharadis opened his eyes. He didn't know which one had spoken, but he supposed it didn't matter, so his eyes locked on the one in front of him. Though the sheggam's face was calm, its body twitched with anticipation. It seemed its master's control only went so far.

"You're right." Tharadis nodded wearily. "I'm no mere warrior." Grimacing in pain, he slowly levered himself to his feet with Shoreseeker's help. Then he held his sword high, gripping the hilt with what little of his strength remained. "I am the Warden of this land, and I have sworn to protect it."

"How quaint." Another one had spoken, this time directly behind him. "Yet that doesn't explain how you knew to come here, nor does it explain how you outran my ferals." Every few words, the speaker changed, though it was so seamless Tharadis almost thought it was a trick of the air. He was surprised to find that, even now, he could be unsettled.

"I wish I knew." Tharadis let his arm fall. It was all he could do to keep Shoreseeker in his grip.

The sheggam in front of him looked down at his bandage-wrapped hand. "I hear a faint echo of the song within you. Yet incomplete you remain."

"Incomplete, you say." Of course. This sheggam obviously thought of itself as the pinnacle of human development. Seeing what it had become, Tharadis wasn't sure he would agree. "I can't explain that either."

448

"The fundamental aspect of the World Pattern is balance," said the sheggam, all of them, in unison. "Darkness is the balance to light. Death, too, is the balance to life. This Rift is the balance to the hated Wall. Each defines the other. Without one, the other cannot exist." A single voice, almost plaintive, added, "What are you the balance to?"

The sheggam's words triggered something deep within Tharadis, some knowledge he had, on some level, already gained but had yet to fully accept. Understanding flooded through him. Not about himself or what was happening to him, but about the Patterner and what it intended.

The Rift. The Runeway. Andrin's Wall. They were all connected. An intricate system of parts, fitting together.

A Pattern. A *fragile* Pattern. And Tharadis could see it all.

But what did that change? His mind raced. He spoke if only to buy him a few more moments to think of something. "Why haven't you killed me yet?" Probably not the wisest question to ask then, but it was all that came to mind.

"I'm not sure what will happen if I do," came the chorus again.

Tharadis looked beyond the ring of sheggam to the writhing mass of flesh at the Rift's edge. With every moment it was immersed in the flood of power, it grew.

It was all connected. A fragile Pattern. A delicate spiderweb.

Tharadis smiled inwardly. He knew which thread to cut to bring it all down.

He also knew that if he so much as twitched, the sheggam would shred him apart. In order for his plan to work, he'd have to kill them all. Which meant he had to do something they would not expect.

He knew exactly what he had to do. He squeezed his eyes so tightly they hurt.

Then he used his newfound power to summon a light brighter than a hundred suns directly over his head.

The sheggam snarled as they backed away from the light. Even with his eyes closed, it was almost too much for Tharadis himself to bear.

But he didn't hesitate. He moved among the sheggam, cutting them down. As their brethren cried out in death, the others began blindly lashing out. Chaos erupted. Yet even though Tharadis couldn't see his enemies, he still knew where they were and where they would be next as if their attacks were a dance he'd seen performed a hundred times—as if he'd created the dance himself. It was all so obvious to him then. Every breath of the wind told him of their movements before they even made them. Why were his enemies so careless? How had they ever defeated anybody?

Once he sensed all of the sheggam were dead, Tharadis spun to a halt in the center of the Runeway and extinguished the light. He opened his eyes.

Blood-drenched chunks of sheggam lay everywhere.

Panting frantically, Tharadis collapsed to a knee. The only thing that kept him from falling flat on his face was Shoreseeker as he jammed its tip down into the swirling metal designs of the Runeway. It took everything he had just to hang on to the hilt.

As he realized what he'd just done, the feeling he'd had just a moment ago, that sense of heightened awareness, was gone—fled as if he'd only imagined it. Fear crashed back into him, even though all his enemies were dead.

Save for one.

"Impressive."

Tharadis frowned, wondering if he'd actually heard the word. Then he found the speaker, a sheggam that had been cut in half at the shoulder. Its neck was bent at a painful angle, its eyes fixed on him as its lips peeled back. With each word, blood oozed out from between its teeth. "Skill ... beyond that ... of a mere swordsman ... A true ... Blade Patterner ..."

Tharadis said nothing, but simply leaned against Shoreseeker. He was too exhausted to do anything else.

"... and magic ... I have never ... before witnessed." Blood spurted out of the sheggam's wound as it swallowed. "Alas ... for I must ... destroy you now ..."

A pale, fleshy tentacle lashed out at Tharadis, nearly faster than his eyes could track. The blow threw him through the air and sent him sprawling onto his stomach. His chest ached where it had hit him, and he coughed blood as he crawled back towards Shoreseeker. More and more fleshy protuberances rose up out the monster, some like tentacles, others more like human limbs, still others simply shapeless knobs. There had been bones in the tentacle that struck him; Tharadis had felt them. He could see bones in the other nightmare shapes rising up all around him.

He stopped crawling when he was a pace away from Shoreseeker, which still stood where he had plunged it into the Runeway. It stood straight, looking immutable and formidable, the flats of the blade perfectly parallel to the length of the Runeway. But no matter what anyone else said, it was still just a sword. Without a hand to wield it ...

Feeling his bruised rib cage creaking, Tharadis stretched his hand towards it. Shadows fell over him as more of the Patterner's limbs towered above him, poised to strike. He knew his hand wouldn't reach the hilt, not from this distance. But it wasn't the hilt he needed to grasp.

He summoned another tiny point of light—too weak to blind anything, and besides, he wasn't sure the Patterner even had eyes anymore. Tharadis fought to keep his own eyes open, to stare at the point of light as it traced a Pattern around Shoreseeker's blade.

The hearthsflame.

The disk formed in the air, with Shoreseeker's crossguard and hilt protruding out the center. The edge of the disk formed right beneath Tharadis's hand.

He seized the edge of the disk and shoved it upward before rolling himself off the Runeway.

Metal groaned as the disk tried to move. Shoreseeker, with its blade in both the disk and the Runeway, wouldn't let it—nor would the torque of the disk's relentless motion snap Shoreseeker's indestructible blade.

The disk and the sword were virtually indestructible. The Runeway was not.

Like a massive tree being yanked out of the ground, the edge of the Runeway nearest Tharadis lifted out of the ground, spraying him with loose dirt and pebbles with a deafening shriek. Levered by the combined force of Shoreseeker and the disk, the mangled and bent form of the Runeway dragged across the ground, grinding and ripping through the creature's vast body.

As Tharadis watched from where he lay, he had thought—no, *hoped*—that he had finally defeated it.

But then the ear-splitting racket suddenly stopped.

The movement of the Runeway also stopped.

Tharadis realized why. Just like the last disk, which had gotten too close to the Rift, the torrent of shegasti power had untangled its Pattern.

The creature's scream was inaudible, yet it shook the ground beneath Tharadis. The Runeway hadn't killed it. Only wounded and enraged it. He rolled to his back to stare up at the fleshy limbs flailing in agony all around him. He knew that wouldn't last. If the creature took control of its body once more, it wouldn't hesitate to pulverize Tharadis.

But that didn't matter anymore. A small smile formed on his lips as he shut his eyes. Whatever happened to him, at least he had won. He had the made the world a little safer for Nina.

Even though the sun was now fully above the horizon, Sherin Firnaleos just wanted to sleep. She couldn't, however. The overturned hay cart she had found and now lay under couldn't stop the daylight from reaching her and keeping her awake.

And after all that had happened the night before, she wasn't sure if she'd rather never sleep again or never wake again. Each was too terrible to contemplate.

The constant chatter, though, was what really kept her up. She was sure that everyone who had come to the caravan—which, at last count, was over twenty thousand, spilling out far beyond the outer ring of wagons—was awake now and chatting away.

Sherin hugged her knees to her chest, tugging the edges of the cloak she had found so it covered her still-booted feet. She had no interest in listening, but a single word, uttered over and over, made her ears perk up.

"Look! Andrin's Wall! It's changing—"

"No, that's just a trick of the light. The Wall is … wait."

"Shores take me. Has this ever happened before? Has the Wall ever turned *yellow?*"

"It's getting darker! The Wall—"

A groan from deep within the earth shook the ground. Sherin threw the cloak off her and sat up quickly, eyes wide now. Metallic shrieking, like a million tons of metal twisting, abruptly split the air. Only one thing could sound like that. The Runeway.

But that was not what had captured Sherin's attention. She stared, mouth hanging open, as the first crack formed in Andrin's Wall.

Then the Wall began to rain chunks of stone.

Enslavement was no longer the plan.

No. Orthkalu wanted to destroy *everything*.

The rage he felt as the Runeway tore free from the ground and swept through his corporeal form, ruining half of it, was immense. He wasn't certain how the Runeway had been turned against him so easily, but it was clear he had underestimated this human—and overestimated his own power. He had been too cautious, merely sipping from the deep well of shegasti in the Rift, when what he truly needed to do was drink deep. He needed torrents of power, not only to repair the damage done to him, but to ensure the human's absolute annihilation.

Consequences be damned.

Orthkalu shifted his sprawling form towards the Rift. Agony shot through him as shegasti energy poured into his open wounds, but he was beyond caring. With a final heave, he threw the rest of himself into the Rift, completely submerging himself in concentrated shegasti power.

It was only then that he noticed the Rift's color changing once more.

To white. To the same color as the hated Wall.

His agony doubled, then trebled, and then there was only the agony. Then nothing.

The Patterner Larril sat on the blue tile roof of his house in the early morning sun, watching the northern horizon with weary eyes. A wooden pipe hung from his fingers, but the spark within had long since gone out. He'd been waiting here all night, after all. Waiting for what he dreaded to come, waiting for the inevitable.

His stomach tightened as it came.

A great white line of light flared into existence, as if another sun had chosen to rise this morning. Larril couldn't normally see the Rift from the roof of his house—it was too far, with too many hills and drytrees in the way—but with how bright it was now, he doubted anyone in Naruvieth would miss it.

The white light died moments later, marking the death of the Rift itself. Just a crevasse from here on out. Just as Andrin's Wall would now be a pile of rubble.

Larril heard a scream then, an inhuman scream that only he could hear. Others would sense it as a mere shifting of the wind, a rustling of the fine hairs on the backs of their arms, but none could hear the Pattern like Larril could.

"So much for all your plans, Orthkalu," Larril muttered as he clambered down off the roof. Where had he put his manacles again? He'd need them if he was going to look for Tharadis. Once Larril found him and healed him—at least enough to ensure there was no permanent damage, anyway— Tharadis would want to put that sword through Larril's belly for sending his daughter off to Falconkeep. He hoped that the manacles would serve as a suitable compromise. After all, it wasn't Larril's time to die. He knew that for a fact. He just had to make sure Tharadis understood that as well.

Larril found the manacles in the first place he looked of course, and he stuffed them in his sack before heading out the door and down to where the Rift used to be.

"All right, O Great Warden," Larril murmured dryly. "Time for you to lead us all to our doom."

Chapter 87: Shoreseeker

In the two weeks that followed, so many reports of disaster came in that Rannald could hardly keep track of them all. And he was nearing the point that he no longer wanted to. It was simply too much for one man to deal with.

Shoulders bowed, he stood in the Sentinel field house, a small, rickety structure hastily built out of the ruins of Garoshmir, reading one such report now. The sheggam invasion, he was learning, had spread far beyond Garoshmir. Dozens of villages and small towns would need to be erased from all maps. Caney Forks, where Rannald had been born, where he had once fought and bled before becoming a Sentinel, had been decimated. The dead were beyond reckoning. This report had specifically mentioned that neither of Rannald's cousins had been found.

After a while, the words on the report seemed little more than indecipherable smudges. He let the hand holding the paper drop to his side. Rannald was beyond tears, even for those he loved. He crumpled the paper and threw it in the wicker basket in the corner of the poorly-lit room, where all his other reports sat crumpled. Many of them had only been partially read as well.

Those reports, too, outlined tragedies beyond reckoning. According to what he'd read, the citizens of Twelve Towers had been slaughtered to a man. He knew most were innocent and shouldn't be blamed for Shad Belgrith's treachery, but he simply couldn't summon any sympathy for them. He had so little sympathy left to give.

The other cities were much the same. Not even Falconkeep had been spared. Rannald was glad that he hadn't been the one to come across that grisly scene. He was even happier that Nina and Chad had been spared such a fate. From what he'd heard, no one was left alive in that place. He shuddered as the image of a killing field full of children passed through his mind, and he quickly turned his mind to something else.

Nina. Rannald wondered if her father was still alive, and if so, whether he knew she and her aunt had survived after he had left them. Of all the reports Rannald had received, the one he'd hoped for most still hadn't come.

What of Naruvieth? What of Tharadis?

He shook his head. Thinking about that report wouldn't make it arrive any faster. Maybe getting some fresh air would do him some good, help him clear his head. Rannald touched the pommel of the sword at his hip to reassure himself it was still there—a constant habit he had taken up since that night, one he didn't feel like breaking any time soon. He stepped outside.

The caravan had grown from a humble handful of wagons to the beginnings of a sprawling settlement. Tents covered the ground, but some squat buildings had been erected, with a couple more on their way. Few Garoshmiri wanted to move back into their homes, but some, especially those with no loved ones to bury, did. Rannald had hardly ever stepped inside a temple, but he found himself wondering what kind of place Farshores really was. He supposed he would find out someday, when it was his turn to cross the Astral Sea. *May that day be a long time off*, he thought.

A few raindrops fell from the dark clouds scattered throughout the afternoon sky, plinking against his breastplate. Involuntarily, Rannald glanced north. The sight filled him with anguish, as it always did, but it was impossible not to look at the rubble where Andrin's Wall had stood for so long. It was also hard not to wonder when the next sheggam army would come along to finish the job the last one had started.

The thunder of galloping hooves approaching pulled Rannald out of his grim reverie. He turned to see one of his Sentinels, panting and red-faced from the hard ride, slide out of his saddle and salute. Rannald saluted back, trying to make sense of the man's strange expression. It was one he hadn't seen in so long. Was he … smiling? "Report, soldier."

"Yes, captain. It's about Naruvieth."

Rannald perked up. "You have news? How do they fare?"

"I don't know, sir." The man's grin widened. "But you can ask them yourself."

"What? Tharadis is here? He's alive?"

"Not just the Warden, sir. All of Shores-damn Naruvieth is on its way."

Two more days passed before the long train of Naruvians came into sight of the settlement outside Garoshmir, and nearly dusk that night before they began to gather at the base of the hill just south of the city's ruins. It turned out not to be all of Shores-damn Naruvieth, but nearly ten thousand of them, several crowded in wagons or mounted on mules, with Tharadis walking at the head. They hadn't the weary, beaten look of refugees. Something else shown through their expressions, something that looked as out-of-place as the smile on that Sentinel's face had. But Rannald couldn't figure out what it was.

When Tharadis's eyes met his own, Rannald couldn't help but smile.

Favoring his right leg, the Warden crossed to him, and they clasped arms. His grip was firm. Rannald didn't want to let go; he was nearly convinced that if he did, Tharadis would prove to be nothing more than a vain wish and disappear before his eyes.

"Captain," Tharadis said when Rannald finally did let go. "It's good to see you're alive and well."

"It's good to see you're alive too, Warden." Rannald stroked his chin as he looked Tharadis over. "Though I'd be hard-pressed to call you 'well.'"

Tharadis nodded but said nothing. His face was a lattice of faint scars. His left hand was tightly bandaged, leaving only his fingers bare. Whatever wound he had suffered did not seem to be healed yet. A deep exhaustion hid behind his eyes as well. Rannald didn't want to ask what the man had been through. He assumed Tharadis would tell him if and when he wanted to.

"My daughter," Tharadis said, his voice quiet. "Where is she?"

Rannald gestured to a nearby tent. "She's there with your sister."

Tharadis didn't even wait for Rannald to finish speaking before heading for the tent. Over his shoulder, he called, "Gather everyone at dawn. I have something to say."

Rannald frowned. "Everyone?"

"Everyone with an ear." Tharadis lifted the tent flap and disappeared within.

Word spread quickly. Everyone wanted to see this man. Conflicting rumors flew about, some saying he had single-handedly destroyed the sheggam threat, while others declared he had brought down the Wall himself. Yet no matter the rumor, Rannald heard it spoken with an unsettling mix of fear and awe.

So, when the sun broke over the horizon, everyone with an ear did indeed gather in front of a large flat-bed wagon, now used as a dais. Rannald stood with ten of his Sentinels in front, ostensibly as protection, but also because Rannald wanted to be close enough to see. Tharadis went up the steps and stood there, wearing his headband with the Warden's symbol, dark waves against a pale blue sky—a sky the same color as the Warden's blade, Rannald realized. And though he had been down in Naruvieth, he was dressed for colder weather, as were many of his people. Earlier, Rannald had heard mutterings that the disappearance of the Rift had completely changed the climate down there, so that it wasn't all that different from Garoshmir's. If that were true, life as these people had known it was over. *Then they're in good company,* Rannald thought grimly.

But he didn't think that was the full explanation of their clothing. Something else was going on here.

Tharadis scanned the thousands of faces watching him. Tharadis had a bearing about him, one different from anyone else here. His face didn't have the glazed eyes, the slack expression that so many here wore. His face wore the opposite. His jaw was tight, his back straight. His green eyes were sharp with focus. Something burned within those eyes. Something dangerous.

Hope.

In the past weeks, Rannald had talked to people, had listened to them. He knew how desperate they were to make sense of the madness their lives had become. Centuries-old institutions had crumbled overnight; their very world was flipped upside-down. They were lost, as if already afloat in the Astral Sea with nothing to guide them to shore. If they saw so much as a flicker of light on the horizon, Rannald knew they would swim for it. No matter where it led.

With a sinking feeling in his gut, Rannald suddenly wondered at the wisdom of yoking his fate, and the fate of his Sentinels, to that of this man.

Tharadis spoke.

"I don't need to remind you of what you've lost," he began, his voice carrying out over the heads of the assembled. "Everywhere you look you see reminders. The institutions you've relied upon for so long are gone. We thought they could keep us safe, but they couldn't. Nothing could have kept us perfectly safe. Perfect safety is an illusion, a lie we tell ourselves. There were always cracks in Andrin's Wall, even if they couldn't be seen."

Beneath the folds of his cloak, Tharadis clasped his hands behind his back and began to pace. "The Restless Sea is no longer restless." Low murmurs rose up as the implications sank in. "Not only can the sheggam come again by land, but they can come by sea. Their Patterners and their commanders will soon learn of our vulnerability and they will work to exploit it."

Rannald didn't know what he had expected from Tharadis, but this certainly wasn't it. His speech was less a general's call to arms and more a funeral service.

Tharadis halted and studied the crowd, and it almost seemed as if his gaze met every pair of eyes looking his way, if only for the briefest moment.

"War has come to us. It is an ancient war, and history shows us that it is a war we cannot win. But when it comes to fighting, we will not have a choice. They will come again, and we will need to prepare ourselves for that day. Everyone fit to hold a weapon must learn how to wield it, simply because there aren't enough trained fighters left to protect you all. You will have to learn how to defend yourselves." Again, murmurs filled the air, this time tinged with anger. "Understand that this is not some command I am issuing. It is merely an observation. You will either learn to fight and perhaps survive, or you will die, helpless and afraid. This is the reality we are faced with, and your acceptance of it has become a matter of life and death.

"Yet," Tharadis continued, "like any walls we build, fighting will only hold them back for a time. Even if we win a battle, we cannot win this war. And knowing that, we may despair, and in that despair our resolve will weaken, hastening our demise.

"This is because our enemies have chosen the field of battle. It is the realm of pain and suffering and death. And though many have died at their hands, death is merely a tool to them, a tool to cause pain to those who remain. Pain is their god, and we are their offering. And as long as we continue to let them choose the battlefield, they will crush us."

"What are you saying?" someone cried out from the crowd, incredulous. "Invade their lands?"

Tharadis shook his head. "We are not tribes disputing mere claims of land. We can't simply drive them back and hope they forget about us. They want to destroy our spirits." He clenched his fist before him. "They want to destroy our will to live! As long as we treat this like a traditional dispute between equals, we are bound to lose."

Tharadis let his hand drop to his side. "Most of you believe in a place called Farshores." Several nodded in assent, though far fewer than Rannald expected. He supposed many had had their faith tested of late. "So do I," he continued. "But in a different way from most of you, I suspect. Most believe it to be a world beyond this one, a place our souls go when we die." He paused. "But I believe that Farshores is real, that it exists on this world, and that the Astral Sea is nothing more than an ocean filled with water that ships can cross."

Anger filled his voice. "But most of all, I believe that we do not have to wait for the sheggam to deliver us to paradise on the points of their swords. I believe that we can deliver *ourselves* on our own two feet!"

All around, the crowd erupted in a roar. Rannald's hand fell to the hilt of his sword in case things turned bad, but the crowd didn't seem upset at Tharadis's heresy. Actually, quite a few of the raised voices were shouting for him to keep speaking. As his hand fell away from his sword, Rannald gaped in astonishment. Were people taking this madness seriously?

However, Rannald wasn't the only one who wasn't convinced. A woman about five heads deeper in the crowd cupped her hands around her mouth to be better heard over the din. "Why should we believe you?"

Tharadis waited until the crowd settled before answering. "An excellent question." He shrugged. "I'm afraid I can't give you much reason to. We don't know much about Farshores aside from the name. But we know that the idea of Farshores is newer than the sheggam scourge. The first one, that is," he added with a sidelong glance to the ruins of Garoshmir. "We know our people were not native to these lands. Our ancestors fled from *somewhere*, and that they flourished there, with wonders beyond our reckoning. At least they did before the sheggam drove them out." He gestured to a small cluster of men and women wearing the brown of the Academy, who flinched at his sudden attention. "Ask your scholars if you must, but I'm not telling you anything you don't already know."

Despite his misgivings about everything else, Rannald had to admit there was some plausibility to the idea. The exploits of a Great Fleet were told to every child in the Sutherlands. Wouldn't those ships have had to come from somewhere?

"I'll be honest," Tharadis said. "I don't know if such a place still exists, if it ever did. But if Farshores does exist, *it is not here.*"

Silence stretched before a new voice called out. "You simply expect to cross the sheggam lands and survive?"

"Do you expect to *live* in Sheggamur and survive?" Tharadis spread his arms. "This is a conquered land, waiting for its occupiers. The only thing stopping them before was Andrin's Wall. It's gone. These are now sheggam lands.

"Maybe I am a fool," Tharadis went on. "Maybe Farshores is just a myth, or a place that no longer exists. Maybe I'll die out there in a hostile wilderness. But if I die, let it be on *my* terms, not on the terms of my enemies!"

Scattered cheers broke out again. Tears even glistened on some faces. Rannald shook his head. He couldn't understand it. Why was anyone taken in by this foolishness?

It *would* be simpler to stay, to try to rebuild rather than strike out into the unknown. Perhaps they'd never build another wall like Andrin's, but they would try. They *had* to.

Rannald lifted his head to look at the sky, blue, spotted by only a sprinkling of clouds. Few gulls flew in the sky now; only the odd crow or raven.

This was not the world he had always known. Even the birds were different.

It seemed such an odd thing to note, but it suddenly made him realize that he was afraid, deathly afraid, of the dangerous, unknown world that lay beyond the rubble of the Wall. That realization, more than anything else, decided it for him.

Fear, I confront you. You can only take what you are given.

And I give you nothing.

Flipping the edge of his cloak back, Rannald ascended the steps to stand at Tharadis's side. The crowd went silent and still at the sight of him. His eyes flicked to the side as he searched for Sherin's face. He suddenly wished he had spoken to her first. *Oh well,* he thought with a grim, inward chuckle. *One more fear to face.*

Tharadis turned to face him. Their eyes met, and he nodded. A small smile appeared, and he pitched his voice for Rannald's ears alone. "We meet again, captain. Just the two of us, in front of everybody."

"Yes. Just the two of us, again deciding the future of our peoples."

Tharadis shook his head. "We can't this time. They have to choose for themselves."

Rannald stared at him a moment longer before raising his voice to address the crowd. "I don't know if Farshores can be found in this life or the next. But I for one will join the Warden in his quest to find out.

"Sentinels," Rannald said, looking down to where they were gathered, "I give you a choice of orders. Stay and help rebuild, or go with me and the Warden to find Farshores."

"Sir!" Major Metsfurth snapped to attention, the rest of the Sentinels following suit in perfect unison. The sound of their bootheels clapping filled the air. "I request permission to speak freely."

"Granted, major."

"We are, to a man, incensed that you would even think of leaving without us. Sir." Again, they saluted, even crisper than before.

It was all Rannald could do to hold back the tears. He didn't dare test his voice. He merely gave a small nod.

Tharadis clapped Rannald's shoulder, gratitude clear in his face, before turning back to the people. "To those who choose to stay behind, I wish you all the best. Rebuild as best you can. Live for as long as you can. I hope you find some measure of peace here. There is little that would make me happier. But I know that we shall never meet again, so here, now, we must say farewell."

Tharadis drew his remarkable sword, Shoreseeker, from its sheath. *It's no longer the sword that deserves that name,* Rannald thought, *but the man who wields it.*

Perhaps they both do.

"But to those of you who embrace this uncertain future." Tharadis raised his sword above his head, parallel to his shoulders, the flat of its sky-blue blade facing forward. Andrin's salute.

"Let us go together," Tharadis shouted as he swung Shoreseeker until it pointed north.

To the land beyond the Wall. To a land of possibility.

Then, as if everyone could see the Pattern of his words, they all thrust their fists in the air and shouted as one, *"To Farshores!"*

Epilogue: Dust and Bones

Noredren lay on his back among red dust and red stones, his fingers laced behind his head as he stared at the eternally starry sky.

The world, once his home, now beyond his reach, loomed large directly above him, though not as large as it had the night he last visited it. The night he had met his savior in person for the first time. The name rang in his mind like the echo of some cosmic bell.

Tharadis.

Even from the immense distance, Noredren could still see the faintest ripples in the Patterns of the world—not as much as he could sense if he were still on its surface, but enough for his purpose. What they told him was that without his future savior, Noredren would be trapped here on Aylia, living out his punishment, for all time.

With a sigh—an affectation, really, since there was no air on Aylia's surface—Noredren rose to his feet and brushed off the dust that clung to his long, white jacket, which still remained nearly pristine after all these centuries. The dust drifted down slowly, as if reluctant to return to the ground. Noredren sympathized. He knew that once he left this cursed moon, he would never return.

He walked to where he knew Kirulk, one of Noredren's three remaining companions, would be. Kirulk knelt with his huge hands on his knees. The twin braids of his gray beard reached beyond his chest, bare save for a thicket of coarse brown hair, down to his ample belly. The sand around where he knelt was etched with thousands of intricate Patterns that Noredren had etched with the tip of his finger. They were inert now, having served their purpose, yet Kirulk had stomped many of them out anyway. As if he could have changed what they had done, what they had taken.

"Did it have to be her?" Kirulk asked, his voice hoarse. Even after all this time, Noredren still was not used to how loud the man's voice was in the otherwise absolute silence of their moon prison. Still, Noredren was not so bored that he would tinker with the Pattern that let them speak in the first place.

Noredren cocked his head and regarded Kirulk with amusement.

463

"Would you rather it had been you?"

Kirulk looked away.

In front of Kirulk lay the charred remains of Shivelca, the one companion who was no longer among them.

Kirulk stared at her blackened bones, his fingers clawed as if he ached to touch them but dared not for how fragile they were. "She always loved that rhyme of us," Kirulk said, more to himself than to Noredren, it seemed. "'The five faces in the moon.'"

"Now there are only four," Noredren said. "But she sacrificed herself to give the rest of us a chance to leave."

Kirulk's eyes flashed as he turned them to Noredren. "No. *You* sacrificed her." He gestured to the Patterns, which only Noredren could have made.

Noredren shrugged. "It was necessary. It was what our savior required. It was what *we* required."

"Damn them." Kirulk's finger joints creaked as his massive hands curled into quivering fists. "Damn them all for what they drive us to do."

"And damn them we shall. Worse than we have ever damned them before." Though, in truth, it would be hard to top the loosing of the sheggam on the world.

The sheggam. For some reason, thinking of them and how Noredren and the other four had unleashed them all those centuries ago always made him feel hollow. He suspected it had something to do with the gaps in his memory. There were so *many*.

Such as why he was the way he was. And why he had done the things he had done.

On the surface, such questions had easy explanations. But even after convincing himself of them, the hollowness remained, and it was an emotion he did not understand. It made him feel even more helpless than being imprisoned on this cursed moon.

Kirulk's broad chest rose and fell with a deeply indrawn breath. "Go. Leave me to my vigil."

Noredren clasped his hands behind his back and left without a word. Once he was alone again, he lifted his gaze back to the world looming above.

"Savior," he whispered. "Find your Farshores. The sooner you do, the sooner I can take my vengeance on this world."

Here ends Book One of *The Farshores Saga.* The story continues in Book Two, *Drawingpath.* Read on for a sample!

Prologue: Councilor of Nothing

ozens of rusty cages swung languidly in the breeze, hooked to poles tilted at odd angles. The poles had been punched into cracks in the stones on either side of wide, crumbling stairway leading up to the top of the pyramid. Some of the cages were occupied, though few by actual living people; most held corpses in various states of decay. The living people only seemed that way in comparison to the corpses. With how little they moved and how blankly they stared, they might have already died too, if only a bit more recently than the others.

With his hands bound in iron shackles, Yarid took each step one at a time, trying his best not to cover his nose against the overwhelming reek of rot carried by the breeze. He was a guest, and he didn't want to offend his hosts.

Presumably, that's how one ended up in a cage.

The flat of a spear head cracked into the small of Yarid's back, sending him stumbling forward. He barked his knees on the next step. Without thinking, he quickly bowed his head and picked up the pace. He didn't complain about the pain or look back at the one who had struck him. He didn't want to look into the sheggam's eyes.

There was madness in their eyes. Every time Yarid looked into those crimson orbs with their tiny yellow pupils, he felt a little piece of his own sanity stripped away.

Not mad yet, he muttered silently. *Not dead yet.* It had become a sort of mantra for him and calmed him when things started to look bleak.

It was a constant litany humming in the back of his mind.

He did his best to ignore the sheggam, but their massive bulk made it so damn difficult. That, and it was hard to ignore the constant threat of their black talons, each one as long as Yarid's little finger, or that of their long muzzles lined with sharp teeth. Ignoring an axe as it descended on your neck would be easier than ignoring the sheggam.

To his side walked Gorun, who had been Yarid's Greater Councilor counterpart on the Council of the Wall—back when there had *been* a Council of the Wall. *But Andrin's Wall has been reduced to rubble,* Yarid thought. *No need for a Council then, is there?* The weathered old man wore no shackles, but then Gorun had been the one to orchestrate the sheggam invasion of the Sutherlands in the first place. He had earned the trust of the sheggam—if the sheggam were capable of such a thing as trust—and so was allowed to walk unfettered.

Yarid had always thought Gorun looked decrepit, nearer to death than the people in the cages. But now there was a fire in the old man's step, a sparkle in his eye. He had been able to keep up with the rest of them during their two-week trek here. It's almost as if coming to Sheggamur filled the man with vitality.

On the other side of Gorun was Jordin, who had been Yarid's own manservant. Before Gorun had somehow bought him, or threatened him, turning him against Yarid. At first, Yarid had been incensed at the betrayal. But Jordin seemed to have aged five years in the past two weeks, almost as if Gorun were somehow sucking the life out of him. Jordin's eyes were sunken and haunted, his frame thinner than even their harsh journey should warrant. The gray in his beard was closer to white now—at least where it wasn't smeared with mud and soot. Even back in Garoshmir, Yarid had always pitied the man, but now that pity had become acute. Whenever fear seized Yarid and seemed like it would never let go, all he would need to do was look into Jordin's eyes and realize things could be worse.

And it was hard to hate a man when your hatred changed nothing.

They continued to climb the steps that were too high and too long for a normal human gait, better suited to a sheggam's stride. The troop of eight sheggam, armored in battered mail shirts and armed with spears, had no problem with the steps. Yarid felt like his thighs were on fire. At least they were almost to the top.

An open pavilion with a flat roof supported by thick stone pillars was their destination. When they finally reached it, the sheggam soldiers behind them roughly herded Yarid and Jordin forward, letting Gorun walk forward at his own pace. Yarid was just glad there were no more steps.

Stretched out beyond the pyramid, nestled into the crook of the valley below, was a gray city.

Eleankuron.

Buildings of gray stone rose up above the perpetual gray mist blanketing the streets, obscuring them. Yarid had caught a glimpse of Eleankuron from a distant, poor vantage point as they made their way to the pyramid. But now the city sprawled before him as if for inspection. As if to flaunt the fact that yes, even the sheggam were capable of building cities.

Yet the mist obscured much. As if to display only that a city was there, yet hide its condition.

Yarid pulled his attention from the city. It wasn't worth thinking about, not now anyway. He instead glanced about the pavilion.

More sheggam guards stood at attention between the pillars on either side of the pavilion. Unlike those that had accompanied Yarid and the others until this point, these had the look of discipline about them—an unsettling thought, considering they were sheggam. Gripped by their taloned hands, the wide, flat blades of their swords had an oblong, padded hole about halfway up—a handle. Yarid imagined such weapons could be used as battle axes as easily as swords with a mere change of the grip. These sheggam seemed at ease with their weapons—though, with sheggam, *at ease* was a relative term—and they wore thick wrought-iron breastplates, hammered with simple designs. Soldiers.

The beasts that had overrun the Accord had been that—feral beasts. Lacking much in the way of direction, lashing out randomly in whatever way seemed to cause the most damage in that moment. Those feral sheggam had nearly leveled the entire Sutherlands in a single night. Yarid shuddered to imagine what an organized sheggam force would look like.

I don't have to imagine, he thought wryly. *They're standing right in front of me.* Still. He wouldn't want to see what they were like in battle.

If there were soldiers, then there were commanders—or at least some sort of hierarchy. Yarid wondered who gave these sheggam soldiers their orders.

Behind a white marble block threaded with veins of green stood another sheggam, this one even taller than the soldiers. Greasy strands of black hair spilled out from under the headdress it wore, which was fashioned from a variety of feathers which were bound into a cone by leather strips, nearly brushed the ceiling. It wore no armor, but rather a red silk brocade robe that made its sickly pale flesh appear even more sickly by contrast.

No, not a regular brocade, Yarid realized. The embroidery was not a simple repeating pattern. The robe was stitched with *Patterns.*

Yarid felt his mouth go dry. Why had they brought Yarid here? What kind of twisted magic was this creature going to perform on him? Yarid was no Patterner himself, but he had seen enough of them to recognize them. And he had often seen their effects. More often than not, they caused ruin.

The sheggam Patterner pulled back its thin lips to reveal its muzzle. It almost seemed to sense Yarid's fear, and revel in it.

On the marble block—an altar of some sort, judging by the intricate scrollwork carved into it, as well as its placement in the center of the pavilion—was another of those strange weapons like the soldiers carried. Only this one was etched with Patterns. The sheggam Patterner rested both of its hands on the sword as it watched him, then turned its regard to Gorun a moment, teeth still bared, before motioning to one of the soldiers.

The soldier barked something wordless—or was it? After hearing Orthkalu, Sheggamur's supposed ambassador, speak in front of the Council of the Wall just before the sheggam invasion, Yarid had never suspected that the sheggam had developed their own language.

From the opposite side of the pyramid, which apparently had another set of steps, three humans walked up, prodded along by spear-wielding sheggam much as Yarid had been. The humans—*no*, Yarid thought, correcting himself, *just people*—the people walked slowly, arms hanging limply, eyes ahead, focusing on nothing. How long had they been here, among the sheggam?

Long enough to see their hope vanish, Yarid thought. The thought chilled him, but he was made of stronger stuff than these three. He had seen many fail where he had flourished; this place would not get the better of him, no matter how hard it tried.

Yarid inspected them. A woman and two children, a young girl and an even younger boy. They wore little more than tattered rags, hanging on withered frames. Soot streaked their faces and darkened their hair, making it difficult to know what they'd look like when washed. Yarid was horrified to realize that on all three, their left arms had been chopped off at the elbow. All that remained were scarred stumps. The wounds looked too clean, too similar to be mere accidents.

Yarid thrust that from his mind, lest he lose what little food was in his stomach, and studied their faces. They looked like a family. But if that were so, who was the father?

Jordin, by falling to his knees and erupting in hysterical sobs, answered that question. The former manservant's eyes were pleading, hands stretched out in front of him uselessly. He had the look of a man suddenly succumbed to madness, a madness that had lay hidden and just out of reach, waiting for just the right moment to rush up and sink its fangs into him.

"Moira!" Jordin cried. "Nori! Peyte!" Spittle flew from his lips on the last name. The three watched him impassively as if watching a beggar in the street.

The guard behind Jordin cracked him across the shoulders with the haft of his spear, sending Jordin sprawling onto his face. The man lay there, with only his continued sobs to indicate he was still conscious.

"As promised," Gorun said, "you may have your family back, Jordin. If you want them."

Weeping suddenly ceased, Jordin lifted himself up to his hands and knees, eyes wide as his gaze bored into Gorun. "And why would you think I wouldn't want them?"

Gorun shrugged and gestured at them. "There isn't much left of them, as you can see. The sheggam have had them for several months."

Yarid thought about that. Andrin's Wall, the only thing that separated the Sutherlands from Sheggamur had stood until just a couple weeks ago. Yet the sheggam invasion happened because the sheggam had come up through volcanic tunnels crossing underneath the Wall. Since the Wall was still standing at that time, these three humans—*no, people, dammit!*—had to have been taken through those same volcanic tunnels.

Yarid couldn't imagine what that must have been like. Trapped in dark tunnels of sharp rock, air reeking of sulfur, being passed along by an army of monsters that were only supposed to exist in songs and stories and nightmares. Then to be trapped in a *city* full of them. For months.

Not for the first time, Yarid wondered if he was mad for following Gorun here. *No*, he thought in sharp reprimand. *I am made of stronger stuff than them. I will survive. I will flourish!*

I was a Councilor of the Wall, he reminded himself.

Then a small voice whispered in the back of his mind, *Councilor of nothing now*.

Jordin rose to his feet, grinning and beckoning. "Come here. Papa's come to take you home. You want to go home, don't you? Just take my hand, and we'll go home. As easy as that." The look of wildness hadn't left his eyes.

His family didn't look like they were going to take a step towards him, but Jordin's wife turned to the sheggam Patterner.

From within the folds of his robe, the Patterner drew a horn-handled iron knife with a curved blade and set it on the altar.

Jordin seemed not to have noticed. His voice grew more panicked, though. "Come on, then! That's a good boy, Peyte. Take your sister and your mother and bring them over. Let's go home and eat something.

Whatever you'd like. I'll even make it myself."

Jordin's wife took the knife in her right hand, gripping it tightly, and walked over to Jordin to thrust the blade into his stomach.

Jordin's eyes bulged. Speckles of blood flew from his mouth to dot his wife's shoulder. He collapsed to his knees, then to his side, breath rattling wetly as he clutched his wound. Jordin's wife then went down on one knee, pressing her other knee against his face, then dragged the blade across his throat. Blood blossomed red.

Yarid looked away. He had seen murder—even done a bit of it himself—but this was something else. A wife, murdering her own husband. Not for greed or revenge or any motive that Yarid could fathom.

Murder for its own sake. Murder for no reason at all.

But that wasn't quite right, was it? Reasons surrounded them, glaring at them with unconcealed hunger and hatred in their crimson eyes.

Would the sheggam break Yarid like they broke Jordin's family?

He squeezed his eyes shut when he heard the sawing sounds begin. After the sounds ended, Yarid opened his eyes to see a pair of wicker baskets, produced from somewhere, sitting near the blood stain. In one basket were severed arms and legs, pointing in various odd angles, and Jordin's head, his neck a bloody, ragged stump.

Yarid spewed up his meager breakfast onto his own feet and collapsed to his hands and knees. He heaved until there was nothing left in his stomach, then heaved some more.

Gorun strode his Yarid's side, twined his fingers in Yarid's long, unbound hair, and yanked him to his feet with surprising strength. The old man's breath was hot on Yarid's ear. "I brought you here because I believed there was something of worth in you."

Yarid wiped the vomit from his chin. *I am made of stronger stuff!* He smiled, albeit weakly. "Consider that a purging of my weakness."

Gorun searched his eyes, nodded, and released Yarid's hair before stepping back.

The sheggam Patterner motioned to the two children. "Take that to the Stitchers," the sheggam said, pointing at the basket with Jordin's remains in it. The sheggam's voice was harsh and guttural, yet articulate.

"The Stitchers?" Yarid wondered aloud as he rose to his feet, then realized he didn't want to know.

In no hurry, the two children grabbed the handles on either side of the basket—awkwardly, as they both had to use their right hands—and carried it back down the steps they had come from. Without a word, Jordin's widow replaced the bloody knife on the altar and followed her children without exhibiting a flicker of emotion.

At Yarid's side, Gorun nodded. "Civilization always comes with a cost. With a human civilization, we have to stifle our emotions and our impulses, surrender them to the laws and to our betters, who best know how to direct such impulses." He gestured to the blood stain that was once the man named Jordin. "Sheggam civilizations … operate under different rules. The costs to maintain order are different, but the necessity for costs is the same." He began walking toward the altar. "Come."

Frowning, Yarid shuffled after.

In front of the altar, Gorun pivoted smartly. Yarid was amazed at how fooled he had been by the man. All those years, Gorun had seemed like such a feeble old man; now Yarid knew it had been an act. To his eyes, Gorun's stiff posture and confidence seemed to remove decades of wear from his body.

It was a dramatic change from the Gorun he had sat next to, almost daily, in the Council Chambers. So dramatic, that Yarid wondered if part of the change was genuine. If Gorun was, somehow, imbued with more energy and liveliness than before. *This place can't be doing it for him*, Yarid decided. *No one can feel good—truly good—about being here.* But if not that, then what?

"Place your left hand on the altar," Gorun said.

Yarid blinked, remembering Jordin's disfigured family. "Have you lost your mind?"

Gorun's expression darkened. "This is the cost I told you about. In order to be a part of sheggam society, you must literally become a part of it."

Yarid couldn't make any sense of that. But he knew right away that he didn't like the sound of it. "And if I refuse?" Yarid asked, voice pitched low so that hopefully only Gorun would hear.

Gorun's answering smile was joyless. "Who knows."

Yarid looked down at the altar, at that bloody knife. Then at the hulking sheggam soldiers. *Not mad yet*, he reminded himself. *Not dead yet.*

But for how much longer?

With a deep, quivering breath, he placed his hand on the altar.

Instead of picking up the knife, as Yarid expected, the sheggam in the headdress snatched the wide-bladed sword by the hilt and handle, and in the same smooth motion, brought it down quickly.

Bone crunched. Yarid screamed.

To be continued in Drawingpath ...

About the Author

Brandon M. Lindsay was raised on a steady diet of science fiction novels from the time he was a wee lad until the age of twenty-two, when he overcame his snobbery and read his first fantasy novel. He quickly discovered that fantasy is actually pretty awesome and has never looked back.

While he has always loved books, he also loves video games. He started his own indie game development studio called Hearthsflame Studios, where he is developing a series of video games that tie directly into *The Farshores Saga*. That series is called *The Birth of Maelstrom*. For more information about it and all of Brandon's other projects, please visit his website:

www.brandonmlindsay.com

Other places to find Brandon online:

Twitter: @BrandonMLindsay, @hearthsflame
Facebook: www.facebook.com/brandonmlindsay.author/
Itch: hearthsflame.itch.io

To learn more about the World of Farshores:

www.worldanvil.com/w/the-world-of-farshores-brandonmlindsay

Made in the USA
Middletown, DE
07 November 2020